Wyoming #2

F
LIN

Lindsey, Johanna.

Savage thunder

16045

DATE			
2-9-91			
2-28-91			
8-19-91			
10-21-92			
1-26-94			
7-8-97			
11-25-97			

16045

Savage Thunder

Savage Thunder

Johanna Lindsey

Thorndike Press • Thorndike, Maine

Library of Congress Cataloging in Publication Data:

Lindsey, Johanna.
  Savage thunder / Johanna Lindsey.
      p. cm.
  ISBN 1-56054-029-X (alk. paper : lg. print)
  1. Large type books. I. Title.
[PS3562.I5123S28   1989]   90-38576
813'.54--dc20   CIP

This work is a novel. Any similarity to actual persons or events is purely coincidental.

Thorndike Press Large Print edition published in 1990 by arrangement with Avon Books.

Cover design by James B. Murray.

The tree indicium is a trademark of Thorndike Press.

To Martha and Bill
for the inspiration of enduring love

Chapter One

Wyoming Territory, 1878

The Callan Ranch was silent that summer day except for the ominous crack of a whip. More than a half-dozen men were gathered in the grass-patched front yard of the ranch house, but not one made a sound as they watched Ramsay Pratt wield the whip with the expertise he was known for. An ex-bullwhacker, as stock drivers were frequently called, Pratt loved to show off his skills. He could knock the revolver out of a gunman's hand with the flick of his wrist, or a fly off the rear end of a horse without touching the hide. Where other men carried guns on their hips, Pratt carried a twelve-foot-long bullwhip coiled on his. But this demonstration today was a mite different from his usual tricks. This one was stripping the flesh off a man's back.

Ramsay did it at Walter Callan's behest, but he derived a good deal of pleasure from it, for it wasn't the first time he had whipped a man to death, or found that he enjoyed doing it, though no one here in Wyoming knew that. He didn't have it easy the way gunmen did. If they wanted to kill a man, they could pick a fight that would be over in a matter of seconds, then claim self-defense after the smoke cleared. But with Ramsay's choice of weapons, he had to disarm a man first, then proceed to whip the life out of him. Not too many people bought self-defense in that case. But in this case, he was following the boss's orders, and the victim was a no-account half-breed anyway, so no one would care.

He wasn't using his bullwhip, which could take a half-inch chunk of flesh with each stroke. That would end the entertainment too soon. Callan had suggested a shorter, thinner horsewhip, still capable of making mincemeat out of a man's back, but taking much longer to do it. Ramsay was all for that. He could drag this out for a good hour or more before his arm got tired.

If Callan weren't so mad, he would probably have just had the Injun shot. But he wanted him to suffer, to scream some before he died, and Ramsay meant to oblige. So far he was just playing with the victim, using the same cracking technique he used with the bullwhip, slicing an inch here, an inch there, not really doing much damage but making each little cut felt.

The Injun hadn't made a noise yet, not even a sharp indrawn breath. He would, though, when Ramsay started slashing instead of flicking. But there was no hurry — unless Callan got bored and called it off. That wasn't likely to happen, not as furious as the boss was. Ramsay knew how he'd feel if he just found out the man courting his only daughter was a damn breed. All these months he'd been fooled, and Jenny Callan too, from the look of her when her father confronted her with it. She'd turned right pale and sick-looking, and she stood on the porch now with her father, looking just as mad as he was.

It was a damn shame, for she was a real pretty gal. But who'd want her now after they heard who she'd kept company with, let touch her, and it was anyone's guess what else he'd done to her. She'd been deceived just as her father had, but who could have guessed that the Summerses' close friend was half Injun? He dressed like a white, spoke like a white, wore his hair shorter than most whites, carried a gun on his hip. It was just plain hard to tell what he was by the look of him, for the only things Injun-like about him were the straightness of his black hair and the darkness of his skin, which, truth to tell, wasn't much darker than that of any other man who rode the range.

The Callans still wouldn't have known if Long Jaw Durant hadn't been there to tell. Durant had been fired from the Rocky Valley Ranch and had only signed on the Callan spread yesterday. He had been in the barn when Colt Thunder, as the breed was calling himself, had ridden in on that big-boned Appaloosa, a son of Mrs. Summers' prize stallion. Naturally Durant was curious enough to ask one of the men what Thunder was doing there, and when told he'd been sniffing 'round Jenny Callan's skirts these past three months, he couldn't believe it. He knew Colt from his previous employment as being a close friend of the boss, Chase Summers, as well as his wife, Jessica. He also knew him to be a half-breed who until three years ago had been a full-fledged Cheyenne warrior, though that knowledge hadn't gone much farther than the Rocky Valley, apparently — until today.

Durant had wasted little time in finding his new boss and apprising him of this news. Maybe if he hadn't done it in front of three other hands, Callan would have handled it differently. But with his men aware of his daughter's shame, there was no way in hell he could let the breed live. He had gathered up the rest of his men, and when Colt Thunder stepped out on the porch, having collected young Jenny for an afternoon picnic, he was facing a half-dozen nervous revolvers trained on his belly, enough firepower to keep his hand away from his own gun, which he was quickly relieved of.

He was a tall man, taller than any of the men surrounding him. Those who had seen him come and go over these past months had never had reason to be wary of him, though, for he smiled often, laughed often, gave every indication of being a man of easy temperament — until now. Now there was little doubt that he had been raised by the Northern Cheyenne, those same Cheyenne who had joined with the Sioux to massacre Lieutenant Colonel Custer and his battalion of two hundred men just two years ago in the valley of the Little Bighorn up in Montana Territory. Colt Thunder, in the blink of an eye, became a Cheyenne brave, lethal, dangerous, the savage wildness of the Injun unleashed, striking fear into the hearts of civilized man.

He did not go down easily once he realized that shooting him was not their intention. It took seven men to get him tied to the hitching post in front of the house, and of those seven, not one came away from the scuffle unscathed. Bruises and bloody noses tamped down any qualms the men might have felt when Walter Callan ordered Ramsay to fetch a horsewhip so the breed would die slow. The

Injun hadn't even flinched at that order. He still hadn't, even though his shirt was now torn and soaking up blood from the many small cuts Ramsay had inflicted.

He was still standing, his hips against the five-foot-long hitching rail his only support, his arms stretched out to either end of it. There was room to bring him sagging to his knees, and he would go down eventually, but right now he stood straight and tall, his head defiantly erect, only the sure grip of his fingers curled around the rail an indication of pain — or anger.

It was that posture, so damn proud, that reminded Ramsay this wasn't like those other times his whip had bitten into human flesh. The two Mexicans he had done the same to down in Texas had crumbled after only three or four licks. That old prospector Ramsay had relieved of his gold and his life in Colorado had started screaming even before the first stroke of the lash. But this was an Injun, or at least he'd been raised like one; hadn't Ramsay heard somewhere about the Northern Plains Injuns putting themselves through some kind of self-torture ceremony? He'd wager the breed had a couple of scars on his chest or back to prove it, and that riled him. It meant it would be a long while and a lot of hard work to get any screams out of this one.

It was time to get serious.

The first true stroke of the whip was like a red-hot iron laid across the breed's back, branding him, the only difference the absence of the stink of burning flesh. Colt Thunder didn't blink, nor would he as long as Jenny Callan was standing up on that porch watching him. He kept his eyes locked to hers. They were blue like his own, though much darker, like that sapphire ring Jessie was fond of wearing. Jessie? God, she was going to be angry about this, but then she had always been protective of him, especially since he showed up on her doorstep three years ago and she took it upon herself to turn him into a white man. She'd even had him believing it could work. He should have known better.

Think of her . . . no, he could only envision Jessie crying when she saw what was left of his body after they were done with him. Jenny — he had to concentrate on her.

Damn, how many strokes was that now? Six? Seven?

Jenny, beautiful, blond, sweet as Jessie's home-made candy. Her father had settled in Wyoming only last year, after the Indian wars were over, the beaten Sioux and Cheyenne confined to reservations. Colt had been in Chicago with Jessie and Chase during the worst of the war, Jessie conspiring to keep the news from him, thinking he would want to go back and fight with his people. He wouldn't have. His mother, sister, and younger brother were already dead, found and killed by a couple of gold prospectors heading for the Black Hills just two months after he had left the tribe in '75. The area had been swarming with prospectors ever since gold was discovered there in '74.

It was the start of the end, that gold in the heart of Indian territory. The Indians had always known it was there, but once the whites did, you couldn't keep them out. And even though they were breaking the treaty by being there, the army finally came in to protect them, and so the last great Indian victory at Little Bighorn, but then the end.

Colt's mother, Wide River Woman, had seen it coming. That was why she had instigated the fight between him and his stepfather, Runs With the Wolf, pretty much forcing Colt into leaving the tribe. She would have sent his sister with him if Little Gray Bird Woman hadn't already married.

She told him that only after it was over and done and too late to mend the breach, that and her reasons for doing it. He had been furious with her at the time. Her fears for the future meant nothing to him. He saw only the end to his way of life. But she had already seen that end, was giving him a new life in forcing him to go.

It was galling to see her proved right, to know that he would be living on a reservation now if he had survived the wars, just as his stepfather and older brother were — if they had survived. But it was even more galling to be saved from that degradation for this.

Twenty-five? Thirty? There was no point in counting, was there?

He had seen Ramsay Pratt's skill with the whip several times before when he had come to visit Jenny. The man took pride in what he could do. And he was showing off now for the men who stood behind him, slashing the whip down in the exact same welt as many times as it took to lay the welt open, again to deepen the cut, then again just for the hell of it, and the pain of it.

Colt knew Pratt could go on indefinitely wielding that whip. He was a big bear of a man, looked like one too, with a nose so flat it was almost unnoticeable, a shaggy mane of dirty brown hair floating wild about his shoulders, and a long, full beard and mustache that blended right into it. If any man looked like a savage, Pratt did. And Colt had seen the gleam in his eyes when told to fetch that whip. This was a chore he was enjoying.

Fifty-five? Sixty? Why was he still trying to

15

keep track? Did he have any skin left? Was the damage as bad as it felt, or was it only Pratt's skill that made it seem as if his back were going up in flames? Just barely, he was aware of the blood seeping into his boots.

How much longer would Jenny stand there and watch, her expression as hard and unemotional as her father's? Had he really thought about marrying this girl, of buying a ranch with the pouch of gold he had found in his belongings when he arrived at the Rocky Valley, his mother's parting gift to him?

From the first time he had seen Jenny he had wanted her. Jessie had teased him about his interest and encouraged him to do something about it. She had also instilled enough self-confidence in him so that he didn't hesitate long.

When they actually met for the first time, he found the attraction was mutual, so mutual that in less than a month, Jenny gifted him with her innocence. He asked her to marry him that night, and they had been making plans ever since, were just waiting for the right moment to tell her father. But the old man had to suspect what was coming. With the Rocky Valley cattle grazing across the open range, practically right up to the Callan Ranch, it was an easy matter for him to come visiting three or four times a week at midday,

16

as well as in the evenings. Walter Callan's knowledge of how serious Colt's suit was probably had a lot to do with his outrage now. And Jenny's outrage?

He realized that he should have told her about his past, that White Thunder was his real name, that Colt for a first name was Jessie's idea. The trouble was, he had known Jenny wouldn't believe him, would think he was only teasing her. Jessie had done too good a job on him; most of the time he even thought like a white.

But to Jenny, he was no longer white. He had seen her fury before she closed it off and matched her father's hard visage as the torture began. There were no tears, no thoughts now of his hands and mouth on her body, of begging him to make love to her each time they found themselves alone. Now he was just another Indian getting what he deserved for presuming to aspire to the affections of a white woman.

His legs were getting weak. So was his vision. The fire had worked its way up to explode inside his brain. He didn't know how he was still standing, how he was keeping his facial muscles from twitching spasmodically. He had thought he had experienced the ultimate in pain during the Sun Dance ceremony, but that was child's play next to this. And

17

Jenny hadn't closed her eyes or looked away yet. But then she couldn't see his back from up on the porch. Not that it would matter. And it no longer mattered that he keep eye contact with her. It wasn't working to block out the pain.

Walter Callan signaled Ramsay to stop a moment when Colt's eyes closed and his head dropped back on his shoulders. "You still alive, boy?"

Colt made no response. The screams were there, in his head, in his throat, just waiting to escape if he opened his mouth. He'd bite his tongue off before he let them out. And it wasn't the fierce pride of the Indian that had decided he would make no sound. The Indian respected the white man who could face death with courage. He didn't expect any such respect from these men for his courage. His silence was for his own sake, his own self-respect.

But the silence around him had been broken by Callan's question. There were exclamations of amazement that he was still on his feet, a debate on whether it was possible to faint without keeling over, a suggestion that a bucket of water be fetched to dump over him, just in case he really had fainted. At that point he opened his eyes, still cognizant enough to know that water touching any part of his mangled back would send him over the edge of control. It was harder to lift his head, but he managed that too.

"Wouldn't believe it if I wasn't seein' it with my own eyes," someone said next to him.

The whir and slap of the whip resumed, but no one was paying much attention to it now except the recipient and the wielder.

"I still don't believe it," a voice grumbled behind Colt. "It ain't possible he's still on his feet."

"What'd you expect? He's only half human, you know. It's the other half that's still standing."

Ramsay tuned out their voices, concentrating on lashing only the raw wounds now. He was furious that he hadn't broken the Injun yet, and his anger was affecting his aim. The bastard couldn't do this to him. He couldn't die without making a sound.

Ramsay was so angry he didn't hear the riders who came tearing around the side of the house, but the others did. They turned to see Chase and Jessica Summers and about twenty of their cowhands descending on them.

If Ramsay heard them, he must have assumed they were some of Callan's men coming in off the range, for he still didn't pause. He was in the process of drawing back his arm for another slash when Jessie Summers palmed her gun and fired.

The bullet that was aimed to shatter Ramsay's skull flew over his head instead, Summers having hit his wife's arm up into the air at the last second when he saw her intent. But that shot was like a signal, every Rocky Valley man drawing a rifle or revolver upon hearing it. The Callan hands didn't move a muscle, didn't even breathe.

Walter Callan began to realize he might have made a serious mistake. Not that he didn't want the breed dead, but maybe he shouldn't have gone about it so publicly.

Ramsay Pratt stared in horror at the barrage of weaponry aimed mostly in his direction. A whip wasn't worth a damn against so many, even his bullwhip. He carefully lowered his arm until the blood-soaked leather was like a red snake curled about his feet.

"You bastard!" Jessie Summers was shouting, but she was shouting at her husband. "Why'd you stop me? Why?!"

Before he could answer, she had slid from her horse and run forward, pushing men out of her way who still didn't dare move on their own, and none too gently. She was in a towering rage. In all her twenty-five years she had never been killing mad like this. Not her father, her mother, or her husband, all of whom she had been at odds with at one time or another, had ever made her lose control like this. If Chase hadn't stopped her, she would have emptied her gun into Callan's men, and saved the last bullet for him.

But when she reached Thunder and saw close up the actual damage that whip had done, the fury drained right out of her. She doubled over with a keening moan that ended abruptly as she emptied her stomach in the blood-splattered yard.

Chase was there before she finished, putting his arms around her. But he was staring at Thunder and feeling kind of queasy himself. He had come to think of the man as a friend, though Colt was closer to Jessie. She loved him like a brother. They had shared a special relationship for more than half their lives. Colt had always been there for her when she needed a friend, and Jessie was going to blame herself for not getting here in time. And Chase had a strong feeling they were too late. If the shock didn't kill Colt, the loss of blood would.

"Nooo!" Jessie was crying now as she raised up and looked at Thunder again. "Oh, God, oh, God! Do something, Chase!"

"I've already sent a man for the doctor."

"That'll take too long. Do something now. You have to do something now. Stop the bleeding — oh, God, why isn't he cut loose yet?"

21

It wasn't really a question. Jessie wasn't aware of what she was saying just then. Almost in a trance, she walked around the post. That was better. He looked all right from the front — except for the paleness of his skin, the deathly stillness of him, his shallow breathing. She was afraid to touch him. She wanted to take him in her arms, but didn't dare. Any touch was going to hurt him. Any movement was going to be excruciating.

"Oh, God, White Thunder, what have they done to you?"

It was said in a tearful whisper. Colt heard her. He knew she was there in front of him, but he didn't open his eyes. If he saw the pain etched on her face, he would lose the slim thread of control he had left. As it was, he was terrified she was going to touch him, and yet he needed her tenderness, needed it desperately.

"Don't . . . cry . . ."

"No, no, I won't," she assured him as the tears continued to pour down her cheeks. "But don't try to talk, okay? I'll take care of everything. I'll even kill Callan for you."

Was she trying to make him laugh? He'd made the same offer to her once, only the man he would have killed for her was now the husband she loved with all her heart.

"Don't . . . kill . . . anyone."

22

"Shhh, all right, all right, anything you say, but don't talk anymore." And then, "Dammit, Chase, hurry up with those ropes! We've got to stop the bleeding."

Colt didn't move his arms when they were freed. Chase stood in front of him now. His voice was gentle as he explained, "Jessie, honey, that whip was trailed through the dirt time and again. His back is going to have to be cleaned first if infection isn't to kill him."

There was a heavy silence. Colt would have tensed if he wasn't already holding himself so rigid.

"Do it, Chase," Jessie said quietly.

"Christ, Jessie — "

"You have to," she insisted.

The three knew each other well enough that both men understood she wasn't talking about cleaning wounds or even moving him yet. Colt's body almost sighed with relief. It was about time she had thought of something sensible.

"We'll need a mattress first, and a couple men to hold him so he doesn't fall."

Jessie was in her element, issuing orders, but when she sent two men into the house for a mattress, Walter Callan recollected whose property they were on and stepped in front of the door to block their way.

"You ain't wastin' one of my mattresses

on that dirty . . ."

He didn't finish. Jessie had whirled around at the sound of his objection, and he now had her full attention, and every bit of the fury she had felt earlier. She mounted the porch steps, and before anyone realized her intent, she had hefted the gun from one of the men Callan was blocking. Chase wasn't there to take it away this time. No one else would dare try.

"You ever been shot before, Callan?" she said conversationally as she motioned the two men into the house and casually caressed the barrel of the old Colt .44 Dragoon. "There are parts on the body that can be shot off that won't bleed too seriously, but will sure hurt like hell. A toe, for instance, or a finger . . . or what makes a man a man. How many bullets do you think it would take to shoot off an inch at a time? Three, maybe? Not even that many? Would that equal your own savagery, do you think?"

"You're crazy," Walter said in a horrified whisper.

His hand had gone to his gun in a protective gesture. Jessie did nothing to stop him, just stared at his hand, hoping he would draw the gun. He saw that hope in her eyes and slowly took his hand away.

"Coward," she hissed, done playing with

24

him. "Pack your gear and be gone by sundown, Callan, you and your men. Ignore my warning and I'll make your life a living hell. There won't be anywhere in the territory you can hide from my vengeance."

He wasn't expecting that. "You got no call — "

"The hell I don't!"

He looked beseechingly to her husband. "Summers, can't you control your wife?"

"I already did you one favor, you son of a bitch," Chase shouted up at him. "I kept her from blowing your head off. Whatever else she has a mind to do is the least of what you deserve, so don't press it. It's lucky for you one of your men who overheard what you were planning is a drinking buddy of my foreman. And it's damn lucky for you he didn't have to ride all the way to the Rocky Valley, but found us out on the range. But that's where your luck runs out. What you did here is the lowest kind of savagery, fit only for animals."

"I had every right," Walter protested. "He defiled my daughter."

"That cold bitch you got for a daughter encouraged him," Jessie spat, moving to the side as the mattress was pushed out the door. A wagon had already been confiscated from the barn. "All I got left to say to you is, if he dies, you die, Callan. You better do some powerful praying on your way out of the territory."

"The sheriff will hear about this."

"Oh, I hope you're that stupid, I really do. If I didn't suspect you'd get no more than a slap on the wrist, I'd turn you in myself. Go against me and I'll take the law into my own hands, I swear to God I will. I ought to anyway," Jessie ended with a measure of self-disgust as she turned away.

"Shit," Walter grumbled behind her. "He's only a damn half-breed."

Jessie swung around, her turquoise eyes blazing. "You bastard! You lowlife, worthless bastard! That's my brother you nearly killed! Say one more word to me and I'll put a bullet between your eyes!"

She gave him two seconds to see if he would call her on this last warning, then turned away to return to Colt. His eyes were open. They stared at each other a long moment.

"You . . . knew?"

"Not always. Did you know?"

"When I . . . left."

She put a finger to his lips very gently. "I'm surprised she told you at all. I had always wondered about the affinity I felt for you, but not for your sister or brothers. I finally asked your mother right out. She wouldn't answer.

It couldn't have been something she would have wanted to admit, that her oldest daughter wasn't the only one to bear my father a child. But that she wouldn't deny it was answer enough for me, especially since I so wanted it to be true."

"Jessie, don't you think this conversation ought to wait for a better time?" Chase said.

She nodded and let her finger trail away in a loving caress across Colt's cheek. It was the signal for the two men standing behind him to step forward and grasp his arms. Colt closed his eyes again when Chase moved directly in front of him.

"Sorry, my friend."

"Don't be an ass, Chase," Jessie said matter-of-factly, earning an I'll-get-you-later-for-that-crack glance from her husband, which she typically ignored. "It's the only thing he'll have to be grateful for on this hellish day. Get it over with."

Chase did, drawing back his fist and letting fly with it toward Colt's jaw.

Chapter Two

Cheshire, England, 1878

Vanessa Britten ignored the embroidery in her lap and watched the duchess complete another circle of the room. She wouldn't exactly call it pacing the floorboards. She doubted the girl was even aware that she was wearing a path in the fine Eastern carpet.

Who would have thought the duchess would even care about the little tragedy taking place upstairs. Vanessa certainly hadn't thought it was possible when she had accepted the position as companion to the nineteen-year-old duchess just last month. It was such a common thing, young girls wedding older lords for their wealth and titles. And Jocelyn Fleming had latched onto one of the best catches, Edward Fleming, sixth Duke of Eaton, in his late middle years and already ailing when they wed last year.

But it didn't take long for Vanessa to change her opinion of the young Duchess of Eaton. Oh, she had certainly been destitute

28

when the duke had proposed to her. Her father had owned a stud farm in Devonshire, one of the finest in England, if Jocelyn could be believed. But like a great many of his contemporaries, he was a man who had a detrimental fondness for gambling, and when he died, he was so in debt that Jocelyn was left without a farthing. Edward Fleming had literally saved the poor girl from what was considered the worst of the worst for a gently reared lady — seeking employment.

Vanessa could only have said "Good show" to such a feat. She loved success stories, wasn't the type to begrudge another a little good fortune or a lot, as in the duchess's case. But Jocelyn Fleming wasn't the fortune huntress she had first assumed her to be.

Vanessa had lived too many years in London, where her peers were a cold-blooded lot, out for anything and everything they could get. Jocelyn wouldn't know how to be cold-blooded if she tried. She was too naive by half, too open and trusting, too innocent to be believed. And yet she really was exactly what she seemed. The most amazing thing about her was that she really loved the man who was at this moment upstairs dying.

Vanessa had been hired for this very contingency. The duke had taken many unusual precautions over the past months, selling unentailed properties, transferring money out of the country, buying the essentials needed for traveling. He had taken care of all the necessary details. The only thing Jocelyn and her rather large entourage needed to do was leave. Even the packing was already done.

Vanessa had been quite skeptical of the reasons for this foresight on the duke's part until she met his distant relations, the "vultures," as he called them, who were waiting to descend on his estate and pick it apart.

If ever a fellow could be termed avaricious and on the hard side of ruthless, it was Maurice Fleming, present heir to the dukedom. Edward had no immediate family. Maurice was a mere cousin, once removed, whom the duke could not tolerate to be even in the same room with. But Maurice had a large family of in-laws to support, as well as a mother and four sisters, and to say he had been avidly awaiting Edward's demise would be putting it mildly. He also had spies in Fleming Hall keeping him apprised of Edward's condition, and the moment the duke was pronounced dead, the knocker would undoubtedly sound at the front door.

Poor Jocelyn was in the middle of what could only be termed a family feud of long standing. Edward's relations had done their best to convince him not to wed her. Failing that, they had made certain threats, not in Edward's hearing, but he had nonetheless learned of them. He was not just being over-protective in all the preparations he had made for his young wife's future.

Vanessa would be the first to agree now that it would be folly to remain in England to tempt the fates. The new duke was not going to sit by idly while the bulk of the Fleming estate flew out of his reach. He would do everything within his power to get it back, and in his position as the new Duke of Eaton, his power was going to be immense. But Edward was bound and determined that Maurice and his greedy family should have nothing of his that was not entailed, that it should all belong to Jocelyn for her loyalty and selfless devotion to him.

If anyone needed Vanessa's advice and guidance, this young girl with the teary eyes did. Jocelyn didn't want to leave England and all that was familiar to her. She had been arguing with her husband since he first suggested it, to no avail. She was like a child in that respect, fearing the unknown. She couldn't grasp the danger to herself if she stayed and fell under Maurice's control. Vanessa could. Good Lord, it didn't bear thinking of. Jocelyn might be the duchess, soon to be the duchess dowager, for Maurice had a wife who would be the new Duchess of Eaton, but Jocelyn's title would give her no protection at all if Maurice managed to get his hands on her.

"Your Grace?" The housekeeper appeared hesitantly in the doorway, the queen's own physician at her side. "Your Grace?"

It took one more "Your Grace" before Jocelyn could be called back from her gloomy thoughts to the present. Vanessa could see that she had still held hope, however small. But one look at the physician's expression and that hope died a final death.

"How long?" Jocelyn asked in a tiny voice.

"Tonight, Your Grace," the old physician replied. "I'm sorry. We knew it was only a matter of time . . ." His voice trailed off.

"May I see him now?"

"Certainly. He is asking for you."

Jocelyn nodded and squared her shoulders. If she had learned anything from her husband this past year, it was poise and a certain self-confidence that came from a position of importance. She wouldn't cry, not in front of the servants. But once alone . . .

He was only fifty-five years old. His brown hair had been sparsely peppered with gray four years ago, when Jocelyn had first met him. He had come to Devonshire to purchase a hunter from her father. She had recommended a less showy mount, and Edward had taken her advice over her father's trainer's. The hunter she had favored had more heart, more stamina. Edward wasn't sorry.

He came back the next year for a pair of racers. Again he bought only on her recommendation. She was terribly flattered. She knew horses, had been raised with them, but no one would take her seriously because of her tender age. Edward Fleming, though, had been impressed with her knowledge and confidence. The Thoroughbreds she had sold him had since earned him a great deal of money. Again he wasn't sorry. And somehow, they became friends, despite the vast difference in their ages.

He came immediately when he learned of her father's death. He made her an offer she couldn't refuse. It was not a salacious offer. He already knew he was dying. The physicians had given him only a few more months to live. What he wanted was a companion, a friend, someone who might care and shed a tear or two at his passing. He had friends, but no one close to him.

He was fond of saying she had given him a reason to live a bit longer. Jocelyn liked to think that was so. She was so grateful for the extra months she had been granted with him;

he was everything to her, father, brother, mentor, friend, hero, everything except lover, but that could not be helped. He had been incapable of making love to a woman for many years before he even met her. But being an innocent bride of eighteen, she didn't know what she was missing, and so had no regrets that there was an area of their relationship she wasn't able to explore. She would have been more than willing, but didn't feel cheated. She simply loved Edward for everything else he was to her.

She sometimes felt she had been born when she met him. Her mother had died before Jocelyn had any real memories of her. Her father spent most of his time in London. Occasionally when he came home he might notice her, but she never felt a closeness to him. Hers had been a lonely, isolated life in the country, her only true interest the horses her father bred. Edward had opened up a whole new world to her, of sports, and socials, and women friends, of fancy clothes, and luxuries she never dreamed of. Now she was about to embark on another new life, but without him to guide her. God, how was she going to face it without him?

Jocelyn adjusted her breathing to the smell of sickness as she entered the state bedroom. She would not use a scented kerchief to mask the unpleasant odors. She could not do that to him.

He was lying prone in the huge bed in the center of the enormous room, to make his own breathing easier. She saw him watching her as she approached, his gray eyes dull, nearly lifeless already, the skin sunken beneath them, and so deathly pale. It brought tears to her eyes to see him like this, when up until only a few weeks ago he had still been reasonably active, a few weeks before that, hale and hearty, or so he had made her believe — while all along he had been making plans and arrangements for her, knowing his time was coming to an end.

"Don't look so sad, my dear."

Even his voice didn't sound the same anymore. God, how was she going to say goodbye to him without breaking down?

She reached for his hand lying on top of the velvet cover and brought it to her lips. When she took it away, a smile remained for his benefit, but it lasted only a second.

"That's cheating," she admonished herself and him. "I am sad. I can't help it, Eddie."

A little of the humor that was so much a part of him returned to his eyes at the name no one else had ever dared to call him, even in childhood. "You were always deplorably honest. It's one of the things I most admired about you."

"And I thought it was my excellent horse sense — about horses, that is."

"That too." His own attempt at a smile also failed.

"Are you in pain?" she asked hesitantly.

"Nothing I'm not used to by now."

"Didn't the physician give you — "

"For later, my dear. I wanted to remain lucid to say my good-byes."

"Oh, God!"

"Now, none of that." He tried to sound stern but had never been able to be stern with her. "Please, Jocelyn. I can't bear to see you cry."

She turned her head away to wipe at the tears, but when she looked back at him, they came rushing down her cheeks again. "I'm sorry, but it just hurts so much, Eddie. I wasn't supposed to love you, not like this," she said baldly.

A remark like that would have made him laugh even a few days ago. "I know."

"You told me two months, and I thought — I thought I wouldn't get that attached to you in such a short time. I wanted to make your last months comfortable, to make you happy if I could, because you were doing so much for me. But I wasn't going to get so close that it was going to hurt when . . . It didn't matter, did it?" A wry smile crossed her lips and then was gone. "Before those two months were up, I already cared too much. Oh, Eddie, can't you give us a little more time? You fooled the doctors before. You can do it again, can't you?"

How he longed to say yes. He didn't want to give up this life, not when happiness had come so late to it. But he had never deceived her, and wouldn't now. He had been selfish to marry her when there were so many other ways he could have helped her instead. But it was done, and he couldn't really regret the time he had had with her, short as it was, even though it was causing her this grief now. He had wanted someone to care, and she did. He just hadn't realized his own heart would ache because of it, now that he must leave her.

He squeezed her hand in answer to her plea. Seeing her shoulders sag, he knew she understood. He sighed, closing his eyes, but only for a moment. Looking at her had always given him so much pleasure, and he needed that right now.

She was incredibly beautiful, though she would be the first to scoff if he said so, and rightly so, since her looks were not in the least fashionable. Her coloring was too flamboyant for the ton, her red hair too bright, like a bursting flame, her lime-green eyes too unusual in their paleness, and much too expressive. If Jocelyn didn't like you, her eyes said so, for she was too honest for her own good and didn't know the first thing about duplicity. Nor did she conform with other redheads, as there wasn't a single freckle on her flawless ivory skin, skin so pale it was nearly translucent.

Her features were more acceptable, a small oval face graced with gently arching brows, a nose small and straight, a soft, delicate mouth. There was a stubborn lift to her chin, though it was not indicative of temperament, at least not that Edward was aware of. The only stubbornness he had ever been treated to was her objection to leaving England, but in that she had finally given in.

As for the rest of her, well, even he had to admit her figure could have been a bit fuller. She was a touch over average in height, though still several inches shorter than his own medium frame. She had always been an active girl, even more so once she came to Fleming Hall, which would account for the narrow slimness of her shape. And she had lost weight this past month in her worry over him, so that her clothes no longer fitted her properly. Not that she cared. She was not a vain girl by any means. She accepted what she had to work with and did not go to great lengths to improve on it.

Edward, in his folly, had found himself extremely jealous of her, at any rate, and so was glad that other men did not find her as lovely as he did. And since his attachment to her was not sexual, her lack of figure was not at issue.

"Have I told you how grateful I am you agreed to be my duchess?"

"A hundred times, at least."

He squeezed her hand again. She barely felt it.

"Are you and the countess packed?"

"Eddie, don't — "

"We have to talk about it, my dear. You must leave immediately, even if it's the middle of the night."

"It's not right."

He knew what she referred to. "Funerals are depressing things, Jocelyn. No purpose can be served by your attending mine, other than to ruin all I've done to see you safe. Promise me?"

She nodded, if reluctantly. He was making it so real, her imminent departure. She had tried not to think of it, as if ignoring it could keep him with her longer. That wasn't possible anymore.

"I sent a copy of your will to Maurice." On seeing her widened eyes, he explained. "I hope it will stay his hand from anything drastic. I am also hoping that once he realizes you've left the country, he will let the matter go and be satisfied with the entailed properties that will come to him. Eaton is rich enough to support him and his large family." She didn't need to stay for the reading of the will, since he had already transferred everything else he owned to her name.

"If you had just given him all of it — "

"Never! I would give it to charity before I let that . . . Jocelyn, I want you to have it, all of it. That's one of the reasons I married you. I want to know that you will never lack for anything. And I have seen to your safety. The men I have obtained for your guard are the best available. Once you leave England, Maurice will be unable to manipulate the courts against you. And after you come of age, or if you should marry — "

"Don't mention marriage now, Eddie . . . not now," she said brokenly.

"I'm sorry, my dear, but you're so young. The day will come when — "

"Eddie, please!"

"Very well. But you do know that I just want you to be happy?"

He shouldn't have said so much to her. He was tired now; he could barely keep his eyes open. And yet there was so much more

40

he wanted to say.

"The world is yours . . . to enjoy."

"I will, Eddie, I promise. I'll make it an adventure, just as you've said. I'll see it all, do it all." She was speaking rapidly now, because he seemed to be fading right before her eyes. She squeezed his hand tighter until his eyes focused on her again. "I'll ride camels and elephants, hunt lions in Africa, climb the pyramids in Egypt."

"Don't forget . . . your stud farm."

"I won't. I'll produce the finest Thoroughbreds in the . . . Eddie?" His eyes had closed, his fingers gone slack. "Eddie?"

"I love . . . you . . . Jocelyn."

"Eddie!"

Chapter Three

Arizona Territory, 1881

It was not a road so much as a mule trail, so narrow at points that several times the lead coach had gotten wedged, once between the ridge of the mountain and immovable boulders, another time between two high, rocky slopes. Each time a good many hours were wasted in widening the path with shovels and picks, tools fortunate enough to have been included in the supplies. Not many miles had been covered this hot morning in October.

Hot. It was that, but Mexico had been worse, much worse, especially in July, an unfortunate time of year to enter that particular country. The cavalcade of coaches and wagons had crossed the Mexican border last night, and that was when their guide had disappeared — the reason they were not on a decent road now. They were lost, in the middle of mountain ranges that seemed to go on forever, though the trail they followed surely must end somewhere.

They were on their way to Bisbee. Or was it Benson? They really did need a guide for this area. The Mexican they had hired several months ago had done an admirable job of getting them over the border without incident, but he obviously had lied about his knowledge of this North American region, or he wouldn't have run off and left them without warning.

Of course, there was no hurry to get anywhere. They had supplies enough to last a month, gold enough to replenish the stores when they did finally reach Bisbee, or Benson, whichever came first. Any town would do, actually. It didn't really matter.

There had been a lot of coin tossing lately to decide on the next direction to travel in, something Jocelyn had started in Europe when she couldn't make up her mind what country to visit next. She had every intention of eventually reaching California this time, where she had sent her ship, the *Jocel*, to meet her. Of course, if something came up to change her mind in the interim, she could always send a message to the captain to meet her elsewhere, as she had done many times before.

She had been debating whether to spend some months exploring this country, as they had done in Mexico, or whether to go on to Canada or South America once she reached California. It was a matter of priorities, really, safety versus pleasure. She wanted to see more of these Western territories, and more of the states, too, and their cities. She had only been to New York and New Orleans so far. And she had especially wanted to visit the stud farms in Kentucky she had heard about, to see how their Thoroughbreds would compare with hers, and if they had any mares she might want to buy for Sir George, the prize stallion she had brought with her.

But if she did as she wanted to do, John Longnose was likely to catch up to them. He was the chap who had been following them about the world ever since they had left England three years ago, hiring cohorts in different countries as he needed them, so that they never really knew whom to suspect, or whom to watch out for. They had never seen the man, nor did they know his actual name. John Longnose was simply the name they gave to him because he was so often a topic of conversation, and they needed some name to call him by.

The safe thing to do would be to take to sea again once they reached California. There was a good chance that Longnose would lose the scent that way, at least for a while. Unless, of course, he had already tracked her ship to the West Coast and would be there waiting for her. And blast it all, she was tired of playing it safe, she really was. It was all she had been doing since this mad adventure had begun, often having to leave a place before she was ready, changing hotels frequently, changing her name even more frequently.

"Oh, dear, I see you're brooding again," Vanessa remarked, looking pointedly at the fan Jocelyn was using with increased speed. The frown she got in answer had her amending, "Of course it is terribly hot, isn't it?"

"We've been in hotter countries, including the one we just left."

"Indeed we have."

Vanessa said no more. She even looked back out the window, as if the subject were closed. Jocelyn knew better. It was an affectation of the countess's to give the impression of retreat, when that was rarely if ever her intention. It was an annoying habit, though Jocelyn was quite used to it by now, even ignored it most times. It was easier to just tell Vanessa what she wanted to know than to try to put her off.

You would think two women would get on each other's nerves after being constant companions for so long, but that had never happened. The friendship begun in England had grown until there wasn't anything they didn't know about each other, anything they couldn't speak of.

45

They made an odd pair, Jocelyn with her vivid coloring, Vanessa pale with ash-blond hair and light brown eyes. The countess was thirty-five now, but she looked ten years younger, with a full figure that turned men's heads. Jocelyn was still thin, all the rich, exotic foods she had sampled in every country they visited not helping at all to increase her curves. When they stood together, Vanessa's shortness made Jocelyn appear taller than her five and a half feet in height, and skinnier than she really was. Vanessa was approachable, conventional in appearance, not at all intimidating, while Jocelyn was the exact opposite simply because her looks were so unusual.

Jocelyn wouldn't know what to do without the countess. She often marveled that the older woman hadn't abandoned her long ago, or at least in New York, where their pursuit had taken on a more sinister aspect with the murder of Jocelyn's American solicitor. But Vanessa had seemed to thrive on the adventure. And unlike Jocelyn, she had always wanted to see the world, so she was enjoying every minute of their travels. She rarely complained, even when their accommodations were less than adequate, or the weather was the worst that it could get.

Vanessa wasn't the only one who had remained loyal through it all. They still had Babette and Jane, their lady's maids from Fleming Hall. The three grooms who saw to the horses, and Sidney and Pearson, the two menservants who came in most handy whenever they camped out in the open, were the same men Edward had picked for Jocelyn's entourage. They had lost their first cook and her two helpers, but Philippe Marivaux, the temperamental French chef they had found in Italy to replace her, was still with them, as were the Spaniard and the Arab who were later hired to assist him, as well as drive the wagons when necessary. And only four of the original sixteen-man escort had left Jocelyn's employ. Those weren't so easy to replace, for there weren't that many men skilled with weapons who were also willing to leave their homes and countries for what was beginning to seem like a never-ending journey.

At the most, five minutes had passed when Vanessa began again. "You aren't worried about this tiny road we're on, are you?"

"It's only a trail, I believe, and no, we seem to be descending now, so it shouldn't go on much longer."

"Then you *were* brooding again," Vanessa said with an I-knew-it smugness to her tone. "Not about that chap you had to leave behind

in New York, I hope. I thought you had concluded you couldn't marry him until you had
disposed of the little matter of your maidenhead?"

Jocelyn didn't blush as she had the first
time her unusual predicament had become the
topic of conversation. They had spoken of it
so often since then, there was nothing left to
blush about.

"I haven't changed my mind," Jocelyn replied. "Charles knew of Edward, had even
met him on his European tour. Under no cir-
cumstance would I allow Charles to become
aware of Edward's affliction. I won't have
Edward's memory besmirched like that. And
there isn't any way Charles wouldn't know of
it if I married him — unless of course he has
the same affliction, which is hardly likely as
young as he is."

"And as sexually aggressive. You did say he
cornered you in that bedroom and nearly — "

"Yes, well, we both agreed he is more than
capable of claiming all marital rights."

Jocelyn was blushing now. She hadn't
meant to confide that incident to Vanessa, but
the older woman had pried it out of her as
usual. Not that she was ashamed of what had
happened. Charles had already proposed to
her. And if she had drunk a little bit too much
at that party and had let Charles seduce her

48

because of it, there wasn't anything so wrong in that considering how they had felt about each other. But that night she had forgotten about her predicament, and if Vanessa hadn't come looking for her, which put an end to Charles' passionate embraces, there wouldn't be a problem anymore. Charles would have found out that the Duke of Eaton's widow was still a virgin.

"If you had loosened up in Morocco," Vanessa reminded her now, "you could have had a nice little affair with that sheikh what's-his-name who kept pursuing you. *He* didn't know Edward, didn't even know you were a widow, could barely even speak English, so it wouldn't have made any difference. And all it takes is one lover, my dear, and your problem is over."

"It was too soon, Vanessa. I was still in mourning, if you'll recall."

"I don't see what that has to do with it. I hope you don't think I waited a year after the earl passed on to take a lover. Goodness, no. A woman has needs every bit as strong as a man's."

"I wouldn't know."

Vanessa grinned at that prim tone. "No, you wouldn't — but you will. Or are you getting nervous again?"

"Not at all," Jocelyn said, and meant it,

though it was one thing to talk about and something else again to actually do. "It's time to find out what all the fuss is about. Just knowing how it's done isn't enough anymore to satisfy my curiosity. But it can't be just any man."

"No, of course not. A mild attraction isn't enough for the first time. You have to be knocked off your feet at the very least."

"I've been looking," Jocelyn said defensively.

"I know you have, dear. Obviously those dark, swarthy men of Mexico just weren't your cup of tea. If only you had made this decision sooner, before you met someone like Charles, whom you were seriously considering for marriage."

"But how could I know I would want to get married again?"

"I warned you these things just happen. No one plans on falling in love."

"Still, I honestly thought I wouldn't marry. After all, I will have to give up a good deal of the freedom I've come to enjoy if I do."

"With the right man that won't matter at all."

They had decided between them, on that long sea voyage from New York to Mexico, that now that marriage was a possibility for the future, Jocelyn had to get rid of her maidenhead. It was the only way she could keep Edward's name from being blackened with ugly gossip. And after all, a widow had no business being a virgin. That she was one at twenty-two was nothing to be proud of, not when it was the last thing anyone would expect her to be.

Her virginity had at last become a hindrance, and as Vanessa had said, something she should have seen to long ago. Her options now were limited. Having a doctor do it was one. But the thought of instruments being poked inside her to cut her membrane left her shuddering with distaste. The only other option was to take a lover, someone not in her social sphere, someone who had never heard of Edward, and especially someone she wasn't likely to ever encounter again when it was over. Whether she then returned to New York and Charles Abington the Third, or whether she met someone else suitable to her station and means, she could marry without worry. Edward's affliction would never come to light.

Jocelyn was ready, had been ever since they had docked in Mexico. And Vanessa was wrong. She had found several Mexicans quite attractive. Unfortunately, her interest was not returned, or if it was, she was too inexperienced to have read the subtle signs. She was not at all adept at flirting.

It wasn't going to be easy, this matter of finding a lover. Besides being so inexperienced, she had Mr. Longnose to consider, and being unable to stay in any one place long enough to develop a relationship to the point where she could entice a man into her bed. She supposed she should hope to be pursued again, as she had been in the Middle East, and on the East Coast of America. Some countries bred men more aggressive than others, or at least more bold in their desires. She could use a little of that boldness now, boldness she had heretofore considered sheer arrogance and audacity.

Recalling the bloodhound who was still dogging their trail, Jocelyn said, "I wasn't brooding about Charles, you know. In fact, it's been quite some time since I've even thought of him. Do you think I mightn't have been as fond of him as I supposed?"

"My dear, you really hadn't known him long enough. They say some loves are rather instantaneous, though I've never experienced one of those myself. Most love takes time to grow. We might have spent several months in New York, but you didn't even meet the man until three weeks before we were forced to leave. I find the fact that you were interested at all a very good sign, since you have tended to ignore men for the most part these past years. Now . . . tell me why our persistent friend the Longnose is troubling you. You can't seriously think he's discovered our whereabouts this soon, not after all that zigzagging we did across Mexico?"

Jocelyn had to smile at Vanessa's assurance that there were only two things she could possibly brood about. "No, I don't see how he could have known we sailed south, when we could just as well have returned to Europe."

"We don't know how he found us in New York either, but he did. I'm beginning to wonder if he hasn't got one of our people in his pay."

Green eyes flared with alarm, for if Jocelyn couldn't trust the people she depended on, then she was in serious trouble. "No! I won't believe that."

"I don't mean any of your escort, my dear. But you know the crew keeps changing on the *Jocel*. In just about every port, the captain loses a number of men he has to replace each time. There were six new men on the trip from New Orleans to New York, and another ten when we sailed to Mexico. And what with the telegraph being used in more and more countries, if Longnose has access to inside information as to our whereabouts, it wouldn't take him long to get it."

Surprisingly, the implications of that reasoning didn't cause fear so much as anger. Blast the man! She had only been worrying that he might locate the ship in California before they got there. Now it was conceivable that he might know where they were at this very moment, or at least where they were heading. The only thing in their favor was that he didn't have a ship at his command to make following them easy.

"Well, that just settled the matter of where we're going," Jocelyn said in a tight voice. "It won't be to California."

Vanessa raised a brow. "I was only speculating, my dear."

"I know. But if it's true, it would certainly explain why he's constantly been able to find us, even when we've left the ship to travel overland, and that just to throw him off the scent. I swear, Vanessa, I've really just about reached my limit. It was bad enough when Longnose was just trying to kidnap me, to return me to England. But since I've turned twenty-one, he has twice tried to kill me. Perhaps it's time I accepted the challenge."

"I hesitate to ask what you mean by that."

"I don't know what I mean, but I'll think of something," Jocelyn assured her.

Chapter Four

"I don' like the idear of killin' no woman, Dewane."

"Wha'd'ya care? It ain't as if'n ya'd ever get a chance at 'er yerself, Clydell. An' she's a fur'ner, jes like hisself thar. Look at 'im, calm an' patient as ya please. He don' dress like us, don' act like us, don' talk like us. An' he claims she's English too. So wha'd'ya care?"

Clydell did spare a glance for the foreigner. Tall, slim, dressed in those fancy Eastern duds — or were they fancy English duds? — and a good ten years older than any one of them. The man was so out of place he stood out like a nose wart. And clean, even after sleeping out with the rest of them on the bluff last night. How did he stay so clean?

"Still . . ." Clydell started again, only to glance back and catch his brother's narrowed gaze.

"Look, he got us outta Mexico, did'n he, when we thought fer sure we'd never scrape up enuf ta get back over the border? I don' mind tellin' ya I'm right glad ta be back whar a man can spit an' piss without givin' offense. We owe him, Clydell, ain't no two ways 'round it. An' ya don' see none o' these other boys gripin', do ya? It's jes' a job, fer Gawd's sake!"

When Dewane took that tone, his younger brother knew it was time to shut up. Dewane could be pressed only so far to explain why they were doing something. Robbing stages hadn't been so bad; neither had rustling a little cattle. And of course raising hell and picking a fight or two was normal whenever they hit a town. Clydell might have complained some about that bank job, but he'd done it anyway. That job had brought a posse after them that wouldn't let up.

They'd been chased into Mexico, where they were safe at last, or thought so, until a lousy band of hill bandits had left them with barely their lives and not a cent to their names. The Englishman had been a godsend, coming along when they were at the bottom of the barrel, so to speak, working just for bread and board in a dirty little cantina where they didn't even understand the lingo. The months had passed by, and Clydell had come to think he'd be dying down there.

He really shouldn't complain or think twice about it. Dewane was right as usual. Those four boys they picked up in Bisbee, two of them ex-rustling partners they'd known in New Mexico, hadn't even blinked when told what needed doing. Clydell was the only one who felt it just wasn't right, killing a woman. And the way it had been decided she'd be killed, that kind of made him sick to his stomach. Of course, it might not work out that way, and thank God he wasn't one of the two assigned to go after her if the boulder didn't manage to smash her to bits. A piece of lead was a much cleaner way to go if someone had to go. But he was one of the four who would be shoving that boulder over the bluff, which was why he groaned inwardly when the Mexican, who had been stationed further back in the hills to watch for the victim's arrival, showed up to say it wouldn't be long now.

Elliot Steele opened his pocket watch to check the time. It was nearly noon. The duchess was late — as usual. But then she always managed to do something to disturb his well-laid plans. Why he should think this time would be any different, he didn't know. But the hour, fortunately, was of no importance. There was only one trail and she was on it. There was no place else she could go except forward, directly into his trap.

How many times had he said that before, and yet she was still going about her merry way. The girl had the luck of the Gods. How else could she have escaped his traps time and again?

Elliot was good at his line of work, or had thought he was, until the Duke of Eaton had hired him. He had made a small fortune over the years working for the gentry in whatever capacity was necessary, no matter how unsavory, so he *had* been good at what he did. And what Maurice Fleming wanted done had been so simple. Just find the girl and return her to England, where he would then have complete control over her and her money, which was all Fleming had wanted.

Elliot had contacts in other countries, men in the same line of work. And he knew how to go about hiring the kind of men who came cheap and didn't ask questions about what they were told to do. The job should have taken no more than a few months, just long enough to find out where the *Jocel* came to port. And yet for nearly two years, the length of time the duke continued to pay all of Elliot's expenses, his men had only once gotten their hands on her.

It was preposterous, because she was so easy to locate wherever she went — if not her ship, then her large entourage of coaches and wagons and mounted guards. It was not a caravan that could pass unnoticed, and she never tried to conceal it or change it or leave it behind. Her coach alone was the finest made, large, bright teal blue, and pulled by six high-stepping mares all a matched gray in color. She might as well have the ducal crest emblazoned on the doors, the vehicle was so memorable.

Yet no matter how many times he was able to locate her, it was never an easy matter to actually get to her. In point of fact, her small army of servants and guards made it frustratingly difficult, and she was never, ever, very far from them. The one time his men had been able to steal her away, she had been found and rescued the very same day, with his four men dying and not one of hers even wounded.

But those days were over. Now that the girl had come of age, Fleming would no longer have an easy time of manipulating the courts to give him control of her. He no longer wanted her, was no longer paying Elliot's expenses to find her, and Elliot had earned nothing for all his time, trouble, and frustration before he was dismissed. Two years he had wasted with nothing to show for it. He was not a man to accept that with a shrug of nonchalance. Not by any means.

His purpose now was twofold. He was going to kill that red-haired bitch for the pleasure of it, but also for all the feelings of incompetence she had made him feel, and for the ruin of the reputation he had built up, of being a man who could be counted on to see a job done quickly and without mistakes. And when he informed the duke that it was done, and that he had seen to it that she left no will, that Fleming could now claim her wealth simply by being her only relative, Elliot would finally be compensated.

He didn't care how long it took or how much of his own money it cost, he would see it done. And killing her was much easier than trying to abduct her. It could be done from afar. It could be done in any number of ways. That he had twice attempted it and twice failed only proved she had not lost her luck yet.

Even the bloody countries she chose to cross were more often than not to her advantage. Mexico had been ideal for his purposes, or so he thought; huge, sparsely populated outside its cities, miles and miles of nothing but wilderness where a massacre could go unreported for days, weeks. And the duchess conveniently set up camp in the middle of nowhere time and again. It was the perfect opportunity to attack in force, to hire an army to match hers. And hiring the army would have been easy and cheap — if it were for any other purpose. But getting a Mexican to agree to kill a woman was nearly impossible. He had tried and tried, and was turned down every time. She had beaten him again without doing a thing, simply through the character of the Mexican people.

Then he had found Dewane and Clydell Owen, two down-on-their-luck Americans who had that look Elliot always recognized as being available and willing for anything. He had sent them north across the border, and they had come up with four others just like themselves, as well as a likely spot for an ambush. They were to meet up in the mining town of Bisbee, which he had finally located yesterday. He had spent the remainder of the day riding back and forth over the narrow mule track below, looking for the ideal spot for what he had in mind.

The spot wasn't as perfect as he could have hoped for: nearly out of the mountains, and with the slope that the trail cut across extending on down to the bottom. Trees were in this area, at least below the trail on the lower slope, not in any great abundance, but enough to stop a rolling coach if the boulder should do no more than knock the vehicle off the track. That wasn't likely to happen. With as steep a drop as there was directly below the boulder, and with the path wide at that point, the boulder was almost guaranteed to drop hard and go no farther.

If there had been time, he would have moved the bloody big rock to a better spot on the trail, where it would have wedged itself between two slopes and been impossible to move, making the trail impassable for horse or coach. He might have let the duchess pass through first if that were the case, simply for the pleasure of killing her with his own hands. But as it was now, if the boulder didn't do as it was supposed to and land directly on the lead coach, the trail would still be blocked enough to keep the rest of the escort trapped behind the boulder, with Elliot's men providing gunfire to hold them there for a while. As long as the duchess was on the opposite side of the boulder, the two men he had prepared for that contingency could sneak down and take care of her without a problem.

They could just hear the horses approach now, coming slowly down the trail. "How many lead riders did you count?" Elliot asked the Mexican.

"Six, senor."

Elliot nodded. He should have known her guards wouldn't break habit just because the trail was narrow and not what they were used to. Six always rode ahead, and six behind the coach. It was just as well there was room below on that ledge for the lead riders to maneuver past the coach when the Mexican started the shooting, to draw their attention to the back of the train. There was little that could be done if they didn't move back to investigate, for it was doubtful all six could be picked off before they had a chance to find cover. And if the coach did escape the boulder, that would leave too many guards to still protect it.

"Go back to your position," Elliot ordered the man, "and wait for the signal to begin."

Dewane watched him go before sneering, "Ya ain't tol' the Mex she's ta die, have ya?"

Elliot stared coldly at the older Owen brother. It was his policy to explain himself as little as possible to his hirelings, and he saw no reason now to mention his experiences with the Mexicans and that he wasn't taking any chances with the one he had hired to guide the duchess away from the main roads so she would be forced to come this way.

"Quite right," was all he said, and that was enough.

These men were leery of him and that was as it should be. They shared a camaraderie of nationality from which he stood apart, which was as he would want it even if their differences did not enter into it. When you employed men as cold-blooded and merciless

63

as yourself, a separateness had to be maintained so there was never any question of who was in control.

Elliot turned to watch the Mexican hurrying along the upper ledge to his assigned position. This spot really was ideal. With two ledges, the upper one concealed from below, it was absolutely perfect for ambush. There was even a path leading down the other side of the bluff to where their horses were hidden. And those below could not give chase even if they wanted to, because the two separate trails didn't meet until they reached the bottom of the mountain on this side. The path leading down the other side of the bluff met the foothills on the western face of the mountain, but horses couldn't maneuver up or down it.

Soon . . . soon he could get on with his life. Nothing was going to go wrong this time. It couldn't. He was due some luck of his own.

He moved into his own position, which allowed a clear view of the trail below. He could see the lead riders now, and Sir Parker Grahame, captain of the guard, out in front as usual. He knew all of her people by name, and some of their histories too. He had spoken with them, bought them drinks, almost managed to seduce that silly French maid, Babette, while they were in Egypt. That they had no idea who he was or what he looked like

64

made it easy. As long as he never approached one of them unless they were alone, and never approached the same one again in another town or country, they never suspected a thing.

"Best get ready, gentlemen," Elliot said quietly to the men behind him.

He lay stretched out to the left of the boulder. He would not relinquish his place, wanting to see the devastation firsthand. The huge rock sat on the very edge of the bluff. They had had to do no more than loosen it from the mountain's grip beforehand, so all it needed now was a push.

The four men ready to do the pushing set their hands to the boulder and waited. Elliot waited for the lead guards to pass and the first of the coach horses to be directly below before sending the Mexican the signal to begin his part. Dewane joined him, a gun in each hand, though he laid one down for later use. The last man took out the mirror that would flash the signal to the Mexican.

"I want the driver of the coach eliminated before he applies the brake." Elliot repeated this particular order. "He'll stop the coach as soon as the guards up front start to turn around to investigate the shots from the rear, but whether the guards have passed behind the coach yet or not, the driver must be prevented from applying the brake. Without the driver, the coach horses will then move forward on their own."

"No problem." Dewane grinned, able to see the big man now who was driving the lead coach. "He's no easy target ta miss."

Elliot saw it was one of the grooms driving the duchess today. Too bad it wasn't the Spaniard. That man was a devil with knives, and had killed one of Elliot's men in New York who had been caught tampering with the duchess's coach.

The guards were passing now. In another moment, another . . .

"Send the signal," Elliot ordered over his shoulder.

He waited tensely, holding his breath. The first pair of matched grays had passed, the second pair was nearly past. Bloody, bloody hell, if that Mexican . . .

They heard the shot. So did the guards below. They were all turning about, but Grahame sent only two back to investigate. The vehicles were all stopping. There were shouts filling the air, demanding to know what was happening. The driver of the lead coach was standing up to look back.

The third matched pair of grays was below the boulder now.

Another two shots were fired successively. The remaining four guards began to maneuver past the coach on the side of the slope, the only place there was room for them to go. Grahame stopped, however, undoubtedly to reassure the duchess. Watching him, Elliott didn't see the driver reach for the brake handle, but Dewane did. The shot fired right next to him gave him a start, but not enough to miss seeing the driver drop the reins as he began falling, right off the coach. He hit the ground behind Grahame's mount, making the horse rear up out of control. The driver hit the ground close enough to the third set of grays; they likewise tried to rear, couldn't, and set their harness mates into fright.

From a dead stop to a frightened surge forward, it was too fast. "Now!" Elliot shouted, then swore a blue streak as he watched the boulder crash to the ledge below, break apart on contact, and do no more than scatter dust on the rapidly fleeing coach.

He got to his feet with a snarl, and narrowly missed being shot. The guards were already returning the fire his men were raining down on them.

The two men who were supposed to have climbed down to the ledge below to get to the coach if it was missed, were standing there awaiting new orders.

"Get your horses and come around to where these trails end," Elliot instructed. "With her bloody luck, that coach will miraculously make it to the bottom of the mountain without going over the side. Follow it with all speed, stop it if you have to, but make sure no one is left alive inside it. No one."

Chapter Five

"Vanessa? Vanessa, are you all right?"

"You may ask me that later. Right now I honestly couldn't say."

Jocelyn was lying on the floor, or to be more exact, on the door. After that horrifying ride that had seemed as though it would never end, the coach had somehow tipped over on its side. Jocelyn had fallen against the door when the coach began to tilt, and presently had her back flat against it, with her long legs stretched out on the actual floor, which was now straight up in the air. Vanessa had not fared much better, though she had remained in her seat, which was now against the side of the coach above Jocelyn's head.

They both sat up at just about the same time, Vanessa with a moan, Jocelyn with a grunt. "I imagine we'll have a few bruises to show for this experience."

"Is that all?" Vanessa replied, sounding not at all herself. "It feels — "

"You *are* hurt," Jocelyn said accusingly,

seeing how the countess was pressing her hand to the side of her head.

"Just a bump, I think. I was trying to brace myself, but my arm slipped."

"Turn around and rest your back against the seat. It's more cushiony than the wall."

Jocelyn helped her until she was settled, then got to her knees. They were both a mess, clothes askew, coiffures falling down. Jocelyn removed the few remaining hairpins that hadn't rattled loose, then tossed her hair back out of the way. She would have grinned at that point for having escaped this experience intact, if Vanessa weren't grimacing in pain from the bump on her head.

"What do you think happened, Vana?"

"I think John Longnose was up to his old tricks again, that's what."

"Do you really?" Jocelyn's teeth worried at her lower lip a moment as she considered that possibility. "But how could he have gotten in front of us? How could he know which way we would come, for that matter?"

Vanessa didn't open her eyes to answer. "We weren't exactly hurrying through Mexico, my dear. There was time aplenty for him to get ahead of us. And as to his knowing where we were going, well, I wondered about that guide's sudden disappearance, I really did. Rather convenient, wasn't it, leading us right to the start of that mountain trail?"

"Why, that little traitor!"

"More likely he was in Longnose's pay first, my dear. He came to us, if you recall; we didn't find him. Besides, I know an Englishman's voice when I hear it, and that shouted 'Now,' just before that crash we heard, was decidedly British. What was that crash, anyway?"

"I have no idea. A better question would be, what's become of our driver?"

Here Vanessa sighed. "I really don't think he was with us on that insane ride, or we would have heard him shouting at the horses, even if he couldn't stop them. That shot that was so close —"

"Don't even think it!" Jocelyn cut in sharply. "If we lost him, he no doubt only lost his seat — as we both did innumerable times."

"No doubt," Vanessa agreed, to keep the peace. They would learn soon enough what had really happened. "But I think we've lost our horses too."

Jocelyn had also felt the difference in the pull of the coach just before they tilted over, so she didn't argue that comment. "They'll be found," she said with confidence. "And so will we be shortly. In the meantime . . ."

Vanessa opened one eye to see the duchess getting to her feet. "Whatever are you doing?"

71

Standing on one door, Jocelyn realized that her head didn't quite reach the other. "I was going to see how we might get out of here, but even if I could throw that door open — "

"Don't even bother, Jocelyn. It won't be that long until our people reach — " She didn't finish, because they could hear someone approaching at a gallop. "You see? That didn't take long at all."

Ears attuned, they heard the first horse skid to a sudden stop very near, probably one of the guards ahead of the others, probably Sir Parker Grahame himself. He was ever diligent, and besides, he was sweet on Jocelyn, and so was prone to get more upset than the others each time Longnose made one of his attempts.

After another moment the coach groaned as their rescuer climbed on top of it, and then the door was lifted and dropped back with a bang. The overhead sun had been pouring in through the window, but nothing like what was now coming in through the open door. Jocelyn was momentarily blinded when she looked up, but as soon as a man's silhouette appeared to block some of the glare, it was easier for her to see, though not to recognize who he was at first.

"Parker?"

"No, ma'am," came a deep, lazy drawl.

If he had said more in that moment, Jocelyn wouldn't have begun glancing about for her reticule, where she kept the little derringer she had purchased in New Orleans. Not that she couldn't have been shot in the time it took her to locate it, hidden as it was under the hats and jackets that had been removed earlier that morning.

When he did speak again, it was with some impatience. "Do you want out of there or not?"

"I'm not so sure," Jocelyn said honestly, looking up again, and wishing she could see more than a black silhouette framed in the opening.

How did you ask a man if he was there to kill you? But would he have offered to get them out if he meant to shoot them? He could just do it. Then again, he might be under orders from John Longnose to bring them to him. It was too much to hope that he was just a stranger passing by.

"It might help, sir," Vanessa intervened in the prolonged silence, "if you would tell us who you are — and what you're doing here."

"I saw your team of horses racing toward the river and figured they'd left a stagecoach behind, though I've never seen horses like that hitched to a stage before."

"And you just thought to investigate? You aren't associated with — the Englishman?"

"I'm not associated, as you put it, with anyone, lady. Christ, what is this with all the questions? Either you want out of there or you don't. Now, I can understand if you feel you'd be dirtying your hand putting it to mine for a lift up" — the impatience turned distinctly bitter here — "but I don't see much alternative just now — unless you want to wait for the next fellow who comes passing by."

"Not at all," Jocelyn said with relief, certain now he meant them no harm. "A little dirt can be easily washed off," she added with a smile, having misunderstood his meaning.

She surprised him good with that answer, enough that he didn't immediately grasp the hands she raised to him. And then it dawned on him that she couldn't really see him. She'd change her tune when she did, quicker than spit. He'd be lucky if he even got a thank-you for his help.

Jocelyn gave a little gasp, she was grasped and lifted so fast. She ended up sitting on the coach with her legs still dangling through the door opening. She laughed then at how easily that was accomplished, and glanced back inside to Vanessa, who hadn't moved yet.

"Are you coming, Vana? It was really quite easy."

"I'll stay here, if you don't mind, my dear. I'd rather wait until the coach can be righted — if it can be done gently, that is. Perhaps this headache will have lessened somewhat by then."

"Very well," Jocelyn agreed. "It shouldn't be *that* long before Sir Parker finds us." She looked around, but her rescuer stood directly behind her. She started to rise, turning and saying to him, "She won't need a lift up. She hit her head, you see, and isn't feeling . . . quite . . ."

The words simply trailed away, forgotten. Jocelyn hadn't been struck so with awe since her first sight of the pyramids in Egypt. But this was totally different, for more senses than sight were affected. Her whole system seemed to go wild for a moment, sending off signals she wasn't quite familiar with — breathlessness, accelerated heartbeat, a rush of adrenaline, signs of fear when she wasn't in the least bit frightened.

He stepped back from her, she wasn't sure why, but it gave her a better look at him, since he was so tall. Too handsome by half, had been her first impression, followed now by strength, which she had felt firsthand, darkness, and strangeness, in that order. Hair as black as pitch, perfectly straight, and falling well past incredibly wide shoulders. Skin darkly bronze with lean, hawkish features, a nose straight and chiseled, deep-set eyes under low, slashing brows, lips well drawn, and a firm, square jaw.

A long, sinewy body finished the picture, encased in a strange animal-skin jacket with long fringes attached, and knee-high boots without heels, of the same soft tan skin and also with fringes. Jocelyn was getting used to seeing the gun worn on the hip after her sojourn through Mexico, so his was no surprise, and the wide-brimmed hat that shaded his eyes so she couldn't determine their color, except that they weren't dark like the rest of him.

His trousers were dark blue and fairly tight around nicely shaped legs. Nothing unusual in that. But he wore no shirt. The jacket hung nearly closed, but still, there was no shirt beneath it, just the same smooth bronzed skin as on his face — smooth, hairless skin. He actually had not a single hair on the several inches of chest and stomach that she could see, definitely unusual as far as she knew, though of course, how much did she really know about Americans, and how much about a man's chest, for that matter?

Truthfully, she had never seen anything quite like him. His strangeness unnerved her, but not nearly as much as his swarthy handsomeness.

76

"Do you always go about — half dressed?"

"Is that all you have to say to me, ma'am?"

She could feel the heat seeping into her cheeks. "Oh, dear, please don't take offense. I can't imagine where that question . . . I'm not usually so impertinent." A loud "Ha!" came from inside the coach, and Jocelyn grinned. "I believe the countess disagrees with me, and rightly so. I suppose my outspokenness does border on rudeness more times than not."

"Ask a stupid question . . ." the man mumbled as he turned away and jumped to the ground.

Jocelyn frowned, watching him move toward his horse, a beautiful, big-boned animal the like of which she had never seen before, with black-and-white spotted markings on its rump and loins. She would love to look the horse over, to ride it even, but at the moment, her only concern was the man's intentions.

"You're not leaving, are you?"

He didn't bother to look back. "You mentioned someone would be along shortly. No point in my — "

"But you can't go!" she cried in alarm, not certain why it was alarm she felt, but it was. "You haven't let me thank you yet, and — and how am I supposed to get down from here if you don't assist me?"

"Shit," she heard, and felt her cheeks heating again. But he was coming back. "All right, jump."

She looked at his hands reaching up to her and didn't hesitate. He had already proved his strength. Not for a moment did she consider how likely he was to miss her if she just threw herself down at him. He didn't miss her. But she did slam into him. Only that wasn't so startling as being set on her feet and away from him almost in the same breath. And again he turned away.

"No, wait." She put out a hand, but he didn't stop to see it, so she lifted her skirts to follow him. "Are you really in such a hurry that you must rush off?"

She plowed into his back when he stopped this time, and heard him swear again before he whipped around to glare at her. "Look, lady, as it happens, I left my gear, *and* my shirt, back at the river, where I was fixing to wash up before heading into town. You can't just leave things lying around in this country and expect them to be there when you get back."

"I'll replace anything you might lose, but please don't leave us yet. Since my people haven't come along by now, they must have been trapped in the mountains behind us. We honestly need your — "

"You've left a trail anyone can follow, ma'am."

"Yes, but we were separated when some men set upon us, men who mean to do me harm. They are as likely to come along as my people."

"Your 'people'?"

"My entourage." When that failed to erase his frown, she added, "My guards and servants, those I travel with."

His eyes moved over her at that, taking in her velvet skid and ruffled silk blouse, the kind of clothes he had only seen worn back East. And then he spared another look at the shining teal-blue coach that one glance inside had made him think he was doubting his eyes. Them fancy private railroad cars didn't come as luxurious as this.

When he'd seen it downed, he hadn't expected to find women inside, especially women like this, one a countess of some kind. Wasn't that royalty or something? Whatever it was, it wasn't from this country. And this one with her flaming hair and, Christ, eyes brighter than new spring leaves. His first sight of her had brought back all the old bitterness. But it didn't stop the surge of sexual awareness he'd been hit with. That scared the shit out of him, because he hadn't been attracted to her kind in years.

"Just who are you, lady?"

"Oh, I'm sorry. I should have introduced

myself right off. I'm Jocelyn Fleming," she said, determining there wasn't much point in using a false name this time with Longnose so close behind them.

He stared at the hand she held out to him, just stared, until she was forced to lower it.

"Maybe I should have asked, what are you?"

"I beg your pardon?"

"You one of those rich miners' wives from Tombstone?"

"No, not at all. I've been widowed now for several years. And we've just come up from Mexico, though our travels originated in England."

"That mean you're English?"

"Yes." She smiled at the way he had of chopping up the mother tongue, though she could understand him perfectly, and rather liked the slow drawl to his words. "I assume you are an American?"

He knew the word, but he'd never heard anyone use it before. Folks usually associated themselves with the state or territory they were from, not the country. And now he recognized her accent too. Though he'd never heard a woman speak with those cultured tones before, he'd met several Englishmen touring the West. But her nationality explained why she hadn't minded touching him.

She hadn't been in the West long enough to recognize what he was. So that wasn't why she had stared at him for so long up on that coach, as he'd assumed. Again his body tightened with a familiar hardness.

For half a second he considered not telling her. He'd probably never see her again anyway, so why put the distance he was accustomed to between them? Because he needed that distance. She was off limits, and this hell-cursed attraction he felt for her was dangerous. But he wasn't used to saying it. He dressed as he did so he wouldn't have to, so there'd be no mistakes.

"I was born in this country, but folks got a different name for me, lady. I'm a half-breed."

"How interesting," she said, aware his tone had turned bitter again, but choosing to ignore it. "It sounds like something to do with stock and cross-breeding. What does it have to do with people?"

He stared at her for a moment as if she were crazy; then he swore under his breath before snarling, "What the hell do you think it has to do with people? It means I'm only half white."

His tone gave her pause, but still she asked, "And the other half?"

Again he gave her a look that said she ought

81

to be locked up for the safety of others. "Indian," he bit out. "Cheyenne, in my case. And if that doesn't set you back on your toes, it ought to."

"Why?"

"Christ, woman, you ought to learn something about a country before you visit it!"

"But I always do," she replied, only slightly wary that he had shouted at her. "I know a good deal about this one."

"Then you must have missed the part about Indians and whites being sworn enemies," he sneered. "Ask in the next town you come to. They'll give you an earful about why you shouldn't be standing here talking to me."

"If you have something against the whites, as you call them, it hasn't anything to do with me, does it?" she replied, undaunted. "I'm not your enemy, sir. Good Lord, how could you even insinuate that I might be, when I feel nothing but gratitude for your timely assistance?"

He shook his head at her, and then he actually chuckled. "I give up, ma'am. You'll learn better if you stay here long enough."

"Does that mean we can be friends now?" At his grunt, she added, "You haven't told me your name."

"Colt Thunder."

"Colt, as in the revolver? How unusual to be named after a gun."

"Well, Jessie has an unusual sense of humor."

"Is Jessie your father?"

"My father's daughter, though neither of us knew it until a few years back. Before that she was my best friend."

"How interesting. I take it, then, that Colt Thunder isn't your real name? I have had to use false names myself quite frequently, though it isn't necessary now that my nemesis has found me again."

He wasn't going to ask. If it killed him, he wasn't. The less he knew about her, the sooner he would forget her — Christ, if he could. That hair, flowing down past her waist, like hot flames licking at her hips. He was going to see that hair in his dreams for a long time to come, he knew damn well he was. And those eyes too. Damn, why did she keep looking at him like that, as if she were as attracted to him as he was to her?

She had said something else to him, but he hadn't heard a word, for she had stepped closer when she said it and put a hand to his arm. Her touch, deliberate, unnecessary, sent his heart pounding against his ribs. It gave him ideas he didn't dare dwell on. Damn it to hell, she was playing with fire and didn't even know it.

The shot took his hat off, bringing him out of the mesmerizing spell she had cast. He whirled and fired without thought, two rounds that both struck home. One of the two men who had been racing hell-bent toward them hit the dirt but didn't stay there, his foot caught in the stirrup. The other had dropped his gun when the bullet struck his right shoulder, and was now whipping his horse around to head back the way he had come. Colt let him go. He didn't shoot men in the back, didn't shoot to kill either — most times.

The riderless horse still came on. The easiest way to stop him was to mount him as he passed, which Colt did.

Jocelyn had seen it all, but she still didn't believe it, especially how fast that gun had come out of Colt Thunder's holster and fired. Nor had she ever witnessed anything as incredible as someone mounting a racing horse. The odds on his not falling flat on his face in the attempt were astronomical, yet he did it by simply twisting a hand in the animal's mane and leaping on.

Bemused, she answered Vanessa's worried inquiry that she was all right, and hurried toward the horse that had already been brought under control only a few yards away. She got there just as Colt ground-tied the animal and moved to release the man's foot from the stirrup. He then bent down to check on the man's condition, and she was treated to another one of his colorful swear words. She could see for herself the man was dead of a broken neck, though Colt's bullet had grazed his temple, so he was likely unconscious when it happened.

"The bastard ducked," Colt said in disgust as he rose to his feet.

"You were aiming at something in particular?"

"The right shoulder bone. Easiest way to disarm a man who's coming right at you. You know him?"

He looked directly at her then, treating her to the full force of his eyes. Without the shadow cast by his hat, she could now see that his eyes weren't light or dark, but the clearest, purest blue, so very startling in such a deeply bronzed face. They quite literally took her breath away, forcing her to lower her own eyes before she could answer him with any degree of normal intelligence.

"No, I've never seen this man before, nor the other. But I have little doubt that they were both John Longnose's hirelings. It's his habit to employ the natives of whatever country we're in at the time to do his dirty work. It looks like your assistance now includes saving my life."

"Lady, no man in his right mind would want to kill you. There's many things I could think of that a man would want to do to you, but killing isn't one of them."

He had turned away to say the last of that as he moved to retrieve his hat, but she had heard him anyway and blushed pleasurably. Not many men found her attractive with her wild coloring, but she could usually tell when one did. Not so with this man. He had glowered at her, shouted at her, couldn't wait to ride off and never see her again. So it was a distinct surprise to find that he might, just might, be as aware of her as she was of him — that was, if she could construe those comments as complimentary.

She quickly followed behind him again to try to explain. "It's only been this last year that he's been trying to kill me, you know. Before that his purpose was just to return me to England. Mine was to avoid that at all costs. It's rather a long story, but the gist of it is that I have been running from that man for three years now, and quite frankly I'm tired of it."

He dusted his hat off by hitting it against his leg, then set it back on his head with the brim tilted forward rather rakishly. "It's none of my business, ma'am."

"No, of course it isn't. Indeed not. And I

wouldn't dream of embroiling you in my problems, especially after all you've done for me already."

He gave her a level look after so many words when a simple nod of agreement would have covered. "Glad to hear it," he replied dryly.

"I wasn't exactly finished, Mr. Thunder."

"Look, don't tack any 'mister' on my name. Call me either Colt or Thunder. I answer to both."

"As you wish. But as I was saying, I couldn't help noticing how superbly adept you are with that revolver you carry."

"Superbly adept?" He grinned. "Lady, you sure have a fancy way of calling the kettle black."

"I beg your pardon?"

"Never mind. So what about it?"

"What about — oh, yes. So are you by any chance for hire?"

"You want Longnose killed?"

That disturbed her, how easily he said it, without the least bit of emotion, but she tamped down the feeling. "No, just apprehend him and turn him over to whatever law officials there are in this territory. He's wanted in New York for the murder of my solicitor."

"Your what?"

"My American lawyer."

"Why'd he kill your lawyer?"

"We have only been able to determine that the unfortunate man discovered him in his office, in the process of stealing the will I had just had executed that same day. It was the only thing missing from his office, according to his partner. And there were several witnesses whom he asked for directions to the lawyers' office. They all swear it was an Englishman who questioned them. And besides, it's not the first will I have made that has turned up missing."

"Sounds to me like all you need is a bounty hunter, ma'am, and that I'm not. Or better yet, just report what happened here to the town marshal over in Tombstone when you have the body turned in. All that's needed is this fellow's name and a description."

"But I don't know his name or what he looks like." At his frown, she quickly added, "John Longnose is just what we call him. All I know about him is that he's as English as I am."

"Well, chances are there's not another Englishman within a hundred miles of here, but you never know. I've seen others passing through, so it'd be easy enough to make a mistake. Your best bet, then, is to entrench and let him come to you. You did say you have guards?"

"Yes, but — "

"Then you don't need another gun."

Before it registered that he was refusing her offer, *his* gun was out again and going off. Jocelyn turned to see a long snake now minus its head, though the body was still wiggling, and she shuddered at how close it was behind her. She hadn't heard it or sensed the danger. She didn't need another gun? He had just proved that statement false.

Colt glanced at her sideways after he tossed the snake away from them. He had to hand it to her. She'd been shot at, near snake-bit, and that was after her coach had crashed. And no telling what had happened before then. Yet she hadn't made a fuss about any of it. Of course, that snake had managed to shut her up. She was the talkingest woman he'd ever met. Not that he minded. That accent of hers was real soft on the ears.

He turned to stare at the dust cloud making its way toward them. Her people, he hoped, considering the size of that cloud indicated quite a few riders. He replaced the rounds in his gun just in case.

He glanced at her again and saw that she had produced a small lacy square of cloth from somewhere and was dabbing it at her forehead. That sweet scent of hers drifted more strongly to him, stirring his blood again.

Damn, but she was dangerous. Each time he looked at her, she somehow got prettier and definitely more desirable. And each time she looked at him with those beautiful green eyes, he had to fight down old instincts. If he had come across her six years ago, he would have simply ridden off with her and made her his. But he was "civilized" now and so couldn't follow his natural inclinations anymore.

But those instincts were strong, too strong, the reason that he didn't dare stick around to help her out with her troubles. It'd be different if she didn't already have help, more than enough help from the look of it. Then he would have no choice, because he damn well didn't like the idea of someone wanting to hurt her. She might not belong out here, but she was here, and she had crossed his path. He was going to worry about her now until she was safe. Just what he needed.

"Those your people riding in?"

Jocelyn started at his question, barely heard through the ringing in her ears from the gunshots. She had been trying to think of some way to change his mind about working for her. She didn't want him to just ride off to where she might never see him again. That was imperative, though she had yet to wonder why.

She saw the riders now, and recognized Sir Parker Grahame out in front. "Yes, my escort, and quite a few of the servants, by the look of it."

"I'll be taking off, then. Your men can find your team staked out at the river, less than a mile east of here — that is, if someone hasn't come along and stolen them by now."

The unspoken words were implicit in his tone. If her horses were gone, so would be his gear.

"Thank you. I'm sure they will be easily recovered. But are you certain you won't change your mind and — "

"Ma'am, that's a small army you have bearing down on us. You don't need me."

"We will need a guide, however."

"You can find one in Tombstone."

Jocelyn gritted her teeth as she followed him to his horse and watched him mount. He obviously wasn't for hire, for any reason.

"Where is this town you mentioned?"

"About six miles or so directly across the San Pedro. It's big enough that you can't miss it."

"Do you live there, by any chance?"

"No, ma'am."

"But will I see you there, do you think?"

"I doubt it."

He hadn't looked at her since he headed for

his horse, but he did now, and had to grip his saddle horn. The disappointment was vivid in her expression, pulling at his gut with invisible cords. What the hell did she want from him? Didn't she know she was courting trouble with that look?

"I really wish you would reconsider," she said in a soft, imploring voice that wrapped around him, making him groan.

It was too much on top of everything else she made him feel. He had to get the hell out of there.

"Forget it, lady. I don't need that kind of trouble."

She didn't know he was referring to her and not her problems. She stood there and watched him ride away, feeling guilty for trying to embroil him in what was a very dangerous situation. He was right to refuse her. He had helped her enough as it was. But blast it all, she didn't *want* to see the last of him.

Chapter Six

Ed Schieffelin had been warned by the post commander at Fort Huachuca when he set out into the Apache-infested wilderness of southeastern Arizona that all he would find was his tombstone. The long-time prospector ignored the warning, and when he found the "strike" of his dreams, promptly named it the Tombstone. Other strikes followed in the area, but Ed's Tombstone was the one that lent its name to the town that sprang up around it in 1877. Four years later, the town boasted some five hundred buildings, with at least a hundred having been granted licenses to sell hard liquor, and maybe half that number operating as brothels and cribs on the east end of town past 6th Street, a small number really, when you considered the town's population had grown to more than ten thousand.

Colt made a habit of learning about a town before he entered it, and he had found out all he needed to know about this one when he had passed through Benson, just as he had learned enough about Benson when he had passed through Tucson. Seeing it for himself now, he could understand why a seventeen-year-old boy on the run toward Mexico might linger here awhile. It was where he expected to finally find Billy Ewing. It was where he damn well better find the boy. After picking up Billy's trail in St. Louis four months ago and losing it time and again, Colt was at the end of his patience and his temper. The things he did for Jessie . . .

It wasn't going to be easy, however, locating a seventeen-year-old kid in a town this size. He'd been told there were five good-sized hotels and six boardinghouses, but who was to say Billy would be using his own name? He'd also been told now was not a good time to visit, that the town was heading for an explosion of violence between the outlaw element operating in the area and the town marshal and his brothers who had been clashing and feuding for some time now.

Colt stopped dead still in the middle of Toughnut Street, remembering that. Where had that piece of information gone hiding when he had spoken to the redhead? He had been heading for Tombstone with every intention of getting Billy out of there as quickly as possible, and yet he had steered a woman like that in the same direction. Had she shaken him up that much, or had he subconsciously wanted her going in his direction? Dumb, plain dumb. Now he'd have to see her again to tell her it'd be healthier if she didn't remain in town for long. No, seeing her again would be even dumber. He'd send Billy with the message — once he found him.

He urged his horse on, his expression black with self-disgust, seeing nothing of the town for several minutes until his senses returned and he realized he'd passed 3rd Street, where he'd meant to turn left. Fly's Lodging House had been recommended to him, located on Fremont Street between 3rd and 4th, so he headed up 4th Street rather than turn around.

The town was laid out in square blocks, with the intersecting thoroughfares being Toughnut, Allen, Fremont, and Safford streets running south to north, and 1st through 7th streets running west to east. Crossing Allen Street, he continued north up 4th, passing Hafford's Saloon on the corner, the Can-Can Restaurant next to it, a coffee shop across the street. The variety of eating establishments was a welcome relief. Some of the smaller towns he had passed through were lucky to have even one.

Most of the businesses along the street had vacant lots between them where he caught a glimpse of a stable he could make use of later.

But he wouldn't need it until after he was first assured of lodgings, and after he had covered all the other lodgings in town looking for Billy, so he continued on, passing a tinsmith's, an assay office, a furniture store. Spangenburg's Gun Shop was almost at the end of the block, then the Capital Saloon on the corner, where he turned left onto Fremont, heading back toward 3rd Street. Next to the saloon was the Tombstone *Nugget*, one of the town's two newspapers, with the other, the Tombstone *Epitaph*, competing just across the street.

He finally caught sight of Fly's almost at the end of the block and nudged his horse a bit faster. It was too much to hope Billy would have a room there, so he imagined the rest of the day would be taken up with his search. And with the way his luck was going, the search would probably take him through a number of saloons too before he was done, where the chances of trouble coming his way were always greatest. In his present mood, he didn't particularly care.

Billy Ewing ran a nervous hand through his golden-brown hair before pouring another shot of the Forty-rod the Oriental Bar and Gambling Saloon served as whiskey, aptly named since you weren't expected to get more

96

than forty rods before paralysis set in. He was in deep shit and knew it, but couldn't think of any way to get out of it without getting his head blown off. He had thought the Oriental would be the last place his new "friend" would show up, since Wyatt Earp was part owner of this particular establishment, and one of the things he had just discovered was the feud going on between the Earp brothers and the Clanton gang. But there weren't any Earps around just now, and Billy Clanton, the youngest of the Clanton brothers and his new friend, had found him anyway.

How deceiving appearances could be, but how would anyone who didn't know better have guessed that young Clanton, who couldn't be more than sixteen if he was even that, was already a cold-blooded killer? Christ.

Billy had met Clanton in Benson, and upon discovering they were both heading for Tombstone the next day, they had decided to ride together. Billy had been grateful for the company of someone with knowledge of the area, even more grateful for the job offered him at the Clanton Ranch near Galeyville. He knew ranching thanks to all the summers he had spent up in Wyoming with his sister, and he definitely needed a job, since his money had just about run out. But his ignorance had really come through on this one. He had tried pretending he was something he wasn't, hadn't asked the questions he should have, and found himself hired on, not to a ranch, but to a gang of cattle rustlers and stage and pack-train robbers. The ranch near Galeyville was merely their headquarters.

A couple of miners who worked the Mountain Maid Mine and had seen him ride in with Clanton had smartened him up that very first night in town. Not that he was willing to take their word for it. But anyone he asked after that told him about the same thing. The Clanton gang had been operating in this area for years, and also clashing with the authorities in Tombstone because of it. They were still known by the same name even though Old Man Clanton, who had started the gang, had been killed a few months ago, leaving Curly Bill Brocius in charge.

Besides Bill Brocius and the three brothers, Ike, Finn, and Billy Clanton, there were other well-known members of the gang who were also well-known troublemakers here in Tombstone. John Ringo was one, known to have participated in the Mason County War down in Texas before joining the gang, and who had not long ago killed Louis Hancock in an Allen Street saloon. Frank and Tom McLaury were also members whose names came up frequently. And Billy Claiborne, another young glory-hunter, who insisted he be called Billy the Kid now that the real Kid was dead. Claiborne had killed three men already for laughing at such grandstanding, and Ike and the McLaury brothers broke him out of the San Pedro jail just the other night after being arrested for that third killing.

Young Billy Clanton had been involved in what was now being called the Guadalupe Canyon Massacre, which had led to his father's death. Ewing had really heard an earful about that particular deed of the Clantons. The gang had attacked a mule train that was freighting silver bullion through the Chiricahua Range in July of this year, slaughtering the nineteen Mexicans leading the train. Old Man Clanton died a few weeks later when friends of the dead muleteers ambushed him and some of his gang as they were leading a stolen Mexican herd back through those same mountains. Young Clanton had missed that deadly encounter, even though from the reports, he had been rustling cattle since he was twelve.

This was who Billy Ewing had gotten tangled up with? He still couldn't believe it. And he plain and simply didn't know how to extricate himself from the situation. He had tried. He had told young Clanton he had changed his mind. But the allusions to cowardice and the way the kid kept resting his hand on the six-shooter he wore had made Billy rethink that decision. Next he had tried to just avoid Clanton. But he was supposed to head out to the ranch with him tomorrow. If he didn't show up, would Clanton come looking for him? If he took off tonight, would the whole damn gang come looking for him?

"This place is dead, man. Whyn't we try the Alhambra, or Hatch's place?"

Billy glanced around at the crowded tables and bar, and at the casino area that was more than half filled with miners from an earlier shift. Dead? He was afraid his "friend" was just looking for trouble his last night in town.

"It's early, not even near sundown," Billy replied. "I just stopped in here for a drink before trying out the New Orleans Restaurant for dinner. Care to join me?"

He had made the offer only out of politeness, so he was glad to hear the answer, "Ain't hungry, an' you sure ain't much of a drinker, are ya? Ya talk funny too, like some Eastern dude. Don't know why I didn't notice 'fore now. Where'd you say you was from?"

"I didn't," Billy hedged. "Does it matter?"

"Guess not, but . . . well, lookee here." Clanton straightened up in his chair, his right hand moving automatically down to caress the handle of his gun as he stared at the tall stranger who had just swung through the bat-wing doors. "Ain't 'Pache or Comanche, but I can smell Injun a mile off, an' I sure as hell know a breed when I see one. Maybe this place'll liven up some — "

"Oh, shit," Billy groaned, and then again as he yanked his hat down low over his brow and sunk down in his chair. "Oh, *shit.*"

Clanton looked at him with a measure of disgust. "Ya know him, or are ya just scared of breeds?"

And they claimed his brother Ike was the loud-mouthed braggart? Billy had had about enough of this Clanton, killer or not.

"Don't be a fool, kid," he hissed aside to the younger and much shorter boy. "He's not your normal half-breed raised with the whites. That one was a full-fledged Cheyenne warrior until only a few years back. And since he left his tribe, he's made a point of learning how to use that gun he's toting. I've never seen any-one faster."

The warning went right over his head, for Clanton considered himself pretty fast. "So ya do know him. He lookin' for you, by any chance?"

One look at the kid's grin of anticipation and Billy groaned again. "Don't even think about it."

"But he's comin' right to us."

Billy chanced a look up and found himself stabbed with those blue eyes so much brighter than his own. If he could crawl under the table, he would.

"Colt," he said miserably in greeting.

He didn't get so much as a nod in reply, and Colt was no longer looking at him, but watching Clanton coming up out of his chair. Before the kid had even straightened fully, Colt's gun was palmed and directing him to sit back down, which he did with eyes now widened and a good deal of color gone from his young face.

Billy stood up slowly, very slowly, but relaxed some when Colt put his gun away. Colt still hadn't said a word, and Billy didn't think he would, not in here anyway. But later . . .

The color was rushing back into Clanton's face to show how angry he was at being bested so easily, but he didn't make a move to get up again. Still, he didn't keep quiet either, not when there had been witnesses, including Earp's bartender, Buckskin Frank Leslie. Not a word had been said, but the breed had gained notice when he walked in, notice that was still on him when he had silently forced young Clanton to back down.

"Ya don't have to go with him, Ewing, whatever ya done. Ya got backin' now. When

I tell my brothers — "

"Forget it, kid," Billy said with a sigh, more relieved really than not, now that he realized Colt's appearance had gotten him out of his predicament. He even grinned at his short-time friend. "I do have to go with him."

"Like hell — "

"Oh, I've no doubt there will be hell to pay," Billy interrupted, his grin widening before he added, "He's my brother, you see."

Chapter Seven

Billy had had his fun. He wasn't grinning as he stepped out onto the boarded walkway in front of the Oriental, waiting for Colt to back out of the swinging doors and step quickly to the side before relaxing his gun hand. Now he felt kind of sick to his stomach. Colt Thunder here? He didn't even begin to hope it was a coincidence.

"Where's your horse?" Colt asked curtly.

Billy grimaced, noticing the big-boned Appaloosa down the street in front of yet another saloon. "I walked from Noble's Hotel, where I'm staying."

"Come on, then."

They were almost the same height, but Billy felt like he was tripping over his own legs trying to keep up with Colt as the taller man took off down the boardwalk. "I didn't think she'd send you after me, Colt, I swear I didn't."

"You thought she'd hunt you down herself?"

"Of course not! I knew she'd write Jessie, and I guess I figured she'd ask Chase to find me. She always depended on him for help."

"That was before he married Jessie. But he probably would've been elected if he was home at the time, only he wasn't. And it wasn't your mother sent me, it was Jessie. She had the dumb idea I'd have no problem tracking you."

"I'm sorry," Billy said lamely.

"Wait until I decide whether or not to beat the shit out of you, kid, before you're sorry."

Billy flinched. He wished he had seen Colt's expression when he said that, but the man was still walking several paces ahead and hadn't looked back to speak. He had little doubt he was serious, though. Which way he decided on the matter would depend on just how angry he was. But come to think of it, seeing his expression wouldn't have told Billy the answer to that. You just couldn't tell with Colt, not with his ability to conceal his emotions when he chose to.

The past years had been one surprise after another for Billy. He had been raised in Chicago by his mother, Rachel, and his stepfather, though he didn't know Jonathon Ewing was only his stepfather. He didn't know he had a sister either, until Jessie's father died and Rachel went to Wyoming to be her guardian. He had been only nine at the time, and meeting someone like Jessie had been an impressionable experience. Her father had raised her like a boy, and she was running the ranch he had left her as well as any man could. She wore britches, toted a gun, and knew everything there was to know about raising cattle. Billy had worshiped her and was delighted when he learned she wasn't just his half sister, but his true sister, that Thomas Blair was his father, too.

But Rachel returned to Chicago, taking Billy with her, and it wasn't until a couple of years later that Billy got to visit the Rocky Valley Ranch again. In fact, he was there the day Colt first showed up, though he was called White Thunder then.

Billy had heard of him, of course. The Cheyenne brave had been Jessie's closest friend for many years, though he had never been to her ranch before. But Billy didn't know who he was at first, and after hearing about all the trouble the Sioux and the Cheyenne were causing at that time, seeing an Indian ride in as bold as you please was frightening, to say the least, especially when he was so obviously not one of the tame variety.

Half naked, with hair that flowed midway down his back, no, there was nothing tame about White Thunder — until you saw him with Jessie and heard him speak English. And not a clear and precise English, as you would suppose an Indian would be taught, but a Western drawl that was an exact copy of Jessie's own speech, which wasn't that surprising after all, since he had learned English from her.

Billy, at eleven, had been fascinated by Thunder just as much as he had been by Jessie. He hadn't gotten to stay to watch his transformation into a "white man," so he had barely recognized him when Colt came east with Jessie and Chase for Rachel's wedding to Chase's father, Carlos Silvela, less than a year later. But there was still something about him that had kept Billy from being able to relax completely in his company, even though he was open and approachable then. And Billy didn't think that would ever change, especially since Colt was no longer easy-going, and hadn't been since that trouble he had back in '78 when he nearly died.

That was when Billy found out that Colt wasn't just Jessie's best friend, but her half brother, and Billy's too; that Thomas Blair had fathered them all. Unfortunately, it didn't make him feel he could get close to Colt, not the way Jessie was, anyway. Brother or not, Colt could scare him worse than ten Billy Clantons, without even trying.

As if Colt had read his mind, he asked, "Who was your hot-tempered little friend?" Billy answered without thinking and found himself pressed up against the wall of the saddle shop they were passing, Colt's fists locked in his shirtfront. "You leave your sense back East, kid? I heard enough about that bunch before I was even halfway through the territory, enough to know they're to be avoided."

"Well, I didn't," Billy said defensively. "At least not until it was too late." He was unable to meet Colt's piercing stare when he added, "I sort of hired on, thinking I'd be doing ranch work."

"You dumb sh —"

"For God's sake, Colt, I didn't know what I was getting into! I was running short of money."

"All you had to do was wire home."

"If I did that I would have to *go* home, and I doubt my mother is ready to see my side of things."

"Whether she is or isn't — shit, never mind." He let Billy down, glancing back at the Oriental, but no one else had exited the place since they had. He continued on to collect his horse, tossing back over his shoulder, "Did you quit?"

"I tried, but you said yourself young Clanton's hot-tempered. He didn't exactly want to take no for an answer."

"All right, forget it. If anyone wants to object to you leaving town, they can take it up with me. We'll check you out of the Noble, and . . ."

Colt's thoughts took flight when he spotted a teal-blue coach coming down the street in their direction, surrounded by a dozen mounted, armed riders. It was followed by another coach, not quite as large, and then still another. Bringing up the rear were three large wagons piled high with baggage and supplies, and being led alongside them, four of the most magnificent Thoroughbred horses to ever show up west of the Mississippi.

"Christ, what in the hell . . . ?"

Colt only vaguely heard Billy's question. It had to be the same question running through everyone else's mind too, except his. All along the street folks had stopped to gawk, or were coming out of stores for a better look or leaning out of windows. What had to be half the children in town were running along beside the cavalcade, as if it were a circus come to town and they didn't want to miss a moment of the excitement.

"I thought she'd have arrived long before now," Colt said absently, his eye on that lead coach.

Billy looked sideways at him, as if he had

said the moon was green. "You know these people?"

Colt recalled himself and stepped off the boardwalk to untether his horse, turning his back on the street — and her. "I met up with the ladies in that lead coach across the San Pedro. They'd gotten separated from the rest and their coach turned over, so they needed some assistance."

Billy didn't miss how Colt was deliberately ignoring the spectacle in the street. "Across the river, huh? What were you doing that far west of here?"

"I'll follow a river anytime, rather than the roads. You meet up with less undesirables that way."

Billy grimaced, the point taken. "So who are they?"

"The ladies are English. I didn't meet their escort, but from the looks of them, they're all foreigners."

"I'll say," Billy remarked.

He was staring at one of the wagon drivers decked out in a flowing white robe, and wearing some kind of large kerchief over his head instead of a hat. The twelve-man guard was also dressed strangely in that they all wore identical red coats with short capes attached, navy blue pants with a black satin band down the outer seam, and tall hats of a military bent.

"Hey, they're stopping," Billy said with some surprise.

Colt swung around and swore. "Christ, she wouldn't — and in front of a damn saloon?" She did, and one of her guards even rushed forward to open the door for her. He caught a glimpse of that glorious red hair before he quickly mounted up. "That woman hasn't got any more sense than you do, Billy."

"Why? All she's doing is getting down and . . . and I think she's coming to talk to you."

Colt refused to look at her again. His blood was already heating, just by his knowing she was only a few feet away.

"She won't if I can help it. I'll meet you in front of your hotel."

Billy's eyes widened. "You're not going to wait and — "

"You know how these people will react if they see her talking to someone like me."

Billy bristled, hating it when Colt degraded himself like that. "Maybe she could teach folks a thing or two about judging a man by his worth."

Colt didn't even bother to answer that. He jerked his horse to the side and took off down the street. Billy was left staring at the most beautiful redhead he had ever laid eyes on. She had stopped in the middle of the street, and the expression of keen disappointment on

111

her face as she watched Colt ride away made Billy want to kick his half brother on the seat of his pants — not that he would ever actually dare, but he sure wanted to.

And what had Colt accomplished anyway, when everyone watching her — and everyone on the whole street *was* watching her — could see who *she* was watching, who she had intended to speak to? It sure wasn't Billy, for after Colt rode off, the elegant redhead turned about and, after a few words to one of her escorts, got back in her coach and continued down the street.

Chapter Eight

Vanessa opened the door of their suite in the Grand Hotel to find Babette giggling in the hall with Mr. Sidney, one of the two footmen constantly vying for her attention. "Well, come along, girl," Vanessa said impatiently, giving Sidney a look of stern disapproval that had him quickly leaving. "I managed to get her to lie down with a cold compress, but she won't relax until she hears what Alonzo has to report. You *do* have his report?"

"But of course." Babette grinned, her artfully arranged blond ringlets bouncing as she hurried into the room. "Alonzo, he finds where the 'Merican goes, but how long he stays there . . . " The French maid shrugged.

"Well, as long as he stays put for whatever it is she intends, though I can't imagine what that is. She did say he refused employment." Vanessa frowned then, staring at the closed door of Jocelyn's bedroom. "On second thought, maybe it would be better if she didn't see him again. I haven't seen her burst

113

into tears like that since those first months after the duke passed on."

"Is no wonder, after everything that is happen today — "

"Oh, I know, I know," Vanessa replied, still amazed that none of their people had been seriously hurt during the ambush. Though two men had been wounded and put to bed under a doctor's supervision, they could travel again if the need arose. "But *that's* not why she cried. The nerve of that rogue, to snub her like that."

"Maybe he did not see her, yes?"

"Maybe."

But Vanessa didn't believe that for a minute. And although she was surprised at how keen Jocelyn's interest was in this man, she wasn't sure it was wise for her to pursue that interest, not after all she had told Vanessa about her encounter with him. He sounded much too . . . unusual.

"Did Alonzo also find out what a half-breed is?"

Babette's pale blue eyes rounded, remembering that part of the report. "Oh, yes, but you will not like it, I think."

"I didn't suppose I would," Vanessa remarked dryly. "Come along, then."

The countess knocked softly before the two women entered the darkened bedroom. The sun had just set, though there was still a lavender sky visible through the open windows, with just enough light to show that Jocelyn was not sleeping; was, in fact, sitting up and looking expectantly at her young maid.

Vanessa motioned Babette to turn on the lamps before saying, "I took the liberty of ordering a light repast that should be delivered shortly. I don't know about you, but I certainly don't feel up to changing for dinner tonight."

Jocelyn frowned at her dear friend. "You should have been the one to lie down, Vana, especially after that terrible headache you suffered this morning. There's certainly nothing wrong with me — "

" — that a little food and rest won't see to," Vanessa finished, her tone brooking no argument.

Jocelyn sighed. It was easier to give in to the countess when she got into one of her mothering moods, which she had been in ever since Jocelyn had succumbed to that silly burst of emotion just after they were shown to their suite. She looked at Babette again, who was still flitting from lamp to lamp. There were six of them in this room alone.

The accommodations were very adequate, considering what they had been led to expect: that most Western towns were small, their hotels even smaller. This being the first Western town they encountered, its large size was a welcome surprise, as was the selection of hotels they had had to choose from. The Grand was not on a par with the luxurious hotels on the East Coast, but it certainly tried to be. And they had been able to rent the entire second floor here, which was ideal for security purposes.

"Enough, Babette," Jocelyn ordered with impatience. "How much light does Alonzo's report warrant?"

The French girl grinned cheekily now that her stalling ploy was seen through. "Is not so bad. At least Alonzo, he say is only a matter of prejudice. The half-breed, he is considered the same as the Indian, and the Indian, he is treated with contempt and loathing."

"Contempt?"

"To hide the fear, you understand. The Indian, he is still greatly feared in this place. He still raids and kills and — "

"Which Indian — ah, Indians?"

"Apaches. We hear of them in Mexico, no?"

"So we did, but I don't recall hearing they were still so hostile."

"Is only Geronimo. Alonzo say he is a renegade with only a small number of followers who hide out in Mexico, but they raid this side of the border too."

"Very well, but Colt Thunder is not an Apache half-breed, he's Cheyenne," Jocelyn pointed out. "What did Alonzo learn of the Cheyenne Indians?"

"They are not known in this area."

"Then why would Mr. Thunder think I should be leery of him?"

"I believe you have missed the point, my dear," Vanessa interjected. "Prejudice is not particular. It sounds like all half-breeds are treated the same in these Western territories, no matter which Indian tribe they are associated with."

"But that's preposterous," Jocelyn insisted. "Not to mention unfair. Besides, there wasn't the least little thing contemptible about Colt Thunder. I found him very polite — well, mostly polite. And he was exceedingly helpful. Good Lord, in less than an hour's span the man twice saved my life." He was also impatient, short-tempered, argumentative, and stubbornly opposed to having anything more to do with her, but that wasn't worth mentioning.

"Jocelyn, dear, we are all grateful to this fellow for his timely assistance. Indeed we are. But his feelings in the matter couldn't have been more plain this afternoon. He won't even talk to you."

"I understand that now. He behaved the same way this morning, as if I were committing some grave faux pas just by being in the same vicinity with him. It's so silly."

"He obviously doesn't think so."

"I know, and he thought he was protecting me by avoiding me in town, which is very commendable, but hardly necessary. I'm not about to let someone else's prejudices influence me. Nor do I give a fig for public opinion. If I want to associate with the man, I will. No one will tell me that I can't."

Vanessa raised a golden brow as Jocelyn's chin went up stubbornly. The duke had told her once, during their initial interview, that his duchess was of the sweetest nature, biddable, and flexible. Vanessa was in a position to know differently.

"Just what sort of association did you have in mind?" Vanessa asked reluctantly, afraid she already knew.

Jocelyn shrugged, though there was a definite sparkle in her lime-green eyes. "Oh, I don't know. Perhaps what we were discussing early this morning."

"I was afraid you were going to say that."

Chapter Nine

"I'll get it," Billy called and bounded off the bed, where he had been stretched out watching Colt shave off the few errant whiskers that he was in too much of a hurry to pluck out, as was his custom.

But before Billy's hand touched the doorknob, he heard the distinctive sound of the hammer being pulled back on Colt's revolver and knew he had blundered once again. You just didn't open your door in a town where trouble was anticipated, not without finding out who was knocking first, or as Colt had done behind him, being prepared for any possibility. And Billy Clanton hadn't left town yet. Though it was unlikely he had tracked Billy down to this lodging house, it wasn't impossible.

He thought Colt would lash into him again as he had last night when Billy forgot to lock the door of the room they shared, but he was obviously in a better mood this morning. "Go ahead," was all he said after Billy hesitated at the door. "Just stay out of the line of fire."

Billy swallowed once at that advice before unlocking the door and swinging it open wide, keeping himself behind it. When he had been on his own, he hadn't worried about such things, hadn't looked for danger around every corner. To do so was a lesson Jessie had taught him, but one he had conveniently forgotten this trip west. It was a wonder he had survived to get this far.

But this was one time caution was apparently unnecessary. There were two men out in the hall, neither of them young Clanton, and both immobilized by the clear view they had of Colt across the room with a gun trained on them, wearing nothing but his pants and his knee-high moccasins. That Colt immediately turned to slip the gun back in the holster hooked over the washstand made Billy wonder, until he too recognized those red jackets. The men still hadn't spoken, however, even though they were no longer looking down the barrel of a Colt .45, but that was understandable. The gun might have startled them, but a glimpse of Colt's back when he turned to put it away had rendered them speechless.

It wouldn't do for Colt to know that, though. If anything could make him spitting mad, it was having his scars looked at with horror. Jessie said it had a lot to do with pride in that he didn't want anyone knowing about the kind of pain he had to have suffered to have a back that looked like his did. Whatever it was, Billy knew how defensive-mean he could get if he detected even the slightest empathy coming his way. He'd rather be hated than pitied.

Billy stepped out from behind the door, forcing the two men to look at him instead of Colt. Dredging up his manners, he asked pleasantly, "Can we help you with something, gentlemen?"

The taller of the two was Billy's height but looked more Colt's age, with chestnut hair cropped short and eyes about the same shade. He was still disconcerted by what he'd seen when he answered with the question, "I say, *you* wouldn't happen to be Colt Thunder, would you?"

It was asked so hopefully Billy couldn't help grinning. "Afraid not."

The two redcoats glanced at each other, their discomfort palpable, but then the taller man said, "Didn't think so, but — well, never mind, then." He leaned to the side to get another glance at Colt before straightening and saying with more force, "We've a message for your mate, if he's Mr. Thunder."

Billy's grin widened. He couldn't resist repeating the way he knew Colt hated being addressed. "Mr. Thunder, they're here for you."

"I heard, but I'm not interested."

Billy swung around, no longer amused, to see Colt shrugging into his shirt. Colt might not be interested, but Billy was damn curious, knowing full well who the message had to be from.

"Ah, come on, Colt, it's just a message. It wouldn't hurt you to at least hear it."

Colt came forward, his expression inscrutable, though Billy recognized the subtle signs of impatience when he saw them. Colt hadn't bothered to button his shirt, just tucking it into his pants. That both pants and shirt were black might account for the two Englishmen taking a wary step back when Colt filled the doorway, but it probably had more to do with his intimidating height and size.

"Let's hear it," he demanded curtly.

The taller fellow cleared his throat, still apparently the spokesman for the two. "Her Grace, the Duchess Dowager of Eaton, requests the honor of your — "

"The what?" Colt interrupted at the same time Billy swore, "Christ, an English duchess!"

Colt gave Billy a sharp look. "What the hell's a duchess?"

"You mean you don't . . . no, of course you wouldn't . . . how could you — ?"

122

"Just spit it out, kid, before you choke on it."

Billy flushed, but he was too excited to be subdued. "A duchess is a member of the English nobility, the wife of a duke. The nobility of England have different degrees of importance — barons, earls, and such. A comparison would be your minor chiefs and war leaders. But you can't get any more important than a duke or duchess, unless you're a member of the royal family."

Colt frowned, but directed the expression at the two messengers. "That right, what he says?"

"Close enough," the spokesman replied, deciding estate size and degree of influence weren't worth mentioning when all he wanted was to get out of there. "But as I was saying, Mr. Thunder, Her Grace requests the honor of your presence this noontime at the Mais — Maisy — "

"Maison Dorée," his nondescript companion supplied in a whisper.

"Right you are, the Maison Dorée Restaurant."

When the man finished, he smiled. Colt looked at Billy, who was grinning widely again. "She wants to meet you for lunch," he explained.

"No," Colt said simply and started to turn away.

"Wait, Mr. Thunder! In the event you declined the first invitation, I was instructed to extend another. Her Grace would be pleased to receive you in her suite it the Grand Hotel, at your convenience, of course."

"No."

"No?"

"I'm not meeting the woman anywhere, at any time. Is that clear enough for you?"

Both men appeared shocked, but not by his refusal, as he found out when the spokesman said, "There are proper modes of address for a duchess, sir. You may refer to her as Her Grace, or Her Ladyship, or even Lady Fleming, but she is never referred to as 'the woman.' It just isn't done, sir."

"I don't believe what I'm hearing," Colt mumbled and did turn away this time. "Get rid of them, Billy."

Billy didn't know whom he was more disappointed in, Colt for his indifference to a genuine duchess — a gorgeous genuine duchess — or her man for his snobbery. "That wasn't too smart, Mister . . ."

"Sir Dudley Leland, sir," the redcoat supplied importantly. "Second son of the Earl of — "

"Christ, man, you've missed the point, haven't you? You're in America now, and if you'll recall, we fought a war with your ances-

124

tors about a hundred years ago to get rid of class distinctions. Your titles might impress the society matrons back East, but they don't mean a thing to a Cheyenne warrior."

"Ah, right you are, sir. Apologies tended. But I've still one more message for your friend there."

Billy glanced back to see Colt standing at the single window the room offered, looking down at the vacant lot next to Fly's Lodging House. There was nothing but an assay office beyond, no view to hold anyone's interest, so he knew Colt had heard Sir Dudley. He just wasn't going to acknowledge it.

"Maybe you better give me the message and I'll pass it on," Billy suggested.

Sir Dudley could see well enough that Colt had divorced himself from the conversation and so nodded. He was also aware that Colt could hear him quite well, but he still addressed the message to Billy.

"Her Grace anticipated both invitations might be declined. That being the case, my final instructions are to inform Mr. Thunder that Her Grace has asked, as he suggested, and has received a full report on the prejudices associated with his bloodlines. She wishes him to know that those prejudices are not hers and mean nothing to her. She hopes Mr. Thunder will take that into account and reconsider one of her invitations."

That Colt didn't turn around after that mouthful was proof that he wasn't going to reconsider anything. Billy noted, however, that he was now gripping the windowsill, that his whole body had gone taut.

"I think you have your answer, gentlemen," he said in a lowered tone. "You may inform the duchess — "

"Don't put words in my mouth, kid," came from behind Billy in a near snarl. "There's no reply. Now shut the damn door!"

Billy shrugged at the messengers, as if to imply Colt's lack of manners was not his own. But he did shut the door in their faces. And he calmly and silently started counting numbers, trying for fifty but getting no further than ten before exploding, "That was the rudest, lowest, most outrageous behavior I've ever been sorry to witness. And deliberate too, I'll wager. But why, for Christ's sake? You know they're going to report back to her, and . . . and that's it, isn't it?"

"You talk too much," Colt said as he turned and reached for his gun belt.

Billy shook his head. "You know, I didn't understand it yesterday, and I sure as hell don't now. I got a good look at the lady and I felt like I'd been dropped through the board-walk. She's beautiful — "

126

"And white," Colt cut in. He finished buckling the belt on and moved for his saddlebags at the foot of the bed.

Billy had gone very still, Colt's behavior suddenly making perfect sense. And he hated it. He had never been able to deal well with Colt's feelings of bitterness, feelings that went back to that painful time when he had almost died. Billy loved his brother, thought there was no man finer, more courageous, more loyal, and so it cut him to the quick when Colt belittled himself, taking the attitude of those ignorant, prejudiced whites who put him on a par with the scum of the earth.

"Did I miss something? I could have sworn I heard that the lady doesn't give a damn what kind of blood flows in your veins."

"She's feeling beholden, Billy," Colt replied in an even tone. "That's all there is to it."

"Is it? That's why you were so mean-tempered rude to her lackeys? You just don't want her gratitude? And that's why she's so eager to meet you again, just to express that gratitude? Be serious, Colt — "

"I am. I'm letting you keep your teeth. Now take yourself down to the O.K. Livery and collect our horses. I'll meet you out on the street in fifteen minutes. If we ride fast enough, we can make Benson for a late lunch."

Yeah, and kill our horses, Billy grouched to himself. Since it was almost noon already, and Benson was a good twenty miles north, that was probably just what they'd do. No, he was being unfair. Colt would never take a bad mood out on his horse. But he was damn determined to quit Tombstone and fast. Before the duchess came up with some other way to see him?

Colt had already left the room to settle the bill, so Billy gathered up his things and went out the back way to do as he'd been told. The stable wasn't far. Camillus S. Fly had a photographic gallery at the back of his lodging house, and the O.K. Livery and Corral was behind that, right in the center of the square, accessible from any vacant lot along 3rd and 4th streets, or Fremont and Allen.

Billy was back on Fremont with time to spare, but without the horses, as Colt noticed when he stepped out of Fly's Lodging House. "Now don't look at me like that," Billy protested quickly. "My horse threw a shoe just as I was walking her out. It'll only take a couple hours — "

"A couple?"

"The smith's busy," Billy explained. "That was his estimate, not mine. So what do you say to an early lunch instead, and I'll challenge you to a few games of billiards over at

Bob Hatch's on Allen Street."

"You're just asking for trouble, aren't you, kid?" Colt replied, but his expression wasn't half as dark as it had been earlier.

"I don't think we'll run into young Clanton, if that's what you mean." Billy grinned. "Fact is, I just heard his brother Ike was buffaloed by one of the Earp brothers this morning, then hauled before the judge and fined. It must have been Wyatt. They say he has a fondness for bending his gun barrel around hard heads. Billy has probably taken his brother back to their ranch by now. So where would you like to eat? The Maison Dorée?"

Colt's answer was a soft kick to Billy's backside.

Chapter Ten

Mrs. Addie Bourland's Millinery Shop was sandwiched between the offices of a stage line and a doctor on Fremont Street. The last thing Jocelyn needed was a new hat, but she had come here to order one, two, or a dozen, however many it took to keep her there until she caught sight of Colt Thunder either coming or going from his lodgings, which were just across the street. Vanessa had suggested she simply present herself at his door, but she was hesitant to do that. The men she had sent there that morning had not been received well, and she had no reason to think she would be any more welcome. No, a chance encounter on the street was the thing, and although there would be little "chance" to it, Mr. Thunder wouldn't know that. She would not let him ignore her again.

She had arrived in her coach just before two o'clock, but since she had sent it away, the curious it had gathered had also departed, so there was nothing to indicate she was ensconced within the millinery shop. The guards were a necessity she could not get rid of, though, six for this outing. They were stationed at the front and rear exits, those in the front room trying to be inconspicuous but failing. They had quite flustered Mrs. Bourland to begin with. She was not accustomed to so many men invading her small shop. Even one at a time was a rarity. But she was ignoring them now as the prospect of such a large order caught her full attention.

With Vanessa stationed at the window to watch for Colt, Jocelyn kept Mrs. Bourland busy with the vast selection of feathers, flowers, colors, and materials available. Never had she been so indecisive in her choices, but then she had no idea how long she would need to stay there. To describe the elaborate European styles she favored in hats accounted for some time, but not enough. Pretending to be unable to make up her mind was going to become quite frustrating for the proprietress, for Jocelyn too, but it was necessary. If Colt didn't show up before closing, however . . .

"Jocelyn, dear, I think you had better come have a look at this," Vanessa called from the window. "There seems to be something . . . unusual about to happen."

Jocelyn joined her at the window, with Addie Bourland stepping up behind her. She

131

saw immediately what Vanessa meant. Walking slowly but purposefully right down the center of the dusty street were four black-garbed gentlemen looking identical with their black Stetsons, thin bow ties, and drooping mustaches, not to mention an assortment of lethal-looking weapons. Not so finely dressed were the five men in the vacant lot across the street who appeared to be waiting for them.

"Lan' sakes, this is it, the big one!" Addie Bourland said excitedly.

"The big what?" Jocelyn inquired.

"Showdown," Addie said without taking her eyes off the street. "It's been comin' a long time now."

"Whatever is a showdown?" Vanessa asked the proprietress.

The woman looked at Vanessa strangely for a moment, but then chuckled. "I thought you ladies talked kinda funny. You ain't from around these parts, are ya?" But she didn't wait for an answer. "A showdown's a shoot-out. That's Virgil Earp, our town marshal, and his brothers Wyatt and Morgan coming down the street. The one carryin' the shotgun is Doc Holiday, Wyatt's good friend."

"A doctor about to participate in a shooting spree?" Vanessa had never heard of anything quite so unethical.

"He used to be a dentist back East, ma'am.

He makes his livin' now at gamblin'. Surprised to see him up and about so early in the day. He's a night owl, that one."

"And the gentlemen who seem to be hiding in wait?"

"Them no-accounts?" Addie snorted. "Rowdy troublemakers, every one of 'em. Thievin' outlaws too. They're members of the Clanton gang." At Vanessa's blank look, Addie clarified, "Ike and Billy Clanton, Frank and Tom McLaury, and looks like young Billy Claiborne's with 'em today. You must not've been in town long if you ain't heard tell of the Clanton bunch. They're arch enemies of the Earps."

"Actually, we only arrived yesterday afternoon. But if, as you say, that is an official of the law out there, why should there be a showdown, as you called it? Isn't it more logical to assume the marshal just intends to arrest those men?"

"Oh, he might intend to, probably does intend to, but it don't make no never mind. Those boys across the street wouldn't be waitin' around to get themselves arrested. Their waitin' there means they're plannin' to shoot it out. I'd stake my shop on it, 'cause like I said, it's been buildin' up to this for a long time now."

Vanessa exchanged a glance with Jocelyn.

133

Neither of them knew whether to take the woman seriously or not. It was true they had never before seen quite so many men sporting weapons on their persons in such a visible manner as here in Tombstone. Everywhere you looked in the town it was the same. But there must be a reason for this, other than to be prepared for a possible "showdown."

The four dark-clad gentlemen had nearly reached the vacant lot. Jocelyn watched in fascination as they pivoted, spreading out in front of it, their backs to the millinery shop. The five men on the lot spread out also in a half circle, facing them. There was a shouted order, something about giving up arms. It was ignored, and before Jocelyn realized what was going to happen next, the shooting began.

She found herself yanked away from the window and nearly shoved to the floor by one of her guards, as were Vanessa and a protesting Addie Bourland. Jocelyn had no thought to protest, not after hearing at least one stray bullet strike the front wall of the shop. The shooting seemed like it would never end, though actually the terrible noise continued for only thirty seconds or so. She was not allowed to rise, however, until one of her men had ascertained that it was truly over.

Addie had worked herself free before then and was back at the window, avidly counting

134

bodies. "Looks like both the McLaurys got it, and young Clanton too. I ought to pity that boy. He couldn't've been more'n sixteen. But his daddy was a bad 'un and raised him bad too, so what can you expect."

Jocelyn didn't expect to be regaled with the gory details. Good Lord, was there really a sixteen-year-old boy dead out there?

"I — I think we should return to our hotel," she suggested in a shaky voice.

"Best wait a bit," Addie replied. "Ike and young Claiborne took off, but you never can tell. At least wait until the Earps leave the scene. They're helpin' Morgan up now. 'Pears to have taken one in the shoulder. 'Pears the marshal and Doc are wounded too, but they're still on their feet, so it can't be serious." She chuckled then. "No, their wounds ain't serious. They're walkin' away and the street's fillin' up with the curious. Think I'll go have a talk with Mr. Fly. Looks like he seen the whole thing up close."

She had forgotten her order, but didn't forget to give poor Sir Dudley a fulminating look for his unwelcome efforts to protect her before she sashayed out of her shop, leaving the door open behind her. The smell of gunsmoke intruded then, making Jocelyn sick to her stomach. Vanessa was positively pale and holding a scented kerchief to her nose.

135

"I don't know about you, Vana, but I don't care to stay here another moment. Would you mind walking? It will take too long to fetch the coach."

Their transportation had been sent to wait inconspicuously around the block on Safford Street, but Vanessa was quick to agree to depart without it. Even one more second there was too long for her. And Jocelyn's guard, ever diligent and attuned to her wishes without being told, was already stepping out of Mrs. Addie Bourland's Millinery Shop to clear a path on the now crowded boardwalk.

It was the sight of those red-coated figures that drew Billy Ewing's attention from across the street. He had been jostled away from where he had stood staring down at the body of his short-time companion, Billy Clanton, bloody from both chest and stomach wounds, and it was all he could do to hold down the lunch he had finished not long ago. He needed a distraction, desperately needed it, and the figure he fully expected to see next would provide it, so he wasted no time in crossing the street, and was there when the two ladies joined their guard on the boardwalk.

From the look of them, they weren't used to seeing bodies lying around dead any more than Billy was. Both were pale, and the older woman looked close to fainting. Neither glanced across the street, though it was doubtful anything could be seen now with the crowd surrounding the bodies. It was obvious, however, that they knew full well what had happened, if they hadn't seen it happen firsthand.

Billy jumped up on the boardwalk as soon as he saw in which direction they were going, and refused to be shuffled aside by the two guards who led the way. Those two and the other four formed a tight circle around the ladies, and none of them looked too agreeable at the moment, making Billy wish he had Colt standing behind him. But Colt was only just now skirting the crowd on the vacant lot, leading their horses out to the street. Even if he saw where Billy had gone, he wasn't likely to join him.

When one of the guards got physical, picking Billy up by his shirtfront before he could get a word out, to set him out of the way, Sir Dudley, at the back of the group, stopped him. "Let him go, Robbie. He's the gent was with that Thunder chap this morning."

Luckily for Billy, red-haired Robbie listened to his friend and immediately set Billy back on his feet. He even went so far as to smooth out the shirt he had wrinkled in his big fists, offering a grin in apology. The man was the largest of the guards present, nearly six feet tall and brawny besides, not someone a lean seventeen-year-old kid would want to tangle with under any circumstances. But Billy hadn't been looking to cause a disturbance. He had simply wanted to meet the duchess, hoping that a few words with her would help to wipe out the lingering image of death from his mind. Unfortunately, he hadn't stopped to consider her own upset, and that this was not the time to stop for a friendly chat, even if she would deign to speak to him.

She did speak to him, however, not so distracted that she hadn't heard Dudley's remarks. "So you are a friend of Mr. Thunder's?"

The two front guards had instantly moved aside so she could step up to Billy. Seen close, she was even more beautiful than he had thought. Those eyes were something else, so light a green they almost glowed. It registered in his mind that a much darker green silk molded over delicate curves on a lithe figure, but he couldn't take his eyes off her face. And several long moments passed before he recalled that she had asked him something.

"I don't know that 'friend' is the appropriate word, Lady Fleming. I'm Colt's brother."

"Brother!" she said with surprise. "But you don't look anything like him. Are you a half-breed too?"

Billy almost laughed. Folks in the West wouldn't ask that question. They took it for granted they would know one if they saw one, and whether a man was a half-breed or not, if he was thought one, he might as well be one.

"No, ma'am," Billy answered her, surprised to find he had dropped the abbreviated speech he picked up each time he came west, his Eastern schooling coming through in response to her own cultured tones. "Colt and I share the same father, but not the same mother."

"Then it would be his mother who is Cheyenne," she remarked more to herself. "Yes, he must take after her. But then you both have blue eyes, though not quite the same. . . . Forgive me. I didn't mean to go on like that."

Billy grinned at the slight blush that came to her cheeks when she realized she had been rambling. "Not at all, ma'am. And Colt inherited his eyes from one of our father's ancestors, since Thomas Blair had eyes of turquoise himself, I'm told. Jessie is the only one who took after him in coloring, in both hair and eyes."

"Jessie . . . yes, your brother mentioned her to me when we met yesterday. But if you don't mind my asking, what do you mean you were *told* about your father's eyes? How could you not know?"

"My mother left him before I was born, so I was raised back East. I was half grown before I even knew about him, or that I had an older sister. And it was still a few more years before I found out I had a half brother too. None of us were raised together, you see. Jessie was raised by our father on a cattle ranch in Wyoming, Colt grew up with his mother's people in the Northern Plains, and I lived in a mansion in Chicago. The whys of all that are kind of complicated."

"That is all very fascinating, young man," Vanessa commented at this point, "and I don't mean to be rude, but we *are* in a bit of a hurry to leave this . . . this location. The duchess, I am sure, will be delighted to continue this conversation, but in quieter surroundings. You may accompany us, if you like, back to our hotel — "

"Much as I would enjoy that, ma'am, I'm afraid I can't. Colt's waiting for me" — his quick glance across the street said where Colt was waiting — "and, well, I just wanted to explain about his behavior this morning and let you know it had nothing to do with you personally, Lady Fleming. He has these set ideas, you see, and . . . "

Billy's words trailed off, for the lady was no longer listening to him. She had followed his look across the street and was still looking there, staring at Colt, who was likewise staring at her. But it was obvious he wasn't going to do anything more than that. He didn't nod to acknowledge her, didn't move a muscle, just stood there holding the horses' reins, patiently waiting for Billy to finish his socializing and join him. Patiently? Not likely. Colt was probably furious. You just couldn't tell it by looking at him.

"He's not leaving town, is he?"

It wasn't hard for her to have drawn that conclusion, with both horses Colt was leading packed for traveling. The alarm in her voice and expression took Billy by surprise, however. He couldn't figure out what possible interest a woman like this could have in someone like Colt. She barely knew him, certainly not enough to generate such concern.

Billy grew uncomfortable, knowing the answer he had to give, and guessing the reaction it would bring. "Colt doesn't like towns much, ma'am, especially those he doesn't know. He only came to this one to find me, and now that he has, he can't wait to be on his way. We would have been gone already if my horse hadn't thrown a shoe."

"Mr. Thunder has the right idea," Vanessa remarked. "I'm all for leaving *this* town myself — immediately."

"We don't have a guide yet," the duchess replied absently to her friend.

"Where were you heading, ma'am, if you don't mind my asking?"

Jocelyn hesitated only a moment before saying, "Wyoming," and Billy wasn't the only one surprised by that answer. But he was the only one to comment on it, and without the least suspicion.

"Imagine that," Billy said with boyish delight. "That's our destination too, or at least Colt's, since he hasn't said yet whether he'll be shipping me back home somewhere along the way or not. It's too bad we can't all . . . "

He didn't finish that thought, realizing just in time that he had no business inviting anyone along, especially not a woman Colt had done everything possible to avoid. But he had said too much as it was, and she pounced on the idea without gi ing him a chance to correct the mistake.

"But that's a splendid notion, Mr. — Blair, is it?"

"Ewing," he replied with a distinctly unpleasant feeling curling in his belly. "I took my stepfather's name."

"Well, Mr. Ewing, you really are a lifesaver," she rushed on. "I agree with the countess that we can no longer remain in a place of such violence. And it will take us no time at all to be ready to leave."

"But — "

"Oh, you needn't feel that we mean to take advantage of your good nature, sir. Not at all. Since we *are* in need of a guide, you must allow me to hire you and your brother for that purpose. I can pay you extremely well to make it worth your while to put up with us for however long it takes to reach Wyoming."

"But — "

"No, no, you can't refuse payment. I really must insist. I wouldn't feel right about imposing, otherwise. So if you will meet us in front of the Grand Hotel within the next hour, we won't delay your departure any longer than that. Until then, Mr. Ewing."

She passed by him with a nod of farewell and was gone before he could get another "but" out, not that one more would have done any better than the others. He was left standing alone on the boardwalk — and facing Colt across the street. Christ! What the hell had just happened? He hadn't actually agreed to escort the duchess and her party to Wyoming, had he? But he hadn't refused either.

His thoughts whirling, Billy didn't move from his spot. But now that he was alone, Colt crossed to him, still leading their horses.

"Mount up, kid."

Just like that. He wasn't even curious about

Billy's conversation with the duchess, or if he was, he wasn't going to appease it. It would have been easier on Billy if Colt had yelled at him and called him ten kinds of fool for going near the woman. He certainly *felt* like a fool. The lady had talked circles around him, and now he had to try and do the same to Colt.

"We, ah . . . we can't leave just yet, Colt."

"Wanna bet?"

Billy groaned inwardly but plunged ahead. "I sort of agreed to take the lady to Wyoming with us."

There was a long silence crackling with tension as he waited for the explosion. When Colt did comment, his voice was barely a whisper. "As in, you sort of agreed to hire on with the Clantons?"

"Well, actually, she never gave me a chance to agree or not. She sort of took it for granted."

"Get on your horse, Billy," was all Colt said to that.

"But this is different! She's gone to her hotel to pack. She expects us to meet her there out front in the next hour."

Colt calmly mounted his horse before he replied, "Then she'll realize she's made a mistake when we don't show up, won't she?"

That was true enough, and the easiest way to get out of it, except . . .

144

"You don't understand, Colt. Those ladies are scared to remain here after what they witnessed. They mean to leave town today, with or without a guide. Would you really let them cross this country alone when they don't know anything about it, don't know what dangers to watch for, how to recognize Indian signs or anything else? They'll end up getting lost, or drowned crossing a river where they shouldn't, or robbed. You know there's hundreds of petty outlaws who operate in this area alone. All it would take is their asking directions of the wrong people to end up in a trap. They're tenderfoots, Colt, a hundred times worse than I am."

Something must have gotten through to Colt, for he lost his temper at that point. "Dammit, I told her I wasn't for hire!"

"But did you know she was going to Wyoming? And she says she pays very well. You might as well get something out of this trip for the trouble I've put you to."

Bringing Colt's thoughts back to the reason for his being there perhaps wasn't the wisest thing to do. Billy felt flattened by the look he got, but then Colt yanked his horse — and headed for the Grand Hotel.

Chapter Eleven

Billy should have known that Colt wasn't so easy to talk around. He had no intention of seeing the duchess and her entourage north. As he put it, while they waited for her to appear outside her hotel, she'd been traveling for three years and was still in one piece. She had all the protection she needed in her own little army, and there were stage lines they could follow to keep from getting lost. If they had to have a guide, they could probably locate one in a matter of hours and still be on their way out of town today. What they did not need, and were not getting, was him, and he was there to make sure the lady was left in no further doubt of that.

How he intended to do that, Billy didn't know. Colt had said his piece and then said no more. But as they sat their mounts in front of the Grand Hotel, watching the baggage and trunks being loaded in the wagons that had been pulled up in front of the building when they got there, Billy was afraid that Colt was not going to be pleasant about it. And Colt could be very unpleasant when he wanted to be. But he also wasn't behaving in a normal fashion. As they waited, his jaw kept working as if he were gritting his teeth, he changed the angle of his hat a half-dozen times, and he seemed to tense each time the hotel doors opened. If Billy didn't know better, he would think Colt was nervous, but that just couldn't be. There wasn't a thing alive that could intimidate Colt, as far as Billy knew. He just didn't have the same reactions to things as other men did.

Inside the hotel, there was no doubt about nervousness. Jocelyn was nearly trembling with it when she neared the hotel entrance. She had been told that Colt Thunder was outside waiting with his brother. She hadn't really let herself believe he would show up, but that he had didn't mean she would be getting what she wanted. Far from it. He had every right to be furious with her for the way she had manipulated his brother. *He* wouldn't have let her get away with it, and was likely there only to tell her what he thought of her high-handedness.

"Stop a moment and take a deep breath before you make yourself sick," Vanessa said in a stern voice, putting her hand on Jocelyn's arm to make sure she did halt, and motioning

147

their guards back. "What's done is done. All you can do now is apologize."

"I could beg."

"You will do no such thing!" Vanessa snapped indignantly. "We aren't desperate for his help, and you aren't desperate for his body, not yet anyway. You're suffering a powerful attraction, but out of sight, out of mind. You will forget him sooner than you think."

"And remain a virgin forever," Jocelyn sighed.

Vanessa couldn't help it. She had to smile at such a forlorn expression. "That isn't likely to happen, dearest, and you know it. You forget that you have only just decided to take a lover. You were not actively seeking one before, but now that you are, you will be surprised how many men you will find appealing that you otherwise wouldn't have noticed."

"But I've made my choice."

"Your choice isn't being cooperative, dear, or did that escape your notice?" Vanessa said dryly, only to regret her words when Jocelyn flinched. "Now, none of that. There's probably a very good reason why these American Indians are called savages, you know. It's doubtful you would have liked his form of lovemaking, so be glad it hasn't worked out."

"He's not a savage, Vana."

"Reserve that opinion until after you face him. And best we put it behind us, so come along."

As they continued forward, the four guards Vanessa had motioned back moved up behind them again, and the two who had been stationed in the lobby fell into step beside them. The remaining six were already outside. They would have thoroughly checked out the area, even the buildings across the street. If there was even one person of a suspicious nature anywhere around who couldn't be warned away, Jocelyn would not be allowed to leave the hotel. Hours could be wasted, and had frequently been wasted, on just such precautions. If Longnose ever hired a decent marksman, those precautions would be pointless, but fortunately, none of his hirelings had ever been competent with firearms, at least not from a distance.

Sir Parker was there to open the door for them with a ready smile. He adored Jocelyn, but only from afar. She was like an ideal to him, safe to worship, but he would never presume to make his feelings known to her. As if everyone didn't know, including Jocelyn. She was the stuff of dreams, whereas earthy creatures like Babette were reality, and Parker and half the guard frequently took advantage of the French maid's brand of reality. But it was amusing to watch Parker and Jocelyn both take such pains not to acknowledge his feelings for her.

It really was too bad he felt that Jocelyn was beyond his reach, Vanessa thought, for his age was perfect at thirty, he owned considerable property in Kent, and he was quite the most handsome of the guards with his black hair and dark green eyes. The trouble was, he would never settle for just being her lover, even if she would consider him as a candidate. He wasn't ready to settle down — the reason he so enjoyed the job the duke had offered him — but if he thought Jocelyn would have him, he would offer for her in a minute.

No, Jocelyn would never consider any of her own men for her first experiments with amour, for that would defeat her purpose of protecting the duke's memory. But Vanessa's misgivings about her Mr. Thunder had grown considerably today, and she was now firmly of the opinion that he was not right for her either.

A virgin needed gentleness and sensitivity for her first sexual experience, and it was highly doubtful that Mr. Thunder possessed either of those qualities. They had assumed, given his appearance and speech, which was easier to understand than that of most of these Westerners, that despite his ancestry, he had been raised in what passed for civilization here in the West. It had been a surprise to hear his brother state otherwise. If a man was raised by savages, didn't that make him a savage? Colt Thunder's civilized veneer was very likely only skin-deep, which was why it was a blessing he didn't return Jocelyn's interest.

Vanessa was forced to change her opinion yet again when they stepped out onto the walkway fronting the hotel and saw the man, still mounted on his horse. Skin-deep? Not even that. There was nothing civilized about the look he directed at Jocelyn. It said more clearly than words that she would have been in serious trouble if they were alone just then. Did she realize that, or was she still blinded by the dark handsomeness of the man? And he was that. Vanessa had not gotten a good look at him before, but it was easier to understand now why he had affected Jocelyn so strongly.

Jocelyn did not mistake the meaning behind the look Colt gave her, but then she had been expecting something like it. The man was angry with her and wanted her to know it. Still, he wasn't shouting at her, not yet anyway, when she had expected that too. Of course, she wasn't alone with him this time. She had her guard surrounding her. But somehow she didn't think that would stop

151

him if he *wanted* to shout at her.

The silence stretched on as he continued to stare at her, shredding her nerves. She ought to apologize. That was what he was probably waiting for. But the words wouldn't come, and then his did.

"Fifty thousand dollars, Duchess. Take it or leave it."

It was fortunate that Jocelyn couldn't see the expressions of the men behind her just then, or she would have thought there was going to be bloodshed. She did hear Vanessa's gasp and was aware that the countess put a hand on Parker's arm to restrain him from reacting to the insult Jocelyn had been dealt. And she did realize she had been insulted, not only by the words, which implied nothing short of a fortune could get him to work for her and that he didn't care one way or the other, but also by the tone in which those words had been delivered.

Oh, he was clever, was Colt Thunder. He fully expected her to be outraged at such a fee. He was counting on it. He was also positive she would refuse; had named such a high figure so she would be forced to refuse; otherwise he wouldn't have made the offer. She had to bite back her smile. She could hire a hundred guides for that price and they both knew it, but what he didn't know was that

that wasn't what she wanted him for. He would likely be the most expensive lover anyone had ever bought, but what else did she have to spend her fortune on?

"Done, Mr. Thunder," Jocelyn said with a good deal of pleasure. "You now work for me." She had to turn away quickly before she laughed aloud at the expression of utter disbelief that appeared on his handsome face.

Chapter Twelve

"He has done this for spite, you know," Vanessa complained angrily as she wiped the dust from her face with a damp cloth. "We passed that town no more than three or four miles back, and it was almost evening then. There was no conceivable reason for us to go on and end up camping out for the night, except that he means to get even with you for calling his bluff today. Mark my words, Jocelyn, that man intends to make you regret crossing him."

"I didn't cross him. I agreed to his terms."

"Don't be obtuse, dear. Those ridiculous terms weren't meant to be agreed to and you know it. You should have seen his face — "

"I did." Jocelyn grinned with such delight that Vanessa couldn't help sharing in her amusement. "I don't think Edward's money has ever given me quite so much pleasure before. He asked for the moon, and I was able to give it to him. Good Lord, that was satisfying."

"I hope you still think so when we end up spending the next several weeks in this tent."

"Oh, stop fussing, Vana. I wouldn't exactly call this a tent." The thing was huge, with ample headroom, a soft Persian carpet covering the ground, silken pillows to recline on, thick furs to sleep on. "We have all the conveniences we could possibly need."

"Except a bath," the countess retorted, revealing the source of her annoyance.

"You can have a bath and you know it."

"After Sidney and Pearson loaded the wagons not so many hours ago, I wouldn't dream of asking them to lug water up from that river we've camped near. I like to think I have more consideration than that."

"The footmen aren't the only ones who can fetch water, Vana. You're just being difficult, and I'd like to know why."

"I'm not the one being difficult. There's simply no reason for us to rough it with a town only a few miles away. Your monstrously expensive guide is the one who's proving difficult."

"And if he has a legitimate reason for avoiding that town?"

"I'd dearly love to hear it. Why don't you go ask him? Well, what are you waiting for?"

"He's not here," Jocelyn had to admit. "His brother said he's scouting the area."

"Humph! More likely he's gone back to Benson for a soft bed and you'll see him in the morning, well rested and ready to heap more hardship on us. That would be just the sort of revenge that would appeal to someone like him."

"Now, there you're wrong, Vana. If he wants revenge, it wouldn't be anywhere near so subtle, and it would be against me, not everyone."

"You saw that in his eyes, too, did you?" Vanessa asked in a much softer tone and came to kneel down among the pillows where Jocelyn was sitting. At Jocelyn's unhappy nod, she placed a gentle hand on her cheek. "Have you finally realized he isn't like any man you've ever known before? He's hard and dangerous and — "

"I still want him," Jocelyn interrupted in a soft whisper. "Even when he was frying me with his eyes, I still felt all funny inside, just as I did the first time I looked at him."

Vanessa sighed. "He won't be gentle with you, dearest; you know that, don't you? And if you tempt him when he's still angry at you, he may hurt you — deliberately."

"You don't know that," Jocelyn protested, even as her eyes filled with uncertainty. "He's not a cruel man. I would have sensed it if he was — wouldn't I?"

"Perhaps," Vanessa allowed. "But I still don't think he has it in him to be gentle. He's a product of a life and culture that we can't even begin to conceive of. Will you at least keep that in mind?"

Jocelyn nodded, then fell back against the pillows with her own sigh. "I don't know what you're worried about. He isn't likely to forgive me for being rich enough to afford him."

Vanessa had to laugh. "Which just proves how different he is. What other man would be furious at finding himself the recipient of such a windfall? And we're not even taking him out of his way. For his convenience, we're going where he's going. By the way, where the devil is this Wyoming?"

"What the hell is that?"

Billy chuckled when he saw what Colt was staring at. "The ladies' accommodations. They got it from a desert sheikh when they were traveling through the Arab countries over in Africa. You wouldn't believe all the places they've been, Colt. The stories they have to tell ought to keep us entertained all the way to Wyoming."

Colt gave Billy a disgusted look before dismounting. "Where'd your sense go this time, kid? I expected to ride in and find a camp, not a damn village. Do you have any idea how many men it's going to take to cover an area this size?"

There were other tents besides the main one, not as large but big enough, and spread out all over the place, as were the vehicles. The only thing that had been done right was that the animals were contained together in an area downwind of the camp.

"Why don't you relax, Colt, and come have some of this dinner I saved for you? They have a French cook, you know, and I can safely say I've never tasted anything . . . so . . ."

The words trailed off when Colt swung around from unsaddling his horse with a dangerous look on his face. "You're enjoying this, aren't you, kid?"

Billy swallowed hard. He'd rather Colt shouted at him any day than use that soft, controlled voice. He was so damn unpredictable when the Indian side of him was dominant. Billy needed to pacify him and quick.

"They knew what they were doing, Colt. They're old hands at camping out. They had everything unpacked and set up in less than twenty minutes. And you forget how many men there actually are. They've already got the watch covered . . ."

Again Billy's words trailed off. Colt had turned away to finish with his horse, but the very inflexibility of his movements spoke volumes. He was wound up tighter than a bowstring about to snap, and Billy finally realized the camp had nothing much to do with what was wrong with him, that it was only an outlet for the anger that couldn't be directed at its proper source. It was a good thing the "source" had already retired for the night.

Billy still couldn't quite believe that Colt was now working for the duchess. Those five little words, *Take it or leave it*, had trapped him but good. It was likely that half his anger was self-directed for having given the woman that option when it hadn't been his intention at all. Fifty thousand dollars. Billy had nearly fallen off his horse when he heard that figure, but that was nothing compared to his shock, and Colt's, when the duchess accepted it.

It was funny now, after the fact; at least he thought so. But he knew Colt wasn't likely to find any humor in it — ever.

Colt might have a small fortune in raw gold that his mother had given him, but Billy doubted he had ever used any of it. Riches had no meaning for someone like Colt. He still lived off the land just as he always had. Jessie had failed to civilize him in that respect. He sometimes slept in the huge ranch house that Chase had built for Jessie after the old one burned down, and sometimes in the cabin he had built up in the hills overlooking the ranch. But most nights would find Colt's bed laid out under the stars somewhere, especially in warmer weather. And he had never worked for anyone before, not even for Jessie.

She had tried to teach him cattle ranching, but it was not something he wanted to do, so his heart hadn't been in the learning of it. What he had finally settled down to do was what he had always had the most skill with, horse training. He now supplied the Rocky Valley, as well as the other ranches in the area, with all the work horses they needed, animals that used to have to be shipped in from Colorado or farther afield. And the stallion he had given to Chase had won the annual horse race in Cheyenne these past two years, so his racers were now in high demand too.

But money still meant nothing to him. He caught and trained wild horses because it was something he enjoyed doing, not for the lucrative living it provided. Nonetheless, he understood money and the price of things. Jessie had rounded out his education in that respect. He'd gone on buying trips with her and Chase to Denver and St. Louis. And during his stay in Chicago he'd been in some of the finest homes, been dragged through some of the more expensive stores, seen firsthand the way the rich lived and played and what they spent their money on. He had been perfectly safe in believing that the fee he had named for his services was so outlandish, no one in their right mind would take it seriously, and that was his mistake.

Oh, he had known the duchess was wealthy. That couldn't be missed. Her equipage, her quality horseflesh, her clothes, and the amount of people she already had in her employ, all shouted wealth. What was incomprehensible, even to Billy, was the kind of wealth that made fifty thousand dollars a paltry sum not worth batting an eye over. Even Billy didn't know anyone that rich.

But even the rich didn't squander away their money frivolously, and that was exactly what the duchess was doing. Why? She might be eccentric, but she didn't strike Billy as being incompetent or crazy. Far from it. Was she just so spoiled that she couldn't tolerate being denied something she wanted?

That made no sense. What she wanted was a guide — or was it? It seemed more like Colt in particular that she had to have as a guide, even though he'd told her he wasn't for hire. He might be an excellent choice to get her safely where she was going, but so could any number of other men, men who would want the job. Colt didn't want it and had made that perfectly clear, but that didn't seem to matter to the duchess. So there had to be a particular reason why she had to have Colt working for her, no matter what it cost her, only Billy couldn't see it.

Neither could Colt, and he'd gone over it in his mind much more thoroughly than Billy had, and with more facts available to him. He knew that she'd first wanted him to go after her enemy. Being her guide had been her second offer. He wondered if she would have had a third if he'd agreed to meet with her earlier today. Likely. Did she think he was the answer to her problems? Didn't she know you couldn't force someone to help you? She'd bought herself a guide and that was all she was getting.

So why did it infuriate him that her camp was wide open to attack? Damned woman was going to get his protection whether he wanted to give it or not. But he wasn't going after her enemy. If she thought she could talk him around to it, she was in for a rude awakening.

And yet that couldn't really be the reason for such stubborn persistence on her part to have him along on this journey of hers. She could hire a dozen bounty hunters for the price she was willing to pay him. Or maybe she wasn't really willing to throw that kind of money away. Maybe she'd called his bluff with a bluff of her own and had no intention of actually paying up. And maybe he could get out of this mess by demanding the money up front — and look like a fool again if she just happened to have that kind of money lying around? Damned if he would. Once today was one time too many.

Colt dropped his saddle on the ground so close to the fire Billy was poking at that sparks went flying and the kid had to do some quick slapping at his clothes. Colt didn't notice. He was staring at that huge cream-and-white-striped monstrosity that stood less than twenty-five feet away, and he wasn't even seeing the tent, but imagining the woman inside it. Was her hair let down and loose again as it was the first time he'd seen her? Had she peeled off those fine, expensive clothes of hers and put on something — what? What did a woman like her sleep in?

Colt gnashed his teeth and turned back to his horse again. He would have much preferred that Billy not set up their fire near her tent, but it was done. He didn't expect to get much sleep tonight anyway, so it didn't really matter how near he was to her.

"I'll be back in a minute, kid. Get rid of that foreign food. I'll make my own."

Billy started to protest, but wisely thought

better of it. Colt had had enough forced on him for one day. *Her* provisions would likely stick in his craw at this point, no matter how good they were.

Billy sighed as he watched Colt lead his Appaloosa off toward the other animals. He wasn't the only one who watched him. Ever since he had ridden in, every eye in the camp had been on him in varying degrees of curiosity, suspicion, and animosity. These people didn't know what to make of him, and they certainly didn't know how to treat him. All they knew was that their lady was determined to have him among them. Billy had been approached, treated in a cordial, even friendly, fashion, but Colt's manner didn't invite such overtures. Even if he hadn't insulted the duchess within hearing of half her men, which was reason enough for them to dislike him, his demeanor fairly shouted, "Don't get close." And the one who ought to stay the farthest away was the duchess herself, but even as Billy thought it, she left her tent to follow Colt toward the horses.

Chapter Thirteen

He knew she was there. He'd heard her approach, though she'd tried to be quiet about it. And he didn't have to turn around and see her to know it was her. Her scent came to him strongly now, but before he'd smelled her, he'd sensed her nearness, almost like an animal its mate.

She stood there just behind him, waiting for him to acknowledge her presence. He shouldn't. The less words he had with her the better. But he didn't think she'd go away without them. She was too stubborn, this woman. Even though her silence proved her nervousness, she had still approached him, her determination stronger than her uncertainty.

"You're wise to keep them close by."

It took Jocelyn a moment to get over the jolt caused by the suddenness of his words, and another moment to understand what he meant. She turned to see *who* had followed her and saw at least four of her guards stationed about the area, and not even trying to be inconspicuous. They had allowed her partial privacy by keeping back a reasonable distance, but they were obviously unwilling to leave her completely alone with their newest guide.

"They don't know you yet. They'll relax their vigilance once they do."

"You don't know me either."

She shivered at the way he said that, as if it implied a threat. Likely it did and she would be smart to take heed and run like hell. She was nervous enough without him saying things like that. But she didn't want to be afraid of him. And she didn't want him to stay angry with her. And she'd never get anywhere with him if she let him frighten her away.

"We could change that," she said hesitantly, wishing he would turn around to look at her. "I would like very much to know you better."

"Why?"

"Because I find you . . . intriguing." *And exciting, and immensely desirable, and blast you, Colt, turn around and look at me!*

He didn't. He continued to rub down his horse with slow and easy strokes as if she weren't even there. She wasn't used to being ignored deliberately. It added nothing to a woman's confidence, and hers was already at a low ebb.

For a while she watched in silence the movement of his hand over the animal's flanks and almost became mesmerized, imagining . . .

Jocelyn shook those thoughts quickly away and stepped to the front of the horse to stroke its muzzle, admiring the animal for a moment instead of its owner — who still wouldn't look in her direction.

She tried again. "Can't we at least talk?"

"No."

For some reason that flat refusal annoyed her enough to spark her own temper. The man was impossible, totally, completely impossible.

"Look, I know you're still angry with me, but — "

"Angry doesn't even get close to what I feel, lady."

He had straightened and was finally looking at her, and now she wished he wasn't. Those blue, blue eyes smoldered with some fierce emotion that took her breath away. Fury? She wasn't quite sure.

Neither was Colt. He tried to hold onto his anger, but other things kept getting in the way, her scent, her voice — memories. Every time he got this close to a white woman he could almost feel that whip tearing the flesh off his back. With her it was even worse, because despite knowing he couldn't have her, he still desired her. It shouldn't be happening at all. It hadn't happened in three years. In all that time her kind had turned him cold with revulsion and remembrance of what he had suffered because of one of them. He was a man who made mistakes only once. So why wasn't he repulsed by her? Why was his body aflame with the need to grab her and draw her even closer? And why the hell didn't she back off before he lost what little control he had left?

"What was it?" he demanded, his tone deliberately cutting. "Had no one ever told you no before?"

"Not — not at all."

"Then why me, Duchess?"

The contempt he put into her title was the last straw. What intimidation she had been feeling was superseded by a burst of indignation.

"Why not you? You did apparently have your price or you wouldn't be here." She was being obtuse and knew it, but wanted one more point made before he got around to telling her that. "I won't release you, you know, even if you do continue with this surly attitude."

"Lady, if I thought there was something I could do to get myself fired, I'd do it," he assured her with a good deal of exasperation.

But then his eyes happened to drop to her lips and stayed there for a heart-stopping moment, and he added, much more softly, "Then again — maybe there is something . . ."

She knew it was going to happen even before his hand reached for her. She even knew it wasn't going to be pleasant, that what he intended was to insult her, or hurt her, or something of the like to get himself fired. But he gave her every opportunity to stop him. There was nothing hurried in his movement as his hand stretched toward her neck. And the first touch of his fingers against her nape was gentle, without constraint.

Up to that point she still could have escaped, but several painful heartbeats later it was too late. His fingers moved up and locked in the thick coil of her hair to trap her and pull her toward him. Yet he did it so slowly that even then she could have done something, begun to struggle, cry out — only she didn't.

He probably thought he was frightening her so bad that she was incapable of speech or movement, but the simple truth was she didn't want to stop him. She wanted the touch of his mouth on hers so much that she was willing to take the hurt with it. She had known that, even when Vanessa had warned her he wouldn't be gentle with her. If she feared anything now, it was that he wouldn't kiss her.

But when he did, it was more brutal than she had counted on. He was serious in his desire to repulse her, perhaps even make her hate him, at the least make her get rid of him. What he didn't know was that the kiss accounted for only half of what she was feeling. The other half, the incredible excitement taking over the rest of her body, sustained her and allowed her to accept what was given without resistance.

"You ready to fire me?"

The question was grated out as his grip tightened painfully in her hair. But she didn't think he was aware that his hold was hurting her. Her lips were numb and throbbing, her breathing ragged, her knees so weak she could barely stand, while his whole concentration seemed to be centered on her mouth, waiting for her answer, as if it alone would decide what he would do next.

"No," she answered breathlessly, surprising him as much as herself. She didn't want him to hurt her any more, but she wasn't giving up on him yet either.

His eyes came to hers, perhaps trying to figure out if she was just stubborn, or just plain crazy. And then his body tensed as reality intruded, and he said in a softly ominous tone, "Tell him to get his hand off me. If I take care of it, he's not going to be much use to you for a while."

She blinked to see Robbie just behind him, his big hand on Colt's shoulder. Colt hadn't looked at him, was still looking at her, but she doubted that Robbie's size would have made any difference in what he'd said. Far from it. He was ready to get violent, wanted to get violent. And she knew it even if the big Scot didn't.

"It's all right, Robbie, Mr. Thunder was just . . . proving a point to me. Nothing for you to be concerned about."

The brawny Scot hesitated in indecision. However much he had witnessed of that punishing kiss in the dim light supplied by the numerous campfires behind them, it was enough to make him doubt her reassurance. How *could* she have forgotten that her men were near? Of course, she didn't have to explain herself to them, but still . . .

And then she realized that Colt's fingers were still twisted in her hair, holding her in place, and that likely was why Robbie was still concerned. It had escaped her notice, and probably Colt's too, when Robbie interrupted them. But when she nudged her shoulder where Colt's wrist touched to subtly remind him, he didn't let go. And one look at his eyes

171

proved he hadn't forgotten he was holding her. He wasn't going to back off, not for any reason.

She didn't understand what motivated him now. Did he want to provoke a fight with her men, hoping *that* would get him fired? Or was this just another means to frighten her, to show her that her men were no real protection, not against him anyway? Whatever his reason, she didn't like it.

If she remonstrated with him and he ignored her, *that* was going to cause a fight. If she forced Robbie to leave while Colt still held her in his grip, then she was giving him free rein to start up again where he had left off. But if she did nothing, then Colt would do something, and Vanessa would never forgive her if she let him hurt her favorite guard. And she had little doubt about *who* would be getting hurt. Robbie might be a big, brawny man who had seen service in Her Majesty's Royal Highlanders, but there was nothing of cold, merciless steel in him, whereas everything about Colt Thunder cried danger.

There was no help for it. "I do appreciate your concern, Robbie, but I'm perfectly safe in Mr. Thunder's company. You may leave now — and take the other gentlemen with you. I will be along in a moment."

Made into an order, he had no choice but to

comply, however reluctantly. "As you wish, Your Grace."

The moment Robbie let go of Colt and turned away, Colt released her. So that was all he had wanted. Blast the man for making her worry about his intentions.

"That was utterly despicable of you," she hissed as she put a hand to the back of her head to rub her sore scalp. "And I don't mean what you did to me, though that was despicable too. I don't doubt that you are capable of meting out a good deal of damage to my men, but to take that means of provoking your dismissal is cowardly, and whatever I thought of you, sir, it was not that you were cowardly."

"And what do you think of me now?" he asked in a low, hard voice.

She took a step back from him, well aware he was referring to what he'd done to her. What did she think, besides the fact that he could be merciless in getting what he wanted?

"I think you are a very determined man, Colt Thunder, but then I am known for that quality myself. And I hate to disappoint you, but your little demonstration didn't work. I still need you."

She walked away from him then, but what she did to him with those last words was ample revenge for that kiss. Her definition of

173

need and the one his body interpreted were not the same, but it kept him awake the entire night anyway, half of which was spent hurting.

Chapter Fourteen

"*Ferme là!*"

"*Hein? Espèce de salaud, je vais te casser la gueule!*"

"*Mon cul!*"

"Good Lord, must we wake up to such swearing?" Jocelyn demanded irritably as she turned over in the furs. "What are they fighting about this time?"

Vanessa, who stood at the tent opening watching the commotion outside, shrugged. "I think Babette insulted his cooking again. You know how touchy Philippe is about his skills."

"She's not really going to smash his face in as she just threatened, is she?"

"She does have hold of one of his frying pans, but then so does he. Right now they're just glaring at each other."

"Do call her off, Vana. I've warned her time and again about fighting with Philippe. Where does she think I can replace him if he quits because of her? *She* is the one I ought to replace. The trouble she causes — "

"She keeps things lively, you'll have to admit, and the men happy, I might add. And why are *you* so touchy this morning?"

Jocelyn ignored that question. "Just call her off before my breakfast is ruined. Why are the lamps still lit? What the deuce time is it, anyway?"

Here Vanessa chuckled. "I would imagine it's about six o'clock of the A.M. Your sweet Mr. Thunder woke the camp about thirty minutes ago. He said something about our pulling out by sunrise so we 'wouldn't waste daylight.' "

"Sunrise! Is he mad?" Jocelyn cried.

"I would hazard a guess that he just wants to reach the end of his obligations with all possible speed. At this rate we ought to reach Wyoming in no time a'tall."

"I'll speak to him."

"Good luck."

"Just *what* do you find so amusing about this, Vana?"

"I warned you, my dear, did I not? That man is going to do his utmost to make sure you regret hiring him. Guide indeed. He's a born slave driver, is what he is."

Vanessa left then to make sure the French in their party did not come to civil war. But she was back in a moment with Jane, who carried in a bowl of warm water and a clean towel. Babette was conspicuously absent, no doubt warned she had incurred Jocelyn's displeasure, so Jane laid out Jocelyn's clothes for the day before departing again.

Jocelyn remained under the covers, fighting with an irritation that had nothing to do with the recent conversation. Her lips felt puffy and sore, and a mirror would no doubt show them to be swollen. How was she going to hide something like that? And if Colt saw it, he would know he had actually hurt her. He would never understand then why she hadn't fired him on the spot. And what could she tell him if he demanded an explanation? That she enjoyed being manhandled? Or the truth, that she wanted so much to have him be her first lover, she could overlook last night's rough treatment?

"Well? He'll be pounding on the — ah, tent flap, if you're not up and ready to leave at his appointed time. Or is that what you had in mind? Should I leave so the coast is clear?"

Vanessa was most definitely not helping matters with her dry humor this morning. She loved to rub it in when she was proved right about something, and Jocelyn supposed she felt this ungodly early rising was proof that Colt was still getting even for the way she had trapped him into working for her.

"If he does come around knocking, that'll be just too bad," Jocelyn grumbled. "I'm not leaving until I'm good and ready."

"What's this? Are we preparing for our first argument with the chap already? Do I get to listen?"

"Vana!"

"All right," the countess conceded as she came to sit at the bottom of Jocelyn's furs. "I've made my point, I suppose. But why *are* you so touchy this morning?"

Jocelyn sighed. "I didn't sleep well."

"Want to talk about it?"

"Not particularly," Jocelyn said as she turned over, and then she flinched to hear Vanessa gasp when she got her first good look at her face.

"Good Lord, it's already happened! When? Why didn't you tell me? And you're still in one piece, thank God. Well, at least now we can dispense with that ruffian's services."

"Nothing happened."

"Rubbish," Vanessa snorted. "I know a well-kissed mouth when I see one."

"That's all he did, and he did that so I would fire him."

"Did you? No, of course you didn't, or he wouldn't still be here. But . . . well, did you at least make some progress?"

"Progress?" Jocelyn felt like laughing.

"Vana, he didn't kiss me because he wanted to. He was trying — "

"Yes, I heard. To make you fire him. But was it . . . what you expected?"

"Expected? Yes. Wanted? No. He made it as brutal as he could, and I hope his blasted lips are just as sore this morning!"

Vanessa blinked at that heated reply. "Well, I guess we can safely say no progress was made," she allowed. "Unless of course you think he might have lost control and that's why he was so savage about it."

Control? His voice *hadn't* been particularly steady when he'd asked her if she was ready to fire him. And now that she thought about it, his breathing had been kind of ragged too. And his fingers *had* tightened in her hair when he ended the kiss, not before. Was it possible some passion had come into that kiss without his planning on it? God, she would like to think so, but she was just too inexperienced to be sure.

"I don't know, Vana, but it doesn't really matter. I ended up thwarting him again, so he would have gone to bed damning me to hell and back, not pining away with desire. And now that I think about it," she added, throwing back the covers to get up, "I would be smart not to get anywhere near him for a few days. I shouldn't have approached him last night, knowing that he hadn't had a chance yet to cool off. I don't care to make that mistake again."

Chapter Fifteen

"Pete's ridin' in."

" 'Bout time," Dewane grumbled.

"Did he bring a doctor with him?" Clay asked from his pallet in the corner.

"Quit yar bellyachin'," Dewane snapped at the wounded man. "I got the damned bullet out, did'n I?"

"Pete's alone, Clay," Clydell offered from the open doorway where he'd spotted the rider coming in. "A doc could'n do much now anyways, an' then we'd jes' hafta kill 'im ta keep his mouth shut. Ya want some more whiskey?"

Elliot watched silently as a bottle of the raw firewater that passed for whiskey in this area was handed over to the man called Clay. The chap was dying and just didn't know it. He had lost too much blood before he had found his way back to them. Instead of making his suffering even worse by removing the bullet, Elliot would have simply put him out of his misery, but he wasn't asked his opinion and didn't volunteer it. He had wanted to kill him anyway for failing in his assignment, but he had kept that desire to himself too. It wouldn't do for the others to know how really furious he was.

The ultimate blame for this latest failure was his and he knew it, for hiring incompetents, for not coming up with a better plan, for not sending more than just two men after the duchess. Luck had come into it again, her infernal luck, this time in finding assistance in the middle of nowhere, and skilled assistance at that. How did she do it every bloody time?

Clay had fallen back into semiconsciousness, which ought to keep his moaning down for a while. It had been driving Elliot crazy, that persistent moaning. But he had said nothing. He was allowing it to get on the others' nerves, too, so no one would object very much when he suggested the chap be left behind to die in peace.

Dewane set the coffeepot down on the table, but Elliot made no move to refill his tin cup with the horrid brew. Their accommodations were deplorable, but at least there was a roof overhead.

Clydell had found the empty hovel which he called a line shack, a place the cowhands of one of the ranches in the area would use when they were out on the range doing whatever it was they did for a living. It sported a table and two chairs, an old cookstove, a few rusted tin goods in a chest, and a moldy mattress on a rope frame. Likely the roof would leak if it rained, but it gave them a place to wait while Pete Saunders was finding out what he could of the duchess's destination.

After two nights of waiting, however, Elliot had begun to think the youngest member of his little group had deserted them. He wouldn't have been overly surprised. After so bloody long having nothing go right for him, he had come to expect the worst. But Pete was back, and now he could finally get down to planning his next move.

Pete sauntered into the one-room shack, grinning and dusting his clothes off with a beat-up hat that was likely older than he was. Elliot had been leery of employing the boy when he first saw him, even though a full brown beard concealed his tender age somewhat. But after being given a list of his accomplishments, which included armed robbery, cattle rustling, and one gunfight where he had emerged the winner, Elliot had reconsidered. He still didn't care for the eighteen-year-old's enthusiasm and jolly manner, though, as if this were only a game he was playing at.

"Thought ya got lost, Pete," Clydell remarked by way of greeting.

"Or too lickered up ta find yer way out of a pisspot," Dewane added with a sneer.

"Didn't have a drop," Pete protested, still grinning as he plopped down across from Elliot in the only other chair. "But I could sure stand a drink now. How's Clay doin'?"

"The same," Clydell said and set his bottle of rotgut on the table.

Elliot allowed the boy only a few swallows from the upended bottle before demanding, "If you have something to report, Mr. Saunders, I would very much like to hear it *now*."

The grin was still there when the bottle was lowered. Elliot would have thought it was a deformity of the boy's mouth, that constant grin, if he hadn't seen him without it when Clay had rejoined them, all covered in blood.

"Sure thing, boss," Pete replied. "When I got to Tombstone, it weren't hard findin' the lady. She'd caused plenty excitement ridin' in the way she did with all those fancy rigs and guards of hers. Just about everyone was talkin' 'bout her, speculatin' who she was and what she was doin' —"

"Yes, yes, that happens no matter where she goes," Elliot interrupted impatiently. "Just get on with it."

"Well, she checked herself and her whole bunch into the Grand, so I figured she was there to stay a while. I was set to ride out the next mornin' after I found out if we had to worry 'bout a posse comin' after us — "

"Do we?" Dewane wanted to know.

"Nah. The fella I asked who sweeps out the jail said we was listed as 'persons unknown' when they turned the body in. They didn't give no descriptions, so the marshal had nothin' to go on. But as I was sayin', it's a good thing I overslept the next mornin' and didn't leave first thing."

"Had some fun, did ya, while we was sittin' here twiddlin' our thumbs waitin' on ya?" Dewane asked in a surly tone.

"Ah, come on, Dewane, what was I supposed to do with time to kill? So I was up a little late that first night. If I hadn't enjoyed myself some, I wouldn't've still been there when the lady left town again."

"She's already on the move?" Elliot demanded with some surprise.

"Sure is. She took off right after the shootout — hey, Dewane, you'll never guess who bought it!" Pete added excitedly. "The McLaury brothers and the Clanton kid."

"The Earps?"

"Who else?"

"Didja see it?" Clydell asked.

"Nah. It happened while I was findin' out what I could at the jail. But you could hear the shots firin' from everywhere. By the time I got there it was all over."

"If you please, Mr. Saunders," Elliot interjected. "I am interested in the duchess, not some obscure shootout in one of your frontier towns."

"Sure, boss, but you see, the lady was there. And right after is when she took to her heels. It don't take much to figure that all that killin' turned her stomach enough to want to get out of there. Anyway, I figured as late as I was, I might as well go by her hotel one more time, and that's when I seen her wagons lined up out front and bein' loaded up."

"I will assume you were smart enough to follow her?"

Pete nodded. "Until they made camp last night a few miles past Benson. They're stickin' to the stage roads even though they picked up some breed for a guide before they left town. He had 'em pullin' out by dawn this mornin' and headin' for Tucson. That's when I come on back here."

"Where is she going now?" Elliot asked.

"Sounds like Tucson," Clydell offered helpfully.

Elliot sighed inwardly. Imbeciles. Nothing but a bunch of imbeciles.

"I assure you the duchess does not intend to remain in this territory, Mr. Owen. It is her ultimate destination I am concerned with."

186

"She's travelin' north now, but it's sure as shootin' she ain't headin' up ta Utah," Dewane said, the only one to grasp what Elliot wanted. "Nuthin' but deserts up thataway. They can either turn off toward Californy or head on over inta New Mexico at any time, then maybe up ta Colirada. Thar's railroads up thar'll take her all the way back East if she's a mind."

"Very good." Elliot finally smiled, though it was a cold, anticipatory smile. "And as long as she keeps to the roads, which is almost assured with those cumbersome vehicles of hers, then we can easily get ahead of her with a little hard riding. How far is this Tucson?"

"Too far fer them fancy rigs ta make it t'day, but if'n we leave now an' ride through the night, we'll get thar first."

"Excellent, but we will also need more men. Would you happen to be acquainted with any in Tucson?"

"I might," Dewane replied. "Ya thinkin' of attackin' in force now?"

"You are forgetting how many armed men she has, Mr. Owen, and now she's added still another to that number. It's too bad about that guide. One of you could have offered your services for the job, and once in her camp, it would have been a simple matter to slit her throat and escape the first moonless night. By the way, what exactly is a *breed?*"

"A half-breed. Ya know, part Injun. What was he, Pete? Apache?"

"Nah, too tall. And I ain't never seen an Apache breed wear a Colt like he really knew how to use it. They stick to rifles."

"Tall, huh?" Dewane said uneasily. "Ya wouldn' happen ta have caught his name, would ya?"

"Matter of fact, I was close enough to hear two of her guards talkin' 'bout him 'fore they kinda insisted I leave the area. They called him Mr. Thunder."

"Ah, shit!" Dewane swore, then added a few more choice words to that. "She's gone an' got herself a fast gun, a *real* fast gun!"

"Am I to understand you know this Thunder chap?"

Dewane forgot himself enough to glare at the Englishman for his calm in the face of his own upset. Colt Thunder, the only bastard who'd ever made him back down from a fight. Shit! What the hell was he doing this far south?

"Ya could say I know 'im, yes. I seen 'im draw on a fella a few years back, and thar weren' no contest to it."

"But, Dewane, that were — "

"Shut up, Clydell!" Dewane growled at his brother. "I know what I seen." And then in a

188

calmer tone: "The Injun's no one ta mess around with, boss. He don' take no crap or insult from any man. He don' hafta, as good as he is. An' ya can bet yer sweet life he's the one shot up our boys. That'd make sense, what with her bein' able ta hire him so quick. She had ta already have met 'im."

"So where is the problem? You simply eliminate him."

"An' how in hell we supposed ta do that? I tol' ya — "

"Don't worry, dear fellow," Elliot replied sardonically. "I'm not suggesting you challenge him to a duel. A bullet in the back ought to do nicely, and then the duchess will need another guide, won't she?"

"I guess she will at that." Dewane grinned. As long as *he* didn't have to get anywhere near Colt Thunder . . .

"If you have nothing else to report, Mr. Saunders, I suggest we be on our way," Elliot said as he stood up to go. "I will need time to survey this next town to see what advantage, if any, might be found in its layout."

"What about Clay?" Pete wanted to know.

"If you think he can survive the ride, by all means bring him along."

Pete glanced at Dewane as the Englishman walked out, but they didn't hesitate long in following. The fifth man of their group, who

189

hadn't contributed to the conversation, did the same. He had known Clay just a few months, but wouldn't waste sympathy on a man careless enough to get shot, since they all took that risk. Clydell was the only one who spared a last glance for the dying man, and as an afterthought, set his bottle of whiskey on the floor next to Clay's pallet before he, too, followed the others.

Chapter Sixteen

They were a beautiful sight, the woman and the magnificent horse. For a short while Colt was mesmerized by the skill that made her seem part of the animal in its wild race across the cactus-strewn basin. He would never have believed she could ride like that, not a woman who chose to pamper herself with fancy coaches. And she wasn't even sitting the horse properly. She sat sideways, for Christ's sake. It made him wonder what other misconceptions he might have formed about her.

But he didn't wonder for long. Quickly his temper started to rise, and by the time she reached him, it was just short of boiling. He didn't even give her a chance to catch her breath, and his voice was so loud he managed to spook her stallion, so that it was several moments more before she got him enough under control to even hear what Colt was shouting about.

"— all the stupid, idiotic . . . you're crazy, right? I should have known! Why else would you pay a dozen men to guard you, then take off without a single one of them beside you?"

"What *are* you talking about?" Jocelyn demanded when she finally brought Sir George up beside him. "I saw you from a distance. I rode directly toward you. If you haven't noticed, there are no hills, or trees, or even bushes that anyone could hide behind. I was perfectly safe in covering this distance alone."

"Is that right? Well, look again, Duchess. That mountain lion over yonder is a mite far from his hunting ground, but he's still there. Whether he caught the dinner that led him this far afield is anyone's guess, but it sure don't mean he'd ignore an easy prey like you if he caught your scent."

He waited a moment for her to stare aghast at the slow-moving cat which was only about three hundred yards south of them. Fortunately, it didn't appear very interested, but she didn't know that, and he wasn't finished with her yet.

"And the snake that spooks that skittish animal of yours into dropping you in the dust will still be there to take a whack at you while your horse is galloping off to safety. You think someone can reach you in time to cut out the poison before you're dead? Think again. Man isn't the only danger out here."

"I believe you've made your point," Jocelyn said in a small voice.

"Good," he replied with a great deal of satisfaction, only to add, "So what the hell are you doing out here?"

"Sir George and I both needed the exercise," she rushed to explain. "He hasn't had a good run since we left Mexico, and besides, it is my habit to ride him for a while each day. In this case, I . . . I wanted to speak to you, and as it didn't appear that you would be returning before nightfall again, I didn't see the harm . . . well, I see it now, but I didn't when I decided to join you."

"Get down."

"I beg your pardon?"

"You gave him his run, Duchess, about three miles' worth. Now give him a breather. Christ, don't you know — "

"Don't you dare tell me how to care for my horse!" she snapped, but immediately dismounted and started walking Sir George in a circle around Colt. "You can instruct me in anything else you please, but not about horses. I've bred and raised them all my life, and no one, *no one*, can tell me a thing about them that I don't already know, and know better."

Colt said nothing to that. The fact that she had a temper surprised him enough to cool down his own. He didn't doubt that she knew horses. Anyone who rode as well as she had to be well acquainted with them. But to have bred and raised them? That wasn't exactly a typical undertaking for a woman to pursue, at least not a white woman.

She really was proving to be other than what he had thought, in some things anyway. But he didn't mind these particular surprises, for they managed to relieve his mind on one score. If it came down to a chase because she happened to be caught out alone, who the hell could catch her on that horse? And she undoubtedly knew that. He wondered why she hadn't mentioned it when he came down on her so hard.

"Did you breed him?"

She had been stewing silently, and glanced up warily at that question. "Yes."

He dismounted then and stepped in front of her so she would stop. The bay stallion drew back nervously, until Colt stretched his hand out and said something to the animal in a language Jocelyn had never heard before. She stared incredulously as Sir George pushed his nose into that outstretched hand and then shouldered Jocelyn aside to get closer to the man.

"That's amazing!" she gasped. "He's nervous enough around people he knows, but he

194

never lets strangers get near him. You've already made his acquaintance, haven't you?" she added suspiciously.

"No."

"Then how did you — Good Lord! You have the touch, don't you?"

"The touch?"

"The ability to make animals trust you. I have it too, but I've never seen it work quite so quickly before."

It annoyed him that she had discovered a common ground between them when he needed to cling to their differences. "What was it you wanted to talk to me about, Duchess?"

"Oh, well, you took off this morning before anyone could ask you why you had started us out on the road we traveled yesterday, only to suddenly turn us east."

"You were followed yesterday," was all he said.

"We . . . how . . . well! They must not have been very close for no one else to notice, but of course you roamed farther afield — "

"There was only one man," he cut in before she went off on another one of her talking sprees. "He bedded down about a mile back, and returned the way he'd come soon after you rejoined the road to Tucson."

"So he'll report we went that way, while

195

we've turned in nearly the opposite direction," she concluded with a laugh. "Oh, I knew you would prove invaluable to me, Thunder. I just hadn't realized how much. Now, don't look at me like that. What did I say?"

"I'm no guide, Duchess, and never professed to be one. Like that mountain lion, I've drifted a hell of a long way from my hunting grounds. I don't even know when we'll run into the next water hole. All I know is that beyond those mountains up ahead is New Mexico and the old Santa Fe Trail that'll lead us to the plains. The plains I know. Between here and there . . . " he ended with a shrug.

"Good Lord, I thought . . . are you saying we could get lost?"

"Not lost, but for a while there'll be no roads to make it easy, and I don't guarantee the way between those mountains will be passable for your vehicles."

"Then how did you get here from Wyoming? That is where you came from, isn't it?"

"The way I came down, your coaches definitely couldn't get through. But then I was following Billy down, and he didn't know where the hell he was going."

"You don't appear very worried about it," she pointed out.

"There's always a way. What it comes

down to is how much time's wasted finding it. That's Apache country up ahead. There's bound to be well-worn trails."

"And Apaches?"

"You were more likely to have run into them in Mexico. Most of them are settled on reservations, just like every other tribe in the country. The time for you to have worried about Indians, Duchess, was when you met me, not now."

She turned away from the bitterness that had entered his voice and moved toward his horse. "Please don't start that again," she told him without looking at him, her attention centered on the big-boned animal that stood docilely while she ran her hand up its neck. "There is nothing you can do that will make me believe you are the uncivilized savage you keep trying to convince me you are."

It was the wrong thing to do, to throw out a challenge like that and not expect him to accept it. But she wasn't used to dealing with men like him. Before she had any warning at all, she was on the ground and he was on top of her, both horses had shied out of the way, and his hand was already yanking her skirt up.

"Nothing, Duchess?" he said in a cold, determined voice. "Let's see how you feel about that after I'm done with you."

She was so stunned she barely heard him, but she felt the sharp tug on her drawers that ripped them open, and then the hard thrust of a finger inside her. "Colt, no, I won't let you —"

"You can't stop me, woman. Hasn't that sunk in yet? You made sure we were alone where the only protection you have is me. So who protects you from me?"

She shoved hard at his shoulders to dislodge him, but he was right, she couldn't stop him. "You're only doing this to frighten me!" And he was succeeding.

"You think it's that many years since I left the life where I took whatever I wanted and killed for the right to do so? Do you know what would happen to you if I had found you then? This — and a helluva lot more. We not only raped white women, we made slaves of them."

She was afraid he wasn't just making a point this time, that he really was going to take her right there in the dirt, with the late afternoon sun broiling down on them. She didn't want it to be like that, and the tears that came to her eyes said as much, but he didn't see them.

It was instinct that made her wrap her arms around his neck as she pleaded, "Please don't hurt me, Colt."

He rolled off her instantly with a vicious curse. Again she was stunned. She hadn't thought it would be that easy to make him stop, but the danger was definitely past. So he *had* just been trying to frighten her again!

"I ought to have you horsewhipped!" she seethed as she yanked her skirt down and scrambled to her feet. "You can't keep doing this to me, Colt Thunder! I won't allow it!"

He glanced over his shoulder at her from where he sat trying to get his overheated body back under control. "Another damn word out of you and you'll find yourself flat on your back again!"

He might have practically snarled that at her, but she was too angry to take heed. "Is that so, you misbegotten son of a — a — an Indian!"

He watched her reach *his* horse, lift her skirt high, and mount it — in the normal way, which hiked her skirt up to her knees. He also watched her pull his rifle out of its scabbard, but still he didn't get to his feet. He didn't know what the hell she thought she was doing, but as long as she didn't point the weapon at him . . .

"I don't mean for you to become that big cat's dinner, but I do hope you will have cooled off before you join us for ours."

With that she fired off two shots that hit the

dust at the lion's feet and sent it racing off into the distance. The noise also scattered a half-dozen nearby jackrabbits, grouse, and even a wild turkey that had previously gone unnoticed. Three more shots in quick succession ended the flight of two of the rabbits and the turkey.

Colt was still staring at the third dead animal when her voice cut through his amazement. "It's only when the danger is camouflaged by its surroundings that it proves a danger, Mr. Thunder. You might want to gather those up before we reach you. Our cook, Philippe, will appreciate it."

He didn't understand half of those last comments of hers until she took off, which she did with a flurry of scattered dust, and then let loose the shrill whistle that brought up the bay stallion's head and had him galloping after her. But Colt didn't get up even then. He was still incredulous over her marksmanship, which damn near equaled his own — another skill he would never have suspected she might possess — so he wasn't quite dealing yet with her audacity in leaving him stranded.

At least she thought that was what she'd done. He could have called his horse back to him just as easily as she had summoned hers to follow her. But that would have put her within arm's reach of him again, and it had already been proved with a vengeance that he couldn't keep his hands off her when she was that close. Christ, he jumped on any excuse to touch her, even if it was only to frighten her so she wouldn't get close enough again for him to find even *more* excuses.

When it did finally sink in that he was still sitting there with three dead animals nearby, almost guaranteed to attract buzzards soon, he let out a stream of curses that would have burned that vindictive redhead's ears. He did need time to cool off, bodywise, and with the caravan still a good mile and a half away, there was little doubt that he would. His temper, on the other hand, was already on the rise again.

Chapter Seventeen

"What are you going to do when the man starts to thrash you?"

Jocelyn waved a hand meant to dismiss that notion. "Don't be silly, Vana. He wouldn't dare." But she stopped in her pacing about the tent, and even she recognized the uncertainty in her voice. "Would he?"

"Don't look at me, my dear. You're the one who keeps playing with fire. I haven't even spoken to the chap yet. But isn't that something you should have considered before you stole his horse?"

"I didn't steal it, I just borrowed it. But he would have deserved it if I had."

She had caused quite a stir returning astride the big Appaloosa, but one look at her sour expression and no one had commented on it, not even Colt's brother, at least not to her. But that was several hours ago.

The cavalcade had passed the point where she had left Colt, but there had been no sign of him. They had also set up camp for another

202

night and there was still no sign of him. Likely her people were beginning to wonder if she hadn't gotten rid of him in a permanent way. After all, they would have heard those shots she had fired. She was beginning to worry herself. There were the snakes he had mentioned, and that blasted mountain lion was still out there somewhere. Of course she hadn't left him weaponless. He did still have his revolver. He no doubt just *wanted* her to worry about him.

"I rather like this carpeting, but it isn't going to last much longer if you keep that up," Vanessa said in her driest tone. "Why don't you come and have a sherry before dinner?"

"I'm sorry," Jocelyn said, but she didn't quit her pacing. "I know I haven't been very good company for you these past few days."

"You must be joking," Vanessa snorted. "Your little clashes with Mr. Thunder have been quite the best entertainment to happen among us since our two strapping footmen tried to kill each other over Babette. You haven't said what happened today, but when you leave in an impeccable condition and return quite the opposite, it isn't that hard to guess. I really can't wait to see what happens next."

For that the countess received a dark glower, but it almost instantly turned into a closed-eyed cringe, for they could both hear the commotion that started up just outside the tent. Mr. Thunder had arrived.

"Now see here, mate," one of the guards said in annoyance, "You can't go in there without an invite."

The only answer was the sound of flesh meeting flesh, likely in the form of knuckles to face. Then another guard's voice was heard, and there was some further scuffling, and two more solid punches.

"You'd better get your derringer, my dear, until he calms down enough to see reason."

But Jocelyn didn't move at Vanessa's prompting, and there really wasn't time. It was ironic that neither of them thought the guards might win the tussle, and they were both right. The tent flap whipped open as Colt came through it without breaking stride, an angry stride that brought him straight to Jocelyn. She braced herself, but still she didn't move an inch. Perhaps that was what made him keep his hands from her when he reached her. He did no more than throw his hat down on the ground between them — and shout.

"I ought to . . . don't you ever . . . "

He didn't finish either thought. Her apparent calm in the face of his fury defeated him. And it was fascinating, watching him fight to regain control of his emotions. He stood there with his eyes closed and she could almost feel the turbulence inside him, the heat and power of it radiating so close to the surface, yet she could no longer see it.

Jocelyn had the feeling that losing control of any kind was alien to him, that he was a man who prided himself on being able to mask feelings of both body and mind, to never give a clue to the inner turmoil he might be experiencing. She had witnessed just such control before. But then, she had also been shouted at before by him.

Was that a good sign, she wondered, that the man seemed to lose his calm only when he was around her? Or was it just the situation he found himself in that he couldn't handle? She wished she knew which it was, but she concluded she'd prodded him enough for one day. Vanessa was right as usual. She had no business playing with fire before first learning the consequences.

Before he opened his eyes the tent was invaded again, by six more guards. "They're late," Colt said quietly to Jocelyn while Vanessa quickly assured the men there was no further need for alarm. "It's too damn easy to get to you, woman."

"Not really," she said just as quietly. "The only reason you got as far as you did is because you're known to them. If a stranger had tried the same thing, he would have been shot instead of merely warned off. Did you do much damage out there?"

"No."

"Good."

She smiled before turning toward her men and adding her assurances to Vanessa's that it was all a misunderstanding. She even took full blame for it, though she did not go into detail, merely admitting that she had provoked Colt unreasonably. The fact that everyone there knew she had returned with Colt's horse, minus Colt, made his upset understandable as well as forgivable. He didn't have to utter a word in his defense, not that he would have.

Sir Parker was the only one reluctant to leave with Colt still there, but as Colt was now calmness itself, and both women insisting there would be no further trouble, he had little choice in the matter. As soon as the last guard departed, though, it was rather disconcerting to hear Colt's comment, quiet, but quite serious.

"I tried walking it off, then running it off, but neither worked one little bit. Nothing short of wringing your neck was going to work."

Vanessa, appalled upon hearing this, opened her mouth to call back the guard, but Jocelyn forestalled her. "Well, my neck appreciates that you came to your senses. Perhaps I do owe you an apology — "

"Damned right." Even that was somehow said in a moderate tone.

" — but you owe me one as well, so why don't we call it even this time?"

He didn't acknowledge her suggestion by word or nod, and Jocelyn grew uncomfortable under his piercing stare. Those eyes of his really were lethal in what they could make her feel, and staring back at him only made it worse. In those blue depths she saw intimate knowledge of her body. His hardness had covered her only hours ago. His hand had seared the flesh on her legs when he had yanked her skirt out of his way. Her knees went weak now as she recalled that he had put his finger inside her. And she had the feeling he was remembering the same thing when he looked at her like that. She prayed not.

She turned away, caught Vanessa's wary look, and almost burst into relieved laughter. It was one thing for Vanessa to make all her snide comments and warnings based on speculation, but now that she was seeing the man for herself and how he could be, she likely didn't know what to think. He certainly wasn't easy to read, especially when he was like this. The fury was probably still there, but buried so deep now that it was harmless — at least for the moment.

"The countess reminded me earlier that I have been remiss in the way of introductions. Colt Thunder, allow me to present my dearest friend and companion, Vanessa Britten."

"Ma'am," Colt said with a nod.

Vanessa was obviously encouraged, enough to say, "Delighted, Mr. Thunder."

"Oh, he doesn't like to be called mister, Vana. He answers to either name."

"Without preference? How odd."

"But it's rather nice, the informality, isn't it? It makes you feel you know a person better than you do."

"If you'll excuse me, ladies."

He said it even as he headed for the exit, prompting Jocelyn to step in front of him. "But you can't leave yet. You must stay and have dinner with us."

"Must?"

She lowered her eyes before correcting herself. "Will you please join us?"

"I don't — "

"At least stay and have a drink," she persisted. "You must be . . . " Wrong thing to mention, his likely thirst. "We have sherry . . . no, you wouldn't like that. Vana, why

208

don't you see what Jane can find in the supply wagon in the way of more potent spirits?"

"Haven't you learned yet that it isn't safe to be alone with me?"

Jocelyn swung around to see that Vanessa had left them without answering, the tent flap still fluttering. They were indeed alone — for the moment.

"She'll be right back, and . . . " She peeked a glance at him. Good Lord, those eyes again. They sent shivers of excitement racing along her skin even when they were so inscrutable. "And haven't you learned yet that I'm not so easily intimidated?"

"What you are is crazy, woman . . . and asking for it," he retorted.

She *was* asking for it, but not in the way he meant. Why couldn't he see that? Why did he try so hard to appear mean and despicable? *Because he really is mean and despicable,* a tiny voice suggested. No, she wouldn't believe that, not for a minute. Besides, Sir George wouldn't have taken to a man who was inherently cruel.

"What I am, Colt Thunder," she said in a soft, whispery tone as her eyes sought his again, "is very attra — "

"Jane won't be but a moment. I told her to find that bottle of old brandy you bought from — oh, I say, I didn't interrupt anything, did I?" Vanessa asked.

Jocelyn was blushing profusely, but managed to shake her head as she stepped away from Colt. "No, not at all," she got out, nearly choking on the words.

She couldn't believe she had been about to confess her attraction for him. That simply wasn't the way things were done, especially when the second party's feelings were not in the least bit clear. Good Lord, how mortifying if she had done so and he hadn't responded, or worse, had replied something to the effect that it was her problem, not his. It *was* her problem, but for once she couldn't plunge right ahead in solving it.

"It's as well you came back so soon, Vana, since I was just getting around to asking Colt why he wanted us to avoid that town yesterday. The answer *was* of particular interest to you, wasn't it?"

"Indeed," Vanessa replied, though with reluctance.

It was all well and good to complain to Jocelyn about their guide's apparent spitefulness, Vanessa thought, but quite another thing to broach the subject with him, especially when he looked anything but friendly. In fact, the way he was looking at Jocelyn while her attention wasn't on him . . . Good Lord, what had happened while she was gone? His eyes were fairly smoldering with passion, but what kind of passion?

He didn't seem to have followed the conversation, so intent was his concentration on Jocelyn, so Vanessa prompted, "Was there a reason, ah — Colt?"

His gaze swung to her with what could only be described as impatience, but the fires were banked now, and then he was looking at the duchess again, almost as if he couldn't seem to help himself. "I kept you out of Benson because your best protection is out in the open, where you can see your enemy coming. In a town, you don't know who the hell to watch out for since you don't even know what this Englishman looks like, or his men. Out here, anyone who approaches is suspect. It's the simplest precaution there is, Duchess, keeping to yourself."

There was a double meaning there. Even Vanessa caught it. Jocelyn chose to ignore it entirely.

"There, you see, Vana, a perfectly good reason. And what's more, Longnose has been temporarily misled thanks to the detour Colt insisted on this morning. We couldn't be in more capable hands, wouldn't you agree?"

Vanessa nodded, but her attention was still on Colt, watching for his reaction. She couldn't fault Jocelyn's age-old tactics. She

211

had let the him know his company was desired, had been shyly avoiding his gaze as if she didn't dare look at him for fear her feelings would be blatantly clear, and now was using flattery. But none of it seemed to be working on the man, at least not as one would expect. If anything, the more agreeable Jocelyn was, the more disturbed he seemed.

Did he grasp the situation and just want no part of it? Or were his the actions of a man who had decided he couldn't have what he wanted? Now there was a thought, but one Vanessa couldn't very well pursue. She wondered if she ought to mention it to Jocelyn. No, best let the girl proceed in her own way. Besides, the answer couldn't be had without direct questioning, and Jocelyn might be straightforward on most subjects, but Vanessa hoped she had sense enough not to broach this one. The embarrassment that could arise didn't bear thinking of.

Neither woman could have known that Colt would have welcomed a little straightforwardness at this point, for he still didn't understand the duchess's motivations in the least. That she could want him, knowing what he was, was the last thing that might occur to him.

But his wanting her was getting out of hand, and being this near to her again was just making it worse. It had been a bad mistake to come in here, even with his anger to sustain him. With the anger gone now, he needed to get the hell away and fast.

He did just that the moment the tent flap opened again with the servant bearing the brandy on a silver tray. "Ladies," was all he said in parting before stalking toward the exit. But he did first snatch the bottle from the startled maid. At least there was something of Jocelyn's that he could have without guilt, and he damn well needed it tonight.

Chapter Eighteen

For the next several days Jocelyn saw nothing of Colt, though she had assurances from others that he hadn't deserted them. He was simply gone before she awoke, and did not return until after she had retired for the night. It was not unreasonable that she should worry about him during these long absences as they moved through what was considered the very heart of Apache country, but it was unusual. There had been much to worry about these past three years, but not since Edward had she focused her concern on one man in particular.

So when Colt showed up one afternoon to ride at the head of the cavalcade, Jocelyn was not the only one who felt there must be a specific reason for it. That he offered no explanation was typical of him. Getting voluntary information out of Colt Thunder was harder than finding water in this arid region. And if she hadn't already guessed that her men had formed a distinct dislike for him, the fact that not one of them would appease his curiosity by questioning him proved it.

She could have done so herself. It would only have been a matter of raising her voice a little since she was riding up with the driver of her coach while Vanessa napped inside. She thought about it for about two seconds. But she had caught a glimpse of his face when he rode up, and quite frankly, he had never looked more unapproachable.

She couldn't help feeling a certain apprehension now, an anticipation of something about to happen, especially as she stared at the rigid set of Colt's back as he continued to lead them forward. It was still another half hour, however, before the tense waiting came to an end.

There was what could only in very generous terms be described as a hill in the near distance, and on top of the tiny mound sat six mounted riders. Jocelyn's front guards drew up the moment the small group was sighted, but when Colt continued on, she indicated they should follow. The strangers weren't identifiable yet, nor were they doing anything except sitting there watching the cavalcade's approach. If it was Longnose . . . well, Jocelyn almost wished it was. To borrow one of the region's more colorful phrases, this was one "showdown" long overdue.

But no such luck. As they drew nearer the

hill, it became clear that they were to be treated to their first sight of some genuine American Indians, but closer still gave an indication that these were not of the tame variety, not with so many cartridge belts in evidence, some used merely as belts, some crossed as bandoliers. Still, there was nothing to be truly alarmed about, not with so few of them. Her guard alone doubled their number. Even so, Jocelyn found herself holding her breath as the Indians began to descend their hill, slowly and in single file, and in a direction that would put them directly in the path the cavalcade now moved.

Colt reined in this time, and everyone behind him immediately followed suit. After a moment, Sir Parker moved up beside him and they shared a few words; then Colt rode forward to speak with the Indians.

Pearson, who was driving the lead coach today, leaned toward Jocelyn to whisper, "I thought these blokes were supposed t' be skilled archers."

She could see what prompted the remark, since not a bow or an arrow was in sight. "These are modern times, Mr. Pearson. It's not surprising they've discovered the rifle to be a more handy weapon for killing — game."

"Game's a mite scarce in this area. Would

they be wantin' some food or such, do you think?"

"That, or perhaps a toll for crossing their land," she replied with a good deal of relief. "Yes, that would seem logical, wouldn't it? What other reason could they . . . have . . . ?"

Her attention centered immediately on Colt as he reached the Indians, who had lined up to face him. Some words were exchanged, but the distance was too far for Jocelyn to hear any of them, and she could only wonder about the excessive use of hand motions between Colt and the Indian leader to emphasize whatever they were discussing.

Fortunately, it didn't take long. Colt yanked his horse about, and Jocelyn had already asked for assistance and was on the ground when he reached her. Unfortunately, his expression was so grim she was back to holding her breath again, at least until he had dismounted, took her arm, and led her a few feet away from the others.

"They want your stallion," he said without preamble.

Equally to the point, Jocelyn replied, "Sir George is not for sale, at any price."

"I didn't say they want to buy him, Duchess."

"But . . . you don't mean they're demanding Sir George in payment to let us cross this way?"

217

"No, I don't. They've got no business in this area themselves. Those are renegade Apaches."

"As in the kind that 'raid across the border,' *this* side of the border?"

The hesitant way she said that almost made him grin. "Now you got the picture."

She sensed his condescension and her chin came up. "And if I don't choose to give them Sir George?"

"They don't usually ask before they take," he replied patiently. "They spotted us yesterday and could've made the attempt to steal the stallion last night. I think they've taken you folks for Easterners, the reason for this brazenness on their part. They're pretty confident you're scared out of your minds right about now and will give up the horse without a hitch."

"Are they indeed?" she snorted.

He did grin this time. "So what's it to be?"

"This is absurd," she said, glaring over his shoulder at the group of waiting Indians. "What can they do? We outnumber them more than three to one. And need I remind you I am also a skilled shot?"

He admired her gumption, but she didn't really know what she was dealing with here. "You ever kill a man before?"

"Certainly not," she replied. "Nor do I

have to kill one to disarm him."

She said that with such confidence he didn't doubt it, so he said no more on that point. "Let me lay it on the line for you, Duchess. You can turn them away empty-handed and they'll go, but you can bet your sweet . . . they'll be back with reinforcements. A few days from now, a week, you won't know when, and it isn't likely they'll give warning either, since it's to their advantage to attack at night, when most of us are asleep. Then they won't just be after the stallion, but everything you've got, especially your lives."

"I won't give up my stallion, for any reason," she said with stubborn determination. "He's the future of my stud farm."

"Lady, it's not as if you need a business to earn your keep, is it? Or was I mistaken in thinking you're so rich money has little meaning to you?"

They were moving into dangerous ground here, if his tone was any indication. "Whatever wealth is at my disposal, life still needs meaning, Colt, and breeding the finest Thoroughbreds gives me that." It was why she had finally allowed Sir George to cover the three mares after she made twenty-one, because she had thought her wandering days were over at last. More fool she.

Suddenly an alternate solution occurred to her. "What if I offer them one of my mares?"

His brows shot up in surprise. "You'd do that?"

"I don't want to, but if it will keep them from attacking us at a later date, yes, of course I will. I won't risk my people needlessly."

He slowly shook his head. "It won't work. The leader of this raiding party has set his sights on the stallion. A horse like that would raise his prestige among his followers so much, he's willing to die to possess it. But I'll make a deal with you. If I can manage to send them on their way with you still in possession of all your horseflesh — "

"Do you mean to tell me you've had another solution to this dilemma all along and failed to mention it?"

"I guess you could say that. But I'm not doing it for nothing, Duchess. It'll cost you — "

"You can't be serious!" she gasped. "After what I'm already paying you — "

" — a filly from one of your mares . . . that is, if your stallion is the one that sired those they're presently carrying."

For a long moment she just stared at him. There was some surprise that he knew the mares were already carrying her future breeding stock, when they weren't due to foal until spring. But mostly she was amazed at his gall.

He couldn't just get rid of those Indians as part of his job, could he? No, that would be too magnanimous of him, the blasted blackguard.

"Is that your deal?" she asked tightly. "Those Apaches leave and bother us no more, and you get a mare from Sir George?" At his curt nod, she added, "Just how do you intend to get them to leave?"

"That's my business, Duchess. Is it a deal?"

"Since you leave me no other choice — "

"Good," he cut her off, impatient now. "Keep your men here, and I would suggest you and the other women stay in the coaches and don't watch."

Don't watch? "Don't watch what?" she demanded, but he had already turned back toward his horse and didn't hear her, or chose not to answer. Whichever, she was annoyed enough not to ask again.

Slowly she walked back to the coach and was about to join Vanessa, who must still be sleeping since she had yet to inquire why they had halted. And then Jocelyn stopped, even more annoyed to realize she was doing just what Colt had ordered her to do.

She moved around the coach to the shaded side and stood there to see how long it would take Colt to convince the Indians to leave. It had better take the rest of the afternoon for what it was costing her. But it was no more than a couple of minutes before Colt was about-facing again.

Jocelyn stiffened. That easy? That no-good, rotten opportunist! But no, he rode only half-way back. And one of the Indians followed him, dismounting when he did, about twenty yards away from both interested parties.

So they were going to talk privately. Very well. She could see where that would be to Colt's advantage. He was probably going to make certain ungentlemanly threats. After all, he was much taller than the Apache, and broader in frame. The full-blooded Indian was in fact short and wiry, to the point of looking undernourished.

But they didn't do any more talking. The Apache, whose bare, knobby knees showed between his high moccasins and a yellowed cloth that hung halfway down his thighs, put his rifle down. His loose, long-sleeved cotton shirt was store-bought or traded, and he was one of them who wore only a single cartridge belt about his waist with a long-bladed knife stuck through it. Now that he was closer, Jocelyn also noted that his skin was much darker than Colt's, his black hair worn much shorter, barely reaching his shoulders, and with a red headband to confine it. Small he

222

might be, but he looked distinctly menacing as he stood there waiting for Colt to face him.

Colt was meanwhile removing his buckskin jacket. Jocelyn hadn't noticed before, but today his shirt was also buckskin, long, and worn outside his pants with a wide, elaborate belt over it. When he turned to hook his jacket over the horn on his saddle, she saw that the front of the shirt held some type of design in . . . Blast the distance. It looked like white-and-blue beadwork topping the shoulders, but she couldn't be sure. The extra long fringes next to it flowed across the top of his arms, as well as all the way down the sleeves to his wrists, and each one seemed to have a bead attached to the end.

He removed his hat next, and Jocelyn could only stare openmouthed as he parted his hair just behind his ears and braided each side. When the gun belt came off after that, she felt her first stirring of alarm. She took a step forward, only to stop as she watched Colt tear off one of the longer fringes and hand it to the Apache before turning his back on the Indian. What the devil . . . ?

A moment later she gasped when Colt faced the Apache again, and she wasn't the only one to make a sound of consternation. Her guards were also whispering among themselves, won-

223

dering why Colt would let the Apache tie his right hand to the back of his belt, rendering that arm useless, but that was exactly what he had done. In another second they had their answer.

The two men drew their knives for what could only be called a very primitive challenge. Colt had allowed himself to be handicapped, severely handicapped, since Jocelyn knew him to be right-handed. They both held their knives in fists, with the long blades facing outward in a stabbing, rather than a slashing, grip, yet it was slashing they did in this backward manner, the Apache first.

He was quick, and agile, and definitely going for blood, but then so was Colt. Apparently the object of this combat was to slash each other to ribbons. Colt had the advantage of a longer reach, but that was all. His disadvantage was in not having that other arm for balance, or for blocking. If he should fall . . . The result didn't bear thinking of.

Obviously, the Apache came to realize that too, for after receiving several slashes across his torso, without scoring any in return, he changed his tactics. He began to leap at Colt, instead of away, and to try to get behind him. When that didn't work, he tried to trip him.

Jocelyn finally came out of her horrified daze and started to run forward, but was immediately blocked by Sir Parker. "You mustn't, Your Grace. He said any interference on our part could draw their fire."

"But we have to stop it!"

"It's too late for that. Best hope those Indians understand some English when we have to deal with them after — "

Her total loss of color silenced him. After Colt was dead? Did they all think he didn't have a chance? No, he couldn't die. She would give them Sir George. . . .

But it was too late. When she looked at the combatants again, it was to see Colt already down, with the Apache on top of him. She nearly fainted with the realization she could never reach them in time to stop it. She could only watch, as the others were doing, as the Apache immobilized Colt's only defense by holding his knife hand to the ground with his own left hand and prepared to stab him with the right.

Jocelyn swung around, unable to bear witnessing the fait accompli, but it was a complete turn she made, for she couldn't bear not knowing either. And in those mere seconds, Colt had pulled off the impossible. He was now on top, his knife at the Apache's throat.

"What? How?"

Sir Parker seemed disgusted by the outcome. "The Indian didn't have the strength to keep his arm pinioned. Thunder managed to bring his knife over to block the stab. The Indian lost his blade in the process, and his balance, since he was still holding onto Thunder's wrist when it happened."

Jocelyn started to smile, but it wasn't over yet. Or was it? Colt got up slowly, reached behind him to cut free his right hand, then offered his left to help his opponent rise. So he hadn't killed the Apache, though the man's lack of movement until then had made her think otherwise. But the defeated man refused his offer, got slowly to his own feet, and moved directly to his horse.

Colt waited there until the Apache had rejoined his companions and they had all ridden away. He then mounted up and returned to the coaches, annoyed to see the duchess still outside hers. When he stopped by her, her eyes seemed anxious as they roved over his body, looking for signs of blood. She also seemed relieved to find none, and that annoyed him even more. He didn't want this woman worrying about him. Her concern worked like talons against his heartstrings, making him feel . . . Christ, just more frustration because he could never have her.

"I'm glad you didn't kill him." She smiled up at him.

Her smile brought out his worst frown.

"Are you? Were he Cheyenne, I would've had to, for my people would rather die than face the disgrace of defeat. But Apache customs differ in many ways from mine. They prefer to live to fight another day, so I've allowed him that."

That got rid of her smile. "And if that other day brings him back to try for Sir George again?"

"It won't. I told him the stallion was mine. That being the case, as he saw it, his only chance to gain him was to kill me, which he failed to do."

"You mean you . . . he . . . Sir George would have . . . " She gritted her teeth for a second in extreme agitation, completely forgetting her soaring relief of a moment ago that he was alive and unhurt. "*What*, pray tell, would have happened if you had lost?"

Colt infuriated her even more by grinning before drawling, "That wouldn't have been my problem, Duchess, now would it?"

Chapter Nineteen

Vanessa gave a weary sigh as she watched Jocelyn through the coach window, stirring up a great cloud of dust as she exercised Sir George. She didn't ride the stallion far anymore, not since that encounter with the Apaches, which Vanessa was still grateful she only had to hear about instead of witness. Against a vivid blue sky the duchess made a splendid picture, despite the drab landscape surrounding her.

It was getting depressing, that drab landscape, though Jocelyn seemed not to mind in the least. At one point lavender mountains had surrounded them on every horizon, but so far in the distance they seemed unreachable. More than anything else had been the endless stretches of flat, parched land, cracked in more places than not, the only green an occasional cactus, everything else, from scrub brush to patches of wilted grass, all washed silver by the blazing sun.

Did it never rain in this part of the world?

Since they had left that violence-invested town of Tombstone — so aptly named, that — there had been nary a drop. And only one little watercourse in all that time, San Simon creek, which was a mere trickle so late in the year, and muddy, that even baths had been out of the question. If they didn't carry their own water barrels, they would have been in quite a pickle.

Vanessa didn't complain, however, not in the least, not since that night she had done so deliberately, just to point out their guide's orneriness. And to be truthful, she wouldn't have wanted to miss seeing this part of the country, for it might be drab and tedious and eternally dusty during the daytime, but twice a day, at dawn and sunset, the most magnificent bursts of color appeared. Sometimes the sky seemed to be wreathed in flames, the reds and yellows were so gloriously vivid. And then the moon would rise in such huge grandeur, you felt you could almost reach out and touch it. With such a monstrously large glowing sphere hanging over the horizon, the sky refused to blacken into true night, and campfires were needed only for cooking and warmth.

Jocelyn never failed to be outside to watch these spectacular entertainments from above at the end of each day, but at the same time she would surreptitiously be scanning the camp, hoping for Colt Thunder to appear. He never did. He was still making himself extremely scarce to everyone except his brother, to whom he would give the general directions for each day's travel.

It annoyed Vanessa no end to see Jocelyn's disappointment at the close of a day when she hadn't seen the guide, even from a distance. But what had started some genuine alarm was hearing Jocelyn describe the encounter with the Apaches, and sensing the underlying emotions she had experienced in the watching, especially when she retold how close Colt had come to dying. The girl had gone from facing a dilemma to having Colt solve it, to horror at the way he solved it, to anguish at the thought of his death, to overwhelming relief that he survived, ending with total vexation with the man that unfortunately didn't last long.

It was the worry and concern for this American half-savage that alarmed Vanessa. Those were feelings that led too easily to love, and although Jocelyn hadn't realized that yet, Vanessa did. Such a happenstance was not to be considered. But it hadn't happened yet; at least Vanessa prayed it hadn't. And since Jocelyn was still determined to have the fellow, the only way to assure that love didn't enter into it was to get the deflowering over with as soon as possible and Colt Thunder sent on his way.

But there was a very big obstacle to seeing that accomplished, besides the fact that Thunder was rarely around. Simply put, he was the only guide they had, and until they came to some sort of civilization where he could be replaced, they were stuck with him.

As it happened, however, the rough terrain they had been crossing at such a brisk speed had played havoc with the vehicles, as well as with the animals, and a blacksmith's services were seriously in need. There was enough work to hold them up for at least several days. Their guide could no longer steer them around towns, if there had even been any to steer around in all this time.

"I'll say one thing for him," Vanessa remarked as they rolled into Silver City late the next morning. "At least it's not a one-street town with a four-room hotel he's brought us to for repairs . . . brought grudgingly, I might add."

Jocelyn didn't turn from the window where she was viewing this newest Western town with interest. "You know he's right about avoiding towns, Vana."

"I suppose," the countess allowed, but she was still chagrined over the fact that they had entered New Mexico several days ago and hadn't known it. "It would have been nice if he had deigned to inform us of the progress we had made in crossing into a new territory. Do you suppose he'll inform us when we reach Wyoming?"

Jocelyn turned with a grin on hearing one of Vanessa's driest tones. "As a guide he's done very well, hasn't he, especially since he never professed to be a guide? We've gotten this far without mishap. And need I add that he wasn't hired to give us a tour of the countryside?"

"Speaking of why he *was* hired, I think you ought to take advantage of our delay here and see the thing accomplished. A room to yourself should help, and you can use any pretext to get him alone in it. After that, one thing should lead to another, and — "

"You're forgetting one minor little point," Jocelyn interrupted, no longer grinning. "He doesn't like me."

"I wouldn't go so far as to say that, my dear."

"I would. He's gone out of his way to prove it. Nor does he find me even a little bit attractive."

Vanessa almost snorted. She settled for "Bosh. Has it occurred to you yet, my girl, that he might be tempted but feel he doesn't dare bestow his amorous attentions on someone of your importance?"

232

"He's not an Englishman, or even a European who would notice class differences, Vana. Didn't his brother give Sir Dudley a dressing-down about the importance Americans place on equality?"

"Indeed he did, but we're talking about an American of a different breed here, one who snubbed you in public to protect your own reputation, or had you forgotten that? And 'importance,' I will allow, was the wrong word to use. What I meant was someone of your . . . color."

"Because I'm what he calls a *white woman?*" Jocelyn gasped with belated understanding. "Good Lord, do you think that's all it is?"

"I wouldn't be surprised. At the very least, it might explain why he's gone to such trouble to, shall we say, frighten you into keeping your distance from him."

"But . . . how do I get around that?"

"A good question. He's already been informed that his half-breed status means nothing to you, so either he is prejudiced himself, but in the reverse, which I sincerely doubt, or he has misinterpreted all your signals for the simple reason that he doesn't believe you could actually desire someone like him."

"I don't like either of those possibilities, Vana," Jocelyn said stiffly in Colt's defense.

"But the second one does seem the most likely."

"I can't believe that he would have such a low opinion of himself."

"My dear, you can't imagine what his life has been like, or what circumstances have formed that life to make him how he is today. So let us just suppose for a minute that I am right. If he still isn't aware that you desire him, the thing to do is make him aware of it."

"I shall simply tell him."

"No — you — will — not!" Vanessa replied with appalled vehemence. "Where in the world did you get the idea that my suppositions are infallible? I will *not* have you suffering the most horrid embarrassment should I be wrong. On the other hand . . . it wouldn't hurt if you were a teeny bit more blatant in the matter of this seduction."

"A teeny bit?"

Vanessa smiled conspiratorially. "One of your French negligees when you receive him alone in your room, perhaps? That ought to take care of the matter most quickly."

"And get me raped most foully," Jocelyn retorted.

"Well, if you're going to take *that* attitude — "

"Now don't get all huffy." Jocelyn grinned. "It's a good idea. I'm just not sure it will bear the right results. He *has* warned me not to be alone with him again, and he does get awfully

234

mean when I don't heed his warnings."

"But that's just it, love. Why would he warn you off if not for his own sake, because the temptation is just too great for him to easily resist? It sounds to me as if that man wants you as much as you do him, if not more. Get past his defenses and you have him."

A tingling excitement rushed into Jocelyn's belly at those encouraging words. "God, Vana, I hope you're right."

I do too, dearest, Vanessa replied, but to herself.

Chapter Twenty

Jocelyn could not sit still as she waited for Colt to knock on her door that evening. He couldn't refuse to come this time. After all, he worked for her now. And she had even come up with a legitimate excuse for summoning him, to ask how much longer it would take to reach Wyoming. In making the decision to go there, she had not once considered where this place was or how long to get there.

Vanessa might have complained that they would be traveling for weeks, but she had been joking. The truth was, neither of them had ever heard of Wyoming before Billy Ewing had mentioned it, and all they knew about it was that it was "up north." Silver City, according to the hotel clerk, was in the southwestern half of New Mexico, and what with the winter months approaching, the time and distance they had yet to travel had become a matter of some concern, especially when Jocelyn needed to be settled someplace before her mares were ready to foal in the spring.

So she had a good excuse for demanding Colt's presence. And if he was crass enough to make some comment about the way she was attired, well, she had an excuse ready for that too. The late hour, fatigue from the long day, and the assumption that he wasn't coming, since she had sent for him hours ago.

Actually, Pearson and Sidney had only just been dispatched to find him and send him to her room. Vanessa had insisted that the scene be completely set beforehand, in case they located Colt immediately.

Jocelyn could not fault that reasoning, or the atmosphere Vanessa had helped to create. The mussed-up bed, as if Jocelyn had already been in it; all but one lamp extinguished, and that one dim. But the crowning touch was herself, bathed and perfumed and draped in shimmering satin so thin, it was utterly indecent.

She would not have chosen this particular negligee if left to herself, but she bowed to Vanessa's judgment since she was more experienced in these matters. It was new, created by a French modiste they had discovered in New York, and ordered on a whim after Jocelyn had met Charles Abington and matrimony had first entered her mind. A lime green that was almost the exact color of her eyes, the gown was simplicity itself, gathered at the shoulders, clinging to waist and hips, without trim, and with a loosely draped neckline so low that the material only covered her breasts as long as she remained in an upright position. The matching long-sleeved robe was bordered with white lace, but had not a single clasp or tie to close it with, not even a belt, since its purpose was not to conceal the gown, but to teasingly frame it.

The final touch was her hair, freshly washed and brushed until its shine rivaled that of the satin. It was left unconfined to flow as it would, down her back or over her shoulders, depending on her movements.

"He saw it like this when you met, but you mark my words," Vanessa had told her after she finished brushing those flaming locks herself. "Tonight he won't be able to resist finding out if it burns to the touch."

Only Jocelyn had not been reassured, had instead remembered that Colt's fingers had already been in her hair, painfully; and along with the nervous excitement she was feeling, there was a certain amount of trepidation. But she couldn't deny she wanted Colt Thunder, so she was willing to risk all on the hope that tonight would be different from those other times she had been alone with him. Tonight he would be the gentle lover she had dreamed about ever since she had made the decision, a few hours after meeting him, that he would be the one to introduce her to lovemaking. If she allowed the uncertainty to intrude, she would never have the courage to open the door when he knocked.

Waiting for that knock had her jumping at the slightest little sound, especially as the minutes turned into hours and the town outside her window quieted. The servants must be having trouble locating him. She should have anticipated that. But one of them would find him, and then he would come immediately, which could be any second now.

So she kept telling herself, increasing her agitation, not by slow degrees, but in leaps and bounds as she walked to the window to look out on the sloping roof of the hotel porch, then over to the bed made up in her own silk sheets. Here she would try to sit, but after a breath or two she was up and moving about, over to the full-length mirror that threw back a reasonably clear image of a pale young woman who looked totally alien to her. She would slap her cheeks for some color, then be off again, over to the door to see if she could hear footsteps approaching, then back to the window to start the whole process once more.

Unfortunately, it was not a very large room, though she had been told it was the largest to

239

be had. No suites here, and only two floors of rooms, so not all of her people had been accommodated, some sent to the boarding-house down the street, some electing to stay with the vehicles. Because she couldn't have the whole floor to herself, a guard was stationed outside her door, but she never heard a peep from him when she listened there, again, and again, and again.

If Colt didn't show up soon, she was going to be a nervous wreck when he did, and how then would she convince him she was surprised to see him, that she had been "sleeping"? Blast the man, what was taking . . . ?

It felt as if her belly dropped several inches when the knock finally sounded, and all she could do was stare at the door, immobilized by a total loss of composure, not to mention courage. So when the door unexpectedly opened to reveal Vanessa instead of Colt, Jocelyn's relief was so great she nearly collapsed with it.

"I'm sorry, dear," Vanessa said in a whisper before she closed the door, then added in a more normal, though regretful tone, "They've looked everywhere, the other lodging houses, the saloons, the — ah — more unsavory establishments. He's being true to form, as elusive as he was on the trail. Not even his brother has seen him since we arrived in town."

"It's all right, Vana. We'll be here a few days. We can try again tomorrow."

"You're taking this awfully well. I would be spitting mad, after all the preparation — "

"What preparation?" Jocelyn grinned in her relief. "It's not as if I spent hours dressing for a ball. I prepared myself for bed — "

"You prepared yourself for a man, which is not the same thing at all." But then the countess added knowingly, "Was it so terrible, the waiting?"

"Excruciating." Jocelyn laughed. "There is much to be said for spontaneity."

"And much more to be said for a well-planned seduction," Vanessa retorted. "You've tried spontaneity without results, if you'll recall."

"True, so I'll try it your way again. Perhaps it will get easier with practice." Again she laughed, for the sheer pleasure of having all her senses back to normal, but there was a discordant note to it too, as if the disappointment was there and she was deliberately ignoring it.

Vanessa suspected as much and so made light of it. "Perhaps we can come up with a better strategy for tomorrow night. After all, a soft bed and a private room do wonders for inspiration, as opposed to a tent that might as well have ears and does have a good dozen pair of eyes trained to watch it at all times, or to the great outdoors." She made a face and a disgusting sound. "Let me tell you, you do *not* want to dally out of doors, no matter how private you think you might be."

"You speak from experience, of course?"

"Well, naturally. Besides nasty insects that just adore bare flesh, you are at the mercy of the weather, and in this part of the country what have you but dust, dirt, and grime to spread your blanket on. And I'll tell you a secret, love. No matter how thick that blanket is, there's going to be a rock, a stick, or *something* directly under your backside to quite detract from the mood. And then there are the wild beasts you must contend with."

A giggle slipped out. "Wild beasts, Vana?"

"Well, there was this rabbit once, only I thought it was my head gardener. It scared me half to death."

Jocelyn burst out laughing. "Now you go too far."

"*Now* I happen to be serious. I was afraid the old man would die of shock."

"After all those wild weekend parties you told me about, where half the couples who got lost in your maze were married to the other half? Your head gardener must have witnessed enough illicit trysts over the years for nothing to shock him."

"But, my dear, my lover at the time happened to be his strapping young son."

"Oh."

"Exactly."

They stared at each other for half a second before they both laughed. When Jocelyn caught her breath, she was smiling fondly at her dear friend. "Thank you. I was taking this seduction too seriously, wasn't I?"

"A trifle. He's just a man, love, who's going to do you a needed service . . . that is, if you haven't changed your mind. There are other men you might want to consider now that we've returned to what can loosely be termed civilization."

"No . . . Colt is still — "

"Say no more." Vanessa sighed inwardly, but replied determinedly. "If he's the one you want, you shall have him. It won't be tonight, though, so to bed with you."

"They're no longer looking for him?"

"There's no point, as late as it is. No, I've sent the servants to bed too. Enjoy a good, long sleep. If your half-breed's as passionate as I suspect he is, you won't get much sleep tomorrow night."

"That's allowing he is seducible."

"With those weapons at your disposal?" Vanessa said, her eyes giving Jocelyn the once-over. She was smiling as she closed the door behind her.

Chapter Twenty-one

Through the open window came the sound of boot-heels clicking softly along the boardwalk across the street, then the startled hiss, barely heard, "Jesus H. Christ, you scared the dickens out o' me, boy!" But there was no reply, and the boot clicking moved on at an even brisker pace. There was a bullfrog making a croaking racket somewhere, a distant sound, heard only when the piano player in one of the saloons down the street took a rest. The music was distant too, the player quite good, the sound soothing rather than disturbing. Every so often laughter was heard, but nothing loud enough to keep the town's inhabitants awake.

Jocelyn certainly couldn't blame the muted sounds for her own wakefulness. Considering the number of times she had been awakened in the middle of the night recently by the shrill yapping of coyotes, or by one of her guards tripping on a tent stake as he patrolled the perimeter of her tent, and swearing a blue streak, these late-night town sounds were peaceful. But they weren't lulling her to sleep.

She had tried, but she was still too keyed up, thinking about what could have happened tonight, and wondering about her relief that it didn't. She had concluded that this deliberate seduction business just wasn't her cup of tea. She would have to tell Vanessa, who was going to be disappointed. She had probably fallen asleep plotting tomorrow's strategy.

Jocelyn gave up and threw off the sheets. The room was exceedingly dark with the moon rising behind the hotel and her only window facing the front, but her eyes were adjusted enough for her to find the lamp and light it. She lowered the wick, however, to give off only a dim glow, enough to find her robe and cross to the window without mishap.

Drawing back the curtains, she was disappointed there was nothing to see. The moonlight was so bright now, what shadows it created were black as pitch. The porch roof was in shadow, and the railing at the edge that supported the hotel sign blocked her view of the street below. Moonlight revealed the buildings across the way clearly, at least the top half of them, but no windows were lit to draw her attention.

What she needed was a long walk to tire herself out. She was sure the guard outside her door wouldn't mind escorting her, but the thought of Sir Parker's outrage in the morning that she should venture out with only a minimum of protection kept her from doing it.

She sighed, annoyed with herself, annoyed with Colt, annoyed with her predicament. If it weren't for Longnose, she could have that walk. If she knew where Colt was, she wouldn't need it. If she didn't care, it wouldn't matter and sleep would have come easily. Blast.

How dare he disappear like that? What if they had to leave in a hurry, a very real possibility, considering how many times they had had to do so in the past? But she was being unreasonable. With the way Colt scouted every day, he would have known if Longnose was close and would have said something. The Englishman was probably still looking for their trail back in Arizona. And to be honest, it was the fact that Colt was likely in some other woman's bed tonight that was bothering her enough to keep sleep away.

This wasn't helping. She would take that walk anyway and worry about Sir Parker later. But just as she turned from the window she heard a loud thump out in the hall, as if . . . as if a body had hit the floor. She stared at the door, then at her reticule clear across the room, and knew without a doubt that by the time she got her hands on her derringer inside it, the door would likely be opened and she would be out of luck. And the derringer was only good at close range. She would have to have it in hand and get behind the door to wait, but another glance at the door showed the handle starting to move.

Without thinking about it, she slipped outside the window and dropped down to the porch roof. Fortunately, the slope of it was not steep, but that was where fortune ended. Too late she realized that whoever was sneaking into her room in the middle of the night was going to look outside the window when they found it empty. She didn't doubt that she would be spotted, even in the shadows. But would they risk a shot to wake the whole town? Hadn't they expected to find her in bed, asleep, and easy to dispose of in any number of quiet ways? Would they follow her out onto the roof?

She ought to be screaming already. One good scream could very well scare them away. But her attire, the blasted revealing negligee she was still wearing, kept her mouth shut for the moment.

She didn't wait to see a head sticking out her window. The end of the roof was a mere few feet away, since only the water closet separated her room from the end of the building on this side. She would have a better chance of not being spotted at all by quickly going over the side of the roof, rather than trying to reach the next window from hers and taking the chance that it was open, since she couldn't tell from her current position if it was or not. The railing that topped the roof in front didn't continue along the sides, so she didn't have anything to climb over. She had only to slip over the side at its lowest point, grasp one of the roof supports with her legs, and simply slide to the ground. Then a mad dash to the back of the hotel where the stable was and she would be safe. Some of her people were there. If she had to be humiliated by being caught out in her nightclothes, at least it could be kept in the family, so to speak.

That was just what she did, even as she thought about it, though she hadn't counted on the impetus she gained in rushing toward the corner of the roof slamming her into the railing there before she could stop. She didn't wait to regain her breath. Slipping over the roof was easier work, with the short railing post there at the end giving her something to hold onto until she could locate the longer support post below with her feet.

That was where her luck ran out, however. She swung her legs this way and that, encountering nothing but air. Belatedly, she realized she had been working on the assumption that every porch roof had support posts to hold it up. How else would the blasted thing keep from toppling over? Then where was the damned post? More importantly now, since it *wasn't* there, how far was the drop to the ground? Blast it all, why hadn't she noticed such things when she entered the hotel? There had been a few steps up to the porch at the front of the building, but that was the most she could recall. She had no idea what kind of height she was dangling from, whether the raised porch extended beyond the end of the building, or if she had ground beneath her and an even greater distance to reach it. A quick glance down showed her nothing but shadows.

She supposed she could work her way around the front of the roof in search of the elusive support post, but her hands were already hurting from bearing her weight just these few moments. She might as well drop where she was, while she had some control over it, as opposed to slipping later and perhaps coming down on her backside instead of her feet. And yet she couldn't dredge up the courage to take the plunge. An insidious panic was taking hold, and getting worse by the moment, adding another foot each second to the distance she must fall, until it was somehow a great bottomless pit below her.

It took several heartbeats for her to realize her hands were no longer her sole support, that arms had wrapped around her legs to hold her up. At the same moment she realized it, she heard a soft, familiar drawl say, "Let go," and so the breath she drew for an ear-splitting scream came out in a long sigh instead. And she let go. Just as she had hurtled herself into his arms from her coach the day they met, she trusted Colt to bring her safely to ground now.

It wasn't quite the same, however. This time she ended up cradled in his arms. And this time he didn't thrust her immediately away from him.

A long silence stretched between them while she tried to make out his features in the shadows, and failed. How it was that he happened to be there right when she needed him she couldn't imagine and wasn't up to asking just yet.

When the silence was broken, it was with a good deal of sarcasm on his part. "Let me guess. You have an aversion to doors, right?"

He let her down as he said it, though he still didn't put her away from him. In fact, he gripped her upper arms now. To steady her? She preferred to think he didn't want to break contact yet. She certainly didn't want to. But then his question penetrated the mush her

250

mind had become, and she forgot how nice it had been, his holding her, and remembered instead the reason for it.

In a rush she explained, "There was someone ... I heard a noise in the hall ... my reticule was too far away ... couldn't possibly reach it in ... I saw the door handle turning. What else was I to do?"

Somehow he got the gist of it. "Are you saying someone tried to enter your room, Duchess?"

"Not tried. The door wasn't locked. I didn't wait around to see it open, but I've little doubt it did."

"What about your guards?"

"There was only one, and I'm afraid he might be dead. That noise I heard — "

He didn't wait for her to finish, but let go of her to shove his revolver into her hand. Nor did he waste time telling her what to do with it. "Stay here," was all he said.

"But where are you going?"

Stupid question, since he had already leaped up to grasp the porch roof and in mere seconds was up and over it — and gone. Jocelyn looked out at the empty moonlit street, at the shadowed hotel porch — which she was standing on, since it *did* extend beyond the building — at the revolver in her hand. It was long-barreled and heavy, not at all like her little

251

derringer. She had never used this type of weapon, and doubted she could at the moment, with her fingers still smarting from holding onto the roof.

The gun dragged at her arm after another few moments, so she cradled it while she waited, staring up at the end of the roof. She just barely made out the jagged remains of the corner support post that had once stood where she had assumed it would be, but at some time or other was broken off and never replaced. She felt better seeing that, and knowing she hadn't been a complete dolt in her impromptu planning. But she didn't once think about following through with her own plan now that she was on the ground, of heading back to the stable and the safety it offered. Colt had said to stay there and so she stayed right there.

Chapter Twenty-two

The room wasn't empty. There were two men inside it, both riffling through the duchess's trunks, carelessly scattering her gowns and belongings on the floor around them. One had found a jewelry case and was trying to pry the lock open with a small knife, while the other was on his knees with his head buried in the largest trunk. Neither of them gave a thought to the window that Colt entered silently. Their only concern was the door, which they glanced at nervously once or twice before Colt reached them.

It was over within seconds, the heavy lid of the large trunk slamming down on the head of one man just as he rose with some find in his fist, and Colt's foot connecting with the jaw of the other — which was a mistake. His foot throbbing, he cursed fluently for not making use of his knife instead, which had been palmed and ready. But he did not need it now, with both men out cold.

With disgust he limped to the bed to inspect

his foot for any serious damage, but no sooner had he sat down than Jocelyn's scent assailed him and he leaped up with another round of curses. He was mad enough at that moment to slit both men's throats, but sanity prevailed. It wasn't their fault he had spent half the night standing in the shadows across the street, nursing a bottle of rotgut and staring at her window like a lovesick fool, imagining a half-dozen fantasies that could come true if he chose to make use of that open window.

It had taken a battle royal with his conscience to keep him from crossing the street. So he was naturally furious that after his conscience had won, he was here anyway, in her room, and inflamed by the fact that she was below waiting on him.

There was the slim hope that she wouldn't be there, that she would have immediately sought out the rest of her guard to inform them of what had happened. But by the time he returned and found she had obeyed him instead, he at least had put a bridle on his lust and was in control again, even of his temper.

"You can come inside now, Duchess."

Miraculously, he sounded almost pleasant calling down to her. She couldn't know his tone was forced.

"You mean no one was in my room?"

"Didn't say that. You had a couple of visitors, but they've been disposed of. I'll meet you in the hall."

"No, wait!" she called up in a frantic whisper. "I can't go through the lobby. What if someone should see me like this?"

Colt stared down at her, glad the shadows didn't allow him to see her too clearly. So she was embarrassed about being caught out in her nightclothes? She ought to worry more about letting *him* see her than some half-asleep desk clerk.

"You like flirting with danger, don't you?"

She misunderstood him completely. "It's not so great a distance. Couldn't you just reach over and lift me up?"

For a long while she saw nothing of his shadow, nor did he answer. Staring anxiously up at the end of the roof, she wondered what the problem was, or if he just hadn't heard her request. It wasn't as if he hadn't done it before. Lifting her up and out of the coach that day hadn't put much strain on him, and there wasn't that much difference in the height here.

She had been lucky so far that no one had come along to see her waiting there at the end of the porch. It had taken Colt more than just a few minutes to "dispose of" the intruders in her room. She shivered, wondering what he had meant by that. But she couldn't continue to wait there indefinitely. As they had traveled north, the temperatures had been gradually dropping, with a marked difference now between day and night. Tonight was downright frigid, or so it seemed in her scanty attire. Chills had begun attacking her the moment her fear had dissipated. She simply couldn't stand out here much longer.

"Colt?"

She didn't bother to whisper this time. If he had gone back inside to await her in the hall as he'd said, she was going to be quite annoyed with him, regardless that he had just — what? Saved her again? She didn't really know what he had done, and wouldn't know until —

She jumped, his hand appeared so suddenly. So he had been there all along — and heard her. Now was not the time to upbraid him for making her wait while he decided whether to lend her a hand or not. In fact, she couldn't afford to upbraid him for anything, not unless she was willing to give him an excuse to quit, which she wasn't. And besides, she had already known how lacking he was in gentlemanly tendencies. Far be it for her to expect him to change his habits now just because she was trembling with cold and loath to show herself in a well-lit hotel lobby half dressed.

She returned his gun first, which he quickly holstered before extending his hand again.

The problem now was that she couldn't quite reach his fingers, even up on tiptoe. She started to tell him so, but she had a feeling this was the most she could hope for, that he wasn't going to lower that hand another inch, even if he could. For whatever reason, he didn't *want* to help her back up onto that roof, but she was more determined than he was.

She made it on the first leap, her fingers locking with his. But her feet went swaying through the air, and her fingers started to slip. She was about to cry out, anticipating a hard landing on her backside, when she was jerked up a bit so his other hand could grasp her wrist.

Dangling by only one arm sent pain shooting through her shoulder socket, but she was up and sitting on the edge of the roof so fast, there was no time to moan about it. Under the circumstances, however, she didn't feel inclined to thank her so-called savior, especially when an insistent tug forced her immediately to her feet.

Again she was about to upbraid him, scathingly this time, when his curt "Come on, dammit" made her grit her teeth instead and follow him up the slight incline to her window.

Here was another unexpected problem. Her hands, raised high, only just reached the window ledge, and she knew without a doubt that with what her arms had already been through, there was no way she could hoist herself up through that window.

She was loath to ask, but there was no help for it. "Could you please accommodate me once more with a boost up?"

She couldn't see his eyes moving down her body to the likely place he would have to touch to shove her through the window. His manhood, already half aroused just from his standing this close to her, came to full attention. There was no way in hell he could put his hands on her body and not do more than that. Nor did he think he could bend down close to her legs to offer her foot the cradle of his hands and not break his control. Enough was enough.

"Not on your life, Duchess," he answered sharply and with finality.

Jocelyn's own control snapped at that point. "Well, I'm sorry, but I just can't do it myself. My arms hurt, I'm freezing, I'm tired . . . do you think I went fleeing out my window and over the roof for the fun of it?"

"It's the middle of the damn night, woman. Who the hell is up and about at this hour?"

"You were," she replied stiffly. "And those gentlemen who stole into my room were. And who is to say there aren't more of them waiting below in the lobby?"

That was a damn good point, but he still wasn't going to put his hands anywhere near that luscious backside of hers. "All right, move over," he conceded with ill grace and vaulted through the window.

This was exactly what Colt had wanted to avoid, being in her room again, being there with her — alone. He used to think there was nothing he couldn't withstand, no pain, no torture, no temptation — until he met her. Christ, even that sadistic bullwhacker Ramsay hadn't been able to break him. But this one little redhead was coming damn close without even trying. And he couldn't even fault her for it. No, he knew exactly where the blame lay — inside his pants.

Lust was making a mockery out of his will, and lacerating his pride and self-esteem to shreds. But it wasn't something that had ever taken control of him before, so he didn't know how to deal with it. All he knew was that he wanted this woman more than he had ever wanted anything before. And each time he saw her, his need seemed to escalate. It was enough to make a man want to cut his own throat.

With self-disgust, he grasped her hands and yanked her up onto the windowsill, far enough into the room for her to be able to climb the rest of the way inside by herself. He then turned on his heel and headed for the door, determined to be out of that room before she was fully into it. But she obviously objected to being left dangling half in and half out.

"Colt!" she wailed.

He didn't stop. "If I touch you again, Duchess, you're going to damn well regret it."

"Just because you manage this with no effort at all doesn't mean . . . oh, never mind!"

Jocelyn lowered the top half of her body until her weight tumbled her forward into the room, ignominiously, she realized, as her legs crashed in behind her and flopped down on the floor. But she wasted not a second in correcting her graceless entry and shot to her feet. Nor did it calm her temper to see that he hadn't been watching. It was in fact the last straw to see him reaching for the door handle.

"You are the most surly, misbegotten . . . Good Lord!" she amended when the shambles of her room caught her attention. "What the devil happened here? Did they think I was hiding in one of the trunks?"

That stopped him. It was a safe enough subject, and she had a right to know. And he did have the distance of the entire room between them. Still, he didn't want to take the risk of looking at her now that she was no longer cloaked in shadows. The mess she was staring at drew his eyes as well, as if he hadn't already seen it.

"They weren't looking for you, Duchess."

"Of course they were. Longnose is the only one — "

"Not this time. Your Longnose hasn't caught up with us yet. I'll know it when he does."

She didn't doubt his certainty, not when she knew he had spent every day on the trail scouting wide circles around them. "Then who were they?"

"A couple of thieves, likely local boys. That guard at your door was probably the lure. Nine times out of ten, if a man sees a room that needs more security than lock and key, he's going to assume there's something worth stealing inside it."

Her eyes flew to him as she remembered the loud thud she had heard in the hall. "Robbie? Is — is he . . . ?"

She couldn't finish, afraid the reason that Colt wouldn't look at her was because the big Scot was dead. But he disabused her of that notion, though he still didn't glance her way. He stooped to pick up a scrap of silk at his feet, staring at the thin blue ribbon in his hand as if it were the most amazing thing he had ever seen.

"Your man was hit from behind. He'll have a helluva headache to show for his carelessness in the morning, but that's about all. It's my guess one of them distracted him long enough for the other to take him out. It's a strategy that works well against a single man."

"And the two brigands?"

"You want the gory details?"

"Colt!"

She had blanched, though he didn't see it. It was her silence after that aggrieved cry that made him relent.

"They got the same as they gave, no more. But I cut up one of your petticoats to truss them with before dumping them out in the hall to keep your Robbie company. Didn't think you'd mind. They're not likely to stir before morning, but you'll need a replacement to guard your door anyway, so he can keep an eye on them as well until they can be turned over to the sheriff." There was a long pause before he added, "You should have had more protection."

She usually did, but tonight there had been special circumstances, because tonight she had planned on receiving a visitor she didn't want anyone to know about. She had agreed to allow Robbie to stand guard outside her door for the simple reason that Vanessa trusted him to keep whatever he saw to himself. But neither of them had thought to add to his number when the circumstances changed.

It was a severe jolt to remember that earlier plan now and realize that it had actually come to pass. Colt was here, in her room. They were alone. And it had come about without a summons, so there was nothing for him to suspect in the way of ulterior motives. Good Lord, she was even still dressed for the part, but there was no longer the guilt of a deliberate seduction to prick her conscience and fill her with misgivings. Whatever happened . . .

Before her heart could accelerate with that thought, Jocelyn realized nothing was going to happen, because Colt hadn't once looked at her since they had come into the softly lit room. And somehow she knew he wasn't going to either. She almost laughed. If she did something to *make* him look at her, that would be tantamount to deliberately trying to seduce him again. She had to face it. Tonight just simply wasn't fated to be *the* night.

"Having only one guard at my door was indirectly your fault, Colt." She smiled at the double meaning that he couldn't possibly guess at. But when she saw him stiffen upon hearing blame placed at his feet, she quickly clarified. "I said indirectly. The fact is I have felt so much safer since you've joined us that I have become remiss in certain precautionary measures. I also felt the men deserved a night off."

"What the hell good is that army that surrounds you if they don't see to your safety regardless of your wishes?"

Now *she* stiffened. "Your point is well taken. How stupid of me to depend on your rescuing abilities simply because you have displayed them so well and so often!"

"Stupid is damned right!"

That was it! He couldn't even look at her when he shouted at her.

"Good *night*, Mr. Thunder."

Seething, she watched him reach for the door handle again and this time slam out of the room.

Chapter Twenty-three

No sooner was Jocelyn alone than she yanked off her robe, wadded it up in her hands, and threw it down at her feet. She just about stomped on it as well. That miserable, detestable . . .

"And when the hell are you going to lock this damned . . . door?"

The "damned door" in question had been opened again for Colt to snarl that question at her. Jocelyn didn't answer it. She had sucked in her breath at his sudden reappearance and seemed to have lost the knowledge of how to breathe, let alone speak, the second her eyes collided with his.

Colt seemed to have the same problem, for he had barely gotten the last word out, nor were any more forthcoming. He stood with one hand gripping the door handle, the other pressed flat against the outside wall, merely leaning into the room, which was as far as he got when he saw her. And he didn't move from that position — at least his body didn't.

His eyes were moving plenty, however, slowly, over every inch of her, from the flame-tinted hair, now in wild disarray, to the bare toes peeking out from the bottom of that incredible sheath of shimmering, clinging green satin, and what was in between — Christ Almighty. What the sight of her standing there like that did to him should have reduced him to ashes.

"I wondered about it . . . often . . . what you slept in."

Jocelyn wouldn't have known what to reply to that even if she could. She had only just started breathing again, and that with difficulty. Speech was still beyond her, as was movement. She was afraid to take a step for fear her knees would buckle. And that wasn't her only fear. His eyes, usually so opaque, were blazing now with such heat she felt scorched by them, thrilled beyond measure — but frightened too. She couldn't help it, not when she recalled that he had never once been gentle with her, and looked anything but gentle now.

Without taking his eyes from her, Colt stepped far enough into the room to close the door behind him. Below the handle was the lock and he turned that too, still with his gaze riveted on her.

If she hadn't already known her time of

waiting was over, that would have confirmed it. But she did know. He was going to have her. She couldn't deny him now even if she wanted to. And she didn't want to. She wanted him, despite the fear, despite knowing she would be getting raw passion rather than gentle lovemaking. Why that didn't change her mind and send her fleeing out the window again she wasn't sure. She just knew he had to be the first, that she couldn't imagine anyone else touching her the way she was going to let him touch her.

Her budding passion and nervous determination were not as pronounced as her fear, which was all Colt sensed in her stillness or saw in her wide-eyed stare. In a primitive way, it only inflamed him the more. But in the back of his mind he was aware that she hadn't instigated this meeting, that if he was lynched for it afterward, he would have nothing to blame but his own weakness. He would be a real bastard to use the same tactics now that he had used previously to frighten her off. Having lost the battle, he had no need for them. But he had a need for fairness, especially when she couldn't stop him, not by herself, not without help. So despite his single-minded determination, he forced himself to give her one last opportunity to escape what he could no longer control himself.

"Scream now, Duchess, while you've got the chance. You won't get another."

Jocelyn wished he hadn't said that. It sounded too ominous by half, as if she wouldn't survive this encounter, or had totally mistaken what was going to happen.

"W — why?"

Her voice acted like a magnet, drawing him across the room even as he answered with brutal clarity, "Because I'm going to lay you on that bed and fill you with my flesh."

God, she hoped so. The words alone sent her blood racing and her heart knocking against her ribs. There was no question of screaming. Moaning maybe. She already felt the need to moan and had to consciously resist it, not wanting any sound to escape that he might mistake before he reached her.

When he did, the opportunity was lost. His fingers immediately threaded into her hair to grasp her head and tilt it back, applying enough pressure so there was no escaping his mouth as it lowered to cover hers. And as she had anticipated, it was a ravaging kiss, fraught with need too long denied, searing and hurting and angry.

But Jocelyn understood the emotion behind it, or thought she did. If Vanessa had the right of it, Colt was probably furious with her right now for breaking his control, but even more furious with himself for letting it happen. It was up to her to tame that fury before it got out of hand.

She shoved desperately against his chest until he raised his head. He even dropped one hand so she could create a space between them. The other hand remained where it was, the fingers closing on her hair. As long as she didn't try to move too far away from him, it didn't hurt. But she knew he could yank her back at any second, that he was merely allowing them both a moment to catch their breath.

Hers was gasping, and instead of calming, it only became more rapid as she watched his eyes drift down her body, taking in everything again at this closer range. When she started to say something, anything that would break the mounting tension in her belly, he knew it without glancing up, and forestalled her with a shake of his head.

"Not now, Duchess." His voice vibrated with warning. "You had your chance."

She swallowed hard, and it was only because his direct gaze still remained diverted that she managed to get out, "Then call me Jocelyn."

In that moment Colt knew she was willing. His eyes shot up to her face to confirm it, and it was there, not fear, or horror, or even disgust, but merely uncertainty, and in her eyes

— arousal. That knowledge acted on him like whiskey poured over hot flames. He groaned and reached for her again, and his hand was trembling as it touched her cheek, slid down her throat, then came to rest on her upper chest, where he could feel the wild tempo of her heartbeat.

Jocelyn released a sigh herself, certain now that there was nothing left to fear. She offered her mouth and he took it, exquisitely, with enough pressure to fan her desire but not enough to alarm or bruise her. Yet when she pressed closer and tried to wrap her arms around him, she found out that the savagery was gone, but not his impatience.

Colt wanted everything at once, to touch her, look at her, taste her. He wanted to be inside her already. At the same time, he didn't want to give up the pleasure of her mouth. So without breaking the kiss, which had become a sensual exploration of taste and texture, he hooked his thumbs in the narrow shoulders of her gown. By the time he had run his hands down her arms, the gown hung at her waist. Only then was he tempted to lean back, and what he saw merely increased his impatience. Her breasts were small but perfectly shaped, the nipples hard little nubs, and he hadn't even touched them yet.

He was so amazed by that that he looked up

at her and was hit with another jolt. The uncertainty was gone. She met his gaze steadily, and there was such naked desire in her look, he couldn't tear his eyes away.

"You want me." He said it in awe, unaware he said it aloud, until he heard her whispered "Yes" and felt her hands on his chest, her fingers working at his buttons, or trying to.

His own hands returned to swiftly finish what he had started, only he had no more luck than she was having with her own efforts to undress him. The gown wouldn't budge past her hips, and Jocelyn was too eager to get her hands on his bare skin to assist him.

"There are ties in the back," she offered helpfully.

"Do you care?"

"No."

The ties broke with his tug and the gown pooled at her feet. He set her back from him then so he could look at her while he got rid of his own clothes, the incentive adding unaccustomed speed and efficiency to his movements.

She wanted to watch him too, to miss nothing of this body she had fantasized about. But the small space between them brought on a sudden shyness, making her acutely aware of her lack of experience. She didn't know what was expected of her at that point, or if anything was. Was it rude to stare at him? Shouldn't she remove his clothes, as he had hers? Or should she have gone directly to the bed to await him? It would be embarrassing if he had to tell her what to do.

Reluctantly, Jocelyn turned toward the bed, but his husky drawl stopped her. "I want to put you there myself. I said I would."

The reminder recalled his exact words, that he was going to fill her with his flesh, and even the memory of those words had the power to weaken her knees. Gladly she gave in to her first desire, to indulge her curiosity about his body, and especially that most mysterious part of the male form, which she had never seen before.

Vanessa had tried to explain what it looked like, had even drawn some sketches that were ridiculously funny but couldn't compare with the real thing. Could it? Just thinking about it made her senses reel, and before she did something really silly, like throw herself at him, she forced her thoughts in a different direction.

She hadn't really noticed what he was wearing tonight, but she did now as each item hit the floor. His shirt and pants were dark, but normal for a change. In fact, with the gun belt, and the bandanna about his throat that she watched him cut off instead of untying, he came close to looking like any other Westerner. Only the boots with spurs were missing, and, tonight, the hat. But then she saw the two thin braids in front. They blended so well with the rest of his flowing black hair that they weren't very noticeable, not in such dim lighting.

His brother Billy had told her about this quirk of his, that he dressed in this manner so no one would mistake him for what he was. Billy hadn't told her the reason, but she had a feeling it had something to do with the bitterness she had sensed in Colt when she first met him, rather than pride in his heritage. She wished she knew the cause, because it came to her, with considerable surprise, that she had a strong desire to rid him of that bitterness, to see this man happy.

She had another immediate surprise, however, to find she had distracted herself so thoroughly she had somehow missed seeing him in all his naked splendor. Being lifted off her feet brought that knowledge home, and she thoughtlessly cried, "Wait!"

"What?" he growled.

Idiot! You can't tell him you want to see his . . . "Nothing."

"Good, because I can't wait."

He did not pause in carrying her straight to the bed or in laying her on it and instantly coming down on top of her. Before she even had a chance to adjust to his unfamiliar weight, her legs were nudged apart by his knees. But more shocking than that was the realization that he really wasn't going to wait another minute. She might not have seen it, but she could feel it, the flesh he meant to fill her with, and it was going to happen *now*.

She tried to hold on, to brace herself, but he caught her hands and held them instead, making her even more frantic — until he kissed her, deeply, making her feel his urgency, making her want it.

And then he was looking down at her with such fierce passion she wasn't even aware he had made his first tentative entry. It was the withdrawal she noticed, that and his second thrust, which gained only another inch.

"Christ, you're tight," he gritted out as if he were in pain. "I think I could spend the rest of my days inside you, but right now I want you too much. Open for me, Duchess, before I explode."

He said this with his lips just barely touching hers, and although he still wouldn't call her by name, he made her title now sound like an endearment. But it was his groan when she did as he wanted that brought an answering sound from her own throat. He had slipped farther inside, but still not enough. She could

274

feel what it was costing him to let her body adjust to his size instead of just plunging into her. His whole upper body was tense and straining, yet his eyes continued to hold her mesmerized with their intensity.

"It'll be a rough ride. Can you take it?"

Jocelyn gulped, but nodded. She was rewarded with a smile of blatant male satisfaction.

"I figured you could," he added in a strained voice. "Has it been three years?"

She knew what he was asking. Other men she had rebuffed had insinuated that as a widow, she should be starved for sex. Colt would have his answer soon enough.

"It's none of my business, right?" This time he didn't give her a chance to respond. "Never mind. I don't want to know."

She didn't notice his harsher tone, or know that the thought of her with other men, like this, had just ended his desire to restrain himself for her sake. He closed his eyes and thrust deep, heard her sharp gasp, felt the barrier he had ripped open, and went still as death.

Jocelyn was tense herself, waiting for the inevitable questions. They didn't come. After a long agonizing moment, he started kissing her instead, his tongue licking at her lips, entreating them to part for him, then slipping inside her mouth to make her a little crazy with wild sensations rippling through her, the heady taste of him. And his hands caressing her — he was so incredibly tender with her now, she wanted to cry.

From her cheek to her throat to her breasts, his touch was so gentle, almost too gentle, until his mouth followed the same path and she was bathed in heat and the abrasion of his tongue across sensitive nipples. She moaned with pleasure. He suckled and she thought she would die.

Tears did come to her eyes as she held his head to her breasts. She felt cherished, precious, and so very desired. She felt beautiful in his eyes, something she had never felt before. And all the while he lavished her body with such exquisite care, she could feel his heat deep inside her, still, patient now, but throbbing with need she desperately wanted to fulfill.

There was no pain left when he began to move in her again much later. There hadn't been from his first shattering kiss. And he had built her desire up to such a fevered pitch, within moments she was dissolving in a white-hot flood of sensation. Through that haze of pleasure she barely heard him reach his own climax, and she was asleep before the last shudder left his body.

Chapter Twenty-four

"His sister, Maura, is quite charming," Vanessa was saying as she put away the green thread and took up the red for the sampler she was working on. "I think you'll like her. She's about your age, I would say, and just dying to see those *Harper's Bazaar* fashion journals we collected while in New York. Did I mention that's where they're from originally? They even know Charles, or at least they've heard of the Abingtons."

"Are you sure Robbie is all right?"

Vanessa didn't raise her head, but her eyes shot up, and her brows met suspiciously over the middle of them. That question had already been asked and answered — twice.

"Actually, the chit's rather brassy, not at all as polished as her brother."

"That's nice."

The countess dropped the sampler in her lap with an exasperated sigh. "Have you heard a single word I've said? Jocelyn? Yoo-hoo, Joc-cel-lyn?" she sing-songed.

Jocelyn turned slightly from the window where she had been standing for the last hour. "Did you say something, Vana?"

With forced calm, the countess replied, "I've been telling you about the Drydens."

"Who?"

"Jocelyn Fleming! You are supposed to be radiant today, not absent-minded. Whatever is the matter with you?"

Jocelyn glanced back out the window, ignoring the censure but not the question. Indeed, what *was* wrong with her? Why couldn't she stop thinking about last night or wondering where Colt was today? Again he couldn't be found. He had been waiting for Robbie's replacement early this morning, or so she had been told, so obviously he had kept watch over her for the rest of the night himself. But in her room or out in the hall?

She had awakened to find the room empty, two long black hairs on the pillow next to hers the only sign that Colt had been there. Well, actually there was one other indication. The smears of dried blood on her upper thighs. But when had he left her? And why had he gone without saying anything?

Vanessa had arrived bright and early and full of worry, after seeing the two apprehended thieves dragged off to the local authorities. She had demanded every detail about Jocelyn's little adventure out the window, as well as what had happened afterward. She had also been vastly relieved to know their planned seduction had come about after all.

"So there's no need to go on to this Wyoming place, is there, or to retain Mr. Thunder's services any longer?"

When Jocelyn had heard that, she had felt strangely bereft and insisted Colt's services were most definitely still in need, if for no other reason than to keep her safe. She pointed out how many times he had already come to her rescue. She pointed out his ability in keeping Longnose from discovering their new direction. And if that wasn't enough, she had announced that Wyoming was where she had decided to locate her stud farm.

Wisely, Vanessa hadn't said any more, though Jocelyn had felt her disapproval at the time and still did. She even understood it, knowing Vanessa was worried that she might form an attachment for Colt that was utterly unsuitable.

"First lovers are inevitably special," Vanessa had told her months ago when they had originally decided she needed one. "But the thing to remember is that they *are* only the first, that you mustn't mistake a simple, healthy attraction for love."

Remembering those words now, Jocelyn

tried to examine what she was feeling, but all she could come up with was confusion, anxiety over her next encounter with Colt, and most of all, a lingering amazement that lovemaking was much, much more deeply satisfying than she had imagined it would be.

Glancing back over her shoulder, she revealed some of those feelings to her friend. "I'm sorry, Vana. It's just that it was . . . it was . . ."

"I know," Vanessa cut in with a snort. "It was so blissful you haven't the proper words to describe it."

"Well, it was," Jocelyn said defensively.

"Then we owe our surly guide our everlasting gratitude, don't we?" Vanessa returned in her most acerbic tone. "Especially when it could have been quite the opposite with someone of his unpredictable temperament, and still could be if you are foolish enough to court his attentions again." Then her voice softened, exposing her very real concern. "What you experienced, my dear, can be had with any man. But it would be preferable, as well as safer, as *well* as less worrisome to me, if you experienced it with a lover you can trust not to erupt into violence at any given moment. I suggest you find another man to prove that, and quickly, before you make this one into something he isn't."

Jocelyn usually heeded Vanessa's advice, but in this case it wasn't necessary. She had needed a lover for only one purpose, and that purpose was accomplished. She didn't need to take another man to her bed, nor even Colt again. Vanessa was getting worked up over nothing. But it wouldn't do to say so. She wouldn't believe it.

"You were saying something about the Bradens?" Jocelyn said pleasantly, but pointedly.

"The Drydens," Vanessa corrected, taking the hint to drop the subject for now. "I told you I met them this morning in the lobby. A very interesting pair of siblings. You could say they are impoverished gentry of the American variety. I swear the run of bad luck they've had since their parents died makes us fortunate we've only got an assassin on our trail."

"That's not funny, Vana."

"No, I suppose not, but I did feel sorry for them."

"They told you their life story while standing about in the lobby?"

"We were sitting, actually, and it was a very shortened version, I'm sure. A few bad investments and the family funds were gone, that sort of thing. They decided to take what little was left and come west to start anew. I believe

281

Miles mentioned something about buying a ranch."

"Miles? Mr. Dryden, I assume you mean? He's *Miles* after only one meeting, yet you continue to call Colt *Mr.* Thunder?"

"Don't change the subject, dear," Vanessa replied, undaunted. "As I was saying, their luck turned from bad to worse when they reached New Mexico. The stagecoach they were traveling in was robbed by some highwaymen — outlaws, I believe they call them here — and one passenger was killed. Then that very same day, in the same coach, mind you, they were set upon by Indians. They would have both been scalped — "

"Scalped?"

"Something unpleasant Indians do to you, I gather, but the cavalry came along — they had been chasing that particular group of raiders — and saved them. At any rate, they've understandably had a change of heart about settling in this part of the country, but they've frankly been too apprehensive about riding the coaches again and so in effect have stranded themselves here. Naturally, I felt compelled to offer them our escort."

"Do you think that's wise? I mean, what do you really know about these people except what they've told you? The brother could be — "

"I'll have you know I have *not* become dotty in my old age yet," Vanessa interrupted indignantly. "Sir Parker has checked their story and confirmed it. They have been living in this very hotel for the past three months. And Miles Dryden has a sister, my dear, a *sister*. If our Mr. Longnose has one, he wouldn't be carting her about with him, now, would he?"

"I didn't mean to imply that *he* might be Longnose, only that he could have been hired . . . oh, never mind." Then, with sudden suspicion: "He wouldn't happen to be handsome, would he?"

"Now don't look at me like that. So he is rather striking in appearance. That doesn't mean I hoped he would take your mind off your half-breed if I invited them along."

"No, of course not," Jocelyn replied with annoyance, for Vanessa's motive was obviously just that.

She was no better at dissembling than Jocelyn was, at least not with Jocelyn. It was time to tell her how unnecessary these machinations were and hope she would believe it.

"I do not intend to allow a repetition of last night, Vana."

"Does *he* know that?"

"*He* was practically raped — "

"What?"

Jocelyn waved a hand dismissively. "The

principle was the same. He had to be forced, didn't he? Seduced? Made to lose control so his baser instincts would take over and he would be powerless to resist? You seem to forget he didn't want anything to do with me, that I did the pursuing, not him. So he isn't likely to want a repetition of last night either, Vana. In fact, I'd be terribly surprised if he isn't furious today, and determined never to put himself in such a position again."

"Attitudes change once the die is cast, my dear. Once the sin is committed, a person tends to overindulge before he's ready to repent."

"I doubt that would apply in Colt's case. Besides, I've already said that I have no intention of letting it happen again. My problem has been solved. I have no further need of a lover."

So says a woman who has been thoroughly satisfied only hours past, Vanessa thought. But she didn't point out that Jocelyn's "need" would eventually be of a different nature, that once tasting the pleasures of the flesh, the body tended to demand more of the same.

She said instead, "If that one wants you again, my dear, I don't think you'll have much choice in the matter."

That prediction caused a tiny thrill in the pit of Jocelyn's stomach, but she staunchly ignored it. "Then I'll just have to make sure I'm never alone with him again. So you can stop worrying — "

"Madame!" Babette interrupted just then, so excited she entered the room without knocking first. "Alonzo, he insists I should tell you Monsieur Thunder is about to have the western duel in the street. He says you would want to know this."

"To have the *what?*"

Vanessa made a tsking sound. "I believe she is referring to what that milliner in Tombstone called a showdown, my dear. Remember we witnessed . . . Jocelyn, don't you dare!" But the duchess had already run out of the room.

Chapter Twenty-five

Standing at the long bar, Colt finished off the whiskey in his glass and slowly poured another from the bottle he'd yanked away from the barkeep earlier. This being the third saloon he'd entered since he left the hotel that morning, by rights he should be drunk already. But he wasn't. His gut was too full of anger to let the whiskey do its stuff.

Looking for a fight also tended to keep a man sober, and he couldn't deny he'd been looking. When the first two saloons had turned up nothing worse than dirty looks, he'd tried this one — and hit the jackpot. Only it wasn't the jackpot he wanted. He'd needed a punching bag for his anger, not an invite to let some lead fly. It was just his luck that the only one to object to his presence with any degree of vocal belligerence was a young man who considered himself a fast draw. Whether he was or not, Colt had little doubt he could take him. It was the quiet ones you needed to worry about, not the show-offs.

It'd be over with already if the barkeep hadn't insisted, with a shotgun to make his point, that they take themselves outside to settle their differences. Colt claimed he'd finish his drink first. Riley, as his friends called him, was magnanimous once his challenge was accepted, and went outside to wait.

The kid was a so-called professional. Still wet behind the ears, but already a gun for hire. He worked for a local mine owner who'd been having some trouble with claim jumpers. In the six months since he'd come to town, he'd already killed two men, pistol-whipped a few more, and forced all others to give him a wide berth. Story was, the mine owner didn't know how to get rid of him now that he was no longer needed.

Colt surmised that much from the bits and pieces of hushed conversation going on behind him. He also heard a number of disparaging remarks about himself, but nothing he hadn't heard before. He'd been called every foul, dirty name there was, so he had to be in a damned ornery mood to take exception to insults that were second nature to the white man when an Indian was around.

It was what he'd been looking for today, those insults. His mood was certainly ornery enough. But folks this far south didn't know what to make of him. They took him for a half-breed, but they'd never seen one so tall, or mean-looking, or with a Colt Peacemaker riding his hip. Things like that tended to make a man think twice before opening his mouth — unless he was a young kid with delusions of omnipotence who'd let a few lucky draws go to his head.

Colt had kept his antagonist waiting about ten minutes now, which was why the customers remaining in the saloon were gradually becoming less wary of him. Riley's shouted "What're ya waitin' on, breed? Or has that red skin o' yourn turned yeller?" had drawn a few snickers from the room, but outright guffaws from the kid's two sidekicks, a couple of cowboys who had been egging him on from the beginning, and both had followed him outside.

Colt's eyes met those of the barkeep's. The man was slowly wiping a glass with a dirty rag. There was contempt in his red-rimmed eyes, mixed with a good deal of sneering pleasure, making his sentiments only too clear. He figured the taunt was true, that Colt would likely be begging for the direction of the back door as soon as he got up the nerve. He figured a half-breed wouldn't have the guts to face a man down, that it wouldn't be his style. Back-stabbing and ambushing were all a breed was good for.

So let him think it. What the hell did Colt care what a barkeep thought, or any of them for that matter? They were all waiting to see him gunned down, hoping to see it. The loudmouthed Riley might be feared and despised in this town, but today he would be applauded if he managed to take down a presumptuous breed.

Colt drained his glass again, then, to match actions to feelings, tossed it to the barkeep. Unprepared, the man dropped the one he'd been cleaning to catch it. Satisfied to hear the glass break and the man snarl, Colt shoved away from the bar and headed toward the entrance. Chairs toppled over in the customers' haste to follow him, but feet came to a skidding halt when he paused just beyond the swinging doors to locate his quarry.

Shade had enticed Riley across the street, where he was lounging against a hitching rail with his two friends. The covered boardwalks on both sides of the street were already filling with eager spectators drawn by Riley's earlier taunt.

The young man had to be nudged to notice Colt's arrival, and he grinned before straightening, making some comment that brought chuckles from his friends. He then walked toward the center of the wide street, slow confidence in his stride.

A muscle jerked in Colt's jaw as he ground his teeth in disgust. He wondered if the good townsfolk would call for a lynching if he happened to kill their resident asshole. Probably. Fair fight or not, white folks didn't like seeing a half-breed defeat one of their own.

At the moment, he didn't particularly care, but he had no intention of killing the kid when this wasn't the kind of fight he'd been courting. Someone else could have that distinction. Of course, if the show-off died accidentally by getting in the way of one of his bullets . . .

Colt tipped his hat back until it dropped behind to hang from the neck strap. He'd once had one pushed forward into his eyes by the wind, at just the wrong moment. He'd be dead now if the other guy hadn't been such a lousy shot.

"Now what're ya waitin' on?" Riley called impatiently from his position in the middle of the street.

"You that anxious to die?"

Riley thought that was funny. So did his friends. So did a number of spectators.

"That ain't no bow an' arrow you're packin', breed, or ain't ya noticed?"

This time the kid bent over double, he laughed so hard at his own sally. There was backslapping and eye-wiping going on on both sides of the street as just about everyone present joined in his humor — except the Spaniard.

Colt noticed Alonzo as he moved out into the street, then the Scot standing with him. So some of her people were present. It made no difference. They were merely spectators like the rest. And yet his eyes suddenly scanned the covered boardwalks — and found her, that bright beacon of red hair hard to miss as she ran toward Alonzo.

Shit! Now he was pissed, well and truly pissed! He wondered who he had to thank for her presence, and when she stopped by the Spaniard, he knew. The look he gave the swarthy man promised retribution, but Alonzo, reading that look correctly, merely shrugged.

Looking at the duchess was out of the question. Colt gave his attention back to Riley, his indifference gone, his anger on the edge of exploding. If she tried to interfere . . .

Jocelyn was about to do just that. She took in the situation at a glance, understood that the two men standing out there in the street were at any moment going to start shooting at each other, and she couldn't allow it to happen. She knew firsthand how skillful Colt was with his revolver, but what if his young opponent was as equally skilled? She couldn't take the chance.

But as she lifted her skirt to step down into the street, Alonzo caught her arm and whispered near her ear, "If you distract him now, he is dead. The moment his eyes turn to you, and they will, the young Riley will take advantage and draw his weapon. Had you come sooner you might have stopped it, but now is too late."

"But . . ." She bit her lip in indecision, staring at Colt. How could she watch and do nothing, when he might be wounded or worse?

But it really was too late to interfere. Even as she looked toward Colt's opponent to assess his readiness, the young man was reaching for his gun.

It all happened so fast, it was no wonder the spectators were collectively drawing in gasps of awe. Colt's gun was already in his hand and aimed at his opponent. The young man, his hand only just gripping his own weapon, still holstered, stared incredulously and didn't move so much as another inch. He looked rather sick. He obviously wasn't sure what to do now, whether to concede the fight or to take his chances and still draw. It was the silence of Colt's gun that made him so undecided.

Colt wasn't waiting for him to make up his mind. With slow, purposeful strides he closed the distance between them until the nozzle of his Peacemaker came to rest against Riley's trembling belly. Riley had broken out in a sweat by then, afraid to look down for fear he would see the trigger being squeezed, afraid to look anywhere but into those hard blue eyes that had never wavered from his.

Colt smelled his fear, saw it, but he wasn't feeling very merciful at the moment. "We tried it your way, you loudmouthed son of a bitch," he hissed low, so only Riley would hear him. "Now you'll accommodate me."

With that Colt removed the gun from Riley's belly, arched it to the left, and brought it across Riley's face in a backhanded swing. The kid went stumbling to the side, and when he touched his hand to his cheek, it came away bloody. He didn't understand. He still didn't, even when Colt holstered his gun and stood there waiting, fingers flexing.

Riley's friends didn't understand either, but they weren't so doubtful about what to do. One reached for his gun. Simultaneously, Alonzo reached for his knife, and Robbie took a step forward. Neither man's assistance was necessary, however, or noted by Colt. He had been keeping Riley's friends in his sights, and out came his gun again, this time to fire.

The bullet struck metal. The cowboy dropped his revolver to the ground with a cry, his fingers numb. The other one spread his arms wide and backed away, unwilling to take Colt on by himself.

Again Colt put his gun away and locked eyes with Riley, who hadn't dared to move even with Colt's attention momentarily directed elsewhere. "Come on, kid, I ain't got all day."

"Come — come on what?"

"You wanted a piece of me. Come and take it."

Riley took a step back instead, his eyes flaring with alarm. "You mean fight you? But you're bigger'n me!"

"My size didn't stop you from shoving insults down my throat, did it?"

"So I made a mistake, mister. Whyn't we forget it, huh?"

Colt slowly shook his head. "I'd rather beat the shit out of you."

Riley took another step back, his eyes like saucers now. "Would — would you shoot me in the back?"

Colt scowled at that fool question. "No."

"Glad to hear it," Riley gulped out and took off down the street.

For a moment Colt simply stared at his fleeing back with a mixture of surprise and exasperation. He'd had men back down from gunfights before when he'd gotten the draw on them, but they'd never turned tail and run when he'd offered them another out to save face, especially with so many witnesses present. Witnesses usually made all the difference in the way a man reacted, turning cowards into brave men, even if those brave men knew they'd end up being dead men.

He could have dropped a few bullets into the dust around those running feet, but since he doubted that would bring Riley back to face him, he didn't bother. He turned away in disgust instead, oblivious to the murmurings of many spectators who were experiencing a full gamut of reactions, from shocked amazement to bitter disappointment to jeering contempt for Riley's cowardice. But mostly they were wondering aloud who Colt was.

It was going to be a source of frustration for the storytellers of the town that they were doomed to never learn his name, for who in their right mind would dare to ask him outright after what they had just witnessed, and there was no one else willing to supply the answer. Jocelyn certainly wasn't, though she heard the question several times on her way back to the hotel. Nor would her people volunteer his name, accustomed as they were to keeping a low profile.

But overhearing a scorn-filled "He's a savage. What else is there to know?" in answer to the same question, brought Jocelyn up short.

Already upset from the scare she had just experienced, as well as frustrated that Colt had disappeared into the crowd before she could speak to him, she turned to the well-dressed young man whose remark managed to rub her on the raw.

"How dare you, sir!" she lit into him without preamble, to the surprise of both the man and his companion, as well as of Robbie and Alonzo, who were close behind her. "They went out into the street to kill each other. That neither is dead is the mark of a civilized man, not a savage."

Feeling a good deal better for having vented a small portion of her anger on the hapless stranger, even though it was Colt she really wanted to upbraid for his careless risk-taking, she marched on without the least notion of the agitation she left behind.

"Nice going, Miles, or hasn't it dawned on you yet that by that accent of hers, it's a safe bet to say you've just offended Lady Fleming herself?"

The sarcasm, delivered so scathingly, put Miles Dryden on the defensive. "Well, how was I to know? The way the countess spoke of her, I was expecting a raving beauty." And then he groaned. "A redhead, and a skinny one at that! I'll never be able to go through with it."

Maura, clinging possessively to his arm, was mollified at hearing that. Personally, she thought the duchess was stunning, but for a moment she had forgotten that Miles wouldn't think so. She knew from experience that his preference in women ran to well-shaped blondes such as herself. The older countess was likely to give her more cause for worry than the younger duchess.

"You'll do just fine, sugar, 'cause it looks like this is the one we've been dreaming about. A real English duchess, traveling just for pleasure, and in such style. She's got to be rich as sin."

"So you said the last time," Miles grumbled.

Maura didn't care for that reminder. "The widow Ames never lied about all her children being dead. She just failed to mention there were seventeen grandchildren patiently waiting to pick her estate apart. So they bought you off with a worthless silver mine that got us stranded in this godforsaken place. At least they never questioned the old lady's death."

"But she was old. This one's young."

"We won't use poison this time to make you a widower again. An accident will do just as well."

"And I suppose I'll have to see to it?"

She was getting tired of his negative attitude. "I took care of your last two wives, sugar. I'd say it's your turn. Of course, if you'd rather find me a husband instead . . . "

"Bitch," he growled jealously, as she knew he would. "The day you even look at another man I'll break your pretty neck."

"Now, now, love, I was only teasing." She grinned up at him. "You know very well I've been faithful to you since the day we met. Besides, I could never do what you do so well. I have enough trouble just pretending to be your sister."

"That was your idea, not mine. This whole lousy scheme has been your idea. 'Marry a rich widow, sugar, and you can give up your gambling,'" he mimicked in a high falsetto.

Maura's eyes narrowed in annoyance. "Your cheating, you mean, which got us run out of one town after another. And you jumped on the idea, if I recall."

"That was before the first wife wasn't rich enough to suit you and you decided she had to die so we could try again . . . and again . . . and again."

"All right!" she snapped. "So all four of them turned out to be bad choices. But this time is going to be different, I just know it is."

"It's already different, Maura, or have you forgotten how young this widow is? I'll likely have to work twice as hard to win her over, and even then my success isn't a foregone conclusion. This could be a total waste of time and effort."

"Not quite, love. We still have that other option to fall back on if the lady doesn't succumb to your fatal charm. But my money is on you. After all, I know how irresistible you can be when you really try. You won *me* heart and soul, didn't you?"

Chapter Twenty-six

"Good morning, Your Grace."

Jocelyn turned to smile at the young man who had caused her such embarrassment the night before when she was first introduced to him. It was laughable now, but at the time it had been quite mortifying to find that the brother and sister Vanessa had taken under her wing were the same pair Jocelyn had practically accosted right after the aborted gunfight yesterday. They had also been invited to dinner, so there was no easy escape from her discomfort.

But somehow, and she still wasn't sure how he had done it, Miles Dryden managed to put her at ease with his profuse apologies, wouldn't accept any she tried to offer in return, and even made her forget the incident for the remainder of the evening. He was, without a doubt, utterly charming. She had suspected he would be handsome too, and indeed he was, with his dark blond hair cropped just below the ears and his eyes the color of fine sherry. On the lean side and slightly above average in height, he had a pair of the most engaging dimples that appeared with every smile, and with a keen sense of humor, he smiled often, as did everyone around him.

Maura Dryden was just as interesting as her brother. There was little family resemblance between them with her ash-blond hair and large, dark green eyes, her much shorter height and voluptuous figure, but there was no denying they had both been blessed with exceptional looks. And where Miles' charm added to his attractiveness, Maura was possessed of a sultriness that enhanced hers, at least as far as men were concerned, if Sir Parker was any indication. He had also joined them for dinner, and to Jocelyn's amusement, had barely taken his eyes off the girl throughout the meal.

Vanessa had certainly been delighted with the whole evening and had no doubt gone to bed with her worries put to rest. As a hoped-for distraction, Miles Dryden was proving eminently successful. Jocelyn had retired conceding that point, and even experienced a measure of relief that it was so — until it occurred to her that Vanessa's scheme could work both ways, for Colt as well as for herself. And the thought of Colt finding Maura Dryden to his liking, just as Sir Parker had, effectively squelched whatever relief she had briefly felt, and even added a new dimension to her confused emotions. To her chagrin, she was afraid it might be jealousy. But since it could just as likely be a misguided sense of possessiveness, what she might feel for anything that had cost her such an exorbitant sum of money, she wasn't going to worry about it.

So she had decided, but even now with Miles Dryden's winsome smile turned on her, she was wondering where his sister was, and what Colt's reaction would be when he first saw the girl. She also wondered if there was any way she might renege on her agreement to allow them to join her entourage, but she supposed not. Their belongings were probably even now being loaded into the wagons in front of the hotel.

"Mr. Dryden." She nodded in reply to his greeting. "I hope this early hour hasn't proved inconvenient. We are more or less at the mercy of our guide, who doesn't believe in wasting daylight, as he so quaintly puts it."

"I know the sort. Our stage driver was a cantankerous old curmudgeon who rushed us in and out of every roadhouse with the threat of leaving us behind if we weren't quick enough to suit him."

She had to smile at that description, which was pretty accurate for their guide, too, except for the old part. Colt was more often than not quarrelsome, irritable, and quick of temper. How would he be today? Would he even be out front watching, or had he already gone on ahead as usual, leaving it to Billy to point the way?

She realized suddenly how anxious she was to see him. She also recalled that she still didn't know what he thought of the gift of her virginity. She didn't try to delude herself that he might not have been aware of the gift. His gentle handling of her that night proved otherwise.

"We aren't nearly so rushed, Mr. Dryden, just roused at an ungodly hour every morning." She hoped she didn't sound as impatient as she felt, but she wanted to find Colt and perhaps have a few words with him before they departed. "You will quickly become accustomed to it, I'm sure. Now, if you will collect your sister — "

"Maura is already outside, Your Grace. If you will allow me?"

She was hesitant in accepting his offered arm. With her guard surrounding her, it was so unnecessary. Besides, she didn't want Colt to see Miles escorting her from the hotel, though she wasn't sure why. But short of outright rudeness, there was no help for it.

Outside, everything was in readiness, Jocelyn being the last to arrive. Miss Dryden stood waiting with Vanessa and the two maids in the shade of the hotel porch, but she wasn't attending their conversation; was, in fact, staring off toward the front of the cavalcade — at Colt.

He was mounted already, as was Billy, who had his attention at the moment. But that didn't mean he wasn't aware of Miss Dryden's perusal. Likely he was, since he was usually aware of everything going on around him, the reason that his eyes turned toward the porch only seconds after Jocelyn stepped out of the hotel. The moment he saw her, he yanked his horse around to take off.

"A moment, Colt, if you please!"

Jocelyn immediately flushed, having thoughtlessly drawn every eye toward her. She had had to raise her voice for Colt to hear her, and even to her own ears she had sounded imperious. She wouldn't have blamed him if he embarrassed her further by ignoring her, but he didn't. He whipped his horse back around and waited, with obvious impatience. That he didn't dismount and come to her as would be expected of one's employee was noted, particularly by her guard, even by Miles, whose arm she could feel tense beneath her hand. But Jocelyn wasn't pressing her luck any further. Excusing herself from Miles, she quickly stepped off the porch.

For an imprudent impulse, however, it went from bad to worse, as she found out when she reached Colt. Billy had moved off to accord them a measure of privacy, but it didn't matter. Looking up at Colt, she knew without a doubt she had made a serious mistake. Although he usually kept his emotions so well hidden you never knew what he was thinking, those emotions were crystal clear right now, and they were anything but placid. She even took a step back, his look was so hostile.

Jocelyn stiffened her resolve, or tried to. So she shouldn't have approached him this soon. It was done. She was there. And although she hadn't the faintest notion of what she had intended to say, perhaps something would come to her that might at least take the edge off his obvious anger.

"Would you get down . . . please?" she asked. "I want to talk to you."

"No, you don't."

"Yes, I — "

"No . . . you don't, Duchess."

She wasn't sure of his meaning, whether he simply refused to hear what she had to say or whether he was warning her that she wouldn't care to hear what *he* had to say in return. Likely the latter, which was why she didn't try to detain him again when he turned about and rode off.

She turned away herself to find all of her people suddenly busy in some unnecessary activity or conversation, which told her plainly that until that moment they had been avidly watching her and Colt. It didn't embarrass her this time, though. Instead her temper flared up, especially when she noticed Miss Dryden's rather smug expression. The woman couldn't have heard Colt's refusal to speak with her, but his disrespect and animosity were unmistakable. Jocelyn could almost read Maura's thoughts: that no man would ever treat *her* so shabbily.

"I — ah, didn't realize he was one of your guards."

That Miles Dryden was there to assist her into her coach did not pacify Jocelyn's now simmering emotions in the least. Nor did she need a reminder of yesterday's foolishness.

But not for the world would she let anyone know how easily Colt could upset her, so she managed a smile, no matter that her lips felt like they would crack, they were so stiff. "He's not. He's our guide."

"A gunfighter for a guide?"

Miles seemed determined to provide an outlet for her temper, but she didn't want a substitute. Colt deserved every bit of it himself.

"His versatility makes him an excellent guide, Mr. Dryden, despite his lack of manners and wretched disposition. But if it bothers you to have such a man leading you through the wilderness — "

"Not at all," he quickly assured her.

"Then I will see you later in the day, sir."

She stepped into her coach to wait impatiently for Vanessa to join her. If Miles had thought he would be sharing her coach, she had just disabused him of that notion. Even if she had intended to give up her privacy, which she hadn't, she would have just changed her mind. Under no circumstances could she spend this day in idle conversation with virtual strangers. She would go mad if she tried.

Vanessa sensed her mood and wisely kept quiet once they were on their way. But the silence merely allowed Jocelyn's awakened ire to feed upon itself. Where she had previously been understanding of Colt's feelings, she now resented his resentment. She wasn't sorry for what had happened between them. She wasn't about to apologize for having wanted him. True, he had resisted her at every turn, but had she held a gun on him and forced him into her bed? No, she certainly had not. So he had no business being angry with her, and she intended to tell him so at the very next opportunity.

Chapter Twenty-seven

Every instinct had warned Colt to stay away from camp that night. Already acquainted with the duchess's stubborn streak, he had little doubt that, having decided on a confrontation, she wouldn't be satisfied until she had it. But he wasn't ready, not by a long shot. The conclusions he had drawn about her might have enraged him enough to send him out looking for trouble, but to have those conclusions confirmed was going to be ten times worse. And if mere suspicions could ride him this hard, what would the truth do to him?

Of course, if he was wrong about her, that would be an entirely different problem, in some ways an even bigger one. It was what had made him take what she offered, despite the fact that he'd sworn never to touch a white woman again. And it would happen again — if he was wrong about her. If it did, he was afraid that he could very easily end up wanting to make her his permanently, when he knew damn well that wasn't possible.

Either way, it was better not to know the truth just yet, at least not until he was certain he could control his reaction to it. Yet knowing that, and also that the redhead would push it as she always did, he still rode into camp that night.

And that was her fault too, for allowing a stranger into their midst at this particular time, when Colt happened to be so pissed off he hadn't been paying attention to any newcomers arriving in town after they had. Even with the precautions he had taken, it wasn't inconceivable that her enemy could have caught up to them in the two days they had wasted in Silver City. With the way danger followed that woman around like a homeless pup, the stranger could, in fact, be one of the Englishman's men. Even if it wasn't at all likely, the merest chance was enough to cause Colt worry. For all his protestations that he wasn't going to protect her, he couldn't bear it if something happened and he wasn't there to prevent it because he was afraid to have a confrontation with the woman.

But when the confrontation came, it came from an unexpected quarter.

As late as it was when Colt rode in, more than half the camp was still up, and it was just his luck that the duchess was one of them. He could feel her eyes follow him as he made his way to Billy's campfire after bedding his horse down with the others. She sat before another fire with a group of her men, her maid — and the stranger.

Billy, who had left that group when he noticed Colt by the horses, handed him the tin plate of food he regularly kept warmed near the fire. Colt had stopped complaining that it was always the fare served up by the duchess's cook. Half the time he was too tired to know what he was eating.

"Didn't think you were going to bed down with us tonight."

With a glance at all the other fires still occupied, Colt replied. "Doesn't look like anyone's got a hankering for sleep."

Billy shrugged. "The new fellow was spinning some pretty gruesome tales. He probably spooked some of them." Remembering those stories, and that Colt wouldn't find them entertaining, Billy quickly added, "Did you see the blonde this morning? She's his sister."

Colt ignored the question, his eyes stopping on the stranger. The duchess sat next to him, too close to him.

"Who is that guy anyway?"

"Name's Dryden, Miles Dryden."

Colt's brow knitted in thought. "He remind you of anyone, kid?"

"Can't say that he does. Why?"

"Seems like I've seen him before some-where."

"Maybe when you went east with Jessie and Chase? He claims to be from there."

Colt shook his head slowly. "No, I've seen him more recent than that. You sure you don't recognize him?"

"Are you sure you do?"

Colt stared hard at the man once more before glancing away. "Yes. It'll come to me in a while." And then, looking pointedly at Billy, "What tales was he telling?"

Billy flushed with the question, having thought he'd neatly avoided it. "Just stories."

"Give," was all Colt said.

"He's an Easterner, Colt," Billy said defensively. "You know how a little Indian attack wouldn't faze a Westerner, but a greenhorn will make it into a big deal every time."

"He was attacked?"

"Him and his sister."

"It took all night to tell it?"

Billy grinned, now that it looked like Colt hadn't taken offense at the subject as he thought he would. "You know how it is. A fellow comes into town and mentions he nearly got scalped, and every other person who's had a similar experience or even heard of one has got to tell him all about it. Dryden heard enough tales to fill a book while he was in Silver City."

"Then he was there before we arrived?"

"Several months. Why?"

"Just wondered."

Colt's mind was put to rest on one score. Dryden wasn't working for Longnose. It still didn't mean he liked the idea of the duchess inviting strangers to join her party. She ought to know better.

Several bites of food later, Colt asked, "What the hell is this stuff I'm eating?"

Billy chuckled. "One of Philippe's specialties. Good, ain't it?"

"You can't taste the meat for the sauce." Colt tossed the plate aside in disgust. "And what's *his* problem?"

Billy turned to see who had drawn Colt's attention now. Parker Grahame was staring right back, and none too amiably.

"He — ah — you could say he's been a mite put out since that night you took care of those two would-be thieves who tried to rob the duchess."

"Was I supposed to let them rob her?"

Billy grinned. "I think he objects to you being the one to rescue her, when that's his job. You *have* been making a habit of it, after all, which doesn't reflect too well on him."

"And that's enough to get him killed?"

Billy tensed. "What are you talking about?"

312

"The man's making up his mind to come over here, and not to pass the time."

"Christ! Well, don't kill him, for God's sake! He's more or less spokesman for all of them, being their captain, and they're kind of fed up with the disrespect you keep showing their lady. *I* know you do it on purpose, but she doesn't, and they don't either. I think this morning was just one time too many for nothing to be said about it."

"Exactly right, Mr. Ewing," Parker said from behind him.

Billy didn't turn to look at the Englishman again. He stared at Colt, dreading his reaction. Considering that he'd been in a foul disposition ever since they'd joined up with the duchess, he couldn't hope for now to be any different. And you just didn't push Colt when he was in such a mood.

Colt leaned back against his saddle in a negligent manner, not at all concerned that the man was standing there bristling. "You got something to say, Grahame, spit it out."

"Your brother has already said it. If you can't behave with a modicum of civility — "

"You'll do what?" Colt cut in with a near sneer. "Call me out?"

"Dammit, Colt!" Billy put in, but too late.

Parker was already stepping around him to get to Colt, so enraged he didn't stop to think,

313

simply hauled Colt to his feet by the front of his shirt. That Colt let him do it, and did nothing to block the fist that was drawn back to clobber him, didn't seem peculiar to Parker because he still wasn't thinking, merely reacting. But years of breeding broke through at the last moment to make him hesitate, if only for a second.

Unfortunately for Parker, in that second their gazes locked and his confidence was nearly shattered. He had the horrible feeling he was looking death in the eye. He'd never backed down from a fight in his life, never had to, never lost one. But he had somehow forgotten just whom he was dealing with here, that the man was in a class all by himself, a man damned close to the savages whom Dryden had been telling them tales of all evening, a man who would know ways of killing that Grahame had never even dreamed of. And he had challenged him?

"Sir Parker, release him at once!"

The voice of authority, reason, and his salvation. Parker obeyed with great relief.

Colt's reaction was just the opposite. "Shit!" He glared at the duchess, standing not far from them. "The man has a genuine grievance to pick with me. Who in the hell asked you to interfere, woman?"

Even if she wasn't rendered momentarily

314

speechless by his verbal attack, Jocelyn had no chance to answer. The scales were tipped for Parker, who saw red again with this latest insolence and let his fist fly.

The blow caught Colt on the side of his face but only slightly turned his head. That it had come when he wasn't looking, however, had everyone who was watching holding his breath, waiting for Colt's reaction. Parker in particular felt rather sick, never having taken a man unawares before. So he was most surprised when Colt turned back to him, slowly, and grinning.

"It took you long enough, English," he said just before his backhanded blow knocked Parker to the ground.

Billy caught Colt's gun and knife, both tossed to him, then simply got out of the way. Jocelyn had to step back also when one charge took both men crashing through the fire, scattering sparks everywhere.

"Come away, my dear," Vanessa said quietly at her side. "You can't stop it now, and shouldn't want to."

"Shouldn't want to? But they're — "

"Behaving atrociously, I know, but your Thunder obviously needs to inflict violence on someone. Better Sir Parker than you. Now come away."

Jocelyn bit her lip, remembering Colt's

hostility that morning, watching his savagery now. Despite what Vanessa said, she didn't think he would hurt her, no matter how angry he got. And she was still angry herself. She was not some vaporous ninny to hide from a man's displeasure.

"I'm staying, Vana," she said determinedly. "I won't try to stop them, but when they're finished I'll have my say."

Chapter Twenty-eight

Colt felt wonderful. He hurt like hell, but inside he was in control again, his emotions spent, his anger leashed, manageable. He could probably even confront the duchess now and get it over with, or so he thought until he saw her standing there watching him.

Back came the irritation, first because she had managed to approach him without his hearing her. He could blame that on the slight ringing in his ears from one of Grahame's punches. He shook his head, but the ringing persisted. He glanced around then to see if anyone else whom he didn't know about had followed him, but she was the only one there. And that was why his irritation increased. She just never learned, this woman. He'd avoided her, he'd warned her off. How much clearer could he get? But it was no more than he could expect with her stubborn streak, so it shouldn't irritate him. It still did.

"What're you looking at?"

Jocelyn let out a sigh, hearing Colt's surly

tone. To think she had actually been concerned when he had stumbled out of camp. Sir Parker had been rendered unconscious, and Vanessa, who was seeing to him, had assured her he would be all right. But Colt still had been on his feet at the end of the fight and had left before anyone could attend to his cuts and abrasions.

He had doused his head in the water hole they had camped next to, and had just finished drying his face with his bandanna when he'd noticed her. Whoever had last toted water from the hole that evening had left a torch behind, stuck in the ground. From that light, she could see the swelling of his left cheek, the cut over his eye still trickling blood down his temple. His clothes were filthy, his pants ripped at the knees. His other injuries were likely hidden, since Sir Parker had concentrated most of his blows to the body. There would be many, however, for the fight had lasted a good fifteen minutes.

"You look terrible. Does it hurt?"

"Does a dog piss?"

Her back stiffened. "I'd appreciate a civil answer, thank you."

"Then go talk to someone else. Here you take your chances."

"I could have sworn you would have had your nasty temper worked off after your exercise this evening."

"Me too," he sneered. "Just goes to show how wrong a dumb Indian can be."

"Don't do that," Jocelyn said angrily.

"What?"

"Belittle yourself like that. You may not be educated in the normal way, Colt Thunder, but you aren't stupid, and we both know it."

"That's debatable, honey. I'm here, aren't I?"

She drew in her breath sharply, "Meaning what? That you shouldn't be?"

"Damned right!"

"Then leave! No one's stopping you."

"Aren't you?" In two long strides he reached her and gripped her arms to shake her. "Aren't you?" he repeated in a furious hiss.

"If I am . . . I'm glad," she said, already regretting that she had offered him an out in the heat of the moment, but relieved that he hadn't jumped on it. "You are needed, after all."

Colt turned away from her, defeated by a single word. Every time she said it, it did crazy things to him inside. Mostly it inflamed his lust, even though he knew full well her use of the word wasn't meant to be provocative. Christ, how he wished it were.

"It takes integrity and honor to keep faith with something you find so disagreeable," she said quietly behind him.

"What is this?" he demanded sharply, glancing over his shoulder with a black scowl. "Soothe the savage beast with a bone of flattery?"

Jocelyn gritted her teeth. "No," she said, wanting to shout it, but afraid now that if she let her temper loose, it would be the excuse he needed to quit. "I'm trying to tell you I'm sorry you don't like the job . . . but not sorry enough to release you from it."

He turned around slowly. "To hell with the job," he said almost conversationally. "That's not the problem and you know it. You're the problem, you and that unexpected little bonus you bestowed on me without warning."

Jocelyn tried to look away at that point, sensing what was coming. Colt brought her gaze back to his with a hard grip on her chin.

"Don't mistake me, Duchess. I'm honored." The sudden sarcasm in his tone said otherwise. "But why don't you clear up the mystery, anyway? Why me?"

She knew exactly what he was asking, but denied it. "I don't know what you mean."

That answer got her another hard shake and a shouted "Why me?"

"I — I wanted you. It's that simple."

"Wrong. A virgin can want every man who comes sniffing, but she won't do anything about it without a ring on her finger, or love clouding her judgment. Now, since neither of those reasons applies to you, let's hear the real one."

It unnerved her that he was so sure those reasons didn't apply to her. How could he know that, or that her attraction to him wasn't the only thing that had motivated her?

"Not that I can see why it matters, but I wasn't just any virgin, I was a widowed virgin. Therefore, I didn't have to wait for love or a ring, as you so put it, if I desired a man. Who is there to tell me that I can't do as I please or have what I want?"

He stared at her for a long moment, running that through his mind, before he finally shook his head. "That was a widow's philosophy, sure enough, but just as you weren't just any virgin, you weren't just any widow. The whys of your special circumstances don't interest me. You were still a virgin, and virgins don't give it away without a damn good reason. I haven't heard yours yet."

"I *have* answered you!" she cried. "I don't know what more you expect — "

"The truth!"

"Why won't you believe me?"

"Because I see it in your eyes, woman."

She paled. "What?"

"That you're hiding something. And now

it's in your face. I pieced it together that night, that you had to have some ulterior motive for accepting me in your bed."

"But I did want you," she insisted. "It had to be you, don't you see?"

"No, I don't see. But I will, if I have to shake it out of you."

Jocelyn stiffened, anger rescuing her from the turmoil his suspicions caused. "You've done quite enough of that, thank you. Now you will release me."

"I don't think so," he said softly and drew her closer instead.

Intimidation had gotten him nowhere. And he recognized that stubborn streak of hers when he saw it. He could throttle her and she wouldn't tell him another thing. But he had to know — one way or the other.

"What the devil are you doing?" she demanded when she felt his lips on her neck.

"All that talk of wanting and you have to ask?"

"But — "

"But what, Duchess?" His lips moved toward her ear while his arms tightened around her until there was no space left between their bodies. "That had to be a powerful need you had to make you give up your virginity to satisfy it. Something that powerful doesn't just go away . . . or does it?"

"No . . . it doesn't," she heard herself saying, to her surprise and his.

But it was true, obviously, since she had felt it the moment he put his arms around her, and it was growing stronger by the moment. He smelled of earth and sweat and man, and she wanted him again, just like before, regardless that she had no reason to indulge the desire this time other than for the sheer pleasure she now knew it would bring her.

His lips had left her skin when she answered him, and his wet hair was dripping on her shoulder and neck, making her shiver. Or was it his breath, which she could still feel warming the sensitive area around her ear?

"Why'd you get rid of it?"

She pressed closer at the sound of his voice. "What? Oh, please, no more questions," she groaned. "Kiss me."

He did, but teasingly, nibbling at her lips, drawing back when she strained to meld their mouths together. He kept it up until she was ready to do anything to bring his mouth crushing down on hers.

"Colt!"

"Why'd you get rid of it?"

Despite the maelstrom of her emotions, it seemed easier to answer. "It was a hindrance."

"Why?" his voice persisted, a husky whisper, while his hands moved all over her.

"It prevented me from . . . from remarrying if I found someone . . . who would suit."

"Why?"

"The duke's affliction mustn't be known."

"But it didn't matter if I learned of it?"

"You didn't know him . . . were never likely to meet anyone who did."

She was suddenly shoved back, his warmth gone, leaving her so frustrated she could have screamed — until she heard him swear. "Son of a bitch! I had to be right, didn't I? Just this once I couldn't be wrong?"

"About what?" she asked, reaching for him, but he knocked her hand aside.

"You used me!"

Jocelyn blinked, jolted out of her confusion, enough to realize what he'd done to her. He'd used her passion against her — just as she had done to him that night. She noted the irony, even supposed she deserved it. But there was a glaring difference in their tactics that caused the outrage now taking over her languor, blinding her to his own. She hadn't withdrawn the moment she got what she wanted, as he just did. She hadn't left him in need.

"So this is what your foul temper has been about these past days?" she demanded furiously. "You feel insulted because I wanted you?"

"Used, woman," he corrected coldly. "Any man would have served for what you *wanted*."

"And you didn't use me? I wasn't there that night, beneath you, filled with your flesh?"

He wanted to hit her for that, for making him burn to get inside her again with the vivid image her words created in his mind, even more than he already burned from holding her. And she wasn't finished.

"Is that what you're trying to tell me, Thunder? That you found no pleasure in my bed?"

"Shut up, damn you!"

"Then what exactly do you resent? That I chose you to be my first lover? Or that I took advantage of your moment of weakness?" And then she went for blood. "That's what's really bothering you, isn't it? I know you didn't want me. You made that abundantly clear every time I got near you. But I managed to seduce you into losing control anyway, and you can't stand that, can you?"

He drew back his hand, but when she didn't flinch from it, he clenched his fist and lowered it. "Answer me one question, Duchess. When did you decide to use me, before or after you forced this damn job down my throat?" When she didn't answer him immediately, he sneered, "Just as I thought. When a man buys a whore, he makes sure he gets his money's worth. Did you?"

She was furious enough to reply, "Of course. You are, after all, a prime specimen of manhood, quite the most handsome I've ever encountered." There was enough sarcasm in her tone to make him doubt there was any truth in her words. And then she added just for spite, "But it was a trifling sum, if you must know. So you needn't worry that you cost me dearly. You didn't. Besides, you have so many other uses, I really did make a splendid bargain, didn't I?"

His answer was to snarl, "I suspected you were a spoiled bitch!"

"And I knew you were an arrogant bastard. So what does that prove? How blind lust can be?"

It was the last taunt Colt could stand without giving in to his urges, and at the moment his greatest urge was to cut out that razor-sharp tongue of hers. The only other thing he could do was leave, which he did.

She misunderstood, however, and shouted after him, "Don't mistake me, Thunder! I have no intention of releasing you from my service until you've finished the job you agreed to. Do you hear me? Don't you dare quit on me!"

He stopped, but only after putting enough distance between them. With the brightly lit camp behind him, she could only see his silhouette, which was just as well, since his expression was now murderous.

"I don't quit, but I give you fair warning, woman. For the last time, stay the hell away from me."

"With pleasure!" she retorted, but his long strides had already increased the distance between them, so she wasn't sure he'd heard her.

She watched until he disappeared behind one of the wagons, then turned about to stare blindly at the far-off mountains. For her ears only she mumbled, "Hateful beast," and then promptly burst into tears.

Chapter Twenty-nine

Jocelyn set her plate aside and then stretched before leaning back against the pillows scattered under the silken lean-to, which was set up for her luncheon each day. It was one of the luxuries she wouldn't need much longer. With the days as cool as they now were in late November, a shaded area in which to eat the noon meal wasn't necessary anymore, was only still being erected at Vanessa's insistence, since she was of the old school that believed a lady's skin should never be touched by the sun, even if it was a cold sun. She clucked her tongue disapprovingly over the slight golden tan Jocelyn had acquired by riding every day now that the torrid southern heat was bowing to winter.

Two weeks had passed since leaving Silver City. They'd dipped south briefly to get around the southern mountains, then ridden almost straight east, until they crossed the Rio Grande River and turned to follow it north. It was much easier traveling after that because they encountered the ancient El Camino Real, or Royal Highway, that stretched from Santa Fe, which they were heading toward, clear down to Mexico City. In fact, they could have used this old road, which had first served as a trade route more than three hundred years ago, if they hadn't originally planned on going to California.

According to Billy, the El Camino Real met up with the Santa Fe Trail, another old trade route. It had been established only some sixty years ago and would lead them out of the mountains, east again, and straight onto the Great Plains, which were the flat grasslands that reached clear into Canada. They'd also found out from Billy just how far away this Wyoming was. If they had known to begin with that it would take nearly two months to reach . . . but that was a moot point now, considering how far they had already come.

The road, however, made for a less bumpy ride, and the scenery was lovely, with the San Andres Mountains on the right, the river on the left with more mountain ranges beyond it, trees now in abundance in magnificent full colors, and even, for several days, the wide-open Jornada del Muerto valley to exercise the horses in.

The desertlike quality of the land had not disappeared entirely, however. There was still cactus to be seen, white and purple sage and creosote bushes, long stretches of parched ground or even white sands, and very little grass other than grama, but they were accustomed to such after traveling so long in these southern regions.

Now, as they neared the Rocky Mountains and Santa Fe, which was only three days away, there were even more ranges on every side, and more lovely valleys to explore. But Jocelyn didn't feel like exploring today. Her sigh must have suggested the same to Vanessa.

"It's not the heat, and the lunch was light enough," the countess remarked beside her. "Didn't you sleep well last night?"

"As well as usual," Jocelyn replied, which wasn't admitting much, since Vanessa was unaware of the many bad nights she'd been having recently.

She knew the cause, though that did nothing to alleviate the problem. She was simply suffering a long-drawn-out case of severe embarrassment over her conduct during the last encounter with Colt.

That blasted fight. She couldn't get it out of her mind, even two weeks later.

The very next day she had begun her monthly time, which she had eagerly used to excuse her uncalled-for tears that night, as well as her horrid behavior. But she still burned with shame every time she recalled how she had allowed Colt to reduce her to the role of a screaming shrew, complete with spite, derision, and malice. She hadn't known she had it in her. Well, how could she have, when she had never in her life acted like that before? But it would never happen again, by God. That she had promised herself, a promise she would keep no matter what that heartless man did to provoke her — if he ever talked to her again.

She had seen him no more than twice in all this time, and then only from a distance when she was exercising Sir George. He had stopped coming into camp at all, not even to sleep. Where he bedded down at night was anyone's guess, though she suspected it wasn't that far away, since Billy rode out before dawn to meet him each morning to confer on the arrangements for the day, and he was never gone long.

She had missed Vanessa's next question. "What?"

"I asked if you were too tired for your ride today. I believe Sir George has already been saddled."

Jocelyn didn't budge from the pillow, nor did she open her eyes to answer. "Not too tired, Vana, but I don't really feel like it. One of the grooms can take him out."

"And what about Miles? You know how much he enjoys your rides together."

With a prickle of irritation, Jocelyn wondered when her friend was going to stop matchmaking. It simply wasn't working.

A very short while ago Jocelyn's interest would have been quite snared by such a man. In personality and looks he outshone Charles Abington, and she had seriously considered marrying Charles. But now there was another man she couldn't help comparing Miles Dryden with, and in her doing so, Miles wasn't quite as fascinating. He became too pale, too charming, too ingratiating. Even his misfortune could be picked apart to reveal a touch of cowardice. Colt wouldn't have run from failure to start over somewhere else. He wouldn't have stranded himself in a town, either, because of a close touch with death. And she couldn't imagine Colt standing by and doing nothing while someone robbed him. Indeed, no.

Devil take it, she had to stop thinking of that man, but she still didn't feel like riding, even for the diversion. "One day isn't going to crush him, Vana."

"I wouldn't be too sure. I believe he is quite smitten. Maura thinks so, and who would know better than his sister, whom he is most likely to confide in."

Jocelyn nearly snorted. The pair were as thick as thieves. If the man was smitten with anyone, it was with his sultry sister. She leaned up to see them walking together near the clifflike banks of the river, deep in conversation.

Glancing at the countess, she said, "I suppose she told you that?"

"Indeed."

"Well, I wouldn't believe everything that girl tells you. I've already caught her in one lie."

"What?"

"The other day she told me that her father had owned some of the finest racers in the eastern states, and that she so regretted their loss when everything had to be sold, even though she doesn't care to ride herself."

"So?"

"So the first time I allowed Miles to try Sir George, he remarked that he'd always wanted to own a Thoroughbred, but that his family had only kept carriage horses, which were all that was necessary in the city."

Vanessa found that merely amusing, if her chuckle was any indication. "It's very common to want to impress someone of your stature, my dear. You should know that by now. The girl is merely a bit prideful and envious. That's nothing to be concerned over."

"I wasn't concerned. I just wouldn't accept everything she says as the literal truth."

"Very well. But in this instance, concerning Miles' affections, I'm inclined to agree with her. I've seen the way he dotes on you myself, after all. In fact, I wouldn't be surprised if you don't get a proposal long before we reach the railroad that will take them back East."

"I wouldn't be surprised either."

Vanessa frowned. "So, you *do* know he's smitten. Whyever have we been arguing about it, then?"

Jocelyn grinned. "I wouldn't call this discussion an argument, Vana. And I didn't agree he's smitten."

"But you said — "

"That I wouldn't be surprised if he proposes. How many proposals have I had in the past three years?"

Vanessa sighed. "Too many to count. So you think he's just another fortune hunter?"

"I'm afraid I do."

"You could be wrong, you know. Look at the attention he lavishes on you. And he's so deucedly handsome — and civilized, I might add."

That stung, so Jocelyn retorted, "He isn't

334

likely to ignore me with my fortune on his mind."

"But what makes you so sure, my dear?"

"His eyes."

"His eyes?"

"Yes, the way he looks at me. There's nothing there, Vana, not even the tiniest spark of interest. Oh, he says all the right words, but his eyes belie every one of them. He's simply not attracted to me. But then few men are."

"More fools they," the countess said in her behalf. "It doesn't matter, dear. We weren't considering him for a husband, merely as an entertaining diversion, so don't let it bother you."

Jocelyn had to force down a smile. "I won't."

But Vanessa was having a hard time letting the idea go. "You're positive?" she asked after a moment.

This time Jocelyn did smile. "Vana!" And laugh. "He looks at *you* with much more warmth than he does me." At the countess's blush, she added, "Ah, you have noticed that, at least?"

"Well, I assumed you were receiving even *more* admiring looks," Vanessa said defensively.

"Now you know better. But don't fret about it. He has been entertaining, and quite amusing, which was partly what you hoped for, wasn't it?"

Again Vanessa blushed. "I meant well, my dear."

Jocelyn leaned over to hug her. "I know, and I love you for it. And you needn't worry about our mean-tempered guide anymore. If you haven't noticed, he's been avoiding me like the plague. It's quite over."

"Is it really?"

She didn't want to explain about the argument, not at this late date, so she said simply, "Yes." But knowing Vanessa wouldn't leave it at that, would start to pick it apart for her own assurance, she cowardly added, "I think I'll have that ride after all."

Chapter Thirty

They rode east toward the Manzano Mountains. The fast gallop brought them to the lower foothills in little time, though Jocelyn was far ahead as usual. She dismounted to wait for Miles to catch up, walking Sir George beneath the golden aspen and ponderosa pines that dotted the area.

She was warm after the ride, but the cold wind kept her from removing her fur-trimmed riding jacket. They had had to dig out some of their winter clothing from the trunks with the recent weather change, a fortunate inclusion since they were likely to see snow before reaching their destination. They were also fortunate that with so many people, there had been only a few minor colds and sniffles to date.

Miles slowed his borrowed mount as he approached the duchess. He was dreading this, but Maura had been after him to get it over with, and she was right, of course. They were running out of time with the railroads close now, and without some definite encouragement from the lady, they had no excuse to continue on with her. And his other option wouldn't wait around indefinitely either.

They had assumed there would be more time, that they would all be taking the train from Santa Fe. They had since learned otherwise. The duchess's party would have to split up to transport so many vehicles on the rails, if the new Santa Fe line even had platform cars to accommodate them. Jocelyn had already decided to wait until the larger depots in Denver were reached before traveling the railroads, if even then, since that half-breed had assured her she could reach Wyoming via the flatlands of the plains.

For the first time, Miles was lacking the confidence so necessary to this scheme, because he had been unable to predetermine the duchess's feelings toward him. Her direct gazes unnerved him, but gave nothing away other than a sense of amusement. He sometimes even imagined that she was laughing at him rather than with him, that she saw right through his campaign to win her.

Of course, his heart hadn't really been in this endeavor from the start. The old broads of the past had been easy prey, susceptible, lonely, gullible, easily won and managed. But this young one lacked all the basic ingredients for a quick and effortless courtship. She also left him cold, despite her youth, which was what was really causing his dread of today's meeting. No matter how much she was worth, he almost hoped she would turn him down.

With self-disgust, he brought forth a smile as he dismounted. "You win again, Jocelyn."

She had allowed him the use of her name, but she still looked at him strangely each time he said it. With so many titles, she likely was simply not used to hearing it. Even the countess addressed her only as "my dear."

"We weren't racing, Miles. The only animals who can give Sir George a decent challenge are his mares, but their condition precludes such strenuous exercise."

He gritted his teeth. He always had the feeling she was condescending to him, and no doubt she was. A poor boy from Missouri, he was out of his depth dealing with an English aristocrat born and bred to wealth. Her damned horseflesh alone was probably worth more than he had gained from all four of his dead wives, especially if you counted the foals she was anticipating in the spring.

"Did you race him in England?" he thought to ask. She was always most agreeable when she talked about her horses, and he needed her agreeable today.

"Dear me, no. He was too young when we

339

left. But his sire . . . what *are* you doing, Miles?"

He had placed his arm around her shoulder as they were walking. Now he turned her to face him.

"Don't be shy," he said gently. "It's natural for a man to want to touch the woman he loves."

"I suppose it is."

That answer confounded him, especially since it was said without the least inflection in her voice. "Didn't you hear me? I've fallen in love with you."

"I'm sorry."

Sorry about what? That she hadn't heard him, or that he loved her? Jesus, it was bad enough he had to propose at all. Did she have to make it even more difficult?

"I suppose you've had many declarations of love."

He wasn't even aware that sarcasm dripped from his words, but Jocelyn was, and it annoyed her. She had intended to treat this anticipated proposal as if it were sincere, to simply refuse gently, without letting on that she knew the only thing he was attracted to was her money. She still wouldn't come right out and call him a liar, but after that sneering comment, she decided to make him wonder.

"You would truly be surprised how many

fortune hunters there are, Miles, who profess to undying love, and they do it so sweetly. Declarations, proposals of marriage . . . there have been so many I stopped counting long ago."

"Are you accusing — "

"Certainly not," she cut in with feigned indignation. "A fine, upstanding man like you wouldn't resort to such a low, despicable means of acquiring a fortune. I never thought that for a moment," she assured him with a pat on the arm. "If I was a bit tepid in my reaction, it's only that it's become rather tedious, having to explain so often why I never intend to marry again. But of course, you weren't proposing marriage, were you? Heavens, of course you weren't. You've only known me for a few weeks, after all."

She had to turn away before he saw her amusement at the flush his pale skin couldn't hide. His hand on her shoulder kept her from walking away, however.

"What do you mean, you never intend to marry again?" he demanded rather sharply.

"What? Oh, that." She managed a heavy sigh in preparation for the whopping lie she was about to tell. "There's simply nothing I can do about it. It was my husband's way of assuring I would always honor his memory. I will lose everything I have, you see, should

I remarry. And I can't very well risk that, now can I?"

"Everything?" he fairly choked.

"Yes, everything."

"But you're so young! What if you want children? What if *you* fall in love?"

"My husband's will doesn't deny me children or lovers. Should I want either, I shall simply have them. Oh, dear, have I shocked you?" His expression certainly said so. It was all she could do not to laugh.

"You must hate his memory," Miles said bitterly. He certainly did.

"Whyever would you think so? He was merely trying to protect me, to assure that no one could ever control me or the money he left to me. I see nothing wrong in that."

"You wouldn't," he mumbled.

"What was that?"

"Nothing." With a supreme effort, his winsome smile reappeared. "As you say, it's too soon to speak of marriage. Tell me, I have wondered, with so many guards, why none accompany you on your daily rides."

Jocelyn laughed at the sudden change of subject, but made him think it was his question she found amusing. "But how could they keep up? The purpose of these rides is to exercise Sir George. My own enjoyment of them is secondary. Besides, I never ride beyond the

342

point that a shot couldn't be heard." She indicated the rifle on her saddle. "And you are along to protect me, after all. If I were alone, I would simply stay within sight of my entourage. Now, shall we return?"

"If you're tired, of course," he said smoothly, his fury well under control now. "But there was a lovely meadow I thought you would enjoy seeing. We passed it, oh, not long before we stopped for luncheon, so it isn't very far from here."

He seemed quite eager to show it to her, and to grant his wish was the least she could do after nipping his plans so neatly in the bud. Truth to tell, she was feeling rather guilty about all those lies she had come up with to avoid the distastefulness of accusations and bad feelings.

"By all means," she agreed with a genuine smile. "It sounds delightful."

Chapter Thirty-one

"This is purely a waste of time, if you ask me."

"So who's asking you?"

Pete Saunders glanced sideways at the new man. He was a strange son of a bitch. He went by the name of Angel, just Angel. It was supposed to be his last name and probably was. Who'd pick such a name if they had the choice? But he didn't look like an angel, not by any means. Oh, he was tidy enough in appearance. Shaved every morning, cut his own hair, and neatly too; cleaned his own clothes when there was no laundry around he could take them to. A real stickler about his appearance, Angel was, just like the boss.

But you didn't seem to notice such things about him, not right off anyway. First you'd see that scar he had running from his chin to his ear along the jawline, as if someone had tried to cut his throat but missed by a few inches. Then you'd see his eyes, black as sin, cold, ruthless, predatory even. You couldn't look into them for very long and not wonder if your days hadn't come to an end.

He wasn't all that tall, but that was another thing you didn't seem to notice, not right off. He always wore a long mackintosh slicker that nearly scraped the ground, and large silver spurs that warned he was coming and made mincemeat of his horse when he was in a hurry. But he rarely hurried about anything. Slow and easy were his movements, and his patience seemed boundless. You never knew what he was thinking either, for he was disturbingly quiet most of the time and never smiled. Even the cold, steely-eyed Englishman had been known to twitch his lips on occasion, but not this Angel.

He'd been picked up in Benson along with two ex-members of the Clanton bunch who didn't want any part of the ongoing feud with the Earps, especially after the Tombstone shoot-out and the new talk of revenge. Dewane had gone to Benson to find a tracker after they'd lost the duchess and her party between there and Tucson. They'd ridden all the way to Tucson first, however, before figuring out that they'd been duped somewhere along the way. With four days wasted, the boss had been pissed some, enough to backhand Pete right off his horse as if it were all his fault.

Pete hadn't forgotten that . . . well, how could he? The bruise on his butt-bone hadn't had a chance to fade with all the hard riding they'd done, and the pink spot on his lip where the scab had only recently fallen off was still tender. He'd almost parted company from this bunch then and there, except Dewane had pointed out where the blame really lay, with that wily half-breed the duchess had hired on. Pete wanted that bastard himself now for making him look bad, and figured the only way he'd get a chance at him was to stick with the Englishman a while more. But with the way things were going, and the boss's new plan — which didn't call for taking out the half-breed just yet, and did call for a helluva lot of patience — it didn't look like he'd get what he wanted.

Patience and revenge didn't mix, leastways not for him. He'd had two clean shots at that breed already, but had been warned off both times. They had to give the new plan a chance first, though Pete was of the opinion the plan had about as much going for it as a snowball in hell.

Revenge wasn't worth all this aggravation, it surely wasn't. He was already regretting not taking off when he'd had the chance. Now they were in New Mexico, where he didn't know a soul, and it was a long ride back to

Arizona. And Angel, whom he was unlucky enough to be riding with today, was getting sarcastic. If he too was losing patience, Pete could anticipate becoming buzzard fodder by sundown.

"Pull up, Saunders," Angel said suddenly.

Pete felt his heart trip over, considering what he'd just been thinking. But when he followed Angel's gaze, he saw what Angel did — two specks kicking up dust in the far-off distance.

"I don't believe it," Pete said. "You think he's finally come through after all this time?"

Angel didn't bother to answer, and Pete didn't press his luck by asking again; they'd know soon enough. He followed the older man to a clump of sagebrush that would keep them from being noticed until they were ready to be noticed.

The deal had been that they'd be waiting with the money, day or night, about a quarter mile east of the road and a good three miles behind. The distance was necessary for them to avoid being spotted by anyone who might drop back, like the half-breed, to make a wide sweep of the area. The boss remained with the others even farther back, so that when they camped each night, there was at least a day's distance separating the two groups.

Each day two of their number would ride

ahead for the rendezvous. Each day they returned empty-handed. The only reason the Englishman hadn't abandoned the plan after two weeks was that he was really savoring the idea of having the woman delivered to him, of seeing to her disposal personally. Getting rid of the half-breed so one of his own men could be a replacement wasn't as desirable as long as he had this other option, since it was doubtful that whoever was sent in would be able to get her away from her guards, but would have to try to kill her in her own camp.

After ten minutes of hard squinting, Pete finally decided it wasn't a long coat he saw flapping on one of the riders approaching them, but a woman's green skirts. "It's really her, ain't it?"

He wasn't actually asking Angel for confirmation, but speaking aloud in surprise. He'd really figured they'd been wasting their time.

Angel answered, however. "That's red hair under that funny-looking hat."

Pete squinted even harder. "Jeeze, you got good eyes. I can't make out no hat, much less the hair under it." But it wasn't long before he could.

Jocelyn was beginning to wonder about this little jaunt that was taking her farther and farther away from her people. She and Miles had ridden several miles already, but there was still no sign of a meadow, valley, or any other scenic spot worth seeing. It came to her mind, belatedly, that Miles might have had some other motive for luring her away — like holding her for ransom. After all, she had dashed his plans for gaining her wealth legally. Mightn't he now think to do it illegally? And she had made it easy for him because of a foolish bit of guilt.

Once the doubt entered her mind, other possibilities sprang to light. What if he hadn't believed her about losing her wealth if she married? Could he be taking her away to get her to agree to a marriage? She shuddered, refusing to think how he might manage that. Coercion came in many forms, none of them pleasant.

That was the thought that had her jerking back on her reins to bring Sir George to a prancing halt. Miles stopped beside her with more ease due to his less spirited mount.

"Is something wrong?"

The innocent inquiry, the concerned expression, had her feeling foolish, but not foolish enough to go on. "Just a headache that's getting out of hand. I'm afraid I'll have to forgo this scenic wonder of yours."

"But it's not much farther," he protested.

So much for that concerned expression, she thought in disgust, annoyed enough to quirk a

brow at him. "Really? All I see ahead is . . ."
Two men moving out from behind a bush not
more than thirty feet in front of them made
her finish with, "Friends of yours?"

Even as she said it she was reaching for her
rifle. Miles' hand came down over hers on the
stock, pinching her fingers against the wood.
She glared at him, only to discover he had
drawn his revolver, which was pointed at her
chest.

"Don't do anything stupid, Duchess," he
warned as he yanked the rifle out of its scabbard and tossed it away.

"You mean, more than I've already done?"
she bit out furiously.

The two men were moving toward them. If
Miles didn't have that blasted gun aimed at
her at such close range, she would have put
her heels to Sir George. But she knew when
she was outmaneuvered. And to think that
this possibility hadn't occurred to her even
once. But how could it with Miles involved? It
was simply inconceivable that Longnose had
gotten to him. When? How? Yet there was no
doubt in her mind whose men these were, or
that Miles had led her directly to them.

"You really gave me no choice with your
unexpected revelation, Duchess," Miles remarked in a low voice just before the two men
reached them. "I would have preferred to

350

have it all, but the five thousand I've been promised will have to suffice."

"Am I supposed to feel sorry that you have to settle for so little? Good Lord, what an utter ass you are!"

He flushed nearly scarlet. "Whatever they want with you, they're welcome to you!"

It was more than galling that he didn't even know what his Judas money was for, but she didn't think it would have made any difference if he did. She knew, but fortunately, she was too enraged by his avarice and her own stupidity to worry about it just yet. Besides, she was almost certain she wouldn't be killed immediately, for she doubted either of the two men was her nemesis. As long as they had her, it was logical to suppose Longnose would want to be present for her execution. After all, he'd worked toward this end too long to be merely told about it.

"So they're welcome to me, are they? And how do you propose to explain my absence to my guards? Did you merely misplace me, or have I met with some dire accident?"

"A fall into the river ought to do it," he replied sullenly.

"Ah, very convenient. But you'd better hope your performance is better than it's been these past weeks. If even one of my people doubt your story, you can be certain you and your sister won't be riding off with your ill-gotten gains."

Suddenly he offered her a smug smile. "You were fooled that Maura was my sister, weren't you? She's actually my mistress."

That information threw her, but only for a moment. "Very clever, Mr. Dryden, but the only part of your scheme that *was* convincing."

"Bullshit!" he snapped. "You believed everything!"

"Just as you did?" It was her turn to smile. "I hate to disappoint you, you fortune-hunting miscreant, but I lied to you today. You don't really think I would have married someone as transparent as you, do you?"

Satisfied to see by his paling complexion that he understood what she meant, she turned her attention to the two men who had reached them by now, heard what she'd said — and also understood it. She didn't care. Dryden didn't deserve to ride away thinking he'd salvaged something from his thwarted schemes. Now he knew his failure to win her was through no fault but his own.

"Didja hear that, Angel?" the younger of the two men asked his partner. "He keeps us waitin' all this time so he could court her. If you ask me, he don't deserve the money."

"So who asked you?" the darker, more dangerous-looking of the two replied. "I didn't figure to waste that much money on him anyway."

Before the others realized what that implied, the man calmly drew the Colt .45 from his hip and shot Miles Dryden right between the eyes, then just as calmly put the gun away.

Jocelyn had her opportunity to flee now that there weren't any weapons trained on her, but she was too shocked by this unexpected turn of events to take advantage of it. One glance at Miles had been enough to ascertain he was dead.

She didn't watch as he slowly slid off his horse and hit the ground, but kept her eyes on his killer, who showed no emotion at all over what he'd just done. She also didn't notice that his companion was nearly as shocked as she was, or that the green velvet of her riding habit was spotted with blood. All she could do was stare at the man, aware that she was at his mercy, aware that he had none. Perhaps he was Longnose after all.

Chapter Thirty-two

He wasn't John Longnose, of course he wasn't. She'd heard him speak in a Western drawl, after all. And his talkative, grinning companion kept referring to him as Angel, as well as alluding to the boss, who *was* undoubtedly Longnose. But Miles Dryden's killer might as well have been the Englishman, for that was whom he was taking her to.

They had been riding for several hours before the numbness began to wear off and Jocelyn's mind had started functioning again. Naturally enough, she was rather horrified at first to find herself sitting on *his* horse, in front of him, his arms caging her on both sides. But after another hour or so of listening to Saunders' busy chatter and Angel's noncommittal grunts in reply, she was less frightened, at least of these two.

Saunders was just a kid, anyway, whose grinning countenance made him seem harmless. And as long as Angel was behind her where she couldn't see him, his hard, cruel features couldn't disturb her. But not for a moment did she forget where she was going and what was awaiting her when she got there.

It wasn't a pleasant feeling, knowing you were going to die. The only reason it hadn't turned her into a gibbering idiot was her natural optimism. Until she breathed her last breath, there was hope that *something* would happen to save her. She could escape, fight back, be rescued. Her rifle was gone, but she wasn't completely weaponless. On her person were numerous long hairpins excellent for poking out eyes, two very hard boots, and ten sharp nails. And she had the past to bolster her courage, the many times Longnose had been foiled before.

Regardless of all that optimism, though, it still took her a while to garner the nerve to address the man behind her. When she did, it was with the most pertinent question first. "How long do I have?"

"For what?"

"To live."

"I wouldn't worry about it," he replied offhandedly in a slow drawl.

Jocelyn was rendered momentarily speechless after that, but gritted her teeth in pique. "I'm not."

"Then why ask?"

"So I'll know when to toss you off this horse and make my escape, of course," she retorted testily.

He laughed, surprising her. "You're all right, lady. But I already figured you had to be something special to get a favor asked of me."

"You're doing this as a favor?" she nearly choked out.

"The pay's good too."

What could she say to that? The man was obviously without conscience. Or was the debt he owed so great that the favor asked of him in return couldn't be refused? For some reason, though, she felt the man couldn't be coerced into doing something he didn't want to do, not for any reason. So indeed, he had to be plainly unconscionable.

That was a discouraging thought that kept her silent for a while. After all, the man represented one of her hopes. He was the stronger, more dangerous of her escort to Longnose. If he could be talked out of turning her over to the Englishman, and talked into taking her back to her people instead, she didn't think Saunders could stop him. But how did she reach someone who told her not to worry about the time she had left to live, who was escorting her to her death as a *favor*, for God's sake? The answer refused to come to her unless . . .

"You *do* know that the Englishman means to kill me, don't you?"

"He hasn't made a secret of it."

So much for thinking he might not know what he was escorting her to. "Do you know why?"

"What's it matter?"

"Nothing to you, obviously."

She heard him laugh again, and again gritted her teeth, but this time to stop herself from calling him every vile, loathsome name she could think of. Unconscionable? Inhuman was more like it. And they called the Indians the savages in this part of the country.

"Since you're such a veritable font of information," she began again in a tight voice, "would you mind telling me how Longnose got to Miles Dryden?"

"Who's Longnose?"

"The Englishman."

"So that's his name." He sounded surprised. "No wonder he didn't want it known."

Jocelyn made a sound of exasperation. "I haven't the faintest notion what the man's blasted name is, nor do you, obviously, but what the devil does *that* matter? I asked you how he got to Dryden. You remember him? The man you killed today?"

"So she has a temper, too."

It was a statement, not a question, so she

357

threw one right back at him, "He understands English."

Another chuckle greeted that dry retort. She really was amusing him for some reason, while he was frustrating her to the point of screaming. But she absolutely refused to rant or rave, no more than she would beg or cry, none of which would accomplish anything, she was sure.

"Dryden?" she prompted once more.

"Why do you want to know?"

"He was suspected of many things, but not once of being one of your little band of miscreants. After all, he wasn't the usual sort of riffraff that Longnose hires . . . no offense intended."

"No, of course not."

She ignored the interruption, though she was pleased to note his thick skin was pierceable. "He was merely a harmless fortune hunter, not a murderer," she pointed out.

"Old Dewane, he seemed to think otherwise, which was why he approached your harmless fortune hunter when he recognized him, before he even cleared it with the boss. And seems he was right on the nose, since your *harmless* fortune hunter came through for us, didn't he?"

"Was this before or after he'd been invited to join our group?"

"After. We caught up with you in Silver City, the morning after you got there. Dewane and his brother were checking out your hotel to see if there was any way to get to you when he spotted Dryden talking to your lady friend in the lobby. The rest you can figure out for yourself."

And she could, not that any of it really mattered except to satisfy her curiosity. You had to have opportunity to learn from your mistakes, and these men were determined to see that she didn't have any more opportunities, of any kind. Or were they — truly determined, that is? Was their loyalty unshakable, or could it be bought?

She decided not to wait to find out. "I can pay you more than the Englishman."

"I know."

"I'm talking about a fortune." There was no answer. "You don't care?"

"No."

"How can you say that?" she demanded incredulously. "You just killed a man for money."

"You talk too much."

"Well, you did, so money must mean something to you."

"Not much."

"Then why did you kill him?"

"You talk too much," he repeated.

"And you not enough!" she retorted.

"Look, lady, it was like this. The man deserved to die. He turned you over to us, didn't he?"

"He didn't know for what purpose."

"Don't kid yourself," he told her in disgust. "He was told you wouldn't be around to point the finger at him afterward. He merely tried his own scheme first — one, I might add, he's made into a profession."

"What do you mean?"

"According to Dewane, he was a card cheat who'd been run out of just about every town west of the Missouri before he changed his career to marrying old widows for their money, then getting rid of them when the money ran out."

"Divorcing them, you mean?"

"No."

"Oh."

"*Now* will you shut up?"

Her jaw was getting sore from so much teeth grinding. "If you don't care for my conversation, sir, you can put me back on my own horse."

"Nice try, lady," was all he said to that.

She did finally fall silent. She wished they had let Sir George go, as they had Miles' horse. She hated to think what would happen to him if her luck actually did desert her this time. She almost asked Angel if he would keep Sir George, but decided he would make no better owner for the magnificent stallion than Longnose would.

Saunders, who had been riding a short distance ahead of them, eager to get where they were going, topped a small rise and let out a shout. Instantly, Jocelyn's blood turned cold, suspecting what she would find on the other side of that rise. She wasn't wrong. There was a steeper drop, enough to conceal the six men in the process of setting up a camp — until now.

Saunders' shout had stopped them at the various tasks they had been doing, so that when Angel topped the rise, they were all looking up in that direction, and every eye was riveted on his prize.

Involuntarily, Jocelyn leaned back into Angel's chest. Thoughts of escape weren't very bolstering at the moment; weren't very conceivable either. All she could do was wonder in what manner Longnose meant to kill her. Would he just shoot her to get it over with quickly, or would he want her to suffer a while first?

She saw him right off. He stood apart from the others, tall, slim, ramrod straight, both hands resting on a silver-handled cane. He obviously hadn't been involved with the camp setup as the others were, an activity likely too menial for his tastes. His clothes also stood him apart from the others. He was wearing not only a dove-gray three-piece suit, but a stylish overcoat of worsted wool as well. He was also a good ten years older than any of his companions, somewhere in his early forties, she would guess.

So this was her nemesis at long last. He didn't look like a cold-blooded killer to her. His men all fitted the mold, but he didn't. He looked perfectly harmless, in fact, and so out of place it was ludicrous.

Jocelyn might have smiled at that thought, for she was rather out of place herself in her heavy velvet riding habit, frothy lace neck scarf, and tall black riding hat, but she didn't feel like smiling. Longnose might not be what she had expected, but he was still the man who had doggedly pursued her for three years with his loathsome intent.

Jocelyn tensed as Angel headed down the slope to join his friends, who were no longer staring in silent awe. Some of their comments broke through her frantic thoughts, and even made her take her eyes off Longnose long enough to notice them. They were all her enemies by association, and if she did somehow manage to get out of this, it wouldn't hurt to know them by sight.

But looking them over only depressed her. They were a hard, dangerous-looking bunch, well suited to this line of work. She'd get no help there, and, she realized now, she really would need some help. She hadn't thought there would be so many of them, or that several of them would be looking at her with lustful gazes. Dear Lord, her courage was fast deserting her, as were her hopes of escape.

"Well, hot damn! I didn't think she'd look like that, did you?"

"Ya whar 'spectin' an ol' broad maybe?"

"As a matter of fact — "

"You can forget what you owe me, boss," someone else yelled out. "I'll take the horse!"

There were a few chuckles, but they didn't stop the personal comments that were unnerving Jocelyn. Unconsciously, she pressed even closer to Angel as he moved slowly toward Longnose.

"Damn, I ain't never seen hair that red."

"Too skinny."

"Who cares?"

"She gonna get passed around first or what? That's all I wanna know."

It was a question more than one of them wanted answered, apparently, for they looked toward the Englishman. But he said nothing yet. He was still staring at Jocelyn, and he was smiling now.

That stiffened her spine. So he was gloating, was he? And he was thinking of handing her over to these lowlifes first for their amusement?

She was ready when Angel stopped and lowered her to the ground. If Longnose had been just a bit closer, he would have had the point of her boot laid to his chin. That would have forced his hand. But there were other ways to provoke him into killing her immediately, before his men got serious in their demands. She was not about to suffer through a mauling and *then* be killed. That was asking too much.

But the moment Jocelyn determinedly started toward her countryman, she was whipped back around to face Angel. He had dismounted behind her, and she saw with some surprise that he wasn't nearly as tall as he had seemed in the saddle. Seeing him for the first time so close, she realized he wasn't much older than she was. But there was a wiry strength hidden beneath that rain slicker that fell to his boots. She felt it in the steely grip on her arm. And he was angry. That she saw in those cold black eyes of his.

The feeling was confirmed by a soft, furious hiss that startled her. "Don't do it."

"What?" she asked warily.

"You were going to sock him one, weren't you?"

364

Her eyes flared incredulously. "How the devil did you know?"

"I could feel you preparing for battle."

She stiffened again, and demanded of him in a terse whisper, "Let go."

"Guess I was wrong when I figured you had some smarts. Figured you'd be working on delaying tactics rather than suicide, to give your guards a chance to find you in time."

She managed to jerk her arm away. "It's a matter of priority, of what one holds most dear."

"And you hold pride dearer than life?"

She blushed to hear it put that way, and to hear his disdain too. Blast the man, he was right. She should be willing to do anything to put off the inevitable. Was there really a chance she might be found in time?

Angel seemed to read her mind. "Don't worry about it. Today's not your day to die, honey."

She opened her mouth to demand he explain that cryptic remark, but another voice spoke first. "So good of you to join us, Your Grace."

She turned around slowly and waited until Longnose had closed the distance between them. She had to look up now, but that was all right. For some reason, even though she didn't understand what Angel had meant, she wasn't afraid with him standing behind her.

"Not at all, Longnose." She gave him a regal nod. "I should thank *you* for inviting me. I would have been quite devastated to have missed your little gathering."

For one reason or another, his men found her remarks hilarious. He certainly didn't. His cheeks suffused with heated color, and his icy gray eyes promised her a truly gruesome death. She had provoked him, and without having to damage her hand doing it. But before he did anything about it, she heard Angel mutter a vile oath behind her, and then she was forcibly moved aside.

Elliot's hands itched to get around her neck, but he wasn't so far immersed in that fantasy that he didn't notice Angel's movement. The man now stood partially in front of the duchess and was very casually folding back his coat to allow easy access to the gun on his hip.

The significance of that was not lost on the older man, but it didn't worry him in the least. Angel was only one man in eight, after all.

Elliot should never have taken him on in the first place, but it was rather late to concede that point. He'd been aware when he met him that he might have trouble with this one, a man so different from the others. But he was the tracker Owen had found in Benson, and he'd picked up the duchess's trail almost immediately, enabling them with some hard riding to catch up with her.

There was really no need for trouble now. Elliot was, in fact, grateful to Angel for distracting him. To end this glorious triumph in a burst of rage was not the least bit fitting, nor what he had envisioned. The duchess deserved much more than that. So if the lad wanted her, if that was the reason for his subtle challenge, he could have her. They could all bloody well have her. And when they were done with their sport, he would slowly choke the life from her while he had her himself.

Elliot smiled, savoring that thought, and was further delighted to see the duchess disconcerted by it. Good. Her previous audacity had been unexpected and not at all appropriate. He wanted to see her fear, needed to see it.

"You have a bizarre sense of humor, Your Grace. I trust it won't desert you too soon." And then Elliot dismissed her for the moment, asking Angel, "Was there any difficulty with Mr. Dryden?"

"None to speak of."

"Excellent. I was beginning to wonder about him, but he's done his part admirably and will now further aid us by buying us time."

"How's that?"

"By sending her people to look for her in the wrong direction, of course. After all, it's to his benefit now, as well as ours, that she isn't found."

"It ain't gonna matter much to him," Pete volunteered at that point. "Angel killed him."

There was a long pause before Elliot said, "I see," then another long moment before he added, "Well, so much for the additional time element. I assume you at least made good time getting back here?"

"Good enough," Angel drawled. "Now you answer me one. Why is it you never said she was a good-looking woman?"

"Because that fact is quite irrelevant."

"Oh, it's relevant, all right. Very relevant. A pretty thing like this shouldn't ought to be wasted."

Jocelyn slapped his hand away when his finger grazed her cheek to the accompaniment of those words. So that was what he had meant by saying she wouldn't die today. It was almost dark. No one was going to find her in the dark. These men would have all night long to rape her, and Angel undoubtedly meant to be the first.

Longnose must have thought so too, for he was smiling again. "There's time enough for that, certainly. I would have suggested it my-

368

self. Just be careful with her. The privilege of killing her is mine, after all."

If Jocelyn were prone to swooning, those words would have had her collapsing. As it was, she was overcome with panic. Sir George was her only chance now. If she could just get to him, she'd earn a swift, merciful bullet in the back, for that would be the only way they could then stop her.

But Angel must have read her thoughts again. His hand clamped on her arm like a vise, keeping her at his side. She would have killed him in that moment if she had the means. She was in fact reaching for one of her hairpins when his quiet voice arrested the movement.

"It don't sound to me like you took my meaning," he was telling Longnose. "I've decided to keep her — until I get tired of her."

"That's out of the question!"

Angel's voice turned softly menacing. "I wasn't asking your permission, Englishman."

The older man's face mottled with color again. He even raised his cane, which was a mistake.

What ensued was becoming quite familiar to Jocelyn, seeing guns drawn at the blink of an eye. She only jumped slightly when the shot was fired, but to her everlasting disgust, Longnose was still standing there. Angel's bullet had merely shot the cane out of his hand.

But the man didn't have the sense to calm down even then. "Mr. Owen!" he bellowed.

That gentleman apparently had more sense. "Ferget it, boss. I ain't tanglin' with the likes o' him."

And when Longnose glanced at the others, he found pretty much the same opinion. One by one, gun belts were slowly being dropped to the ground. It was only when Jocelyn noticed that Angel's gun was pointing from man to man that she realized why. Not one of them cared to try their luck at disarming him, even though they so outnumbered him. Incredible. But then she wasn't the only one who had witnessed how swift he was, or how accurate.

"Bring that horse over here, Saunders." Angel ordered, indicating Sir George.

The boy quickly complied. Jocelyn almost smiled, her relief was so great. Until she recalled that she wasn't actually being rescued, but was merely exchanging one bad situation for another. The odds were better now, though, and her life was no longer in imminent danger, so she supposed she had reason to be grateful to her unexpected savior.

She changed her mind about that, however, at his parting words to Longnose. "For your purposes, man, you can consider her dead.

Her people won't find her where I'm taking her, and when I'm done with her . . . "

"You'll kill her?"

"Why not?" Angel replied with a shrug. "I've got Dryden's money as payment in advance."

Chapter Thirty-three

Jocelyn had assumed she would be put on Sir George, even if Angel was to ride behind her again to assure she wouldn't take off with the stallion. There was a need for speed to quit the area, after all. But after walking both horses up the rise so that he could keep his gun trained on the group below, Angel mounted his own horse and pulled her up in front of him again. Her stallion was merely led along, as Saunders had done before.

There was one surprising moment, however, just as they took off, when he asked her, "That rifle you carried, did you know how to use it?" Since she didn't feel like talking to him then, she gave him no more than a curt nod, only to be amazed when he placed his rifle in her hands with the order, "Shoot anything that appears over that rise."

"I'd rather shoot you."

"Really? Well, save that urge for some other time, honey."

She saw the sense in that, and after resting

the rifle on his shoulder to steady it, did fire off a few shots. Whether it was heads or rocks she shot at, though, she didn't know. The deep rose light of the setting sun was too misleading for her to tell. But there *had* been answering shots that continued long after they were out of range.

She didn't feel that they were safe, however, until Angel took the rifle back. And then he frightened the devil out of her by swinging her around to the back of the horse, without any warning. He rode faster then, forcing her to hold on for dear life. Not once did she consider letting go of the fist-holds she had on his slicker. Even if she could hide with the oncoming dark, with the way her luck had gone today, she likely would break her neck in the fall.

But he did slow up when full dark was upon them, and even when the moon appeared later to give him enough light to avoid shrubs and large rocks, he kept to the slower pace. She had to wonder about that, until it occurred to her that anyone following wouldn't risk a faster pace either, at least not until morning.

She had no idea where they were going. He'd been riding toward the mountains in the east before he changed her position on the horse, but he didn't seem to keep to any direct line. And once the sky blackened, she lost her sense of direction. If there were mountains ahead of them, she could no longer see them.

"How long do you think that guard of yours will look for you tonight?"

Jocelyn was surprised by the question, coming after such a long silence. Was he worried? She certainly hoped so. She certainly wasn't going to volunteer any information that might aid him.

"I'd be more concerned over the Englishman if I were you," she told him. "You don't think he's going to trust you to keep me from escaping, or to kill me when you're done with me, do you? No, he'll be the one to follow, but now to kill us both."

He said nothing to that, nor did he ask his question again, leaving her rather deflated that he didn't give her another opportunity to be uncooperative. But about twenty minutes later he did, when he reached back to try and grab her hands to force them around him. She resisted that quite nicely.

And gained his anger, if his tone was any indication as he snarled over his shoulder, "I'd be nice to me if I were you."

Jocelyn was not impressed. "You don't intimidate me, Mr. Angel. You might as well kill me now, because I will *not* be your mistress or your whore."

"What about my wife?"

That threw her. "*You* want to marry me? But money means nothing to you, as I recall."

"What has money got to do with it?"

What an absurd question. "Very well, suppose you tell me why marriage has entered your mind."

"Besides the obvious reasons, a man's got the right to beat his wife."

"That isn't funny!" she snapped, realizing by his sudden laughter that he had only been teasing her. "Odious man," she muttered to herself.

"Where's that sense of humor you antagonized the Englishman with?"

"Gone to sleep, obviously, which is what I'd like to do. Are you going to ride all night?"

"You want me to stop and wait for my friends to catch up?"

His humor was getting on her nerves. "Don't forget my own people."

"Your guards are probably lost in the hills, honey. There's no trackers among them. 'Course, there's that half-breed guide of yours," he added in a speculative tone. "Would he bother to look for you?"

With the abominable way Colt had been treating her lately? "No," she said without thinking, then realized she should have lied. "But I wouldn't discount my guard so easily."

He chuckled in answer, which was really

too much. Jocelyn started to give him a serious volley on what she thought of him, when she heard the horse approaching. With a gasp she looked behind her to see a gray blur racing toward them at a breakneck speed. Her heart nearly lodged in her throat.

"We're about to be overtaken!"

"I know."

"You — well, do something!"

He did. He stopped, turning his horse about. He even dismounted and pulled her down with him. But he didn't draw his gun, didn't reach for his rifle. She stared at him as if he were mad. She didn't wait around to see if he was. She started running, and got about fifteen yards before she was yanked off her feet. Her frightened scream blasted across the countryside, only to be cut short when she was slammed down on another horse.

"Are you all right?"

Jocelyn blinked, doubting her ears, but it really was *his* voice. She looked up to confirm it, saw his fierce, beautiful face, and wailed, "Oh, Colt!"

She burst into tears for some foolish reason, burying her face against his chest. He came to a stop, and then his arms wrapped more fully around her. For a moment she couldn't breathe, she was squeezed so tightly. The man obviously didn't know his own strength.

"Are you all right?" he repeated.

"Yes."

"Then why are you crying?"

"I don't know!" And she cried louder — until she heard Angel laughing in the distance. She stiffened then and demanded, "Where's your gun?"

"What for?"

"I'm going to shoot that wretched man!"

"No, you're not," Colt said laconically. "I might, but you're not."

With that he jerked his mount around and trotted back to where Angel was waiting — and still chuckling. Jocelyn didn't understand the man's humor, but she was infuriated by it. Didn't he realize she had been rescued, and this time *really* rescued? And then it dawned on her. It truly was over, now that Colt was here. He wouldn't let anything else happen to her. He might not like her anymore . . . who was she kidding? He had *never* liked her. So he might like her even less now, but he would still protect her. And no one could make her feel quite as safe and protected as he could.

She almost felt sorry for Angel, who didn't realize his danger yet. Her annoyance with him dissolved with that thought. After all, he hadn't hurt her, had in fact kept her from harm. Colt might have gotten there in time to prevent Longnose from killing her, but he wouldn't have been in time to prevent the other . . . Angel had done that.

She had to tell him, especially after that remark about his possibly shooting Angel. "Ah, Colt —"

"Not now, Duchess."

"But, Colt . . ."

She was too late. He dropped off his horse before it even stopped and only then, watching him, did she realize that he was furious. Angel must have realized it too. She'd seen both men draw before, and couldn't actually say who was faster.

And then Angel was being lifted off the ground, a good half foot. "If you were a little bigger, you son of a bitch, I'd beat the shit out of you!"

"Ah, come on, Colt, I did what you asked."

"Like hell you did!" That with a shake. "You were supposed to be there to help out if she was brought in, not be the one to *bring* her in."

"I had it covered!"

"You're damn lucky I had *you* covered!" Colt growled before he let Angel go with a shove.

"I figured that was you drawing their fire. When'd you get there?"

"Not soon enough to stop you from taking her over that rise," Colt said in disgust, but then sounded almost anguished when he added, "Damn you, Angel. If I'd found out about that stunt afterward, I'd probably kill you now. To put her in danger like that . . . I still ought to beat the crap out of you."

"All right," Angel said on a conciliatory note. "Maybe it wasn't the smartest move. But it wasn't that dangerous either, Colt. I've been with that bunch long enough to know what to expect of them. Half are nothing but cowards, and the rest wouldn't know their ass from a hole in the ground."

"But why the hell did you do it?"

"So she'd know her enemy. Everyone's got that right, Colt. He's had the advantage all this time because she wouldn't know him if she passed him in the street. Now she knows him."

"You should have just killed the bastard and saved me the trouble," Colt muttered.

"You didn't ask me to do that." Angel grinned. "Besides, I figure that's her right too."

Colt's anger burst again, hearing that. "Who the hell do you think she is, another Jessie? She's a damned duchess, for Christ's sake! They don't go around killing people when they can hire someone else to do it."

"I wouldn't be too sure about that, Colt Thunder," Jocelyn said in a tightly controlled voice. "Would you care to offer me your gun to find out?"

They had both obviously forgotten about her during their discourse, if their expressions were any indication. Angel flinched. Colt swung around, scowling. But damned if he didn't toss her his gun. The least she could do was cock it and point it at him.

"I ought to, you know." She was seething with anger, not enough to shoot him, but enough to shout, "Why the devil didn't you tell me you had sent someone into that nest of vipers? Do you know that your blasted friend didn't once let on he was there at your request? A *favor,* he mentioned, but he let me think it was owed to Longnose. And do you know what he assured Longnose he would do with me? I was to be used until he tired of me; then, of course, he would kill me."

"Whaaat?" Angel complained innocently when Colt's scowl came back to him. "I had to tell him something to make him think twice about coming right after us. Did I know you were there to hold them off?"

"So why didn't you set her straight once you were out of there?"

"Well, shoot, Colt, I figured she knew it was just a bunch of hogwash I was feeding him. I teased her enough about it. I told her she had nothing to worry about. And she

380

wasn't afraid of me. The only time she was upset at all was right after I sent that two-faced Dryden to his Maker. He really turned my stomach, handing her over to us the way he did."

Colt's gaze came back to Jocelyn then, and she had the feeling his anger changed direction too. He was now furious at her for some reason, but she couldn't imagine why.

"Well, splendid," she said on a sigh. "So now I'm at fault, am I? Care to tell me why?"

"You have to ask? You let that bastard work his lies on you, and then you have the gall to be upset over his death. I seem to recall you didn't even bat an eye when I killed one of those scum for you."

She still didn't understand what he was objecting to. "I didn't *know* that chap you killed. I'd never set eyes on him before. Besides, you killed to protect me. Angel killed in cold blood. I hope I know the difference."

His lips thinned out, letting her know she hadn't appeased him. Angel was frowning now, too, at her allegation, but didn't care to argue with her about it with Colt there. Colt was too touchy by half about her. But he felt the need for justification. Cold-blooded, hell.

"Did you know about Dryden, Colt?" he asked, drawing his attention away from the duchess.

"Not everything, obviously," Colt replied brusquely. "When was he recruited?"

"When you all were laid over in Silver City. He agreed to bring the duchess to us, which is why there was no need to get close enough where you could spot us. They said he killed rich old widow women . . . after he married them. You blame me for taking him out?"

"I'd have killed him myself just for handing her over to you. Christ, I wasn't expecting that. I'd finally remembered where I'd seen him before, though. He was run out of Cheyenne a few years back for getting caught cheating at cards. I seem to recall there was a widow preparing for a wedding who was a mite upset at his leaving."

Jocelyn's eyes flared for a moment. "And you didn't bother to tell me that, either?"

"And ruin your little romance? I didn't think you'd appreciate that too much."

Was that *jealousy* snarling at her? The thought was so incredulous it . . . it dissolved instantly. Of course he wasn't. He was likely ticked off because he hadn't known all the facts about Dryden. But she'd had too exhausting a day to put up with his surliness another moment, or Angel's humor. That miserable wretch was grinning again!

"Bother this," she said in disgust, and tossed Colt's gun back to him before the temptation became too great. She ignored him then to address Angel. "Protocol demands that I thank you for your assistance, sir, no matter how despicable the manner of it." He grimaced, but she wasn't quite finished with him. "So allow me to wish you a long and uneventful life — and may you drop dead from sheer boredom. Good evening, gentlemen."

Without another look at either of them, she hooked her leg over the uncomfortable horn of Colt's saddle. She didn't even try to locate the stirrup for support, since it was adjusted to his long legs, not hers. But the precarious perch didn't change her mind. She rode off.

Colt didn't move, prompting Angel to comment casually, "She's going to break her neck sitting that horse sideways like that."

"It's the way she rides."

"Not on a Western saddle, it ain't."

Colt swore beneath his breath before he shouted, "Come back here, Duchess!"

Of course she ignored him. But he still didn't move to follow her. He let out a yipping yell instead, then waited to hear her give out a curse or two herself when his horse turned around. The horse did stop and turn, but instead of cursing, the duchess calmly slid off him. And then Colt heard that shrill whistle he'd heard once before but forgotten about, and was nearly knocked down by her stallion as the animal took off in answer to her call.

He cursed a blue streak then as he ran out to meet the Appaloosa on its way back to him, knowing full well hers would reach her first and he'd never catch up with that lightning bolt she called a horse. Angel mounted up in his own good time to follow, quietly laughing his head off.

Chapter Thirty-four

"I hope you know I aged ten years."

"I likely picked up a few myself," Jocelyn told the countess as she sank deeper into the little tub that had been brought to the room they shared.

"If only I — "

"Oh, Vana, please, *please* stop blaming yourself! No one could have known what a truly despicable man he was beneath all that charm. Colt didn't know what he was capable of, and he knew Dryden was no good."

"Well, I'm glad that nice Angel chap dispatched him, I truly am. He deserved no less."

"Nice? Angel?" Jocelyn choked. "That man — "

"Saved you, dear."

"At the expense of my peace of mind!"

The countess clicked her tongue. "Don't quibble means. It's the end result that counts."

"Colt was there," Jocelyn reminded her sullenly. "He wouldn't have let anyone touch me."

"But his friend didn't know that. His friend risked his life to get you out of there against great odds."

"His *friend* took me there to begin with!" Jocelyn retorted, having heard quite enough. "And, I might add, his friend never said he *was* his friend. Now, not another word about that wretched man. Colt had the right idea. He should have beat the crap out of him."

Vanessa's brows shot up, not only at Jocelyn's show of temper, but that *word*. "Crap?"

"I believe it means Angel wouldn't have walked away from the fight. You know, guts spilled and all that."

Vanessa's frown came quickly with the assumption that Jocelyn was merely being sarcastic. "That isn't funny, dear."

"I wasn't joking."

"Oh . . . well . . ."

Jocelyn waited, but that last had definitely silenced Vanessa. She went back to working her sampler with short, jabbing stitches that would likely have to be redone later. Jocelyn relaxed into the little tub as well as she could and closed her eyes. It was the first chance she'd actually had to relax since Longnose had gotten lucky — well, almost lucky.

She didn't like remembering how close it had been this time, nor did she like having an image to bring to mind of that horrid man.

But she had to allow Angel had been right in one respect. No matter how much it disturbed her to remember the Englishman's face, it was to her benefit that she could.

She had come upon her men that night shortly after the race to outdistance Colt had begun, but then she had almost expected that, since she realized with some surprise after she started that she was on the main road. Angel had been taking her back to her people all along. Colt had been right behind her, and although she had anticipated he would be furious enough to cause a scene, he had merely said to her, "Someone ought to do something about that temper of yours."

It was later that she learned Colt had been the only one to hear the shot that killed Dryden, which was why he'd been able to find her so quickly. Her men had gone out to search for her when she didn't return at the usual time, but they'd been forced to follow her trail into the hills first, and Angel was right again, there were no trackers among them.

Maura Dryden, or whatever her name really was, had disappeared by the time they got back to the wagons. Vanessa had assumed she had stolen a horse and left while it was still daylight, but she couldn't be sure. She and the other women had been too upset to take note. But it was concluded that Maura had likely panicked when Miles didn't return to report Jocelyn's supposed "accident" as he had planned to do. She must have assumed either that he had run out on her or that something had gone wrong. In either case, she'd been wise not to stay to find out.

Jocelyn wouldn't be surprised if she was hiding somewhere in Santa Fe, or perhaps back in that town they had avoided. She didn't think the woman would leave the area until she had learned what had befallen her lover. She didn't particularly care what became of Maura, as long as she never had to meet up with her again.

They had ridden straight for Santa Fe at Colt's suggestion, with only short stops long enough to rest the horses. It had not been pleasant sleeping in the coaches, but they had cut the time in half to reach the old town, leaving the Englishman likely still looking for her and Angel in the mountains. The rush hadn't really been necessary. He wouldn't attack with his small number. But it gave them the opportunity to lose him again. They could leave the trail now, take the railroad, or even let him pass them by.

But no decisions had been made yet. Jocelyn was hoping to discuss the matter with Colt, but the latest run-in with Longnose hadn't changed his habits. She hadn't seen him since it happened.

"You know, I suppose I must admit our guide did acquit himself rather well during that unpleasantness."

Jocelyn's eyes popped open. Good Lord, had Vanessa been milling that over all this time? If she had, then she had probably come to some sort of conclusion that Jocelyn was certain not to like.

"I thought so," Jocelyn agreed hesitantly — at least up until he got angry with her again for no apparent reason, she added to herself.

"I'm rather impressed with the way he went after you," Vanessa continued, "without wasting valuable time in coming for help, without knowing what he would be facing when he found you."

"He knew that Angel would be there."

"Actually, he didn't, if you'll recall. When he went back to Benson that night we camped so near it, and encountered his friend there, he only requested he make himself available to the Englishman if the opportunity arose. He had no way of knowing if Angel had succeeded in joining the brigands, or how many other men Longnose might have acquired between then and now."

Vanessa — defending Colt? Jocelyn really *didn't* want to know what this was leading u~ to. And yet for some reason she was pleas~

to hear Colt being praised, especially by her friend.

"Yes, well, he has never struck me as a man who might worry over odds." And then a twinkle appeared in Jocelyn's eyes. "Do you suppose it might have something to do with his heritage? After all, a good many of those stories we heard about Indians were of small numbers attacking large groups of settlers." Jocelyn had to force back the grin pulling at her lips on seeing Vanessa's quick frown over her observation.

"I believe it is nothing more than courage," Vanessa insisted.

Better and better. Colt was going to become marriage material if the countess kept this up. If he had a sixth sense, he ought to be on his way out of the territory by now.

"I wonder what's keeping Babette with that extra water?"

"Don't change the subject," Vanessa admonished.

"I wasn't. I never doubted Colt's courage, Vana. His sanity, maybe, but never his courage."

"Then why don't you ask Colt to go after Longnose?"

So there it was finally. Jocelyn had known he wouldn't like it. After their fight that ght she had behaved so wretchedly she could never ask Colt for another thing, certainly not to risk his life for her more than he already had.

"So it's 'Colt' now that you've found some use for him?"

Vanessa had the grace to look embarrassed. "I never said he wasn't useful, my dear, only that your particular use for him was ended."

"I don't like that word 'use.' *He* hates it."

"What?"

"He's been used quite enough, Vana."

"But this is different."

"I doubt he'd feel it is. Besides, the day I met him I asked if I could hire him to find Longnose and bring him in. He refused."

"That was before he took an intimate interest in you," Vanessa pointed out.

Heat stole into Jocelyn's cheeks, chasing away the chill from the cooling water. "I would never use our intimacy as leverage against him!"

"I wasn't suggesting — "

"Weren't you?"

They were both silent a moment, Jocelyn furiously so, Vanessa contrite.

"I'm sorry," Vanessa finally said. "It's just that I worry a great deal about you. Longnose has never been quite as successful before. The man had bungled his attempts so often, I'm afraid I began to think of him as an inco petent blunderhead, that he didn't present a really serious threat, just a nuisance. That has been proven false, however, since we came to this savage land, a place which seems to bring out the worse traits in its inhabitants."

"Or the best."

"Yes, well . . . if you don't want to impose on Colt any further, I can certainly understand that. Some men get the absurd notion that if you ask something of them, they can then demand anything they want of you in return, and I don't have to tell you what they most often ask for."

"Yes, I know." Jocelyn nodded sagely. "Dinner."

"No, dear," Vanessa began, but caught the teasing light in those green eyes and knew she was forgiven. "Dinner indeed . . . actually, for some men that just might be first choice. Have you noticed how many eating establishments in the West carry the advertisement 'Home-cooked meals'? That seems to be of particular importance in this country."

They were both laughing before the countess had finished, and still laughing when Babette burst in without knocking. Vanessa sobered first, remembering the last time the maid had come in like that, *and* looking like *that*, her blue eyes wide, her hands aflutter. *t again,* she groaned inwardly, but Babette's first words proved this was indeed a repeat performance on her part.

"Monsieur Thunder, he has been shot!"

Vanessa closed her eyes with a sigh — until she heard the splash. Then she recalled what else had happened the last time and shot out of her chair to barricade the door. And indeed, she got there only a moment before the duchess did.

"You are *not* — "

"Vana!"

The countess refused to budge. "She said he was shot, not dead. He's not dead, is he, Babette?"

"*Non,* madame."

"There, you see? There is no need to rush out of here in a state of panic, without clothes . . . or hadn't you noticed you're stark naked, dear?"

Jocelyn had already turned about to find her robe. Babette was bringing it forward. Vanessa knew it was pointless to suggest she clothe herself a bit more appropriately. Jocelyn barely had the robe drawn together before she was out the door.

Vanessa sighed once more and gave the maid an exasperated look. "Babette, I really must speak to you about this penchant you have developed for melodramatics."

Chapter Thirty-five

Jocelyn hadn't known which room was Colt's, but with a half dozen of her men standing in and about the open doorway, it wasn't hard to find. Pushing through the crowd, she found even more inside, Angel, Billy, and Alonzo. Colt was sitting in a chair with his shirt off, blood dripping down his arm from beneath a wet padding of cloth.

Her heart lurched at the sight of the blood, but only for a moment, then quieted down from the frantic pounding it had been doing since she left her room. He was sitting up, he had been talking, he looked just fine, discounting the blood. It wasn't a mortal wound.

Colt became aware that every man in the room was staring at her at about the same time she did. But for a moment, it was almost as if everyone else had vanished. He saw only her, and her state of dishabille, the white velvet robe molded to damp curves, the glorious red hair piled loosely on her head with long wet tendrils clinging to the velvet about her breasts, beads of water still on her neck and cheeks, the bare feet.

He almost got up to reach for her, so powerful and instantaneous was her effect on him. It was like a fist slamming into his gut when he heard someone clear his throat and realized they weren't alone, that he couldn't touch her, couldn't lick that moisture from her neck as he was dying to do, couldn't even get near her. He could only stare at her and watch her pale, pale skin blossom with color as she too became aware that they weren't alone, that she had breached all manners of propriety, that she was damned near naked. And he had a sudden, fierce need to kill every man there just for seeing her like that.

Jocelyn recovered first, which was fortunate, since Colt was about to embarrass the hell out of her by tossing her over his shoulder and taking her back to her room, where she belonged. If she had known that, she wouldn't have been able to bluff her way through the embarrassment she was already experiencing.

But brazenness had its uses, and pretending it was nothing out of the ordinary for her men to see her in such a state, when they never had before, was all she could do. Allowances would have to be made for the reason she was there. Of course, it would have helped if Colt had looked just a little more injured than he did.

"Has a doctor been summoned yet?" Since she didn't address the question to anyone in particular, she didn't note who replied in the negative. "Then would you be so good as to fetch one, Rob — "

"I don't need a doctor," Colt cut in.

"Perhaps not, but it wouldn't hurt — "

"I don't *want* a doctor — ma'am. What I want is to be left alone."

He said it quietly, but there was so much suppressed anger in his tone, the exodus began immediately. Only Angel was left, sitting on the end of the bed leaning against the bedpost, and Billy, who went back to wringing out the cloth Colt had been cleaning the wound with — and Jocelyn, still standing in the middle of the room.

Colt chose to ignore her, hoping she would take the hint and go away. "Hurry up with that, kid, before I bleed to death."

It was the worst thing he could have said. Jocelyn had been about to leave. She could find out later how he had gotten shot. She never should have come in the first place to see if he was all right.

"You *do* need a doctor!" she said now.

"No, dammit, I don't," Colt snarled, realizing his own mistake. "That was just a . . . what the hell are you doing?"

396

Jocelyn had already crossed over to him and was reaching for the wet cloth covering the wound. "I wish to ascertain for myself — "

He cut her off again. "Leave it alone, Duchess. It's just a scratch."

"Hell, Colt, when did you get to be such an ornery cuss?" Angel commented, coming up off the bed. "Why don't you let her patch it up since she's willing? It's a plain fact women got a gentler touch."

"I seem to recall you yelling your head off when Jessie took that bullet out of your side."

"Your sister is the exception." Angel grinned. "Come on, Billy, he's in good hands."

"Billy, get back here!" Colt demanded when he started to follow Angel out the door.

"But Angel's right, Colt. Lady Jocelyn can bandage you up better than I could."

Colt didn't need him for bandaging, he needed him for a buffer. Couldn't either of them see that? Obviously not, since the door closed behind them, leaving him alone with the duchess.

"I thought I gave you a warning a few weeks back," he said quietly, careful not to look at her standing by his side. "Did you forget it?"

"No, but this is an emergency, wouldn't you say?"

"It's a damned scratch, Duchess — "

"That still needs attention. And since your friends and family have abandoned you to my tender mercies, why don't you let me attend to it and stop being an — an ornery cuss?"

His lips almost twitched. Her arrogance could stand being brought down a peg or two, but he had to admire her tenacity. And he found that as long as he kept his eyes fixed across the room, he could even bear her closeness — for a short while. He also found, to his chagrin, that he liked having her fuss over him. Of course, it was what women did when a man was hurt, but still, *she* didn't have to do it. She had others she could have sent in her stead. So why hadn't she? And why had she looked almost frantic when she had pushed her way into his room?

"What were you told to bring you straight from your bath, without even drying off first?"

Jocelyn blushed clear to her roots. "You weren't supposed to notice that."

"Shit, who didn't?" he grumbled, then, "Ouch!" when she slapped a new wet cloth on his arm without warning. He would damned well tell Angel that here was another exception to his gentle theory.

"Who did you say taught you English?"

"My sister," he replied testily.

"Then *her* English leaves much to be desired."

"I picked up a few words on my own."

"I'm delighted to hear it. But someone should have told you the proper place for them, which is *not* in the presence of a lady."

"You didn't answer my question — lady."

"I was told you were shot."

"Afraid you'd lost your guide?"

"Something like that," she replied dryly.

He frowned then, and sank more deeply into his chair. "Can't you hurry that up?"

"For a scratch, it's rather nasty-looking." The bullet had ripped a deep groove through the upper layer of flesh and muscle. How he wasn't complaining about it, she didn't know. "It could stand a few stitches so it won't leave such a wide scar after it heals."

Was she kidding? "A man doesn't worry about a few scars."

"So I noticed."

He glanced at her sharply then, but she was looking at the scars on his chest. She couldn't see his back the way he was slouched in the chair.

"Aren't you going to ask?"

"I believe I already know," she replied, directing her attention to his arm again. "It's called the Sun Dance, isn't it?"

He was surprised enough to show it.

"Where'd you hear about it?"

"From Miles. He suggested you might bear such marks. I didn't believe him, of course. It sounded so barbaric, the way he described how it was done . . . that wooden skewers were thrust through the flesh of a man's chest, and he was then hung from a tree by ropes attached to the skewers until the flesh ripped open to release him. Is that really how it's done?"

"Close enough."

"But why would you do something like that to yourself, to deliberately torture yourself?"

"I'm just a dumb Injun, remember? We don't know any better."

Her eyes met his for the first time since she started cleaning his wound. "I thought I'd asked you not to do that," she admonished softly. "I was asking a question out of genuine curiosity, hoping to understand something of a culture I'm unfamiliar with. But if you don't care to explain, then please forget that I asked."

How was it he suddenly felt about three feet tall? "It's a religious ceremony," he said after a short silence, staring across the room again. "A ceremony of renewal and prayer for blessing. Not every warrior participates, but those who do wear their scars with pride as an assurance of divine blessing."

"Religion," she mused. "I should have realized it would be that simple." She wanted to touch those scars so badly her fingers almost trembled. "It must have been horribly painful. Was it worth it — for you? Did you feel you had received your blessing?"

"Only for a very short time."

"I'm sorry."

He looked up at her again with surprise. "Why?"

"If someone's going to suffer excruciating pain for a blessing, well, then they ought to be able to expect that blessing to last a good, long while, shouldn't they? Otherwise, why bother?"

"Hadn't thought of that."

She could tell he found her view amusing. He didn't actually smile, but she knew when someone was humoring her. She chose not to take exception to it, however. The man was injured, after all.

"Yes, well, never mind. Why don't you tell me how this happened?" she said, indicating his flesh wound.

The change in Colt was swift and chilling. "I got careless."

When he didn't elaborate, Jocelyn became annoyed, enough to deliberately misunderstand. "You shot yourself? How clumsy c you."

He gave her a baleful look rife with promise. "The shot came out of a dark alley. By the time I got to the end of it, the culprit was on his horse and hightailing it out of town."

"Then you don't know who it was?"

"I didn't see his face, no, but I recognized the horse. I remember horses better than I do people. That one belonged to the kid who rode with Angel to escort you to the Englishman. I believe Angel said his name was Pete Saunders."

"But I thought we beat them here!"

"They're obviously determined not to lose you again, Duchess. They knew where we were headed. And you still had your vehicles slowing you down, even without making camp. It would have been easy enough for them to ride around us and get here first."

"Then what was the point of *our* rushing?"

"On the off chance that Angel's ploy had them wasting time searching the mountains for you. But they must have gotten lucky and found where he doubled back."

"So what am I supposed to do now?" she said, tying his bandage off a bit too tightly in her agitation. "I suppose they'll be watching the railroad, watching the . . . wait a minute. Why did they shoot at you?"

"For the usual reason," he answered dryly. "To kill me."

Now he was the recipient of a baleful glance. "Longnose has never harmed any of my people. Why should he? It must have been a mistake."

In her upset, she had begun to pace in front of him. Colt had to force his eyes away from the bottom of her robe, which kept threatening to open with each step she took.

"There was no mistake, Duchess. What would you do without a guide?"

"Hire another . . . " She didn't finish the thought. Her eyes flared with understanding she didn't want to accept. "But I've seen them all. How can they think — "

"It wouldn't be a man you might recognize. Your Longnose will find someone else, and probably already has. Didn't Angel tell you this was their original plan before they came across Dryden?"

"*Your* Angel was as closemouthed as a sphinx. Of course he didn't tell me anything. But if he told you . . . why haven't you quit?" She got such a fierce look of annoyance, she almost smiled. "Oh, that's right, you don't quit." She was feeling better already. "You see, I was right all along about how much I need you. If anything happened to you, I wouldn't be able to hire anyone to replace you. I couldn't trust him not to be one of Longnose's men."

Colt didn't hear much beyond that "I need you" of hers. If he didn't get her out of his room pronto, she wouldn't be leaving at all.

"All right, Duchess, so you've got few options left open to you right now. The train's out. As you said, they'll be watching it, as well as your vehicles. If you split your men, some to go after the Englishman, some to protect you, you just make it easier for him."

She was frowning. "I know you said *you* wouldn't hunt him down, but what about Angel? Do you think he might be interested in the job?"

He shook his head. "He's got business in Texas that's already been delayed. He's taking off in the morning."

"So where does that leave me?"

"You either hole up and wait until your enemy gathers enough men to attack, or . . . "

He didn't finish, and she could see that whatever that "or" was, he either had changed his mind or hadn't thought it through. She was too impatient to wait.

"Or?"

He gave her a long, considering look that ended in a shrug. "You can strike out alone."

For a moment she thought he was joking. He must be. But she sensed his nonchalance was contrived, that he was tense, even expectant.

"Without protection?"

"With me. I can get you safely to Wyoming, but it'd be just you, me, and the horses, and a lot of hard riding. Your people would have to follow at their own pace."

"Just you and me . . . " she began, but was still reeling over the possibilities. "But you warned me to stay away from you," she reminded him. "Why would you offer — "

"Don't get me wrong, Duchess," he interrupted in a low, mesmerizing tone. "I guarantee you'll get to Wyoming in one piece. I make no other promises. Do you understand what I'm saying?"

She nodded curtly, feeling the color already mounting in her cheeks, and nearly ran toward the door. "I — I will have to consider . . . " She stopped, her hand on the door handle, her back to him. "When would you want to leave?"

"Tonight . . . when it'd be least expected."

Again she nodded, but wouldn't turn to look at him. "I'll have my decision delivered to you shortly."

Chapter Thirty-six

It was absolutely out of the question. It was so improper it didn't even bear consideration. Besides, there was that implied warning that Colt wouldn't keep his hands off her if she went with him.

That was the one point Jocelyn didn't mention when she told the countess she was going, and then spent the next two hours arguing with her about it. In the end, it was her decision to make. And in the end, Vanessa even allowed the plan might have *some* merit to it. After all, if Jocelyn could get away undetected, Longnose wouldn't leave the area, thinking she was still there.

Later in the week the rest of their numbers could be divided, half to take the train to meet her in Cheyenne, the other half to go by the Santa Fe Trail as they had intended. And with Jocelyn in neither party, Longnose wouldn't know which to follow, would likely assume she had been hidden somehow. He might even divide his own numbers, which would make it simpler for the law authorities, whom she intended to have waiting for him when he eventually showed up in Wyoming.

Jocelyn didn't know how Colt had greeted her decision to go with him, for she had sent a servant to tell him. There was the strong possibility his offer hadn't been sincere and he would be furious that she had once again called his bluff. After all, she really didn't understand why he would do this for her when she knew how much he disliked her company. But if he had been sincere, then she could only conclude that he was so fed up with the job she had forced on him — which had now become extremely risky as well as bothersome — that he was willing to do anything to get it over with. Traveling without the encumbrance of the vehicles would get them to Wyoming in half the time, maybe even less.

She was ready when he came for her around midnight, dressed in one of her more sturdy riding habits, with a full-length fur-lined cloak draped over an arm, her rifle in one hand and a small valise in the other. Colt did no more than remove her tall, short-brimmed riding hat to replace it with one he had brought along, a man's wide-brimmed hat in the same style as his, which surprisingly fitted. She didn't object. She didn't dare. She was goir to have to get used to doing things as *he* directed, or risk heaven knew what, a thought that didn't sit well with her, but she supposed she would get used to that too.

She noted right off, despite there being no words exchanged between them, that Colt didn't *seem* furious. But then most of the time it was impossible to tell what he was feeling. However, if anything, he seemed rather relaxed in his manner. He even flipped her new hat down over her eyes after he'd placed it on her head, something a playful relative or friend might do, but not her taciturn guide.

But he wasn't wasting any time in getting started, so she didn't wonder about his attitude for very long. He led her out of the hotel through the back and down several streets, not to the stables, but to an alley where his brother was waiting with the horses.

"You see anyone?" he asked Billy.

"Not a soul."

Billy stepped back as Colt tossed Jocelyn up onto Sir George, then secured her valise for her. She had to spend a few moments quieting the animal, who didn't like such proximity to Colt's stallion.

"Don't forget what I told you, kid," Colt was saying. "Just keep to the flats with the mountains on your left, and you'll have no problem leading the others straight into

408

Cheyenne. I'm trusting you to show up at the Rocky Valley on your own. If you make me come looking for you again, you'll wish to hell you hadn't."

"I'll be there," Billy replied in a somewhat grumbling tone. "But I'm still not going back to school."

"You can take your objections up with your ma when you return to Chicago, which is what you should have done in the first place."

At that point Billy grinned. "She didn't think I was serious about not wanting to be a lawyer, that I mean to take up ranching instead. Now she knows I wasn't kidding."

"You proved your point all right. What good it'll do you is debatable, though."

And then Colt pulled Billy into a brief, bone-crushing embrace, surprising the boy as well as Jocelyn, who was watching. If she had been asked, she would have sworn Colt Thunder didn't have an affectionate bone in his body. Obviously, he had one or two well hidden.

As Billy headed back to the hotel and Colt mounted up, it finally dawned on Jocelyn what was missing. "Where are the supply horses?"

"You're traveling with an Indian, Duchess." For once he didn't say it in a derogatory way. "If I can't survive off the land, there's some thing wrong with me."

They both thought of Philippe Marivaux simultaneously, Colt with satisfaction that he'd never have to smell another meal smothered in French wines, Jocelyn with regret. "I'm skinny enough as it is," she felt obliged to complain. "I'll probably waste away to nothing by the time we get there."

He had the gall to laugh. But after she thought about it, she rather liked the idea of his providing for her. Protection, provision, and whatever else was needed. That had a rather nice sound to it.

Chapter Thirty-seven

They rode throughout the remainder of the night, keeping to the road for the horses' sake, to avoid the hazards of the land. At one point Jocelyn asked when they might be stopping for some sleep and was told they wouldn't be, not until the following evening. Already tired, and it wasn't even close to dawn, she almost turned around. Almost.

But she got it into her mind that Colt was likely testing her. He had probably even made wagers with himself on how soon it would take her to start complaining about something. Of course, she never said she wouldn't complain. If she had made such an irrational promise, then she wouldn't dare to say anything, no matter how difficult he made this journey for her. But she decided that thwarting him would be the only enjoyment she could look forward to in the coming days. She wouldn't complain even if it killed her.

At dawn they stopped briefly to rest the horses. She thought they would have a mea then, but Colt merely dug out some thin strips of dried beef from his saddlebags that she was told to chew on. She tried. She really did. But Westerners must have tougher teeth than duchesses. She ended up sticking the thing in her mouth like a cigar and sucking on it for the rest of the morning.

By noon she had to remove her cloak. Not that the day had warmed up to any great degree, but the steady pace Colt was keeping to was grueling exercise, and there was little wind in the hills where they were riding now.

They had stopped once more, again only for the horses. Sir George was bearing up much better than Jocelyn. Her back felt on fire, the muscles were so stiff. The leg she hooked over her saddle horn for balance had gone to sleep a good half-dozen times. She envied it. She was so tired she was almost sleeping in the saddle. If Sir George were a less frisky mount, she likely would be.

He gave not the slightest sign of having missed a full night's sleep. He didn't bend or stretch his back to work out the kinks; his head didn't drop. His belly probably wasn't grumbling either, as was hers.

She was given a couple of biscuits shortly after noon, and a canteen of water she was allowed to keep. If the biscuits didn't fill her up, the water did, for a while anyway. Colt was pacing the animals now, letting them canter for a while and then briefly gallop, then walking them for a mile or two, then urging them back into a canter. It was during one of the slow paces that Jocelyn fell asleep.

She came awake with a curse ringing in her ears and a band of steel tightening about her waist. "Christ, woman, are you trying to kill yourself?"

It was Colt's arm about her waist. And at her back was a pillow, his chest. She took instant advantage of it, not even caring how she got there.

"Did something happen?" She yawned her question.

"You started to fall off your horse."

"Sorry. Must have nodded off," she said and started to again.

"Sorry? Haven't you sense enough to say something if you can't stay awake?"

Groggily, she wondered why he was shouting at her. "Very well, I can't stay awake."

"Stubbornness, that's what it is," she heard him mumble. "Pure stubbornness."

Whatever that meant, she didn't care. He had loosened his tight hold around her belly, reached forward to pull her leg over the saddle so she straddled it, and shifted his weight until she curved into him like she would into a comfortable chair. Even her legs were supported by his, so there was no tension left in her body. She was so relaxed, in fact, that she didn't feel her hat being removed, or the hairpins being slowly pulled from her hair. She was already nodding off again.

But it wasn't a deep sleep yet, and when the horses picked up their gait suddenly, she became aware of it. "Aren't we going to stop?"

"What for?"

"To sleep, of course."

"I thought you were."

"I meant both of us. You didn't get any rest last night either."

"Don't need it, but I forgot that you do. So go ahead, I won't let you fall off."

Jocelyn didn't need any more encouragement than that, especially when he was much more comfortable than the hard ground would be.

Colt knew, to the second, when her sleep had deepened into total oblivion. It was as if a signal went off in his body, telling him he could touch her now. But he didn't. Knowing that he could, at any time, do whatever he liked with her gave him patience for the time being. She belonged to him for at least a week. He had seen to it.

The peace that came with his decision still surprised him. But he'd been fighting his instincts for so long, as well as his needs, that

414

the turmoil inside him had begun to seem normal. He should have lost the fight sooner. He'd put himself through hell, and for what? There was no getting around the fact that he wanted Jocelyn Fleming. White women were still anathema to him, but the duchess would just have to be an exception.

It still bothered him that she'd used him to prepare the way for another man to have her, but he'd see to it that she made him forget about that. It also still bothered him how quickly she'd turned to Dryden. Before the week was out, she wouldn't even remember that bastard's name.

Chapter Thirty-eight

She climaxed in her dream. She woke up with it, still throbbing, the most blissful languor drifting through her limbs — and not a clue to what she had been dreaming about, though it wasn't difficult to hazard a guess.

Jocelyn stretched deliciously, yawned — and realized she was on a horse. Her eyes popped open to a number of other realizations clamoring for notice. The sun was setting. The horse was just plodding along, its reins wrapped around the saddle horn. Her jacket was wide open, as was her blouse. And the right side of her lacy camisole was tucked beneath her breast, exposing that plump mound to the rosy glow of the sunset. But that wasn't even the worst of it. Her skirt was hiked up to her hips, revealing the unladylike spread of her legs on either side of the horse. And between her legs . . .

"Colt Thunder!"

" 'Bout time you woke up."

"Remove your hand at once!"

"I like it where it is."

"I don't care what you — "

"Stop screeching, Duchess, or we won't have any dinner tonight. You'll have scared away every animal for miles around."

She was close to sputtering, while he offered her nothing but a lazy drawl? "To hell with dinner! You can't — "

He interrupted her again. "I already have. And leave your blouse alone. It took me a damned long time getting it open, and I like it, too, as it is."

When she didn't obey him, his fingers delved more deeply inside her. She gave a tiny moan, of protest or pleasure, he wasn't sure which. Neither was she, but finally her hands fell away from her clothes to grip his thighs instead.

"That's better," he bent to whisper by her ear. "Do you still want me to remove my hand?" She wouldn't answer. "You liked it, didn't you?"

She still wouldn't answer. But her back arched, her head reared back, and her fingers were now kneading his thighs in a desperate manner. He took advantage of her exposed neck to graze his teeth along her skin, sending ripples of excitement down to her belly. His other hand, which had been spread across her middle to hold her against him, came up now to her exposed breast. The nipple was already hard and begging for his touch. He teased it a while before satisfying it with the firm pressure of his palm in a circular motion. The other breast was soon bared for the same tantalizing treatment. And the fingers of his other hand, still slowly moving . . .

"I'm sorry I couldn't wait, Duchess, but you were given fair warning, weren't you?" His hot breath filling her ear was nearly her undoing.

"I didn't . . . expect to be attacked . . . when I wasn't looking," she finally got out, only to hear him chuckle.

"It makes no difference when or how, when it's not up to you. You relinquished all choices when you agreed to take off with me. Actually, you relinquished them a while back. You just didn't know it."

"What are you talking about?"

"If a Cheyenne maiden allows a warrior to touch her body intimately, that warrior wouldn't be criticized if he then treats her in a proprietary manner. It would, in fact, be unusual if he didn't consider her his belonging. You allowed me more than a mere touch, didn't you, Duchess?"

Proprietary? Belonging? Why wasn't she incensed by those words? And why was it the deep timbre of his voice stimulated what she was already feeling? And his fingers . . . dear Lord, she could barely draw breath to answer him.

"I'm not Cheyenne."

"No . . . but I am."

"Only half."

"And the white half has had one helluva time resisting twenty-two years of ingrained customs and beliefs lately. Now turn around."

"What?"

"Turn around. I want you facing me."

"But — but why?"

"Why do you think?"

There was enough insinuation in that to give her the answer. And he had ensured, with the deft movements of his fingers deep inside her and with his possession of her breasts, that she wouldn't object to his intention too strenuously. She just couldn't believe he was serious about the way he meant to do it.

"Why don't you stop the horse?"

"And waste time spreading a blanket? I'd have to take my hands off you to do that, and I don't think I can. Besides, this is the way I thought about it, Duchess, when you were making all those sexy little sounds in your sleep. You rode my fingers to the rhythm of my horse. I want you riding me to the same rhythm."

She was lifting her leg over the horse's neck before he'd even finished talking. He helped her bring the other one around. There was a brief problem with her skirt, but by the time she'd solved it, he was also ready, and before she even thought to wonder how they were going to do this, he lifted her, impaled her, and then dug his heels into his mount. With a gasp, all Jocelyn could do was hold on.

It was the most incredible ride of her life. Arms locked around Colt's neck, legs around his hips, she didn't have to move a muscle, just glide with the motion of the man and the horse. It was when Colt took the animal through its slower gaits that things got really interesting, especially when he no longer moved with the flow of motion, but against it, forcing her to bounce, grind, and slam against him.

By the time the horse came to a standstill, she had climaxed three times with soul-searing intensity. She was also slightly dazed, so it took her a while to realize they had stopped, or that Colt was kissing her in a sweetly tender way.

"Are you all right?"

"I haven't the faintest idea."

He chuckled. God, she could feel it between her legs — they were still connected. She was also still clinging to him. She let her arms slide down his shoulders as she leaned back. Her blush was thankfully indistinguishable in what little light there was left in the day. But he must have sensed it. He tilted her chin up and placed another soft kiss on her lips.

"You'll get used to it, Duchess. I intend to see that you do."

To his lovemaking? Or to his new manner with her? She was so accustomed to his surliness, his bitterness, his pushing her away by deed or word. He'd changed since leaving Santa Fe, and she didn't know quite what to make of the new Colt Thunder. She wouldn't go so far as to call him charming. Proprietary came to mind, and she recalled what he'd said earlier. He hadn't really been serious about considering her his belonging, had he?

"Ah — didn't you mention something about dinner tonight? I'm not certain, but I may be starving."

Again he chuckled, something else that was totally strange coming from him. "I guess I should take advantage of what little light is left," he told her as he set her down on the ground. "You can wash up while I scout around. And if you know how, you can get a fire going. There are matches in my saddlebags." He tossed those down by her feet, as well as a roll of blankets. And then he ur hooked her hat from his saddle horn and plopped it back on her head. "Best cover up, Duchess, before you catch cold."

She stared after him openmouthed as he rode off up the creek. Yes, there was a creek, the reason his horse had halted. And Sir George was there too, munching grass on the bank. She'd completely forgotten about him, as well as everything else, when Colt whisked her onto his horse. But the stallion had, thankfully, followed them.

She called him to her now to retrieve her cloak and valise, and found more blankets strapped to the back of her saddle, as well as a bag of cooking and eating utensils. Well, thank God for small favors. She had pictured herself eating meat off a stick and all manner of other barbaric modes of roughing it in the wilds. No tent, no fat pillows to sleep on, no chamber pot — which reminded her. She ought to take advantage of this small bit of privacy while she could. She had a feeling she wouldn't have much in the coming days.

Catch cold indeed. Good Lord, she hadn't even noticed the cold.

Chapter Thirty-nine

Colt returned with a pheasant and two small quail, some rather large eggs that likely belonged to another species of bird, a leather pouch of greens and what Jocelyn supposed were wild onions, and another one containing an assortment of berries. His pockets had been stuffed with nuts, which he seemed to take pleasure in dumping into her lap as he squatted down next to her.

She was surprised by the variety of his provender. She had been expecting a dead animal she would have to suffer watching him skin. She was also piqued by his long absence, which had allowed her imagination and fears to run wild.

"What, no deer?"

He answered her as if he hadn't detected the sarcasm in her tone. "You scared away all the big game with your screaming. I warned you that might happen."

"That was miles back."

"I meant when you — "

"Don't say it!" she gasped, vaguely recalling how noisy she had gotten at several
points during their passionate ride. She lowered her eyes to the pile of nuts in her lap,
realizing it was her fault it had taken him so
long to find food for them. "I'm sorry I
snapped at you. I had begun to think you
weren't coming back."

His hand touched the side of her head and
came away with one of her hairpins, which
released a long red lock to fall over her breast.
"I see you brought more of these along. Am I
going to have to steal them all from you before
you let your sun free?"

She glanced at him in bemusement. "My
sun?"

"Your hair, Duchess. My people would say
you had captured the sun in it."

"How poetic," she said as he reached for
another pin and another lock fell. She was
unaccountably pleased by his fascination with
her hair. "You're not angry I scared all the
animals away?"

"You didn't." He met her green gaze when
he admitted that. "I don't like to waste food,
and to kill a large animal when we don't have
time to preserve the meat to take with us
would be a waste."

It was amazing how quickly her temper
hot to the surface, but even more amazing

424

how he defused it simply by raising a questioning brow at her. And then he laughed when he saw she wasn't going to explode.

"Are you still afraid I'll quit on you, Duchess?" he asked knowingly.

"No, you don't quit, or so you've assured me. I guess I deserved that little lie about the animals, however. I shouldn't have greeted you the way I did after you went to so much trouble to lay a feast before me."

"Yet you were worried," he said with a slight frown. "I wouldn't go so far off that I couldn't hear you if you needed me. You had nothing to fear in that respect. But how could you think I wouldn't come back to you?"

She lowered her eyes again. "I remembered how much you dislike white women."

"And you're whiter than most, aren't you?" The back of one finger grazed her cheek as he said that.

"You've never tried to hide how you feel."

"I see. Well, I disliked you a helluva lot today, didn't I?"

Her head shot up. "You lost control again, like before. That's perfectly understandable, given the way I fell asleep on you."

She was blushing furiously by the time she had finished explaining away his actions for him. But Colt was shaking his head at her and she had the feeling he was angry now though she couldn't be sure. He was wearing that stoical expression of his that could be so exasperating.

"The only control I lost today was of my patience, woman. And if I disliked you, there's no way in hell you could heat my blood the way you do."

"I do?" she asked stupidly.

"You know damned well you do."

His tone annoyed her, even as his words pleased her. "Well, you dislike *that*, don't you?"

"If you haven't noticed, I've stopped fighting it." He leaned forward to grind his lips against hers as if to prove his point, but his voice was less harsh when he added, "If it hasn't sunk into that pretty head of yours yet, you'll be sharing my blankets until we reach Cheyenne, and that, Duchess, pleases the hell out of me. So don't doubt I'll be back each day. There isn't much that could keep me away."

Jocelyn couldn't think of a single thing to say to that. To have their arrangement spelled out so literally was disconcerting. So was the warmth flowing through her bloodstream after hearing it. She should protest that he had taken too much for granted. She had never agreed they would be lovers for the duration. The very idea . . . was so thrilling it stole her breath away. And what, after all, could she say about it? As he had pointed out, the choices were all his to make for the time being.

As if he had read her mind, Colt smiled at her in what was possibly the most beautiful smile she'd ever encountered — then moved off to see to the food. She found that rather arrogant of him, but still said nothing. What was the point? Even if she tried to argue about their arrangement for propriety's sake, her heart wouldn't be in it, and he would know that. And she wasn't a hypocrite. She had honestly thought she wouldn't want him again, but he had proved her wrong.

Her eyes moved leisurely over his body as he dug a hole next to the small fire she had started. She had heard of people baking things in the ground before, and assumed that was what he was going to do with their birds. Not that she was interested in food just then, for her eyes noticed the way his leg muscles bulged when he squatted like that. She recalled that she hadn't seen him completely without clothes yet, and realized that she soon would, perhaps even tonight. Good Lord, just thinking about it caused a fluttering in her belly. Safer thoughts were definitely called for.

"You aren't going to ask me if I can cook, are you?"

He shook his head without glancing at her. "If you said yes, I'd be forced to give you a try at it, whether you were lying or not. I'd rather have a full belly."

Jocelyn laughed, well aware he wasn't teasing. "So would I, so I'm grateful that at least one of us knows how. I was never allowed near the kitchen myself — the servants' domain, you know. Not that I had any great desire to learn how to cook when I was growing up. I preferred the stables, actually, and no one thought to refuse me access there. But even my mother knew how to make pies, I'm told. I suppose I should have learned to cook at least one specialty, though. Every woman should have one thing she is especially good at, don't you think?"

"You don't do so bad, Duchess . . . at certain things."

His pause brought color to her cheeks. "I meant in the kitchen."

"I meant your way with horses."

She couldn't help grinning. "You're a terrible tease, Colt Thunder."

He caught her grin and returned it. "You're not so bad with a rifle either."

"Well, if we're going to get into talents in general, then I must confess I don't do badly at all. I'm rather good at sailing, archery, tennis, and bicycling."

"And what?"

"Bicycling. You know, that contraption with two wheels and — "

"I know what it is. A damned two-legged horse. I saw plenty of them on the streets of Chicago, spooking the real thing and crashing into buildings. And you're good at that?"

"I can get on the thing and off without a single fall, though I don't like to count the numerous scrapes and bruises I received while learning to master it. But I agree they can be dangerous in the city. In the country, however, they are quite fun to drive. You ought to try it."

"No, thanks, I'll stick to the real thing."

She tried to imagine Colt on a bicycle and almost laughed. No, she didn't think he would like something that was so difficult to control.

The meal they shared was pleasant, the food delicious. The birds might have looked terrible since they hadn't been plucked, but the meat inside was tender and tasty. She teased Colt about making a good wife for someone, but didn't think he appreciated her humor.

Her humor didn't last long, however. After she'd rinsed off the utensils in the creek — she thought she ought to do at least something to help, since he didn't want her near the cook

429

fire — she found herself overcome with shyness, especially when Colt very casually moved his blankets from where she had earlier placed them, to lay them next to hers.

She sat in the middle of hers, fully clothed, not knowing what to do, what was expected. She'd had this problem before, she remembered, but he'd helped her then, told her what to do, led her through it. And desire, hot and impatient, had been present. Spontaneously coming together was different from this, however. Waking up in his arms was different too. Even thinking about going to bed with him wasn't the same as actually doing it.

She wasn't feeling desire at the moment, she was feeling extremely nervous, so much so that when Colt began to remove his jacket, she blurted out, "Shouldn't you leave that on . . . because of the cold?"

"I won't need it."

"Oh."

This just wouldn't do. She needed time to calm her nerves. How *could* he be so nonchalant about it, to stand there in front of her and undress as if he did it every day?

When he unbuckled his gun belt, she quickly racked her brain for a subject to divert him and settled on Angel. "Tell me about your friend Angel."

That arrested his movements. It also made

him frown. "What about him?"

"I was wondering why he would do what he did for you, simply at your request. To insinuate himself with a band of dangerous brigands just to be available to help me in case I was captured, that was a bit much to ask of any man. Yet he did it for you."

Colt stared at her a moment, decided it wasn't actual interest in Angel that had prompted her curiosity, and shrugged. "He figured he owed me, I guess."

"Why?"

"I helped him out of a bad situation a few years back. He'd hired on at my sister's ranch, been there only a week or two when he came across a small gang of rustlers stealing some of her stock. There were only four of them, or so he thought. He also thought he could take them all on by himself. Likely he could have pulled it off, but there were actually five in that bunch. The fifth one shot him from behind."

"That bullet you mentioned your sister removing for him?"

"Yes."

"Then you found him and helped him back to her ranch? That's all there was to it?"

"There was a bit more. When I arrived, a gun was already cocked to finish him off. It was a matter of seconds."

"Then you saved his life," she concluded. "Well, that's worth a favor or two, I suppose. And the rustlers?"

"I saved them a hanging."

"You — oh, well, you needn't go into detail about that."

"I wasn't going to," he said with a knowing grin, having watched the way her eyes were following his hands. "Now, aren't you going to undress?"

"The cold — "

"You won't feel it, Duchess, I promise you."

"But . . ."

"Yes?"

"This feels so — so awkward," she said at last. "You haven't even kissed me or anything."

"That's because I figured we could use some sleep, or did you forget we didn't get any last night? If I kissed you now, we wouldn't get any tonight either."

She started to laugh. "So *that's* why you've been so blasted casual about this."

"If you had other ideas — "

"No, no, sleep sounds most appropriate," she said quickly and rose to fetch her valise. "I'll just change into my nightgown."

"We'll be warmer if we're both naked," he 'd her as she headed for the nearest bush.

"But will we get any sleep that way?" she dared to ask.

"Go ahead and change."

Chapter Forty

After three years of traveling and seeing the world, Jocelyn finally felt as if she were on holiday. She was enjoying herself immensely, and feeling like a tourist. Everything she saw was beautiful and worth remembering, from the mountains that they moved in and out of to the plains that they used to cover greater distances in less time. The sky was beautiful, so blue, with the sun often shining. The rivers and creeks were sparkling and clear. Even the cold was a delight to be in. She could find no fault with anything, except maybe how quickly the time was passing.

They'd been traveling through Colorado for four days now, having crossed the mountains through the narrow Raton Pass, the scene of a near war between the railroads only a few years back, when the Denver & Rio Grande and the Atchison, Topeka & Santa Fe railroads had both raced to claim the route for their lines, the Santa Fe having won, surprisingly without bloodshed.

Traveling near the railroads gave Jocelyn a feeling of being back in civilization, but then Colorado had drawn thousands of prospectors and settlers to its wilderness ever since gold was discovered there in 1858. It was fairly well settled by now and had even earned statehood in 1876. If she didn't see very much of the settled parts, it was only because Colt tended to make a wide berth around farms, ranches, and towns.

That changed today, however. Sitting on the flat plain with the massive Rocky Mountains, topped by Pikes Peak, looking like an impregnable solid wall behind it was the small town of Colorado Springs, which they approached around noon. Colt said they might go on by train from here, and with visions of making love in a comfortable bed in a luxurious Pullman sleeper car, the countryside speeding by outside the window, Jocelyn didn't object. He had intended to catch the train in Denver anyway for the last leg of the journey, and Denver was only two days north at the speed they had been traveling.

Colt paused before they entered the town, however, and Jocelyn was forced to wait while he braided his hair. That morning he had also removed the heavy coat he had been using on the frigid mountain trails, so that he was now wearing only a fringed buckskin shirt with his

435

tight black pants and moccasins.

Jocelyn shook her head at him. "Why do you do that, go out of your way to flaunt your heritage? I know it causes you problems. It's what led to that gunfight in Silver City, isn't it?"

"So?"

"So if you cut your hair, dressed a little differently, you'd look perfectly normal, wouldn't you — except maybe for your handsomeness. There's nothing normal about that."

He grinned at her, surprised that her question didn't annoy him. Perhaps it was the way her eyes were admiring him. It made him feel damned good when she looked at him like that.

"You do things your way, Duchess, and I'll do them mine. Worse things can happen when folks make mistakes about you."

"Worse than gunfights?" she snorted, but didn't wait for an answer. "And if I'm to do things my way, you'll have to give me back my hairpins."

She held out her hand for them, but now he did the head shaking. "When we reach Cheyenne is soon enough for you to go back to being 'Your Royal Grace.'"

She started to frown, until it occurred to her that this was a golden opportunity to do things she couldn't do with the countess or her guard along. "In that case, while we're waiting for the train, I wish to visit a brothel to — "

"Like hell!"

"Just to see what it's like inside, Colt. I've always wondered — "

"Forget it, and I mean *forget it.*"

She did frown now, at his implacable expression. "A saloon, then," she said as a compromise. "Surely you can't object to that."

"Can't I?"

Before he flatly refused this too, she said, "Please, Colt. When else will I ever have such an opportunity? To come to this land and miss viewing one of its cultural phenomena? Once my people rejoin me, I can't be so — bold."

"You willing to wear pants and my coat?"

For a moment, all she heard was that he hadn't said no. "Your pants? You must be joking."

"No one said they had to fit, Duchess."

She grinned suddenly. "You think to change my mind, don't you?"

"Have I?"

"No."

"Then let's hope the train's ready to pull out when we get to the station."

It wasn't. They had about two hours before the northbound train was scheduled to arrive.

Jocelyn was pleased about that, but extremely disappointed to be told there were no Pullman sleeping cars available, until she noticed a small private railroad car in the station yard. She was told that it was owned by one of the more prosperous residents of the town, but newly purchased, so not for sale or rent. That of course meant nothing to her, and after thirty minutes spent in locating the man, exchanging messages back and forth, then a small pouch of gold, she had the car for her exclusive use all the way to Cheyenne.

Colt, having stood back and watched the effect her money and manner had on people — she didn't even have to mention her title — could only shake his head. He stowed their gear in the car, then waited in the parlor section while she changed clothes in the small sleeping compartment. It reminded him of her coach with the velvet-upholstered walls and plush lounge chairs, but was much more gaudy with its silk-tasseled curtains, narrow gilt mirrors between each window, thick carpeting on the floor, ceiling in white oak, paneled and decorated with vines and flower pieces. There was a Baker heater, a lavatory complete with sink and tub, a well-stocked bar, and even a piano off in the corner.

Colt looked around the room and wondered what the hell he was doing there. It suited the duchess, but the trappings of wealth were not for him. His one-room cabin in the hills above Jessie's ranch didn't even have a bed in it. Jessie had insisted on stuffing it with some furnishings, but a bed he had refused, preferring to sleep on the floor. And he had actually toyed with the idea of keeping the duchess? He'd been crazy to even think about it.

What he needed now was to get her off his hands for his peace of mind, which was why they were here. He liked being with her too much, liked providing for her, liked her dependence on him. But the danger had been there all along, that this short time with her wouldn't be enough, that he'd end up wanting to keep her permanently. He'd hoped it would be otherwise, but no such luck. He just hadn't thought he'd feel so strongly about it.

Thinking about it brought back all the old bitterness and anger. It didn't matter what he wanted, he couldn't have her. She was white, he wasn't. White women didn't marry breeds unless they wanted to be ostracized by their own kind. She likely hadn't forgotten that, even if he had for a while. She was amusing herself with him, but she'd walk away without a backward glance when the time came. Hadn't she used him to dispose of her virginity so she could marry someone who would suit? Someone who would suit!

"I'm ready."

Christ, even when she looked ridiculous, she looked good to him. "No, you're not. Stuff that hair under your hat."

She did, frowning at his tone. "Is something wrong?"

"Should it be?"

"You don't really want to take me to a saloon, do you?"

"It makes no difference, Duchess . . . what I want."

There seemed to be a double meaning there and it annoyed her that she couldn't grasp it. His surliness was annoying too, since she'd thought she'd seen the last of it.

"Then if it makes no difference, shall we go?"

She didn't wait for his consent, or for him. She left the car and marched angrily toward the main street. Colt jerked her around before she'd even left the station yard.

"You want to do this damn fool thing, then you'll do it my way. Keep your hat on, your eyes lowered. You stare at some man looking like one yourself, and he'll think you want to fight. Keep your mouth shut, too. And for Christ's sake, don't cling to me if something startles you. Remember you're supposed to be a man. Act like one."

"Like you? I don't think I can manage that particular scowl, but you've got so many to choose from, I should be able to imitate at least one. How's this?"

The face she made was his undoing. He turned her about and shoved her forward before she noticed the grin he couldn't keep back.

They didn't have too far to go to find a saloon. "Do they brew gold here?" Jocelyn inquired after seeing the sign out front that read "The Gold Nugget Brewery."

Colt wasn't ready for any more of her humor just then. "Trouble is what they brew in these places, Dutch. Are you sure you want to do this?"

"Dutch?" She grinned. "I assume that's a manly nickname and not a nationality. Do I really look like a Dutch?"

"You look like something dragged in off the range," he retorted and yanked her hat down to cover her delicate earlobes. "Christ, this will never work. One look at your face and it's all over."

"But what could happen if they know I'm a woman?"

"Anything, dammit."

She could see he was about to change his mind about letting her go inside, so she backed up toward the batwing doors as she said, "Just five minutes, Colt, please. Nothing will happen in just five minutes." And she pushed through the doors before he could stop her.

Chapter Forty-one

The Gold Nugget Brewery hadn't sounded that crowded from the outside, but it was. Jocelyn didn't go very far into the room. She wondered if today might be a holiday of some sort, to account for so many people being there in the middle of the afternoon. But then she noticed most of the men up at the bar had plates of food in front of them, and realized it was still the lunch hour — and that she was hungry herself.

"You didn't tell me it was also a restaurant," she whispered when she felt Colt at her back.

"Who you talkin' to, kid?"

She glanced around with widened eyes to find an old-timer in pants almost as baggy as hers, wearing nothing but long johns and suspenders with them. He was scratching a full gray beard as he eyed the bar rather than her, to her relief.

"I beg your pardon, I was — "

"You beg my . . . "

He cackled before he finished. Jocelyn grimaced and looked over his shoulder to see what had happened to Colt. He wasn't there. And the old-timer was squinting at her now.

"You wouldn't happen to have an extra nickel on you that you wouldn't mind partin' company with, would you, sonny? Food's free as long as you buy a drink with it."

She dug into her coat pocket where she had stuffed a few coins earlier and handed him one. She realized her mistake at once when his eyes bulged and he nearly broke her fingers getting the twenty-dollar gold piece out of her hand before she changed her mind.

"You must be fresh in from the gold fields, kid. Come on and I'll buy *you* a drink. Hell, I'm rich now."

He headed off toward the bar, cackling again. Jocelyn wasn't about to follow him. She had started for the exit, in fact, when she was swung back around to see a very disgusted Colt, who'd been standing behind her the whole while.

"I thought I told you to keep your mouth shut."

"He thought I was a boy," she explained quickly. "We didn't consider that. If I can pass for a boy, mightn't we stay long enough to have some lunch?"

"No, we *mightn't*," he gritted out irritably.

"Have you seen enough?"

"I haven't seen anything yet, actually, but . . . "

Her voice trailed off and her eyes rounded on what she saw just then, a long gilt-framed picture hanging over the mirror behind the bar, of a woman reclining on a sofa, without a single stitch of clothes on. Colt's chuckle made her realize she was blushing — and staring.

"Come on, the view's better from over here. Five minutes, Dutch, and we're out of here."

She nodded and followed him to the bar. It was a long affair, made of carved walnut, with towels draped from it at about eight-foot intervals, so the patrons who were eating could wipe their hands, she supposed. Bootheels were hooked on a brass foot rail which ran along the base of the bar, with cuspidors on the floor by it, placed one to about every four customers. Sawdust surrounded the spittoons, and it was her misfortune to see why as one fellow spat a wad of chewing tobacco toward one, but missed the thing.

When she reached the bar, the man behind it came over to wipe the space in front of her that had some remains of the free lunch on it, and asked, "What'll you have, boy?"

"A brandy, if you please."

"Make that two whiskeys," Colt nearly growled next to her and tossed a dime on the counter.

His scowl was worth a thousand words, making her realize she'd made another mistake. Brandy, very possibly, wasn't even heard of in these parts, much less stocked.

"Sorry," she offered in a small voice.

All he said was, "Hold it, don't drink it," when the shot of whiskey was set before her.

She took the small glass in hand, turned around, and leaned one arm back on the bar as she saw another fellow doing. Colt remained facing forward, but the mirror behind the bar was there and he could see the whole room in that mirror. Jocelyn preferred to view it firsthand.

It wasn't a very large saloon, about the size of the smaller parlor at Fleming Hall. Besides that lewd picture that she refused to look at again, there were other interesting things hanging on the walls: a deer's head, the bleached skull of some large animal, old weapons, the butt end of a buffalo — she blinked twice at that one.

There were a few gambling tables, a faro layout, a roulette wheel, a monte bank, but nothing to take away from the room's main business, which was drinking. In the space of a few minutes she heard such things as

Snake Poison, Coffin Varnish, Red Dynamite, Tarantula Juice, and Panther Piss, all being requested of the bartender, and guessed them to be different names for whiskey. She was almost tempted to take a sip of her own drink just to see why it warranted such colorful descriptions. A glance at Colt, who was still watching things through the mirror, convinced her not to.

There were all manner of men present, in all manner of dress: prospectors, gamblers, businessmen, cowboys, drifters. It was almost a surprise when she finally noticed the women sitting at some of the tables.

Hurty-gurty gals, she'd heard they were called. Actually, she'd heard them mentioned by a few other names as well, though not so nice. They were apparently available for more than a drink or a dance, but the only things Jocelyn could see different about them from the women of the town were that they weren't wearing plain frocks or calico and were wearing face paint.

They were, in fact, dressed in the height of French fashion. She recognized one of those styles herself from her fashion plates, though she didn't remember the bodice being quite so low. It was when one of the women stood up that she saw where the resemblance to current fashion ended. Her dress had no skirt, or

447

what skirt it had ended only halfway down her thighs, not her calves but her thighs, revealing long legs encased in gaudy silk striped stockings.

Jocelyn caught herself staring, mouth open, and snapped it shut. Well, she'd asked to be shocked, she really had, by coming in here. And if these women dressed so scantily, good Lord, what did the women in brothels wear? No wonder Colt had been so appalled at her wish to visit a brothel.

"You got a problem, mister?"

Now she groaned. Colt had warned her not to stare at anyone, and the bearlike man who was looking in their direction appeared mighty disgruntled for some reason. But she couldn't recall staring at him. She didn't even recall seeing him until just then. Perhaps he hadn't been talking to her.

"I asked you a question, mister."

He wasn't talking to her, she realized then, he was talking to Colt. And glancing at Colt, she saw that he was watching the man through the mirror, that he was doing the staring he'd warned her not to do, and the bear, who could also see him clearly in the mirror, definitely didn't like it.

But Colt didn't turn around to answer the man, didn't answer him at all. He had gone still, however, deathly still. Not a muscle moved throughout his whole body.

"Shit, you're a breed, ain't you?" Jocelyn heard next and stiffened herself. "Who the hell let you in here?"

She waited for Colt to turn now, to tell that obnoxious creature where to get off. Why *did* he have to wear those braids along with the buckskin shirt *and* moccasins? One thing alone wouldn't have mattered. There were other men right there in the room who had hair longer than Colt's. There was another man in buckskin. There weren't any others wearing moccasins, but still, all three things together were like wearing a hand-painted sign in large letters anyone could read. It was just *asking* for trouble. So why didn't he turn and meet it?

"I'm talking to you, breed."

The fellow stood up as he said that. He really was a big man. He really did resemble a bear too, with a wild, shaggy mane of brown hair and a face full of beard and mustache. He wasn't wearing a gun and didn't seem to care that Colt was. He did have a coiled whip attached to his belt, however, proclaiming him as some kind of animal driver. A freighter probably, who had to push his animals up the mountain trails. Jocelyn pitied those animals, for the man looked not only mean but rather cruel.

And Colt still hadn't answered him.

"Maybe you need something to get your attention," the bear suggested.

Jocelyn gasped then as that whip unwound onto the floor. The man wouldn't dare! And yet everyone standing at the bar must have thought otherwise, for they scattered, moving far back against the walls. The tables nearest the bar cleared too. Someone even grabbed a fistful of her coat to yank her out of the way. And Colt *still* didn't turn around.

By the time Jocelyn jerked loose of her would-be protector, the whip had cracked. And she could see the dark imprint across Colt's back where it had struck, crushing the nap of the buckskin. Her horror was indescribable. That beast had actually done it, lashed Colt to get his attention. But he didn't get it. To her amazement, and to everyone else's surprise, Colt did nothing. He didn't move, didn't show by the slightest inflection that he'd been hurt. And that blow had to have hurt. The crack had been as loud as a gunshot.

The bear was also surprised that he'd gotten no reaction from his victim, but only for a moment. His eyes narrowed on Colt's back, moved to the mirror where he could see his face, then narrowed even more.

"You look mighty familiar, breed. Did you

450

give me trouble before, maybe when I was too liquored up to remember?" And then he shouted, "Answer me, you bastard!" and let that whip slice through the air again.

"No," Jocelyn gasped when it struck Colt again, and she started forward, only to be held back by a firm hand on her shoulder.

"Stay out of it, boy. He's only a breed."

She lost her reason then. She didn't understand any of this, the prejudice that could make a man say that, the apathy that could let the rest of them just stand there and watch instead of doing something to stop such cruelty. Most of all, she didn't understand what was wrong with Colt that he could remain silent and take it. She couldn't.

She turned on the fellow gripping her shoulder and lifted his gun before he realized that was her intent. It was a long-barreled, unwieldy thing. She had to support it on her forearm, but even then she didn't think she'd have much luck with it. Handguns were not her area of expertise.

The bear didn't know that, however. "Strike him again, sir, and I shall have to shoot you."

More people moved out of the way, those behind her now and those behind the bear. She'd gotten his attention, if nothing else, and it was most definitely unnerving. She spared a quick glance at Colt, but blast the man, even

now that she'd interfered, he remained un-
moving. Did he honestly think she could get
them out of this by herself?

"Were you talkin' to me, boy?" the bear
asked her. "I hope you ain't that stupid."

She gave a little start when he snapped the
whip back to his side. The menace of it was
palpable, the message clear. If she didn't put
the gun down, he'd use it on her.

Her hands began to sweat. It took her two
tries to cock the revolver. The sound of it was
horribly loud in the deathly silence of the
room. And all it did was get the bear angry at
her, so much so that he didn't seem to care
that she had a gun aimed at him.

"You little shit," he growled. "Back off, or
I'll slice you to ribbons!"

"Whyn't you back off, Pratt?" someone
called out. "He's just a baby."

"You want some too?" was the bear's answer.

"Ain't you showed off enough for one day,
Pratt?" This from the other side of the room.

Jocelyn began to take heart, until she realized the man was becoming enraged that he
didn't have total support from the room, and
he turned that rage on her. "Damn your hide,
drop it or use it!"

He gave her no choice, for he was drawing
back his arm in preparation of sending that

452

lash in her direction. She pulled the trigger —
then froze in utter horror. Nothing had happened. She'd confiscated a gun that wasn't loaded!

The savage exultation on Pratt's face told its own story. For her audacity in challenging him, she was going to bleed now, and feel excruciating pain in the process. That knowledge paralyzed her with such fear that she couldn't even scream when she saw the coil of the whip coming at her, much less move out of the way.

The sound of the crack was worse than the bite, in fact — Jocelyn felt nothing. Her heart might have stopped beating, but she felt no pain. And then she smelled the smoke, saw Pratt crash slowly to the floor, and knew someone had saved her, that it was gunfire she'd heard, rather than the whip.

That she didn't automatically assume Colt had come to her rescue this time was understandable, since he'd let things go so far. Yet it was his gun that was still trailing a small stream of smoke, and his eyes she met as she sagged in relief — then almost immediately began to seethe.

But her sudden anger was under perfect control. She slowly turned and handed her useless gun back to its owner, then calmly walked out of the saloon. She was never going to speak to Colt Thunder again. For whatever diabolical reason he had refrained from doing anything until the last possible moment, and she suspected it was just to teach her a lesson, he'd allowed her to be frightened half to death, and she wouldn't forgive him for that.

Chapter Forty-two

Colt watched the duchess walk out of the saloon, but made no move to follow her. He couldn't just then. He felt weak as a baby. His heart was still slamming against his ribs, his skin still clammy with cold sweat. Nothing like this had ever happened to him before, and he wasn't sure what did happen.

He'd noticed Ramsay Pratt looking at him in the mirror, recognized him, and felt such primitive satisfaction he nearly let out a war whoop. So many times he'd imagined coming across the man again, imagined calling him out and emptying his gun into him, not to kill him but to cripple him. He didn't want him dead. He wanted Pratt to live with the same kind of bitterness and pain that had been a part of his own life ever since they last crossed paths.

He'd deliberately let the man get worked up by not answering him. He'd wanted him good and mad, mad enough to break out that whip of his. But when he got what he wanted and started to turn around to face the bastard, he found that he couldn't. It was as if his body had just clicked off when he saw that whip, as if the part of his mind that controlled it had decided not to participate in another confrontation with the whip-wielder, as if he were *afraid* to go through that experience again.

Even when Ramsay had lashed him, he'd been unable to break out of the trancelike stupor that gripped him. Not that there was any pain to help him out of it. With so much damaged tissue and nerves, hot coals could be set on his back and he wouldn't be likely to feel them. He didn't know even now if Ramsay had done any damage this time. He wouldn't know until he could see his back for himself.

But if it was fear that had paralyzed him without his conscious knowledge, it had been stark terror that he'd felt when the duchess had been threatened and he still couldn't move; stark terror that had brought the sweat and debilitation when he thought she'd be hurt. It was only when he saw the whip actually raised against her that the rage had exploded in his head and given him back his mobility.

He watched as Pratt's body was hauled out of the saloon. There were a few comments, but none directed at him. Most of the patrons went back to doing what they'd been doing

456

before the violence began. It was a typical reaction when violence was more or less an everyday occurrence.

Colt felt nothing, no regret, no satisfaction, no emotion at all for the man he'd just killed. It was that look of utter contempt he'd had from the duchess just before she walked out that disturbed him. He didn't have to wonder why he'd received it. And what was he supposed to tell her? That he'd been afraid without conscious awareness of it? That he'd wanted to keep her out of it, had tried, but just couldn't move? Couldn't move? She'd really buy that, wouldn't she?

He returned to the station yard and that fancy railroad car she'd acquired so easily. The duchess was there, but locked in the sleeping compartment. Colt debated for about a minute whether to pound on the door, then decided against it. This just might be for the best. He'd be losing a few days with her, but he had to give her up anyway, so what did that really matter?

He gathered up his gear and headed for the door. He'd buy a ticket for the passenger car and let the conductor inform the duchess where he'd be. There was no reason for them to even see each other again until they arrived in Cheyenne. But on his way out one of the mirrors caught his eye and he remembered his back. He dropped his gear and yanked off his shirt to have a quick look-see. Pratt must have lost his touch over the years, Colt decided. He couldn't detect a single mark.

"Dear God in heaven!"

He swung around, reaching for his gun. "What?!" But he knew from the expression on her face. Pity he couldn't take at the best of times, and from her not at all.

Jocelyn dropped the rifle out of her hand to cover her mouth. She was going to be sick. She'd seen enough violence in the past hour, but this, the result of violence, done to him — to him! She ran for the lavatory.

Colt threw his shirt to the floor with a vicious curse and ran after her, jerking her around before she reached the door. "Don't you dare! It's nothing, do you hear? Nothing! If you wanted to spill your guts, you should have done it when the bullwhacker spilled his, not now!"

She swallowed the bile in her throat, shaking her head. The tears were already starting. She didn't know why he was so angry. She couldn't help the emotion tearing up her insides.

When he saw the tears, he snarled, "Don't!" but her wail drowned him out as she threw her arms around his neck. He tried to break her hold, but couldn't without hurting her.

458

And she wasn't letting go, was clinging so tightly she nearly choked him.

"Ah, shit," he said after a moment and carried her to the nearest chair, where he sat down to cradle her in his lap. "You've got no business doing this to me, woman. What the hell are you crying for anyway? I told you it was nothing."

"You call . . . that . . . nothing?" she sobbed into his shoulder.

"Nothing to you. It happened a long time ago. Do you think it still hurts or something? I assure you it doesn't."

"But it did!" she cried even louder. "You can't tell me it didn't! Oh, God, your poor back!"

He stiffened. He couldn't help it. "Listen to me, Duchess, and listen well. A warrior can't accept pity. He'd rather be dead."

She leaned back then, somewhat surprised. "But I don't pity you."

"Then what's all this crying about?"

"It's the pain you must have felt. I — I can't bear to think of you suffering like that."

He shook his head at her. "You're not looking at it from the proper perspective, woman. It was a whipping meant to kill me. There aren't many men who could have survived it, but I did. The scars represent triumph over my enemies. I defeated them by living."

"If you're proud of those scars, like you are of these" — her fingers brushed against the puckered skin over one nipple, making him jerk — "then why have you hid them from me? And you have, haven't you?"

She recalled now the times they had both been completely without clothes while making love, and every time she had reached for his back, he had stopped her by taking her hands and holding them over her head or at her sides. She also recalled the time she had told him she ought to have him horsewhipped. Dear God, how insensitive! But she hadn't known.

"I didn't say I was proud of them, Duchess. But remember your reaction to these," he said bitterly as he pressed her hands to his nipples, "and your reaction just now, and you have your answer. These bring forth disgust. My back makes women puke."

"Do you know why?" she asked with some heat. "Because you did one set yourself, deliberately inflicting self-torture, and you're *proud* of it. But someone else did the other, mutilating this magnificent body, and that's an atrocity beyond description. Who did that to you, Colt?"

He wasn't sure if he'd just been scolded or complimented. "You just watched him die."

It took her a moment to grasp that, but

then the color drained from her face. "Oh, God, no wonder you couldn't move when you saw him! I couldn't move myself when I thought he was going to hit me, and I didn't know what it would feel like. But you knew . . . oh, God," she groaned and wrapped her arms tightly around his neck again, as if by doing so she could take the memory away for him. "You knew exactly what it would feel like if he struck you . . . and he did! You had to relive that nightmare — "

"Cut it out, Duchess," he said gruffly. "You're making it out to be worse than it was. I felt nothing. It takes live nerves to feel pain, and I've got few of those left."

"Oh, God!" She started crying again.

"*Now* what?"

But she shook her head, aware that he wouldn't want to hear her say that was worse. Only he knew what she was thinking. And he knew what she was doing, trying to smother him with the soothing only a female could offer. She'd have his head at her breast if he'd let her, and trouble was, the thought was too tempting by half.

He had to get her mind on something else, and spotting the rifle she'd dropped on the floor, he asked, "Where were you heading with that rifle?"

"I'm afraid I didn't hear you come in," she

sniffled. "It had finally occurred to me that you might have had more difficulty at the saloon after I left."

"And so you were going back to save me?"

"Something like that."

She expected him to laugh. Instead she felt his hand in her hair pulling her head back so he could kiss her. And she didn't wonder about the almost desperate quality of that kiss, for it could have been more on her part than his. Their time together was running out, and they both knew it.

Chapter Forty-three

There was a light swirling of snow outside the windows of the private car as the train rolled into the Cheyenne depot. After spending nearly a year in the warm Mediterranean countries before sailing to America, Jocelyn had not seen snow in a very long time.

"Is the weather too severe here for horses, do you think?" she asked as she let the curtain fall back into place.

Colt was shrugging into his coat. "Wild horses have lived here for hundreds of years, Duchess. You think folks can get along without their horses?"

She smiled a little self-consciously. She'd told Vanessa she meant to locate her stud farm here, but that decision had been impulsive, influenced by the man casually preparing to leave the train — and her. If she had no other reason to live in this territory, perhaps another part of the country would be better for raising her Thoroughbreds.

"But would you breed horses here?" she asked him.

"I intend to, with that little filly you owe me. If you're worried if she'll survive, don't be. The weather is actually ideal for animals, the summers not too hot, the winters not too cold."

"It was my own stock I was concerned with. Didn't I mention that I am considering staying here?"

"For God's sake, why?"

She turned away from his expression of horror, a lump rising in her throat. It hurt, it really did, and she was about to tell him not to worry about it, that if she did choose the Wyoming Territory for her farm, she'd make sure it was far away from him.

But he came up behind her, placing a hand on each shoulder to tell her, "Forget I said that. What you do now is your own concern, since my job's over."

But how in the hell was he going to get through each day knowing she was close? Colt wondered. He had thought she'd do whatever it was she had come here for, then take the train back East. He could forget about her then. But if she didn't leave . . .

She shrugged his hands away, but he'd felt her stiffness before she did. "I can't imagine why I keep forgetting how eager you are to

464

end our association. If you'll just take me to a hotel, you can be on your way. I'll have your fee delivered to your sister's ranch as soon as it arrives."

"No, you won't."

"Yes, I — "

"No . . . you won't, Duchess."

Jocelyn's lips clamped together. He'd done this to her once before, only then she had merely wanted to talk to him. Now she wasn't so intimidated by that implacable expression. She was also allowing her temper to push aside her hurt. So he wouldn't wait? So he wanted all ties with her broken immediately? After the week they had just spent together, she had thought she had begun to understand him a little better. She had even begun to hope . . .

"If you're worried that I'll deliver the money, I won't. I assure you, you won't have to see me again. But I certainly haven't carried that kind of money in my valise. If you can't wait until my wagons arrive, I suppose I can wire my closest bank and have the money transferred — what is it now?" she demanded when he kept shaking his head.

"You try and pay me that money and I'll burn it. I never wanted the damn money and you know it. You just have that filly delivered when she's ready to be parted from her mama, and we'll be square."

"So you stuck with a job you hated for nothing? At least let me pay you the going fee —"

"No."

She glared at him. "You're determined to make me feel guilty for taking advantage of you, aren't you? But I'll have to disappoint you. If I feel anything, it's certainly not guilt."

With that she swiped up her valise and marched out the door. Colt gritted his teeth, angry enough to spit. His saddlebags were still in the bed compartment, or he'd have been right behind her. Damned women. Was she trying to make *him* feel guilty for not taking her money? All he wanted was to get away from her before he did something stupid, like tell her how he felt about her. He could just imagine her reaction to that. She'd run like hell — if she didn't laugh first.

He recalled what she'd said about visiting that saloon, that she'd never have the opportunity again because once her people rejoined her, she couldn't be so bold. The same thing applied to him and he knew it. She might be willing to share his blankets as long as they were alone and no one else knew about it, but some of her people were bound to be here waiting for her. She'd be appalled if they found out she'd taken her half-breed guide for a lover. If she had a bee under her bonnet now, it was likely because he'd reminded her it was over before she could dismiss him. That was when she had gotten all stiff and huffy.

Slamming out of the private car, Colt had to run to catch up with the duchess. She should have gone directly to the stock car so they could retrieve the horses first, but instead she was moving briskly into town. He had half a mind to just let her go. She was safe enough now. But worrying about her had become a habit. Until he was sure her people had arrived ahead of them by train and he could turn her over to them, he was still stuck with her.

Jocelyn was too angry to notice where she was going, who she was passing, or anything else about Cheyenne, Wyoming. She felt — used. Good Lord, had this past week just been his way of getting even with her? He had felt used by her, and now he'd made sure she felt the same. What a low, despicable thing to do. But what else could she think? Just this morning he had made wild, passionate love to her, had held her tenderly in his arms afterward. Now he couldn't wait to part company, to never see her again. Never? Oh, God, she'd never see him again, never know his touch again. How could she bear it?

Her feet slowed, her chest filling with pain.

She tried to recall where she was, that she couldn't cry on a public street, but the tears gathered anyway. And then her wrist was caught and she was jerked to the side, and her first thought was, *Not yet, he hasn't deserted me just yet.* But a hand clamping over her mouth and a sharp prick on her neck swiftly changed that notion.

"Yer lucky the boss wants ta see ya first, gal, or I'd slit yer throat right now. Make any funny moves an' I'll hafta disappoint 'im."

She understood the warning. She just wasn't sure she cared to heed it. Why wait? Why suffer the Englishman's abuse before she died, when she could see the matter ended then and there?

Besides the man who held her against him with no more than a hand over her mouth and a knife at her throat, there was one other she could see. He was pressed against the side of the building at its corner, his hand stuck inside his heavy coat. She didn't doubt it concealed a gun, since he could be seen from the street. She had been dragged back somewhat, so she was less likely to be seen in the shade between the two buildings, not unless someone passed by this narrow alleyway as she had done.

She didn't understand why they just stood there. Surely they had horses waiting behind the buildings to take her away. All they were doing was giving her time to decide she wouldn't go with them. If she didn't get her throat slit immediately, she might be able to fight free, or at least to scream.

She was just about to kick backward when the other man said, "He's comin', Dewane."

Who was? Not Colt. He should still be at the train getting his horse, or even on his way home already. But she knew it was Colt, and knew they wouldn't be waiting on him unless they meant to kill him. Panic immobilized her, stole her warmth and color. And then he was there, coming around the corner, and brought up short by a gun shoved in his face.

"Don't even breathe," he was told.

Colt didn't, because the rage came up to nearly choke him. How stupid could he get, not to wonder why the duchess had suddenly changed direction to duck between two buildings? He thought she was just trying to lose him, but that was no excuse. One look at her revealed she was so frightened she was even crying. That did it, brought on his killing instinct as nothing else could. Neither of these two bastards was going to walk away if he could help it.

"Ya can relax, Clint. He ain't gonna do nuthin' long's I got this purdy neck in jeppaardy. Ain't that right, Injun Thunder?"

Dewane chuckled. "Don' 'member me, do ya? 'Spect ya've outdrawn so many men, ya cain't keep track, huh?"

"Owen, isn't it?"

"Well, now, I'm purely flattered. An' the shoe's on t'other foot now, ain't it? Betcha thought ya'd pulled one over on us, didn' ya, takin' off with the li'l lady? Butcha see, ol' Miles, he tol' us whar the gal was aheadin'. Weren' no need ta go follerin' after a breed when we could jes' sit tight here an' wait."

"So the Englishman's here in town?"

"Ya oughta be askin' how pissed off he is, not whar he is, since the one don' matter, but t'other shore do."

Clint was the one to laugh at that, since he hadn't been with them then, but had heard all about their last encounter with the girl. Dewane didn't share his humor at that point, though. He *had* been there.

"He like ta kill us all chasin' after Angel, only ta find he done give'er back," Dewane continued. "An' then he were even more mad when my stupid brother an' Saunders caught gold fever in Colirada an' snuck off fer the goldfields." He grinned now. "Ya can bet yer last few breaths he'll be seein' she pays fer every aggervation he's ever knowed. Ya ready ta pay fer yer part in it?"

"My part?"

"Think we don' know it were yer gun holdin' us off, Thunder?"

"That *is* your Injun name, ain't it?" Clint was bold enough to ask. "You got something else goes with it, best spit it out now." And then he snickered. "We wanna make sure we got your whole name for the grave marker."

"The first name's White," Colt replied calmly.

"White Thunder," Dewane sneered. "Figures."

"How's that?" Clint wanted to know. "It ain't as fancy as Mad Dog or Crazy Horse."

"Yer fergettin' he's a breed, dummy," Dewane said with some disgust. "It's fer his white half."

"No, it's for the lightning that strikes with the thunder," Colt said quietly as he drew and put a bullet right in the center of Dewane's forehead.

Clint was staring in shock, forgetting he even had his gun drawn. The duchess started screaming when she went down with Dewane, and that was when Clint looked at Colt — and received the bullet reserved for him. He got off a shot in reflex, but it hit the dirt only moments before he did.

Colt made sure he was dead — there was no doubt about Owen — before he helped Jocelyn to her feet. She immediately took a swing at him, which he just narrowly sidestepped. Her fury he couldn't avoid, though.

"You could have killed me! *He* could have killed me!"

He caught her second swing and yanked her tightly into his arms. "It's over, Duchess," he said gently. "And I don't shoot unless I know exactly what I'm going to hit."

He felt the shudder pass through her before she sagged against him. "I think I've seen one too many bodies drop around me lately. Take me away from here, Colt."

There was nothing he would have liked better, but as he watched the townsfolk running toward them to investigate the gunshots, he knew it'd have to wait. Among the crowd was Deputy Smith, whom fortunately he knew, so at least they wouldn't be detained too long answering questions.

"I'll take you out to the Rocky Valley as soon as I get this mess explained, Duchess. I'll come back to see if any of your guard got here ahead of us, but as long as the Englishman might be about too — and who knows what new men he's had a chance to hire, like that Clint — you'll be safer at the ranch."

She didn't give him an argument. All that mattered was that he wasn't deserting her just yet.

Chapter Forty-four

The first thing the woman said to him was, "Unless he's changed gender, Colt, that isn't Billy you've brought home." And then he was embraced, and looked over, and finally frowned at. "I never thought it'd take this long. Couldn't you find the peabrain?"

Jocelyn did no more than stand back and listen to the brief explanation Colt offered, then the barrage of questions he answered. She didn't think she'd ever heard him talk so much, certainly not at one time. Of course she didn't doubt for a minute that the black-haired beauty with the magnificent turquoise eyes was his sister Jessie, the one who'd named him, the one who'd taught him English — there was no doubt of that either, listening to the two of them talk.

She eventually got introduced, but, typical of Colt, he just called her Duchess. She wondered if he even remembered her name by now, but she didn't bother to correct his sister when she assumed Duchess *was* her name.

Then she met Jessie's husband, Chase, a simply gorgeous man with eyes so dark they appeared black. Although Jessie didn't look more than twenty-one, she had to be a bit older than that with a seven-year-old son the image of his father, a five-year-old daughter, and another boy who was only four, beautiful children who gave Jocelyn a tight feeling in her chest when she watched them crawl all over their "Uncle Colt."

Having arrived at the Rocky Valley Ranch shortly after dark, Jocelyn excused herself early to allow Colt a private reunion with his family. In the morning, however, she found out that he had gone back to town last night. And when she joined his sister in the dining room of the large ranch house, it was to be met with a certain amount of hostility.

"What'd you do to my brother?" were the very first words said to her.

"I beg your pardon?"

"Don't take that haughty tone with me, Duchess, and don't pretend you don't know what I mean. The Colt who came home last night wasn't the same one who left here all those months ago to find Billy."

It dawned on Jocelyn that here, at last, she might learn something about Colt Thunder. She saw Jessie Summers' hostility for what was, upset and concern over someone she loved, so Jocelyn didn't take offense, didn't even acknowledge it.

"Just how was he when he left here?" she ventured.

"Happy, content, and it took me a helluva long time to manage that. Here he can be himself, and let me tell you, Duchess, a more generous, thoughtful man you'll never meet. But last night, hell, he was reserved, he was on edge, he was closed up tight, and damned if he didn't light out of here just as soon as you went to bed. Now I want to know what's going on!"

"I'm afraid I haven't the vaguest notion. The only Colt I've known is the abrupt, surly fellow I first met when he saved my life. No, I take that back. He was more . . . relaxed, shall we say, this past week — up until yesterday, that is."

"And what happened yesterday?"

"We arrived in Cheyenne, of course, and he couldn't get rid of me fast enough. Unfortunately, my enemy had an alternate plan in mind, which is why I'm here, and perhaps *that* is why he seemed different to you. He hasn't been able to divorce himself from my association yet."

"Divorce himself?" Jessie chuckled. "You've got a real fancy way with words, Duchess. Next time my husband decides to disagree

475

with me, I think I'll divorce myself from the argument."

"A wise decision, if he's anything like Colt." Jocelyn joined in her humor.

"Colt argue? Since when?"

"Since forever, or so I thought. Are you saying that isn't usual?"

"It sure isn't. There aren't many folks who'd care to argue with him, if you know what I mean. When I do, he just sits back quietly until I run out of steam, then says something to make me laugh."

Jocelyn shook her head, bemused. "I can't believe we're talking about the same man."

"Neither can I, Duchess."

"Would you mind calling me Jocelyn?"

"What, is Duchess just a nickname Colt calls you?"

"You could say that," Jocelyn hedged, not wanting to explain when she had something more important to find out. "I've often wondered what could account for the bitterness I've sensed in Colt so often. Perhaps you could shed some light on this."

"Are you kidding? It's kind of obvious, isn't it? Folks won't accept him as he is."

"But you said he was happy here, content even."

"That's here on the ranch. He's well known and liked in Cheyenne too, but every once in a while he still draws trouble there from strangers. It'll be a helluva long time, maybe not even in his lifetime, before folks can look at him and not see an Indian, one they feel naturally obliged to hate."

"But that's his own fault with the way he dresses to flaunt his heritage!" Jocelyn protested, her temper pricked by the unfairness of it all. "Doesn't he realize how little he actually resembles an Indian? If he cut his hair — "

"He tried that," Jessie interrupted sharply, some of her own bitterness showing through. "Do you want to know what it got him, looking like a white? It got one of my neighbors so riled when he found out the truth that he set his men on Colt, had him tied to a hitching rail, and ordered him whipped to death."

"Oh, God," Jocelyn whispered, closing her eyes as if she were in pain.

"There wasn't much skin left to stitch together," Jessie went on relentlessly as the memories came back to her. "There wasn't much flesh left either, after more than a hundred lashes. But do you know, he was still standing when we got there to put a stop to it. And they hadn't worked even one scream out of him either, though they tried hard enough, the bastards. Of course, we thought we'd lose him when he ran a fever for nearly three weeks. And it was a good eight months before he really got all his strength back. But what they did to him is not a pretty sight."

"I know," Jocelyn said in a small voice.

"You know? How'd that happen? He never lets anyone see his back."

"I'm afraid I came upon him by surprise."

"Oh," Jessie said, ashamed of what she'd started thinking. "You must have been — shocked."

"That doesn't half describe what I felt. I was very nearly sick."

"His back's not *that* disgusting," Jessie protested.

Jocelyn blinked. "Of course it isn't. I was sickened that someone could do that to him. I couldn't understand it then, and I still don't. That neighbor of yours had to have been a madman. That is the only thing that could explain such a heinous act of violence."

"Oh, he was sane enough. And he even felt he was justified. Colt was courting his lily-white daughter, you see, and he'd let him. That was all the reason he needed to do what he did, because Colt had dared to want his slut of a daughter. And do you know, she stood there and watched it all without saying a word." Then Jessie frowned, seeing Jocelyn's expression. "I'm sorry. I shouldn't have told you all that. I just get so furious every

478

time I remember it."

"Yes, I understand."

But Jocelyn understood even more than that. She now knew why Colt disliked white women so much, and she felt utterly defeated.

"What was all that 'your gracing' about?" Jessie asked her husband as they stood watching Jocelyn ride away with the six-man escort that had come for her.

"I think the duchess is actually a real duchess."

"Well, if that don't beat all." Jessie grinned. "My brother doesn't aspire too high, does he?"

"What's that supposed to mean?" Chase frowned at her.

"Don't tell me you didn't notice the way he kept looking at her last night. I expected to see smoke rise up from the sofa she was sitting on."

"Christ, Jessie, you're not thinking of matchmaking, are you? She's an English noblewoman."

Her eyes narrowed on him. "Are you saying my brother isn't good enough?"

"Of course not," he said in exasperation. "All I'm saying is nobility marries nobility."

"She's already done that," Jessie snorted. "Seems to me she could marry whoever she wants to now."

"And you think she wants to marry Colt?"

A smug smile curled her lips. "I saw the way she was looking at him, too, last night. And you should have heard her talk about him this morning. I won't have to do any matchmaking, honey. Whatever's between them two is already there."

"You sound mighty pleased about that."

"I am. She's nice, but more than that, I think she can heal the scars on his soul."

"Scars on his soul? Christ, woman, where do you come up with such idioms?"

"Are you making fun of me, Chase Summers?"

"I wouldn't dream of it."

Her eyes sharpened on his innocent expression before she humphed. "Good, because if you do, I'll just have to divorce myself from your presence."

"You'll *what?*" he shouted after her, only to hear her laughter as she disappeared inside the house.

Chapter Forty-five

"You know, Chase, time's a-wasting. Winter will be gone before you know it, and then they'll have missed the opportunity to laze the cold days away, snuggled up in front of a fire like this."

"Who will?" he asked, as if he didn't know. His wife had been able to talk of little else lately.

"Colt and his duchess. I really ought to do something about it."

"I thought you agreed they could find their own way."

"Well, I didn't know they were both going to be so pigheaded stubborn about it. She's been over at the Callan spread for three weeks now. She's got the place all fixed up. Furnishings have been coming in every day from the East. She's even got a new stable built."

"And you haven't told her yet whose place she bought?"

"She'd already spent so much money on it before I found out, I didn't have the heart to tell her. But I suppose that could be one reason why Colt won't go over there."

"Honey, if she was interested, don't you think she would have come up with an excuse or two to visit us here, where she might run into him? That she hasn't ought to tell you something."

"Only that she's stubborn — and maybe needs a little encouragement. He didn't even tell her good-bye, you know. The last she saw of him was that night he brought her here. And she was still under the impression then that he was glad to be rid of her."

"Maybe he is."

Jessie snorted. "If you ask me, he's laboring under the same impression."

"Laboring? I see *you've* been to visit the duchess again."

Jessie grinned to herself, running her fingernails down his bare chest under the fur cover. She didn't *always* take the bait when he teased her.

"You're just looking to get something pinched, aren't you?"

Since he knew she wasn't mad — the difference was easy to discern after all these years — he pulled her half on top of him and suggested lazily, "If you'll kiss it to make it better afterward, you can pinch me anywhere you like."

"I figured you wouldn't mind too much." But when her hand drifted down between his legs, he went tense, making her giggle. "What's the matter, honey? Don't you trust your sweet wife?"

"Sweet, hell," he grumbled at her own teasing. "Sometimes I think you're still as wild and untamed as you were the day I met you."

Her head turned slightly so she could twirl her tongue around his nipple. Soft turquoise eyes peeked up at him for his reaction.

"Would you want me any other way?"

"Hell, no."

Later that afternoon, Jessie rode up into the hills to Colt's cabin. It still made her smile each time she passed the spot where she and Chase had first made love, there in the lower hills overlooking the valley. That first time had been wonderful, even though it had ended badly. He'd thought he wasn't ready for marriage yet and settling down. He'd found out differently. He had even brought her back up here after they returned to Wyoming, to do it right this time, he said. Did they ever do it right.

The years had been good to them, exceedingly so. She might still be gruff with him at times — old habits died hard, and she'd always been quick to show her temper — but she knew the man loved her as much as she loved him, which was one hell of a lot.

Colt's cabin was higher up in the mountains near the creek where she used to swim as a girl, with a view of not only the valley but the plains beyond. Even with a few inches of snow covering the slopes this high up, she still found him outside wearing only a pair of old buckskin breeches as he chopped wood. He had a small mountain of wood piling up behind him. He swung that ax with a vengeance too. As chilly as the air was, sweat sheened on his chest and back.

She decided not to comment on his method for working off steam, which she had little doubt was the reason for such exertion. "Any coffee left on the stove?"

He didn't look up as he nodded, having known who his visitor was long before she came into sight of his little clearing. "Help yourself."

She did, taking note that his cabin was a mess and about a dozen bottles of whiskey filled a box in the corner, all empty. She came back out to stand in the doorway, cup in hand. He still didn't stop his chopping.

"You catch any horses lately?"

Since his corral was empty, it was really a question just to annoy him. It didn't work.

"No," was all he said.

"Billy will be taking the train to Chicago next week. I think my mother's actually going to listen to him now about that extra schooling he doesn't want. It wouldn't hurt him none to have it, though. Maybe you and I could talk him into changing his mind."

"The boy's old enough to make his own decisions, Jessie," he said with another swing of the ax.

She let that tack go. "You haven't seen him since he led those foreigners into town. Are you going to at least come down to say good-bye? I notice you've been remiss in that department lately."

She got his attention with that one. "What is that supposed to mean?"

Jessie shrugged. "Just that your duchess remarked on your absence the morning she left. She hadn't realized she wasn't going to see you again."

He swung the ax once more, making no comment other than "She's not my duchess."

"Well, of course not," Jessie allowed. "I didn't mean it *that* way." She moved out of the doorway to sit on a tree stump closer to the woodpile and remarked casually, "She sure is a lady who knows how to get things done. I heard she just walked into the bank and came out less than a half hour later with a deed in hand."

485

"To the Callan place."

So he did know. She hadn't been sure. "Well, there wasn't much else available already built. She's fixed it up so you wouldn't recognize it, but I guess she's still not that happy with it. She also bought land running clear up into the mountains and plans to build a mansion in the foothills come spring. There's already some famous New York architect working on a design for her, and she's got whole crews willing to travel all this way — "

"How do you know so much, Jessie?"

"I've paid her a visit or two. She is my neighbor now, after all, and only a short ride away."

"I know."

She frowned at the disgust in his tone. "Is that a problem?"

"Why should it be?"

"Well, you sure don't sound too happy about it."

"Was I supposed to?"

"Well . . . yes, I kind of thought you might be. Weren't you and she friends?"

"She hired me to do a job. I did it."

"And that's all there was between you two?"

"Jessie," he began warningly, but she cut him off.

"White Thunder, this is me you're talking to. And I saw the way you looked at her, so

486

you can't tell me you don't want her. Why aren't you over there doing some courting? My foreman is, every chance he gets."

"Emmett Harwell?" he snapped. "He's old enough to be her father!"

"Well, now, what's that got to do with anything? I heard her duke was even older than that."

He glowered at her for a moment, but went right back to swinging the ax. Jessie made a sound of exasperation. Directness just wasn't going to work.

She took a sip of coffee, then said, "You know, after hearing all about this English dude who keeps hounding the lady, I figured the first thing she'd do when she moved in was build a wall around the place, but she didn't. I even asked her about it, and you know what she said?"

She waited. It took about twenty seconds, but he finally looked at her and demanded, "Well?"

"She doesn't want to keep him out. She says she's entrenched and waiting for him to come to her. Sounds like something you might have suggested she do."

"Maybe I did."

"That's what I thought, but I couldn't figure out why you weren't there waiting with her."

"She's got enough men —"

"But she doesn't plan to use them. She plans on shooting the Englishman herself, so she's making it easy for him to get to her."

Colt dropped the ax. "Where'd she get *that* crazy idea from?"

Jessie shrugged. "I wouldn't know. Maybe she was just trying to impress me with her courage, since it's something I might do. Like you said, she's got men aplenty. Stands to reason there'd be one or two around to get him before he reaches her."

Colt made no comment to that. He was already heading for his cabin. Jessie followed, trying not to grin.

"You planning to go over there?" she called after him.

"The woman doesn't make idle remarks like that, Jessie," he tossed over his shoulder. "If she said she'd shoot him, she means to do it. Someone's got to tell her it's a damn-fool idea."

"Well, while you're there, why don't you put an end to this silliness of drinking yourself sick each night and ask the woman to marry you?"

He swung around to scowl at her. "Mind your own business, Jessie."

"You want to, don't you?"

"What difference does that make? She's a

white woman, or didn't you notice?"

She deliberately widened her eyes, as if she understood perfectly now. "Well, why didn't you tell me she was prejudiced?"

"Are you crazy? She doesn't even know the meaning of the word."

"Then she's too arrogant for you? I should have known, her being a duchess and all."

"She's no more arrogant than you are," he retorted.

"Well, *I'm* not arrogant, so it must be she's mean-spirited. I never would have guessed."

"Cut it out, Jessie," he hissed. "There isn't a mean bone in her body."

"Then it must be her looks. And here I thought you didn't mind all that ugly red hair."

"Chase should have wrung your neck the last time he threatened to."

"What'd I say?" she asked innocently.

He chuckled then, and caught her about the waist to give her a hard hug. "You've made your point, sister. I guess I can't lose anything by asking."

Jessie stepped back, wrinkling her nose and wiping her hands on her pants. "Best take a bath first. You don't want her to swoon before she has a chance to answer you."

She barely got the last word out before she squealed and started running.

Chapter Forty-six

"You're the first to know, dear. I've decided to get married."

Jocelyn swung around in surprise, nearly knocking the lamp off the table next to her. "Vana! You hardly know Mr. Harwell. He's only been calling on you this past week!"

The countess chuckled. "I'm surprised you even noticed, you've been moping around here so much."

"I have not!"

"Well, I don't know what else you might call it. But never mind. And I'm not marrying that nice Emmett Harwell, though I do have him to thank for making my dear Robbie jealous enough to ask me."

"Robbie?"

"And why not?" the countess said defensively at Jocelyn's bemused look. "If you can fall in love with a man entirely unsuitable to your station — "

"The devil take my station! And I don't love him either!"

"Of course you don't, dear."

Jocelyn glared. Vanessa was blissfully unmoved by it. Jocelyn finally turned away with a sigh.

"It would be rather stupid of me to love a man who doesn't love me, wouldn't it?" she said in a small voice.

"Oh, definitely."

Jocelyn glanced over her shoulder with another glare. "Why aren't you telling me he's too surly, mean-tempered, dangerous — "

"Because he can't be all that bad or you wouldn't love him."

"He's not, but if you haven't noticed, he hasn't come calling."

"You may have to do the calling yourself, dear. I understand he has an aversion to this ranch. His sister confided to me that he nearly died here some years ago — good Lord, sit down! What did I say?"

Jocelyn waved the countess off from trying to drag her to a chair. "I'm all right. It would have been nice if someone had told me, though. What horrid irony."

"What is?"

"That I should have purchased *this* place."

"Yes, well, you're not exactly going to remain here long, only until the spring. And besides, he may want you to live up in the mountains with him, in his rustic little cabin."

"I wouldn't mind."

The countess made a face, for she had merely been trying to bring some levity to the conversation. "Let's not overdo it with the old 'sacrifice for the sake of love' rubbish. Let him do the sacrificing and get used to the finer things in life."

"I would love to, but you keep overlooking the small matter of his absence. He hasn't tried to see me because he doesn't want to."

"I wouldn't be too sure of that, dear. According to his sister — "

"Oh, please, Vana, not confidences from *another* sister. I thought you'd learned your lesson — "

"Don't be obtuse," the countess interrupted right back. "Jessica Summers is not a little liar like that Maura woman was."

"Perhaps not, but she's still biased and — "

Jocelyn broke off at the sound of shouts coming from outside. She moved swiftly to the window. The sight of smoke pouring out of the new stable started her heart pumping in fear.

"What is it?" Vanessa asked.

Jocelyn was already turning and heading for the door. "There is a fire in the stable."

"Dear God — wait a minute!" The countess started hurrying to keep up with her. "You can't go out there. Longnose could have started it to draw you out."

"Don't be ridiculous, Vana. It's still daylight. If he comes, it'll be after dark so he can slither in with the other night crawlers."

"You don't know — "

"Those are *my* horses, Vana!"

The countess didn't say another word after that, just followed Jocelyn outside. It might still be daylight, but only just, and the smoke belching from the long building added to the growing appearance of dusk. Men were already leading horses out; others came charging out on their own. Their cries of fear were pitiful.

"Sir George?" Jocelyn asked the next man to come out of the wide-open doors.

"Red Rob's getting him, Your Grace."

"How bad is it?"

"The loft's caught already."

She panicked, hearing that. Sir George was going to be terrified, so much so that no one would be able to control him enough to get him out.

She was running inside before anyone thought to stop her. Smoke was rolling above her head in great waves, the smell of it so overwhelming the kerchief she held to her nose couldn't keep it out. She was coughing before she reached Sir George's large stall.

Robbie was indeed there, trying in vain to

get hold of the stallion's mane to lead him out. Even as she watched, Sir George reared up with a scream and the Scot was knocked backward. Nor did Robbie get up immediately. He'd been struck hard on the shoulder.

"Are you all right, Robbie?"

"Good God, woman, what are you — "

"Not now!" she shouted as she tore off her blouse, the only thing handy, to wrap around the stallion's eyes. "If you'll get up and get on him, I'll have the three of us out of here in a trice."

She was already pulling herself up onto the animal's back, the horse having calmed somewhat at the sound of her voice and the total darkness. Robbie didn't hesitate to follow suit. Moments later, Sir George burst through the doors almost at a full gallop. Jocelyn managed to bring him about by using her blouse as substitute reins, no mean feat with her directions coming from the top of his head rather than from a bit at his mouth.

She hailed Sir Dudley. "The rest of the animals?"

"All accounted for, Your Grace."

She sagged back against Red Rob's wide chest, but caught herself almost instantly and straightened. Simultaneously, they both remembered the unorthodox way he had addressed her back in the stable. The countess found them laughing when she approached.

"I'll have you know you scared the life out of me, and here you are having a good time."

Jocelyn sobered at that scolding, but not completely. She was still grinning as she offered, "I'm sorry, Vana, but I had a feeling this great skittish beast wouldn't let anyone near him, and I was right. I believe your fiance's shoulder will need some immediate attention. You know Sir George is never gentle with his kicks."

The countess's temper turned to quick concern. "Is anything broken, darling?"

"Just dislocated, sweetheart. Nothing to worry about."

Jocelyn almost groaned, hearing them coo at each other. "I'll just give him a ride to the house, Vana, while you find someone to set his shoulder. I'm feeling a bit of a chill myself."

"And no wonder —"

Jocelyn didn't wait around for more scolding, embarrassment mounting at being caught out in no more than a skimpy white camisole to cover her chest. She nudged Sir George toward the house and left him there with Robbie as she ran up the stairs to repair her state of undress before she went out to inspect the rest of the animals for any injuries. But she didn't get back outside. Waiting in her room, casually reclining on her bed as if it belonged to him, was her nemesis, John Longnose.

She was surprised enough not to scream, then wise enough not to when she noticed the gun he had pointed at her head. The horrid man was grinning. Well, why not? He'd won, after all. Vanessa had been right. He'd set the fire in the stable to draw everyone out of the house so he could then sneak into it. And the bastard had no care for the animals, that some of them could have died. Jocelyn's temper rose before fear had a chance to.

"Shut the door, Your Grace," he fairly purred. "We don't want to be disturbed."

"Shut it yourself!"

He sat up, his gray eyes darkening with annoyance that she wasn't immediately cowed. "I don't think you realize — "

"No, *you* don't seem to realize that I'm fed up to here with you!" She hit her chin with the back of her fingers to show him just where. "So go ahead and shoot me, you miserable little worm. But I promise you, you won't get out of this house alive!"

"I don't intend to shoot you," he growled angrily.

"No? Then give me your gun. I have no such qualms."

"You bloody bitch!" His face was turning

496

quite red in his frustration that she was ruining the way he'd fantasized this meeting. "Remember you said that when I get my hands around your neck!"

"Well, come along then and I'll scratch your eyes out while you're trying!"

But when he did rise with a snarl of rage, she realized she'd forgotten how tall he was. Slim, but not worth risking a physical struggle with. She wasn't stupid, after all.

She darted out the door, racing toward the stairs. She thought she could almost feel his breath down her neck, but hoped it was just her imagination running wild. It was, almost. He was three feet behind her when she abruptly halted at the top of the stairs. Colt was there, halfway up them. He stopped too. So did Longnose, who thought to turn the gun still in his hand on Colt. It was the last thing he ever did.

Even as he was pulling the trigger, Colt was firing his own gun. Longnose's bullet whisked past his ear to embed in the wall behind him. Colt's bullet took the Englishman in the chest. He fell slowly, knees hitting the floor first, mumbling something about bloody hell, then toppling the rest of the way over.

Jocelyn sat down on the top step with a shuddering sigh. "This is one time I don't mind at all your habit of dropping men at my feet."

"Are you all right?"

"Certainly. I'm becoming an old hand at this sort of thing." Yet her voice sounded anything but calm.

His eyes narrowed on her. "You look like you could use a shot of whiskey."

"Make that brandy and I quite agree. I have some in the parlor."

"Then go ahead. I'll join you after I dispose of the trash."

He joined her sooner than that. Her people came running into the house from all directions to investigate the shot. He left the cleanup to them. The countess almost beat him to the parlor, however, but not quite.

"She's all right, Vanessa," Colt told her in a quiet but firm voice. "Leave her to me."

The countess was too shocked at hearing him call her by name to say anything at first. And then the door was closed in her face, so she'd missed her chance.

"Well, I never," Vanessa gasped.

"I thought you were hoping he would show up," Robbie said behind her.

"I must have been temporarily crazy. I'd forgotten what he's like."

"As long as she doesn't mind, sweetheart, why should you?"

She started to frown, but ended up smiling. "How right you are. *I* won't have to live with him, after all."

Inside the parlor, Jocelyn drained the brandy from her glass before saying, "That wasn't very nice of you."

"Wasn't I polite enough?"

She quirked a brow at his innocent expression, not sure whether he was serious or not. Not that she cared. She was more interested in what he was doing here.

He had dropped his coat on the rack in the hall before the shouting had drawn him upstairs. She noted the absence of buckskins and braids. Only his moccasins were familiar. The rest of his attire, the dark pants and open-necked blue shirt, the red bandanna and Western hat, was pretty much what the average cowboy sported.

He was taking in *her* dress, in particular her thin camisole, so incongruous with her heavy wool skirt. She could feel the color mounting and it annoyed her. Good Lord, after all they had been through, how could he still make her blush?

She decided her doubting look was answer enough to his question and asked one of her own. "What are you doing here, Colt?"

"I'd heard you planned to shoot Longnose yourself."

"And you thought to dissuade me from that notion?"

"Something like that."

She remembered saying that to him once and couldn't help smiling, even if she was disappointed by his answer. "Your timing was on the mark — as ever. I don't suppose I'll ever learn his real name now."

"Does it matter?"

"No, he was a Longnose to the end, following my scent across yet another country. I'm liable to miss him, you know. He added an element of excitement to my life."

"You'll have to find something else, then — that can excite you."

Those words didn't do too bad a job. She could feel her heartbeat accelerate. And the way he was looking at her . . .

She moved over to the window so she could watch the activity at the stable and get her pulse under control. The animals were already being taken into the old barn, which fortunately hadn't been torn down yet. She didn't see much more than that, however, once Colt moved up behind her. He had a way of claiming her full attention even when she wasn't looking at him.

"Will you marry me?"

Jocelyn's forehead dropped against the window. It was a wonder her legs didn't give out. She felt such unbelievable relief on hearing those words, and such ecstasy washing over her — and he'd made her suffer for three weeks while he made up his mind.

"I don't know," she said in a perfectly normal tone, though she didn't know how she managed it. "The countess says one shouldn't marry her lover. Ruins the romance, you know."

"And I'm not suitable except to be your lover?"

She swung around, her eyes large with temper. "Suitable? There you go belittling yourself again! I thought I'd warned you — "

He grabbed her to shut her up. "Am I still your lover?"

"If you are, you've been a very inattentive one."

He kissed the pout from her lips, slowly, persuasively. "What if you marry me for the hell of it, but we pretend we're just lovers?"

"That sounds rather nice, especially since lovers tend to love each other."

"And married folks don't?"

"Not always."

"I won't have any problem with that."

"You won't?"

"Don't look so surprised, Duchess. Did you think I was after your money?"

She was chagrined by his grin, and snorted,

"You'll probably ask me to give it all away."

"I might."

"And live in a cabin in the hills."

"I might."

"And have your babies and wash your clothes."

"I'd like to keep my clothes intact, and I warn you now, you're not getting anywhere near my stove. I guess you'll have to have a few servants around after all."

"And the babies?"

"You want some?"

"Most definitely."

"I guess that means you love me, huh?"

"Or I just like your body. Did I tell you what a splendid — Yes!" she squealed when he squeezed her tight. "I love you, you wretched man."

"You could have told me sooner," he growled, holding her close. "Like when I was making love to you or some other appropriate time. Then I wouldn't have gone through hell these last weeks thinking — "

"If you're going to mention something about your heritage, Colt Thunder, I'll hit you."

He leaned back to look at her fierce expression, and then he laughed. "God, I love you, Duchess. You're one of a kind."

"I'm delighted to know it," she said between showering his face with kisses. "But if you can call my closest friend by name, why can't you say mine? It's Jocelyn, if you don't remember."

"I know what it is, honey, but it isn't you. You're the duchess, plain and simple — and mine."

"Well, if you put it that way . . ."